ALSO BY MARY HIGGINS CLARK

Night-time Is My Time
Second Time Around
Kitchen Privileges
Daddy's Little Girl
On the Street Where You Live
Before I Say Good-bye
We'll Meet Again
All Through the Night
You Belong to Me
Pretend You Don't See Her
My Gal Sunday
Moonlight Becomes You
Silent Night
Let Me Call You Sweetheart
Remember Me
Weep No More, My Lady
Stillwatch
A Cry in the Night
The Cradle Will Fall
A Stranger Is Watching
Where Are the Children?

BY MARY HIGGINS CLARK AND CAROL HIGGINS CLARK

The Christmas Thief
He Sees You When You're Sleeping
Deck the Halls

MARY HIGGINS CLARK

No Place Like Home

POCKET
BOOKS

LONDON • SYDNEY • NEW YORK • TORONTO

First published in Great Britain by Simon and Schuster UK Ltd, 2005
This paperback edition published by Pocket Books, 2006
An imprint of Simon & Schuster UK Ltd
A Viacom company

1 3 5 7 9 10 8 6 4 2

Simon & Schuster UK Ltd
Africa House
64–78 Kingsway
London WC2B 6AH

www.simonsays.co.uk

Simon & Schuster Australia
Sydney

A CIP catalogue record for this book is available from the British Library

ISBN 1 4165 0221 1
EAN 9781416502210

Printed and bound in Great Britain by
Cox & Wyman Ltd, Reading, Berks

PROLOGUE

Ten-year-old Liza was dreaming her favorite dream, the one about the day when she was six years old, and she and Daddy were at the beach, in New Jersey, at Spring Lake. They'd been in the water, holding hands and jumping together whenever a wave broke near them. Then a much bigger wave suddenly rushed in and began to break right over them, and Daddy grabbed her. "Hang on, Liza," he yelled, and the next minute they were tumbling under water and being thrown around by the wave. Liza had been so scared.

She could still feel her forehead slamming into the sand when the wave crashed them onto the shore. She had swallowed water and was coughing and her eyes were stinging and she was crying but then Daddy pulled her onto his lap. "Now *that* was a wave!" he said, as he brushed the sand from her face, "but we rode it out together, didn't we, Liza?"

That was the best part of the dream — having Daddy's arms around her and feeling so safe.

Before the next summer came around, Daddy had died. After that she'd never really felt safe again. Now she was always afraid, because Mom had made Ted, her stepfather, move out of the house. Ted didn't want a divorce, and he kept pestering Mom, wanting her to let him come back. Liza knew she wasn't the only one afraid; Mom was afraid, too.

Liza tried not to listen. She wanted to go back into the dream of being in Daddy's arms, but the voices kept waking her up.

Someone was crying and yelling. Did she hear Mom calling Daddy's name? What was she saying? Liza sat up and slid out of bed.

Mom always left the door to Liza's bedroom open just a little so that she could see the light in the hall. And until she married Ted last year, she had always told Liza that if she woke up and felt sad, she could come into her room and sleep with her. Once Ted moved in, she'd never gotten in bed with her mother again.

It was Ted's voice she heard now. He was yelling at Mom, and Mom was screaming. "Let go of me!"

Liza knew that Mom was so afraid of Ted, and that since he'd moved out she even kept Daddy's gun in the drawer of her night table. Liza rushed down the hall, her feet moving noiselessly along the padded carpet. The door of Mom's sitting room was open and inside she could see that Ted had Mom pinned against the wall and was shaking her. Liza ran past the sitting room and went directly into her mother's bedroom. She hurried around the bed and yanked open the night table drawer. Trembling, she grabbed the gun and ran back to the sitting room.

Standing in the doorway, she pointed the gun at Ted and screamed, "Let go of my mother!"

Ted spun around, still holding on to Mom, his eyes wide and angry. The veins in his forehead were sticking out. Liza could see the tears streaming down her mother's cheeks.

"Sure," he yelled. With a violent thrust, he shoved Liza's mother at her. When she crashed into Liza, the gun went off. Then Liza heard a funny little gurgle and Mom crumpled to the floor. Liza looked down at her mother, then up at Ted. He began to lunge toward her, and Liza pointed the gun at him and pulled the trigger. She pulled it again and again, until he fell down and then began crawling across the room and tried to grab the gun from her. When it wouldn't fire anymore, she dropped the gun and got down on the floor and put her arms around her mother. There was no sound, and she knew her mother was dead.

After that Liza had only a hazy memory of what happened. She remembered Ted's voice on the phone, the police coming, someone pulling her arms from her mother's neck.

She was taken away, and she never saw her mother again.

1

Twenty-four Years Later

I cannot believe I am standing in the exact spot where I was standing when I killed my mother. I ask myself if this is part of a nightmare, or if it is really happening. In the beginning, after that terrible night, I had nightmares all the time. I spent a good part of my childhood drawing pictures of them for Dr. Moran, a psychologist in California, where I went to live after the trial. This room figured in many of those drawings.

The mirror over the fireplace is the same one my father chose when he restored the house. It is part of the wall, recessed and framed. In it, I see my reflection. My face is deadly pale. My eyes no longer seem dark blue, but black, reflecting all the terrible visions that are leaping through my mind.

The color of my eyes is a heritage from my father. My mother's eyes were lighter, a sapphire blue, picture perfect with her golden hair. My hair would be dark blond if I left it natural. I have darkened it, though, ever since I came back to the East Coast sixteen years ago to attend the Fashion Institute of Technology in Manhattan. I am also taller than my mother was by five inches. Yet, as I grow older, I believe I am beginning to resemble my mother in many ways, and I try to distance myself from that resemblance. I have always lived in dread of someone saying to me, "You look familiar . . ." At the time, my mother's image was splashed all over the media, and still turns up periodically in stories that rehash the circumstances of her death. So if anyone says I look familiar, I know it's her they have in mind. I, Celia Foster Nolan, formerly Liza Barton, the child the tabloids dubbed "Little Lizzie Borden," am far less likely to be recognized as that chubby-faced little girl with golden curls who was acquitted— not exonerated—of deliberately killing her mother and trying to kill her stepfather.

My second husband, Alex Nolan, and I have been married for six months. Today I thought we were going to take my four-year-old son, Jack, to see a horse show in Peapack, an upscale town in northern New Jersey, when suddenly Alex detoured to Mendham, a neighboring town. It was only then that he told me he had a wonderful surprise for my birthday and drove down the road to this house. Alex parked the car, and we went inside.

Jack is tugging at my hand, but I remain frozen to the spot. Energetic, as most four-year-olds are, he wants to explore. I let him go, and in a flash he is out of the room and running down the hall.

Alex is standing a little behind me. Without looking at him, I can feel his anxiety. He believes he has found a beautiful home for us to live in, and his generosity is such that the deed is solely in my name, his birthday gift to me. "I'll catch up with Jack, honey," he reassures me. "You look around and start figuring how you'll decorate."

As he leaves the room, I hear him call, "Don't go downstairs, Jack. We haven't finished showing Mommy her new house."

"Your husband tells me that you're an interior designer," Henry Paley, the real estate agent, is saying. "This house has been very well kept up, but, of course, every woman, especially one in your profession, wants to put her own signature on her home."

Not yet trusting myself to speak, I look at him. Paley is a small man of about sixty, with thinning gray hair, and neatly dressed in a dark blue pin-striped suit. I realize he is waiting expectantly for me to show enthusiasm for the wonderful birthday gift my husband has just presented to me.

"As your husband may have told you, I was not the selling agent," Paley explains. "My boss, Georgette Grove, was showing your husband various properties nearby when he spotted the FOR SALE sign on the lawn. He apparently fell in love with it immediately. The house is quite simply an architectural treasure, and it's situated on ten acres in the premier location in a premier town."

I know it is a treasure. My father was the architect who restored a crumbling eighteenth-century mansion, turning it into this charming and spacious home. I look past Paley and study the fireplace. Mother and Daddy found the mantel in France, in a château about to be demolished. Daddy told me the meanings of all the sculptured work on it, the cherubs and the pineapples and the grapes . . .

Ted pinning Mother against the wall . . .

Mother sobbing . . .

I am pointing the gun at him. Daddy's gun . . .

Let go of my mother . . .

Sure . . .

Ted spinning Mother around and shoving her at me . . .

Mother's terrified eyes looking at me . . .

The gun going off . . .

Lizzie Borden had an axe . . .

"Are you all right, Mrs. Nolan?" Henry Paley is asking me.

"Yes, of course," I manage, with some effort. My tongue feels too heavy to mouth the words. My mind is racing with the thought that I should not have let Larry, my first husband, make me swear that I wouldn't tell the truth about myself to anyone, not even to someone I married. In this moment I am fiercely angry at Larry for wringing that promise from me. He had been so kind when I told him about myself before our marriage, but in the end he failed me. He was ashamed of my past, afraid of the impact it might have on our son's future. That fear has brought us here, now.

Already the lie is a wedge driven between Alex and me. We both feel it. He talks about wanting to have children soon, and I wonder how he would feel if he knew that Little Lizzie Borden would be their mother.

It's been twenty-four years, but such memories die hard. Will anyone in town recognize me? I wonder. Probably not. But though I agreed to live in this area, I did not agree to live in this town, or in this house. I can't live here. I simply can't.

To avoid the curiosity in Paley's eyes, I walk over to the mantel and pretend to study it.

"Beautiful, isn't it?" Paley asks, the professional enthusiasm of the real estate agent ringing through his somewhat high-pitched voice.

"Yes, it is."

"The master bedroom is very large, and has two separate, wonderfully appointed baths." He opens the door to the bedroom and looks expectantly at me. Reluctantly, I follow him.

Memories flood my mind. Weekend mornings in this room. I used to get in bed with Mother and Daddy. Daddy would bring up coffee for Mother and hot chocolate for me.

Their king-size bed with the tufted headboard is gone, of course. The soft peach walls are now painted dark green. Looking out the back windows I can see that the Japanese maple tree Daddy planted so long ago is now mature and beautiful.

Tears are pressing against my eyelids. I want to run out of here. If necessary I will have to break my promise to Larry and tell Alex the truth about myself. I am not Celia Foster, nee Kellogg, the daughter of Kathleen and Martin Kellogg of Santa Barbara, California. I am Liza Barton, born in this town and, as a child, reluctantly acquitted by a judge of murder and attempted murder.

"Mom, Mom!" I hear my son's voice as his footsteps clatter on the uncarpeted floorboards. He hurries into the room, energy encapsulated, small and sturdy, a bright quickness about him, a handsome little boy, the center of my heart. At night I steal into his room to listen to the sound of his even breathing. He is not interested in what happened years ago. He is satisfied if I am there to answer when he calls me.

As he reaches me, I bend down and catch him in my arms. Jack has Larry's light brown hair and high forehead. His beautiful blue eyes are my mother's, but then Larry had blue eyes, too. In those last moments of fading consciousness, Larry had whispered that when Jack attended his prep school, he didn't want him to ever have to deal with the tabloids digging up those old stories about me. I taste again the bitterness of knowing that his father was ashamed of me.

Ted Cartwright swears estranged wife begged for reconciliation . . .

State psychiatrist testifies ten-year-old Liza Barton mentally competent to form the intent to commit murder. . . .

Was Larry right to swear me to silence? At this moment, I can't be sure of anything. I kiss the top of Jack's head.

"I really, really, really like it here," he tells me excitedly.

Alex is coming into the bedroom. He planned this surprise for me with so much care. When we came up the driveway, it had been festooned with birthday balloons, swaying on this breezy August day— all painted with my name and the words "Happy Birthday." But the exuberant joy with which he handed me the key and the deed to the house is gone. He can read me too well. He knows I'm not happy. He is disappointed and hurt, and why wouldn't he be?

"When I told the people at the office what I'd done, a couple of the women said that no matter how beautiful a house might be, they'd want to have the chance to make the decision about buying it," he said, his voice forlorn.

They were right, I thought as I looked at him, at his reddish-brown hair and brown eyes. Tall and wide-shouldered, Alex has a look of strength about him that makes him enormously attractive. Jack adores him. Now Jack slides from my arms and puts his arm around Alex's leg.

My husband and my son.

And my house.

2

The Grove Real Estate Agency was on East Main Street in the attractive New Jersey town of Mendham. Georgette Grove parked in front of it and got out of the car. The August day was unusually cool, and the overhead clouds were threatening rain. Her short-sleeved linen suit was not warm enough for the weather, and she moved with a quick step up the path to the door of her office.

Sixty-two years old, Georgette was a handsome whippet-thin woman with short wavy hair the color of steel, hazel eyes, and a firm chin. At the moment, her emotions were conflicted. She was pleased at how smoothly the closing had gone on the house she had just helped sell. It was one of the smaller houses in town, its selling price barely breaking the seven figure mark, but even though she had split the commission with another broker, the check she was carrying was manna from heaven. It would give her a few months' reserve until she landed another sale.

So far it had been a disastrous year, saved only by her sale of the house on Old Mill Lane to Alex Nolan. That one had caught her up on overdue bills at the office. She had very much wanted to be present that morning when Nolan presented the house to his wife. I hope she likes surprises, Georgette thought for the hundredth time. She worried that what he was doing was risky. She had tried to warn him about the house, about its history, but Nolan didn't seem to care. Georgette worried also that since he'd put the house in his wife's name only, if his wife didn't like it, she, Georgette, might be wide open to a non-disclosure suit.

It was part of the real estate code of New Jersey that a prospective buyer had to be notified if a house was a stigmatized property, meaning one that might be impacted by a factor that, on a psychological level, could cause apprehension or fears. Since some people would not want to live in a house in which a crime had been committed, or in which there had been a suicide, the real estate agent was obliged to make a prospective client aware of any such history. The statute even required the agent to reveal if a house had the reputation of being haunted.

I tried to tell Alex Nolan that there had been a tragedy in the house on Old Mill Lane, Georgette thought defensively as she opened the office door and stepped into the reception room. But he had cut her off, saying that his family used to rent a two-hundred-year-old house on Cape Cod, and the history of some of the people who lived in it would curl your hair. But this is different, Georgette thought. I should have told him that around here the house he bought is known as "Little Lizzie's Place."

She wondered if Nolan had become nervous about his surprise. At the last minute he had asked her to be at the house when they arrived, but it had been impossible to change the other closing. Instead she had sent Henry Paley to greet Nolan and his wife, and to be there to answer any questions Mrs. Nolan might have. Henry had been reluctant to cover for her, and in the end she had been forced to remind him, rather sharply, not only to be there, but to be sure to emphasize the many desirable features of the house and property.

At Nolan's request, the driveway had been decorated with festive balloons, all painted with the words "Happy Birthday, Celia." The porch had been draped with festive papier-mâché, and he also had asked that champagne and a birthday cake and glasses and plates and silverware and birthday napkins be waiting inside.

When Georgette pointed out that there was absolutely no furniture in the house, and offered to bring over a folding table and chairs, Nolan had been upset. He had rushed to a nearby furniture store and ordered an expensive glass patio table and chairs, and instructed the salesman to have them placed in the dining room. "We'll switch them to the patio when we move in, or if Celia doesn't like them, we'll donate them to a charity and take a deduction," he had said.

Five thousand dollars for a patio set and he's talking about giving it away, Georgette had thought, but she knew he meant it. Yesterday afternoon he had phoned and asked her to be sure there were a dozen roses in every room on the main floor, as well as in the master bedroom suite. "Roses are Ceil's favorite flowers," he explained. "When we got married, I promised her that she'd never be without them."

He's rich. He's handsome. He's charming. And he's clearly devoted to his wife, Georgette thought as she stepped inside and automatically glanced around the reception room to see if any potential clients were waiting there. From half the marriages I've seen, she's a damn lucky woman.

But how will she react when she starts hearing the stories about the house?

Georgette tried to push the thought away. Born with a natural ability to sell, she had progressed rapidly from being a secretary and part-time real estate agent, to founding her own company. Her reception room was a matter of special pride to her. Robin Carpenter, her secretary-receptionist, was positioned at an antique mahogany desk to the right of the entrance. On the left, a brightly upholstered sectional couch and chairs were grouped around a coffee table.

There, while clients sipped coffee or soft drinks or a glass of wine in the early evening, Georgette or Henry would run tapes showing available properties. The tapes provided meticulous details of every aspect of the interior, the exterior, and the surrounding neighborhood.

"Those tapes take a lot of time to do properly," Georgette was fond of explaining to clients, "but they save you a lot of time, and by finding your likes and dislikes, we can get a very good idea of what you're really looking for."

Make them want it before they set foot in it—that was Georgette's game plan. It had worked for nearly twenty years, but in the last five it had gotten tougher, as more and more high-powered agencies had opened in the area, their young and vigorous brokers panting for every listing.

Robin was the only person in the reception area. "How did the closing go?" she asked Georgette.

"Smoothly, thank God. Is Henry back?"

"No, I guess he's still drinking champagne with the Nolans. I still can't believe it. A gorgeous guy buys a gorgeous house for his wife for her thirty-fourth birthday. That's exactly my age. She's so lucky. Did you ever find out if Alex Nolan has a brother?" Robin sighed. "But on the other hand, there can't be two men like that," she added.

"Let's all hope that after she gets over the surprise, and has heard the story of that house, Celia Nolan still considers herself lucky," Georgette snapped nervously. "Otherwise, we might have a real problem on our hands."

Robin knew exactly what she meant. Small, slender, and very pretty, with a heart-shaped face and a penchant for frilly clothes, the initial impression she gave was that of the air-headed blond. And so Georgette had believed when she applied for the job a year ago. Five minutes of conversation, however, had led her not only to reversing that opinion but to hiring Robin on the spot and upping the salary she had intended to pay. Now, after a year, Robin was about to get her own real estate license, and Georgette welcomed the prospect of having her working as an agent. Henry simply wasn't pulling his weight anymore.

"You *did* try to warn the husband about the history of the house. I can back you up on that, Georgette."

"That's something," Georgette said, as she headed down the hall to her private office at the rear of the building. But then she turned abruptly and faced the younger woman. "I tried to speak to Alex Nolan about the background of the house one time only, Robin," she said emphatically. "And that was when I was alone in the car with him on our way to see the Murray house on Moselle Road. You couldn't have heard me discussing it with him."

"I'm sure I heard you bring it up one of the times Alex Nolan was in here," Robin insisted.

"I mentioned it to him once in the car. I never said anything about it to him here. Robin, you're not doing me or, in the long run, yourself any favors by lying to a client," Georgette snapped. "Keep that in mind, please."

The outside door opened. They both turned as Henry Paley came into the reception room. "How did it go?" Georgette asked, her anxiety apparent in the tone of her voice.

"I would say that Mrs. Nolan put up a very good act of seeming to be delighted by her husband's birthday surprise," Paley answered. "I believe she convinced him. However, she did not convince me."

"Why not?" Robin asked before Georgette could frame the words.

Henry Paley's expression was that of a man who had completed a mission he knew was doomed to failure. "I wish I could tell you," he said. "It may just be that she was overwhelmed." He looked at Georgette, obviously afraid that he might be giving the impression that he had somehow let her down. "Georgette," he said apologetically, "I swear, when I was showing Mrs. Nolan the master suite, all I could vi-sualize was that kid shooting her mother and stepfather in the sitting room years ago. Isn't that weird?"

"Henry, this agency has sold that house three times in the last twenty-four years, and you were involved in at least two of those sales. I never heard you say that before," Georgette protested angrily.

"I never got that feeling before. Maybe it's because of all those damn flowers the husband ordered. It's the same scent that hits you in funeral homes. I got it full force in the master suite of Little Lizzie's Place today. And I have a feeling that Celia Nolan had a reaction like that, too."

Henry realized that unwittingly he had used the forbidden words in describing the house on Old Mill Lane. "Sorry, Georgette," he mumbled as he brushed past her.

"You should be," Georgette said bitterly. "I can just imagine the kind of vibes you were sending out to Mrs. Nolan."

"Maybe you'll take me up after all on my offer to back you up on what you told Alex Nolan about the house, Georgette," Robin sug-gested, a touch of sarcasm in her voice.

3

"But, Ceil, it's what we were *planning* to do. We're just doing it a little faster. It makes sense for Jack to start pre-K in Mendham. We've been cramped for these six months in your apartment, and you didn't want to move downtown to mine."

It was the day after my birthday, the day following the big surprise. We were having breakfast in my apartment, the one that six years ago I had been hired to decorate for Larry, who became my first husband. Jack had rushed through a glass of juice and a bowl of cornflakes, and hopefully was now getting dressed for day camp.

I don't think I had closed my eyes all night. Instead I lay in bed, my shoulder brushing against Alex, staring into the dark, remembering, always remembering. Now wrapped in a blue and white linen robe, and with my hair twisted into a bun, I was trying to appear calm and collected as I sipped my coffee. Across the table, impeccably dressed as always in a dark blue suit, white shirt, and figured blue and red tie, Alex was rushing through the slice of toast and mug of coffee that was his everyday breakfast.

My suggestion that, while the house was beautiful, I would want to be able to completely redecorate it before we moved in had met with resistance from Alex. "Ceil, I know it was probably insanity to buy the house without consulting you, but it was exactly the kind of place we both had in mind. You had agreed to the area. We talked about Peapack or Basking Ridge, and Mendham is only minutes from both of them. It's an upscale town, convenient to New York, and, besides the fact the firm is moving me to New Jersey, the added plus is that I can get in some early morning rides. Central Park just doesn't do it for me. And I want to teach you how to ride. You said you'd enjoy taking lessons."

I studied my husband. His expression was both contrite and pleading. He was right. This apartment really was too small for the three of us. Alex had given up so much when we married. His spacious apartment in SoHo had included a large study, with room for his splendid sound system and even a grand piano. The piano was now in storage. Alex had a natural gift for music, and thoroughly enjoyed playing. I know he misses that pleasure. He's worked hard to accomplish all he has. Though a distant cousin of my late husband, who himself had come from wealth, Alex was decidedly a "poor relation." I knew how proud he was to be able to buy this new house.

"You've been saying that you want to get back to decorating," Alex reminded me. "Once you're settled, there'd be plenty of opportunity for that, especially in Mendham. There's a lot of money there, and plenty of big houses being built. Please give it a try, for me, Ceil. You have a standing offer from the people next door to purchase this apartment at a nice profit to you. You know that."

He came around the table and put his arms around me. "Please."

I hadn't heard Jack come into the dining room. "I like the house, too, Mom," he piped up. "Alex is going to buy me my own pony when we move there."

I looked at my husband and son. "It looks as though we have a new home," I said, trying to smile. Alex is desperate to have more space, I thought. He loves the idea of being near the riding club. Eventually I'll find a different house in one of the other towns. It won't be hard to persuade him to move. He *did* admit that it was a mistake to buy without consulting me, after all.

One month later the moving vans were pulling away from 895 Fifth Avenue and heading for the Lincoln Tunnel. Its destination was One Old Mill Lane, Mendham, New Jersey.

4

Her eyes ablaze with curiosity, fifty-four-year-old Marcella Williams stood to one side of the front window of her living room watching the long moving van chug slowly past her home. Twenty minutes ago, she had seen Georgette Grove's silver BMW go up the hill. Georgette had been the agent who sold the house. Marcella was sure that the Mercedes sedan that arrived shortly after that belonged to her new neighbors. She had heard that they were rushing to move in because the four-year-old was starting prekindergarten. She wondered what they'd be like.

People didn't tend to stay in that house long, she reflected, and it wasn't surprising. Nobody likes to have their home known as "Little Lizzie's Place." Jane Salzman was the first buyer of the house when it was sold after Liza Barton went on her shooting spree. Jane picked it up dirt cheap. She always claimed the house had a creepy feeling, but then, Jane was into parapsychology which Marcella thought was a lot of nonsense. But no question, the fact that the house was known as "Little Lizzie's Place" eventually got on the nerves of all the owners, and last year's Halloween prank was the finish for the last owners, Mark and Louise Harriman. She flipped out when she saw the sign on her lawn, and the life-sized doll with a pistol in its hand on her porch. She and Mark had been planning to relocate to Florida next year anyhow, so she simply moved up the timing. They moved out in February, and the house had been empty since then.

That train of thought led Marcella to wonder where Liza Barton was now. Marcella had been living there when the tragedy occurred, and she still could picture Little Liza at age ten, with the blond, curly hair, round Kewpie doll face, and quiet, mature manner. She was certainly a smart child, Marcella thought, but she had a way of looking at people, even adults, as if she were sizing them up. I like a child to act like a child, she thought. I went out of my way to be nice to Audrey and Liza after Will Barton died. Then I was happy when Audrey married Ted Cartwright. I said to Liza that she must be thrilled to have a new father, and I'll never forget the way that little snip looked at me when she said, "My mother has a new husband. I don't have a new father."

I told them that at the trial, Marcella reminded herself with some satisfaction. And I told them that I was in the house when Ted collected all the personal stuff that Will Barton left in his study and put it in boxes to store in the garage. Liza was screaming at him, and kept dragging the boxes into her room. She wouldn't give Ted an inch. She made it so hard for her mother. And it was clear that Audrey was crazy about Ted.

At least in the *beginning*, she was crazy about him, Marcella thought, mentally correcting herself as she watched a second van follow the first one up the hill. Who knows what happened there? Audrey certainly didn't give the marriage much time to work out and that restraining order she got against Ted was absolutely unnecessary. I believed Ted when he swore that Audrey had phoned and asked him to come over that night.

Ted was always so grateful for my support, Marcella remembered. My testimony helped him in the civil case he filed against Liza. Well, the poor fellow *should* have been compensated. It's pretty nasty to go through life with a shattered knee. He still has a limp. It's a miracle he wasn't killed that night.

When Ted got out of the hospital following the shooting, he had moved a few towns away to Bernardsville. Now a major New Jersey developer, the logo for his construction company was frequently seen on malls and highways. His latest venture had been to take advantage of the fitness craze by opening gyms across the state and building town houses in Madison.

Over the years, Marcella had bumped into him at various functions. The last time had been only a month ago. Ted had never remarried, but he'd had a string of girlfriends along the way, and, according to the gossip, the last break-up had been very recent. He always claimed that Audrey was the love of his life, and that he'd never get over her. But he certainly looked great, and he even said something about our getting together sometime. He might be interested to know that new people are moving into the house.

Marcella admitted to herself that since her casual meeting with Ted, she'd been casting around for a reason to call him. Last Halloween, when some kids wrote LITTLE LIZZIE'S PLACE. BEWARE! on the lawn with white paint, the newspapers had called Ted for a comment.

I wonder if those kids will pull a stunt like that on the new owner. If there are any kind of shenanigans, it's a given the newspapers will contact Ted for a comment. Maybe I'll let him know that the house has changed hands again.

Pleased at the excuse to call Ted Cartwright, Marcella headed for the phone. As she crossed the spacious living room, she gave a brief smile of approval to her reflection in the mirror. Her shapely body showed the daily regimen of exercise. Her frosted blond hair framed a smooth face, tightened by several recent Botox treatments. She was confident that the new liner and mascara she was using enhanced her hazel eyes.

Victor Williams, the husband from whom she'd been divorced for ten years, was still dining out on his sardonic comment that Marcella was so afraid she'd miss getting the dirt on someone that she slept with her eyes open and receivers in her ears.

Marcella called information and got the number for Ted Cartwright's office. After instructions to "dial one for this, dial two for that, dial three for . . . " she finally reached his voicemail. He has such a nice speaking voice, she thought as she listened to his message.

Her own voice distinctly coquettish, she said, "Ted, this is Marcella Williams. I thought you'd be interested to hear that your former home has changed hands again, and the new owners are in the process of moving in. Two vans just passed my house."

The sound of a police siren interrupted her. An instant later she watched as a police car hurtled past her window. There's already a problem there, she thought with a shiver of delight. "Ted, I'll call you back," she said, breathlessly. "The cops are on the way to your old house. I'll let you know what develops."

5

"I am so sorry, Mrs. Nolan," Georgette stammered. "I just got here myself. I've called the police."

I looked at her. She was trying to drag a hose across the bluestone walk, hoping, I suppose, to wash away some of the defacing of the lawn and house.

The house was set back one hundred feet from the road. In thick billboard-sized letters, the words

LITTLE LIZZIE'S PLACE.
BEWARE!

were painted in red on the lawn.

Splashes of red paint stained the shingles and limestone on the front of the house. I saw that a skull and crossbones were carved in the mahogany door. A straw doll with a toy gun in its hand was propped against the door. I guessed it was supposed to represent me.

"What's this supposed to be about?" Alex snapped.

"Some kids, I guess. I'm so sorry," Georgette Grove explained nervously. "I'll get a clean-up crew here right away, and I'll call my landscaper. He'll come over and cut this grass out and resod the lawn today. I can't believe . . . "

Her voice trailed off as she looked at us. It was a hot and muggy day. We were both dressed in casual clothes, short-sleeved shirts and slacks. My hair was pulled back, falling loose on my shoulders. Thank God I was wearing dark glasses. I was standing beside the Mercedes, my hand on the door. Next to me, angry and upset, Alex was clearly not going to be satisfied with the offer to get rid of the mess. He wanted to know why this had happened.

I can tell you what it's about, Alex, I thought. Hang on, I told myself desperately. I knew that if I let go of the car door, I would fall. The August sun was streaming down, making the red paint glisten.

Blood. It wasn't paint. It was Mother's blood. I could feel my arms and neck and face becoming sticky with her blood.

"Celia, are you okay?" Alex had his hand on my arm. "Honey, I'm so sorry. I can't imagine what in hell would make anyone do this."

Jack had scrambled out of the car. "Mommy, are you okay? You're not sick are you?"

History repeating itself. Jack, who had only a dim memory of his own father, was instinctively frightened that he would lose me, too.

I forced myself to try to focus on him, on his need for reassurance. Then I looked at the concern and distress on Alex's face. A terrible possibility rushed through my mind. Does he *know*? Is this some terrible, cruel joke? As quickly as the thought came, I dismissed it. Of course Alex had no idea that I had ever lived here. That real estate agent, Henry Paley, had told me that Alex had been on his way to see a house three blocks away when he spotted the FOR SALE sign on this house. It was one of those terrible events that just happens, a horrible coincidence. But my God, what shall I do?

"I'll be all right," I told Jack, managing to force the words out through lips that felt numb and spongy.

Jack ran past the car and onto the lawn. "I can read that," he said proudly. "L-i-t-t-l-e L-i-z-z-i-e . . ."

"That's enough, Jack," Alex said firmly. He looked at Georgette. "Is there any explanation for this?"

"I tried to explain something to you when we first viewed the house," Georgette said, "but you weren't interested. A tragedy took place here nearly twenty-five years ago. A ten-year-old child, Liza Barton, accidentally killed her mother and shot her stepfather. Because of the similarity of her name to the infamous Lizzie Borden, the tabloids called her, 'Little Lizzie Borden.' Since then from time to time, there have been incidents here, but never anything like this."

Georgette was clearly on the verge of tears. "I should have made you listen."

The first moving van was pulling into the driveway. Two men jumped out and ran behind it to open the door and begin to unload.

"Alex, tell them to stop," I demanded, then was frightened to hear my voice rising to a near shriek. "Tell them to turn around and go back to New York right now. I can't live under this roof." Too late, I realized that Alex and the real estate agent were staring at me, their expressions shocked.

"Mrs. Nolan, don't think like that," Georgette Grove protested. "I am so sorry this has happened. I can't apologize enough. I assure you that some kids did this as a joke. But they'll know it's not a joke when the police get through with them."

"Honey, you're overreacting," Alex protested. "This is a beautiful home. I'm sorry I didn't listen to Georgette about what happened here, but I would have bought the house for you anyhow. Don't let some stupid kids spoil it for you." He put his hands on my face. "Look at me. I promise that before the day is over, this mess will be gone. Come on around the back. I want to show Jack the surprise I have for him."

One of the moving men was heading for the house, Jack scampering behind him. "No, Jack, we're going around to the barn," Alex called. "Come on, Ceil," he urged. "Please."

I wanted to protest, but then I saw the blinking lights of a patrol car rushing up the road.

When they pulled my arms away from my mother's body they made me sit in the patrol car. I was wearing my nightgown and someone got a blanket and tucked it around me. And then the ambulance came and they took Ted out on a stretcher.

"Come on, honey," Alex coaxed. "Let's show Jack his surprise."

"Mrs. Nolan, I'll take care of talking to the police," Georgette Grove volunteered.

I couldn't bear having to come face-to-face with the police, so to avoid an encounter with them, I walked quickly along the path with Alex. We headed to the spacious grounds behind the house. I realized that the blue hydrangeas Mother had planted along the foundation of the house were gone, and then I was startled to see that in the month since I had been here, a riding enclosure had been built.

Alex had promised Jack a pony. Was it here already? The same thought must have occurred to Jack because he began running across the lawn toward the barn. He pulled open the door, and then I heard a whoop of joy. "It's a pony, Mom," he shouted. "Alex bought me a pony!"

Five minutes later, his eyes shining with delight, his feet firmly secure in the stirrups of his new saddle, and Alex at his side, Jack was walking the pony around the enclosure. I stood at the split-rail fence, watching them, taking in the expression of pure bliss on Jack's face and the satisfaction in Alex's smile. I realized that Jack had the reaction to his pony that Alex had expected of me about the house.

"This is another reason why I knew this place would be perfect, sweetheart," Alex said as he passed me. "Jack has the makings of being a terrific rider someday. Now he can ride every single day, right, Jack?"

There was somebody clearing his throat behind me. "Mrs. Nolan, I'm Sergeant Earley. I very much regret this incident. This is no way to welcome you to Mendham."

I hadn't heard the police officer and Georgette Grove approaching me. Startled, I turned around to face them.

He was a man who appeared to be in his late fifties, with an outdoorsman's complexion and thinning sandy hair. "I know just which kids to question," he said grimly. "Trust me. Their parents will pay for whatever has to be done to restore the house and lawn."

Earley, I thought. I know that name. When I packed my files last week I read the hidden one again, the file that began with the night I killed my mother. There had been a cop named Earley mentioned in the article.

"Mrs. Nolan, I've been on the police force in this town for over thirty years," he continued. "It's as friendly a town as you'll find anywhere in the world."

Alex, having seen the sergeant and Georgette Grove, left Jack on the pony to join us. Grove introduced him to Sergeant Earley.

"Sergeant, I know I speak for my wife when I say that we don't want to start our life in this town by signing complaints against neighborhood kids," Alex said. "But I do hope that when you find those vandals you'll make them understand that they're damn lucky that we're being this generous. Actually, I'm going to fence in the property and put up security cameras immediately. That way if any kids have ideas of more mischief they won't get very far."

Earley, I thought. In my mind I was rereading the articles in the tabloids about me, the ones that had made me heartsick when I looked at them again only a week ago. There had been a picture of a cop tucking a blanket around me in the back of the police car. Officer Earley had been his name. Afterwards he had commented to the press that he'd never seen a kid as composed as I had been. "She was covered with her mother's blood, yet when I put the blanket around her, she said, 'Thank you very much, officer.' You'd think I had given her an ice cream cone."

And now I was facing this same man again, and once more expected, I guess, to thank him for the service he would now perform on my behalf.

"Mom, I love my pony," Jack called. "I want to name her Lizzie, after the name on the grass. Isn't that a good idea?"

Lizzie!

Before I could respond, I heard Georgette Grove murmur in dismay, "Oh, Lord, I should have known. Here comes the busybody."

A moment later I was being introduced to Marcella Williams, who, as she grabbed and shook my hand, told me, "I've been living next door for twenty-eight years, and I'm delighted to welcome my new neighbor. I'm looking forward to getting to know you and your husband and little boy."

Marcella Williams. She still lives here! She testified against me. I looked from one to the other: Georgette Grove, the real estate agent who had sold Alex this house; Sergeant Earley, who long ago tucked a blanket around me and then as good as told the press that I was some kind of unfeeling monster; Marcella Williams, who had verified everything Ted told the court, helping him to get the financial settlement that had left me with almost nothing.

"Mom, is it all right if I name her Lizzie?" Jack called.

I *have* to protect him, I thought. This is what would follow me if they knew who I am. For an instant the dream I sometimes have about being in the ocean and trying to save Jack rushed into my mind. I'm in the ocean again, I thought frantically.

Alex was looking at me, his expression puzzled. "Ceil, is it okay with you if Jack calls the pony Lizzie?"

I felt the eyes of my husband, my neighbor, the police officer and the real estate agent watching me intently. I wanted to run away from them. I wanted to hide. Jack, in his innocence, wanted to name his pony after the infamous child I was reputed to be.

I had to get rid of all the memories. I had to act the part of a new-comer annoyed by vandalism. Only that, and nothing more. I forced a smile that must have come through as a grimace. "Let's not spoil the day because of some dumb kids," I said. "I agree. I don't want to sign a complaint. Georgette, please get the damage repaired as fast as possible."

I felt as though Sergeant Earley and Marcella Williams were taking my measure. Were either one of them asking themselves, "Who does she remind me of?" I turned and leaned on the fence. "You call your pony any name you want, Jack," I called.

I've got to get inside, I thought. Sergeant Earley, Marcella Williams—how soon will it be before they see something familiar about me?

One of the moving men, a burly-shouldered, baby-faced guy in his early twenties, was hurrying across the lawn. "Mr. Nolan," he said, "the media is out front taking pictures of the vandalism. One of them is a reporter from a television station, and he wants you and Mrs. Nolan to make a statement on camera."

"No!" I looked at Alex imploringly. "Absolutely not."

"I have a key to the back door," Georgette Grove said quickly.

But it was too late. As I tried to escape, the reporters came hurrying around the corner of the house. I felt light bulbs flashing, and as I raised my hands to cover my face, I felt my knees crumble and a rush of darkness envelope me.

6

Dru Perry had been on Route 24 on her way to the courthouse in Morris County when she got the call to cover the story of the vandalism of "Little Lizzie's Place" for her newspaper, the *Star-Ledger*. Sixty-three years old, a seasoned veteran of forty years as a reporter, Dru was a big-boned woman with iron-gray, shoulder-length hair that always looked somewhat unkempt. Wide glasses exaggerated her penetrating brown eyes.

In the summer, her normal attire was a short-sleeved cotton shirt, khaki slacks, and tennis shoes. Today, because the air-conditioned courtroom was likely to be chilly, she had taken the precaution of stuffing a light sweater in the shoulder bag that held her purse, notebook, water bottle, and the digital camera she carried to help her recall specific details of a breaking story.

"Dru, forget the courthouse. Keep going to Mendham," her editor ordered when he reached her on her car phone. "There's been more vandalism at that house they call 'Little Lizzie's Place' on Old Mill Lane. I've got Chris on his way to get pictures."

Little Lizzie's Place, Dru thought as she drove through Morristown. She had covered the story last Halloween when the kids had left a doll with a toy gun on the porch of that house, and painted the sign on the lawn. The cops had been tough on them then; they had ended up in juvenile court. It was surprising that they'd be bold enough to try it again.

Dru reached for the bottle of water that was her constant traveling companion and sipped thoughtfully. This was August, not Halloween. What would make kids suddenly decide to stir up mischief again?

The answer became obvious when she drove up Old Mill Lane and saw the moving vans and the workers carrying furniture into the house. Whoever did this wanted to rattle the new owners, she thought. Then she caught her breath as the full impact of the vandalism registered.

This is serious damage, Dru thought. I don't think you can just cover those shingles. They'll all have to be repainted, and the limestone will have to be professionally treated, to say nothing of the destruction to the lawn.

She parked on the road, behind the truck from the local television station. As she opened the door of her car, she heard the sound of a helicopter overhead.

She saw two reporters and a cameraman starting to run around the side of the house. Running herself, Dru caught up with them. She got her camera out just in time to snap Celia toppling over in a faint.

Then, with the gathering media, she waited until an ambulance pulled up and Marcella Williams came out of the house. The reporters pounced on her, peppering her with questions.

She's in her glory, Dru thought as Mrs. Williams explained that Mrs. Nolan had revived and seemed to be shaken but otherwise was fine. Then, as she posed for pictures and spoke into the television microphone, she went into detail of the history of the house.

"I knew the Bartons" she explained. "Will Barton was an architect and restored this house himself. It was all such a terrible tragedy."

It was a tragedy she was happy to recall for the media, going into great detail, including her belief that Liza Barton at age ten knew exactly what she was doing when she took her father's gun out of the drawer.

Dru stepped forward. "Not everyone believes that version," she said brusquely.

"Not everyone knew Liza Barton as well as I did," Marcella snapped back.

When Williams went back inside, Dru walked up to the front door to study the skull and crossbones that had been carved into it. Startled, she realized that there was an initial carved into each of the eye sockets of the skull—an *L* in the left socket, and a *B* in the right one.

Whoever did this is really creepy, Dru thought. This wasn't slapped together. A stringer for the *New York Post* had arrived and began to study the skull and crossbones. He gestured to his camera man. "Get a close-up of that," he ordered. "My guess is that we have tomorrow's front page photo. I'll see what I can find out about the new owners."

That was exactly what Dru was planning to do as well. Her next stop was going to be the home of the neighbor, Marcella Williams, but on a hunch she waited around to see if anyone representing the new owners came out to make a statement.

Her hunch paid off. Ten minutes later, Alex Nolan appeared before the cameras. "As you can understand, this is a most regrettable incident. My wife will be fine. She's exhausted from the packing, and the shock of the vandalism simply overwhelmed her. She is resting now."

"Is it true you bought the house as a birthday present for her?" Dru asked.

"Yes, that's true, and Celia is delighted about it."

"Knowing the history of the house, do you think she will want to stay here?"

"That is entirely her decision. Now if you'll excuse me." Alex turned, went back into the house, and closed the door.

Dru took a long sip from the bottle of water she kept in her shoulder bag. Marcella Williams had explained that she lived just down the road. I'll go wait for her there. Then, after I talk to her, Dru decided, I'll look up every detail I can find about the Little Lizzie case. I wonder if the court transcripts are sealed. I'd like to do a feature article about it. I was with the *Washington Post* when that happened. And wouldn't it be interesting if I could find out where Liza Barton is now, and what she's doing with her life. If she did deliberately kill her mother and try to kill her stepfather, chances are she's gotten into trouble again somewhere along the way.

7

When I opened my eyes, I was lying on a couch that the moving men had hastily placed in the living room. The first thing I saw was the terrified look in Jack's eyes. He was bending over me.

My mother's eyes, so frightened in that last moment of her life— Jack's eyes were so like Mother's. Instinctively, I reached up my arm and pulled him down beside me. "I'm okay, pal," I whispered.

"You scared me," he whispered back. "You really scared me. I don't want you to die."

Don't be dead, Mom. Don't be dead. Hadn't I moaned that as I rocked my mother's body in my arms?

Alex was on the cell phone, demanding to know why the ambulance was taking so long to arrive.

An ambulance. Ted being carried out on a stretcher to an ambulance . . .

Still holding Jack, I pushed myself up on one elbow. "I don't need an ambulance," I said. "I'm all right, really I am."

Georgette Grove was standing at the foot of the couch. "Mrs. Nolan, Celia, I really think it would be better if . . ."

"You really must be checked thoroughly," Marcella Williams said, interrupting Georgette.

"Jack, Mommy's fine. We're getting up." I swung my legs around and, ignoring the wave of dizziness, leaned one hand on the arm of the couch for balance and pulled myself to my feet. I could see the look of protest on Alex's face, the concern in his eyes. "Alex, you know how busy this week has been," I said. "I simply need to get the movers to put your big chair and a hassock in one of the bedrooms and let me take it easy for a couple of hours."

"The ambulance is dispatched, Ceil," Alex told me. "You'll let them check you over?"

"Yes."

I had to get rid of Georgette Grove and Marcella Williams. I looked directly at them. "I know you'll understand if I just want to rest quietly," I said.

"Of course," Grove agreed. "And, I'll take care of everything outside."

"Maybe you'd like a cup of tea," Marcella Williams offered, clearly unwilling to leave.

Alex put his hand under my arm. "We don't want to keep you, Mrs. Williams. If you'll excuse us, please."

The wail of a siren told us that the ambulance had arrived.

The EMT examined me in the second-floor room that had once been my playroom. "You got kind of a nasty shock, I would say," he observed. "And with what happened outside, I can understand why. Take it easy for the rest of the day, if that's possible. A cup of tea with a shot of whiskey wouldn't hurt, either."

The sounds of furniture being hauled around seemed to be coming from every direction. I remembered how after my trial, the Kelloggs, my father's distant cousins from California, came to take me back with them. I asked them to drive past the house. An auction was going on at which they were selling all the furniture and rugs and fixtures and china and paintings.

I remember watching them carry out the desk that used to be in that corner, the one that I'd used when I drew pictures of pretty rooms. Remembering how awful that moment had been for that little girl in the car who was driving away with virtual strangers, I felt tears streaming from my eyes.

"Mrs. Nolan, maybe you should come to the hospital." The EMT was in his fifties, fatherly looking, with a full head of gray hair and bushy eyebrows.

"No, absolutely not."

Alex was leaning over me, brushing the tears from my cheeks. "Celia, I have to go outside and say something to those reporters. I'll be right back."

"Where did Jack go?" I whispered.

"The moving guy in the kitchen asked Jack to help him unpack the groceries. He's fine."

Not trusting myself to speak, I nodded and felt Alex slip a hand-kerchief into my hand. Alone, desperately as I tried, I could not stem the river of tears that poured from my eyes.

I can't hide anymore, I thought. I can't live in horror that some-one will find out about me. I have to tell Alex. I have to be honest. Better Jack learns about me when he's young than have the story hit him in twenty years.

When Alex came back, he slid down beside me on the chair and lifted me onto his lap. "Ceil, what is it? It can't be just the condition of the house. What else is upsetting you?"

I felt the tears finally stop, and an icy calm come over me. Maybe this was the moment to tell him. "That story Georgette Grove told about the child who accidentally killed her mother . . . " I began.

"Georgette's spin isn't the one I heard from Marcella Williams," Alex interrupted. "According to her, that kid should have been con-victed. She must have been a little monster. After she shot and killed her mother she kept on shooting the stepfather until the pistol was empty. Marcella says that it came out in court that it took a lot of strength to pull the trigger of that gun. It's not the kind with a hair trigger that just keeps going off."

I struggled free from his embrace. With his preconceived notion, how could I possibly tell Alex the truth now? "Are all those people gone?" I asked, glad to realize that my voice sounded somewhat normal.

"You mean the media?"

"The media, the ambulance, the cop, the neighbor, the real estate agent." I realized that I was gaining strength from my anger. Alex had been willing to accept Marcella Williams's version of what had happened.

"Everyone's gone except the movers."

"Then I'd better pull myself together somehow and tell them where I want the furniture placed."

"Ceil, tell me what's wrong."

I will tell you, I thought, but only after I can somehow prove to you, and to the world, that Ted Cartwright lied about what happened that night, and that when I held that gun I was trying to defend my mother, not kill her.

I am going to tell Alex—and the whole world—who I am, but I'm going to do it when I am able to learn everything I can about the full story of that night, and why Mother was so afraid of Ted. She did not let him in that night willingly. I know that. So much of the period after Mother died is a blur. I couldn't defend myself. There must be a trial transcript, an autopsy report. Things I have to find and read.

"Ceil, what is wrong?"

I put my arms around him. "Nothing and everything, Alex," I said. "But that doesn't mean that things can't change."

He stepped back and put his hands on my shoulders. "Ceil, there's something not working between us. I know that. Frankly, living in the apartment that was yours and Larry's made me feel like a visitor. That's why when I saw this house, and thought it was the perfect place for us, I couldn't resist. I know I shouldn't have bought it without you. I should have let Georgette Grove tell me the background of the place instead of cutting her off, although, in my own defense, from what I know now, she would have glossed over the facts even if I *had* listened to her."

There were tears in Alex's eyes. This time it was I who brushed them dry. "It's going to be all right," I said. "I promise I'm going to make it be all right."

8

Jeffrey MacKingsley, Prosecutor of Morris County, had a particular interest in seeing that the mischief that had once again flared up at the Barton home be squelched once and for all. He had been fourteen and in his first year in high school when the tragedy happened twenty-four years ago. At that time, he lived less than a mile away from the Barton home, and when the news spread through town about the shooting, he'd rushed over and been standing there when the cops carried out the stretcher with the body of Audrey Barton.

Even then he'd been avidly interested in crime and criminal law, so as a kid he'd read everything he could about the case.

Over the years, he had remained intrigued with the question of whether ten-year-old Liza Barton had accidentally killed her mother and shot her stepfather in defense of her mother, or was one of those kids who are born without a conscience. And they exist, Jeff thought with a sigh. They sure do exist.

Sandy-haired, with dark brown eyes, a lean athletic body, six feet tall, and quick to smile, Jeff was the kind of person law-abiding people instinctively liked and trusted. He'd been Prosecutor of Morris County for four years now. As a young assistant prosecutor, he'd understood that if he'd been defending instead of prosecuting a case, he often could have found a loophole that would allow a felon, even a dangerous felon, to walk. That was why, when he'd been offered potentially lucrative positions in defense attorney firms, he elected instead to stay in the prosecutor's office, where he'd quickly become a star.

The result was that four years ago, when the prosecutor he'd worked for retired, Jeff was immediately appointed by the governor to take his place.

On both sides of the courthouse he was known as a straight arrow, tough on crime, but with the ability to understand that many offenders, with the right combination of supervision and punishment, could be rehabilitated.

Jeff had his next goal in mind—to run for governor after the incumbent's second term ended. In the meantime, he intended to exercise his authority as prosecutor to make sure that Morris County was a safe place to live.

That was why the repeated vandalisms of property at the Barton home infuriated and challenged him.

"Those kids, privileged as they are, have nothing better to do than to rake up that old tragedy and turn that beautiful home into the local haunted house," Jeff fumed to Anna Malloy, his secretary, when the incident was reported to him. "Every Halloween they tell wild stories about seeing a ghost looking out at them from the upstairs window. And last year they left a big doll on the porch, holding a toy gun."

"I wouldn't want to live in that house," Anna said matter-of-factly. "I believe that places have vibes. Maybe the kids do see ghosts."

The remark made Jeff think, not for the first time, that Anna had a way of sometimes setting his teeth on edge. This was one of those times. Then he was quick to remind himself that she was probably the most hardworking and efficient secretary in the courthouse. Nearly sixty years old, and happily married to a clerk of the court, she never wasted a minute with personal phone calls, as most of the younger secretaries were guilty of doing.

"Put me through to police headquarters in Mendham," he said, not adding "please," which was unusual for him, but signaled to her that he was annoyed.

Sergeant Earley, whom Jeff knew well, brought him up to date. "I answered the phone call from the real estate agent. A couple named Nolan bought the house."

"How did they react when they saw what had happened?"

"He was furious. She was really upset, actually fainted."

"How old are they?"

"He's mid to late thirties. She is probably about thirty. Classy. You know what I mean. They have a four-year-old boy who found a pony waiting for him in the barn. Get this. The boy was able to read the writing on the lawn and wants to name the pony Lizzie."

"I'm sure that went over big with the mother."

"She seemed okay with it."

"I understand that this time whoever did it wasn't satisfied with wrecking the lawn."

"This goes beyond anything that's ever been pulled before. I went straight over to the school to talk to the kids who pulled the Halloween trick last year. Michael Buckley was the ringleader. He's twelve and a smart aleck. He swears he had nothing to do with it, but then had the nerve to say that he thinks it was only fair for somebody to warn the new owners that they bought a creepy house."

"Do you believe he wasn't involved?"

"His father backs him up, says they were both home last night." Earley hesitated. "Jeff, I believe Mike, not because he isn't capable of pulling the wool over his father's eyes and sneaking out in the middle of the night, but because this just wasn't a kid's trick."

"How do you know?"

"This time they used real paint, not that stuff that washes off. This time they did a job on the front of the house, and from the height of the carving it's clear that someone a lot taller than Michael did it. Something else—the skull and crossbones on the door were done by someone who is artistic. When I looked up close, I could see that it had initials in the eye sockets. *L* and *B*. For Lizzie Borden, I guess."

"Or Liza Barton," Jeff injected.

Earley reconsidered. "Oh, sure. I didn't think about that. Finally, the doll that was left on the porch wasn't a beat-up rag doll like the other one was. This one cost money."

"That should make it easier to trace."

"I hope so. We're working on it."

"Keep me posted."

"The problem is that even if we track down the culprits, the Nolans refuse to sign a complaint," Earley continued, frustration evident in his voice. "But Mr. Nolan plans to fence in the property and put up security cameras, so I don't think there should be any more problems."

"Clyde," Jeff cautioned, "if there's one thing that you and I know, it's that, no matter what the situation, you can never assume there aren't going to be any more problems."

Clyde Earley, like many other people, tended to raise his voice when he was on the phone. As Jeff replaced the receiver, it was clear that Anna had caught every word. "Jeff," she said, "a long time ago, I read a book called *Psychic Explorations*. In it, the author said that when there has been a tragedy in a house, the walls retain the vibrations, and when someone with a similar background moves into the house, the tragedy will have to be completed. The Bartons were a young, upscale couple, with a four-year-old child when they moved into the house on Old Mill Lane. From what I heard Sergeant Earley say, the Nolans are an upscale couple about that age, with a four-year-old child. Kind of makes you wonder what's next, doesn't it?"

9

The next morning when I awoke, I looked at the clock and was startled to realize that it was already quarter past eight. In a reflex gesture, I turned my head. The pillow beside me was still indented from where Alex's head had rested on it, but the room had the feeling of being empty. Then I saw that he had propped a note against the lamp on his bedside table. I read it quickly.

"Darling Ceil,
    Woke at 6 A.M. So glad to see that you were sleeping after all that you went through yesterday. Took off for an hour's ride at the club. Will make it a short day and be home by three. Hope Jack takes well to his first day at school. I want to hear all about it. Love you both, A."

Years ago I read a biography of the great musical comedy star, Gertrude Lawrence, written by her husband, the producer Richard Aldrich after her death. He had titled it *Gertrude Lawrence as Mrs. A.* In the six months we'd been married, whenever Alex happened to jot off a note to me, he invariably signed it "A." I had rather enjoyed thinking of myself as Mrs. A, and even now, with the weight of awareness of where I was, I felt a lift of the heart. I wanted to be Mrs. A. I wanted a normal life in which I could smile indulgently, taking pleasure in the fact that my husband was an early bird so that he could have time for the horseback ride that he enjoyed so much.

I got up, pulled on a robe and walked down the hall to Jack's room. His bed was empty. I walked back into the hall and called his name, but he did not answer. Suddenly frightened, I began to call louder, "Jack . . . Jack . . . Jack"—and realized there was a note of panic in my voice. I forced my lips shut, scolding myself for being ridiculous. He probably just went downstairs to the kitchen and fixed himself some cereal. He's an independent little boy, and often did that in the apartment. But the house had a disconcerting silence about it as I raced down the stairs and from one room to the other. I couldn't find a trace of him. In the kitchen there was no cereal bowl or empty juice glass on the counter or in the sink.

Jack was adventurous. Suppose he had become tired of waiting for me to wake up, and had wandered outside and become lost? He didn't know this neighborhood. Suppose someone saw him alone and picked him up and drove off with him?

Even in the midst of those few but seemingly endless moments, I panicked at the realization that if I didn't find Jack immediately, I would have to call the police.

And then, in a moment of breathtaking release, I knew where he was. Of course. He would have hurried out to visit his new pony. I ran to the door that led from the kitchen to the patio and yanked it open, then sighed with relief. The barn door was open, and I could see Jack's small pajama-clad figure inside the barn, looking up at the pony's stall.

The relief was quickly followed by anger. Last night we had set the alarm after figuring out a four number code, 1023. We'd chosen those numbers because Alex and I met on October 23rd last year. But the fact that when Jack opened the door the alarm had not gone off meant that Alex had not reset it when he left this morning. If he had, I would have known that Jack was on the loose.

Alex was trying so hard, but he still was not used to being a parent, I reminded myself as I began walking toward the barn. Trying to calm down, I forced myself to concentrate on the fact that it was a perfectly beautiful early September morning, with just a touch of coolness that hinted of an early fall. I don't know why, but autumn has always been my favorite time of the year. Even after my father died and it was just Mother and me, I remember evenings sitting with her in the little library off the living room, the fire crackling and both of us deep in our books. I'd be propped up with my head on the arm of the couch, close enough to her to touch her side with my toes.

As I made my way across the backyard, a thought flashed into my mind. On that last night, Mother and I had been in the study together, and had watched a movie that ended at ten o'clock. Before we went upstairs, she had turned on the alarm. Even as a child I was a light sleeper, so it surely would have awakened me if that piercing sound had gone off. But it had not gone off, so Mother had no warning that Ted was in the house. Had that ever come up in the police investigation? Ted was an engineer, and at the time had recently opened his own small construction company. It probably wouldn't have been difficult for him to disarm the system.

I'll have to start a notebook, I thought. I'll jot down anything that comes back to me that may help me to prove that Ted broke into the house that night.

I walked into the barn and tousled Jack's head. "Hey, you scared me," I told him. "I don't want you to ever go out of the house again before I'm up. Okay?"

Jack caught the firmness in my voice and nodded sheepishly. As I spoke I turned and looked at the stall where the pony was standing.

"I just wanted to talk to Lizzie," Jack said earnestly, then added, "Who are those people, Mom?"

I stared at the newspaper photo that had been taped to the post of the stall. It was a copy of a snapshot of my mother and father and me on the beach in Spring Lake. My father was holding me in one arm. His other arm was around my mother. I remember that photo because it had been taken at the end of that day when the wave had thrown Daddy and me on the shore. I had a copy of the picture and the newspaper article in my secret file.

"Do you know that man and woman and that little girl?" Jack asked.

And, of course, I had to lie: "No, Jack, I don't."

"Then why did someone leave their picture here?"

Why indeed? Was this another example of malicious mischief, or had somebody already recognized me? I tried to keep my voice calm. "Jack, we won't tell Alex about the picture. He'd be very mad if he thinks anyone came here and put it up."

Jack looked at me with the penetrating wisdom of a child who senses something is very wrong.

"It's our secret, Jack," I said.

"Did whoever put the picture near Lizzie come while we were asleep?" Jack asked.

"I don't know." My mouth went dry. Suppose whoever had taped it on the post had been in the barn when Jack walked in here alone? What kind of sick mind had planned the defacing of the house and lawn, and how did this picture fall into his hands? What might he have done to my son if Jack had walked in while he was here?

Jack was standing on tiptoes, stroking the pony's muzzle. "Lizzie's pretty, isn't she, Mom?" he asked, his attention completely diverted from the picture that was now in the pocket of my robe.

The pony was rust-colored with a small white marking on the

bridge of its nose that, at a stretch, could be interpreted as a star. "Yes, she is, Jack," I said, trying not to show the fear that was making me want to snatch Jack in my arms and run away. "But I think she's too pretty to be called Lizzie. Let's think up another name for her, shall we?"

Jack looked at me. "I like to call her Lizzie," he said, a stubborn note creeping into his voice. "Yesterday you said I could call her any name I wanted."

He was right, but maybe there was a way I could change his mind. I pointed to the white marking. "I think any pony with a star on its face should be called 'Star,' " I said. "That will be my name for Lizzie. Now we'd better get you ready for school."

Jack was starting pre-K at ten o'clock at St. Joseph's, the school I had attended until the fourth grade. I wondered if any of my old teachers were still there, and if so, would meeting me stir something in their memories.

10

By pleading, cajoling, and offering a handsome bonus, Georgette Grove managed to find a landscaper who would cut out the damaged grass and lay sod on the front lawn of the Nolans' house. She also secured a painter that same afternoon to cover the red paint splattered on the shingles. She had not yet been able to hire a mason to repair the stone, nor a woodwork expert to remove the skull and crossbones carved in the front door.

The events of the day had resulted in an almost sleepless night. At six o'clock when Georgette heard the sound of the newspaper delivery service in her driveway, she leapt out of bed. Every night before retiring, she prepared the coffee pot so that in the morning she could simply flip the switch. Without even thinking, she did exactly that as she hurried to the side door of the kitchen, opened it, and retrieved the newspapers from the driveway.

The dreadful worry that was sitting like a slab of concrete on her head was that Celia Nolan would demand that the sale of the house be voided. This is the fourth time in twenty-four years that I've sold that house, Georgette reminded herself. Jane Salzman got it cheap because of all the publicity about it, but she was never happy there. She claimed that there was a popping sound when the heat went on that no plumber could fix, a sound that reminded her of shots being fired. After ten years she'd had enough.

It took two years before it was sold to the Greens. They stayed nearly six years, then listed it with her. "It's a beautiful house, but no matter how much I try, I can't get over the feeling that something terrible will happen here again, and I don't want to be around for it," Eleanor Green had said when she called Georgette to give her the listing.

The last owners, the Harrimans, had a home in Palm Beach and spent most of their time there. When the kids pulled their Halloween trick last year, they abruptly decided to move to Florida full-time instead of waiting another year or so. "There's such a different feeling in our house there," Louise Harriman had told Georgette when she handed her the key. "Around here, I feel as though everyone is thinking of me as the lady who lives in 'Little Lizzie's Place.' "

In the last ten months, when Georgette again had been showing the house and reciting its history, most prospective buyers said they were uneasy at the thought of owning a home in which there had been a fatal shooting. If they lived in the area and were aware of the house being called "Little Lizzie's Place," they flatly refused even to look at it. It had taken a special buyer like Alex Nolan to brush aside her admittedly sketchy attempt to discuss the background of the home he was considering.

Georgette sat at the breakfast bar and opened the newspapers— the *Daily Record*, the *Star-Ledger*, and the *New York Post*. The *Daily Record* gave the picture of the house its entire front page. The follow-up story deplored the vandalism that refused to let go of the local tragedy. On the third page of the *Star-Ledger* there was a picture of Celia Nolan, caught at the exact moment she began to faint. It showed her head bent, her knees buckling, and her dark hair drifting behind her. The picture next to it showed the front of the vandalized house and the inscription on the lawn. The *New York Post,* on page three, had a close-up of the skull and crossbones on the front door with the initials *L* and *B* in the eye sockets. Both the *Post* and *Star-Ledger* rehashed the sensational case. "Unhappily, 'Little Lizzie's Place' has acquired a sinister mythology in our community over the years," the reporter for the *Daily Record* wrote.

That reporter had interviewed Ted Cartwright about the vandalism. He had posed for the picture in his home in nearby Bernardsville, his walking stick in his hand. "I have never recovered from the death of my wife, and I am shocked that someone would be vicious enough to remind us of that terrible incident," he was quoted as saying. "Both physically and emotionally, I certainly don't need a reminder. I still have nightmares about the expression on that child's face when she went on her shooting spree. She looked like the devil incarnate."

It's the same story he's been telling for nearly a quarter of a century, Georgette thought. He doesn't want anyone to forget it. It's a damn shame Liza was too traumatized to defend herself. I'd give anything to hear her version of what happened that night. I've seen the way Ted Cartwright conducts business. If he had his way, we'd have strip malls instead of riding trails in Mendham and Peapack, and he'll keep trying until the day he's lowered into the ground. He may fool a lot of people, but I've been on the zoning board and I've seen him in action. Behind that phony country-gentleman, bereaved-husband façade, he's ruthless.

Georgette continued reading. Dru Perry of the *Star-Ledger* had obviously done research on the Nolans. "Alex Nolan, a partner in Ackerman and Nolan, a New York law firm, is a member of the Peapack Riding Club. His wife, Celia Foster Nolan, is the widow of Laurence Foster, former president of Bradford and Foster investment firm."

Even though I did try to tell Alex Nolan about the stigma on the house, Georgette thought for the hundredth time, it's in his wife's name, and she knew nothing about it. If she finds out about the stigma law, she could demand that the sale be voided.

Tears of frustration in her eyes, Georgette studied the picture of Celia Nolan as she was caught in the process of fainting. I could probably claim that I did tell her husband and let her take me to court, but that picture would have a big impact on a judge.

As Georgette got up to refill her coffee cup, her phone rang. It was Robin: "Georgette, I suppose you've seen the newspapers."

"Yes, I have. You're up early."

"I was worried about you. I know how upset you were yesterday."

Georgette was grateful for the concern she heard in Robin's voice. "Thanks. Yes, I read all the articles."

"What scares me is that some other real estate broker is bound to contact Celia Nolan and let her know that she could easily break the contract, and then tell her they'd be happy to help her find a new home," Robin said.

The last hope Georgette had that somehow everything would work out vanished.

"Of course. You're right; someone is likely to do that," she said slowly. "I'll see you at the office, Robin."

Georgette replaced the phone on the receiver. "There's no out," she said aloud. "There's simply no out."

Then her mouth tightened. This is my livelihood somebody's ruining, she thought. Maybe the Nolans don't want to file charges, but if I lose that sale, somebody's going to suffer. She picked up the phone, called the police station and asked for Sergeant Earley. Even as she was told that he would not be in for another hour, she realized that it was not seven o'clock yet. "This is Georgette Grove," she told Brian Shields, the desk officer whom she had known since he was a child.

"Brian, as you must certainly be aware, I sold the house on Old Mill Lane that was vandalized. I may lose that sale because of what happened there, and I want Clyde Earley to understand that you people have got to find out who has done this and make an example of them. Mike Buckley admitted he painted the sign on the lawn and left the doll last Halloween. I want to know if you've questioned him yet."

"Ms. Grove, I can answer that," Shields responded hastily. "Sergeant Earley went over to Mike Buckley's school and pulled him out of class. He has an alibi. His father backed up his story that he never left the house the night before last."

"Was his father sober?" Georgette asked caustically. "From what I understand about Greg Buckley, he ties one on pretty regularly." She did not wait for an answer. "Ask Sergeant Earley to call me at my office when he gets in," she said.

She replaced the phone, started to walk to the staircase, the cup of coffee in her hand, then stopped abruptly as a faint hope occurred to her. Alex Nolan is a member of the riding club. In the process of looking for a house, he had told her that his law firm had asked him to head up their new office in Summit, so there are a couple of good reasons why he wants to be in this area. There are a few other listings available that might interest him and his wife. If I offer to show Celia Nolan other houses, and even forgo my sales commission, maybe she'll go along with me. After all, Alex Nolan *did* publicly admit that I tried to tell him about the history of the house.

It was a possibility—maybe a forlorn one she realized, but at least a possibility.

Georgette went into her bedroom and began to untie the knot of her robe. Or is it time to close the agency? she wondered. I can't keep on losing money. The frame house on Main Street that she had bought so cheaply twenty-five years ago would sell in a minute. All the other houses around it were now offices. But what would I do?

she asked herself. I can't afford to retire, and I don't want to work for anyone else.

I'll try to interest the Nolans in another house, she decided. As she showered and dressed, another possibility occurred to her. One Old Mill Lane started out as a very happy home when Audrey and Will Barton bought it. He saw the possibilities in that broken-down mansion and turned it into one of the most charming residences in town. I remember driving by to watch the progress of the renovation, and seeing Will and Audrey working together, planting flowers with Liza standing in her playpen on the lawn.

I never believed for a minute that Liza intended to kill her mother or tried to kill Ted Cartwright that night. She was a child, for heaven's sake. If that ex-girlfriend of Ted's hadn't testified that he roughed her up after they split, Liza probably would have been raised in a juvenile detention home. I wonder where she is now, and how much she remembers about that night. I never could understand what Audrey saw in Ted in the first place. He wasn't fit to carry Will Barton's hat. But some women need a man, and Audrey was one of them, I guess. If only I hadn't encouraged Will to take riding lessons . . .

Half an hour later, reinforced with juice, toast, and a final cup of coffee, Georgette left her house and got into her car. As she backed out of the driveway onto Hardscrabble Road, she gave an appreciative glance at the pale yellow, clapboard house that had been her home for the last thirty years. Despite her business worries, she never failed to feel cheered by the cozy appeal of the former carriage house with its quirky arch over the front door, an unexplainable add-on to the original building.

I want to spend the rest of my life here, she thought, then tried to brush off the sudden chill that washed over her.

11

My mother and father were buried from St. Joseph's Church. It was built on West Main Street in 1860. A school wing was added in 1962. Behind the church there is a cemetery where some of the early settlers of Mendham are buried. Among them are my ancestors.

My mother's maiden name was Sutton, a name that goes back to the late eighteenth century, when gristmills and sawmills and forges were dotted among the rolling acres of farmland. Our original home once stood near the Pitney homestead on Cold Hill Road. The Pitney family still owns that house. In the late eighteen hundreds, the original Sutton house was demolished by a new owner.

My mother grew up on Mountainside Road, the child of older parents who fortunately for them did not live to suffer her death at age thirty-six. That home, like so many others, has been gracefully restored and expanded. I have the vaguest of childhood memories of being in that house. One firm memory I *do* have is that of my grandmother's friends telling my mother in no uncertain terms that my grandmother never approved of Ted Cartwright.

When I was enrolled at St. Joseph's, there were still mostly nuns on the staff. But this morning, as I walked down the hall to the pre-K class, Jack's hand in mine, I could see that the teachers were almost all members of the laity, as the non-religious are called.

Jack already had been to nursery school in New York, and he loves to be with other children. Even so, he clung to my hand as the teacher, Miss Durkin, came over to greet him, and with a worried note in his voice, he asked. "You will come back for me, won't you, Mom?"

His father has been dead two years. Surely by now whatever memory he has of Larry has faded, replaced probably by a vague sense of anxiety about losing me. I know, because after the day a priest from St. Joseph's, accompanied by the owner of the Washington Valley stables came to our home to tell us that my father's horse had bolted, and that he had died instantly in a fall, I was always afraid that something would happen to my mother.

And it did. By my hand.

My mother blamed herself for my father's accident. A born rider, she had often said she wished he could ride with her. Looking back, I believe he had a secret fear of horses, and, of course, horses sense that. For my mother, it was as necessary to ride as it was to breathe. After she dropped me off at school she inevitably headed to the stable at the Peapack Riding Club, where she could find some solace for her grief.

I felt a tug on my hand. Jack was waiting for me to reassure him. "What time is class over?" I asked Miss Durkin.

She knew what I was doing. "Twelve o'clock," she said.

Jack can tell time. I knelt down so that our faces would be even. Jack has a sprinkle of freckles across his nose. His mouth is quick to smile, but his eyes sometimes hold a hint of worry, even of fear. I held up my watch. "What time is it?" I demanded with mock seriousness.

"Ten o'clock, Mom."

"What time do you think I'm going to be back?"

He smiled. "Twelve o'clock on the dot."

I kissed his forehead. "Agreed."

I got up quickly, as Miss Durkin took his hand. "Jack, I want you to meet Billy. You can help me cheer him up."

Tears were streaming down Billy's face. It was clear he'd rather be anywhere than in this pre-K class.

When Jack turned toward him, I slipped out of the classroom and made my way back down the hall. As I passed the door of the office, I saw an older woman behind the secretarial desk who somehow quickened something in my memory. Was I wrong, or had she been here all those years ago? She had. I was sure of it, and sure that I would recall her name.

In the month since my birthday, I had avoided coming to Mendham. When Alex suggested that we measure the rooms for furniture and carpets and window treatments, I used every excuse in the book to delay being put in the position of ordering any household trappings that would be suitable for my former home. I said that I wanted to live in the house and get the feel of it before I made any final selections.

I resisted the temptation to walk in the graveyard and visit my parents' graves. Instead I got in the car and drove a few minutes down Main Street, intending to go into the small shopping center for a cup of coffee. Now that I was alone, my mind felt as though the events of the past twenty-four hours were racing through it, endlessly replaying.

The vandalism. The sign on the lawn. Sergeant Earley. Marcella Williams. Georgette Grove. The newspaper photo in the barn this morning.

Reaching the shopping center, I parked, bought the newspapers, and went into the coffee shop where I ordered black coffee. I forced myself to read every word of the stories about the house, and cringed at the picture of me, my knees buckling under me.

If there was any morsel of comfort, it was clear that all the newspapers referred to us only as "the new owners of the house." The only personal information was the brief mention that I was the widow of the philanthropist Laurence Foster, and that Alex was a member of the riding club and about to open a branch of his law firm in Summit.

Alex. What was I doing to him? Yesterday, typical of his thoughtfulness, he had hired enough extra help so that by six o'clock the house was in as good shape as it could possibly be on move-in day. Of course, we did not have enough furniture, but the table and chairs and armoire were in place in the dining room, as were the couches and lamps and tables and occasional chairs in the living room. The bedrooms—Alex's and mine, and Jack's—were in relatively good order. Our hanging bags were in the closets and the suitcases were unpacked.

I remembered how hurt Alex had been and how puzzled the movers were by my refusal to allow them to unpack the good china and silver and crystal. Instead I had them placed in one of the guest bedrooms along with other boxes marked "Fragile," a word that I thought was more appropriate to use describing me than the china.

I could see the disappointment growing in Alex's eyes as I sent more and more boxes to be stacked in the guest bedroom. He knew that it meant our stay in the house would probably be measured in weeks, not months or years.

Alex wanted to live in this area, and I knew that when I married him. I sipped my coffee and reflected on that simple fact. Summit is only half an hour from here, and he was already a member of the Peapack Club when I met him. Is it possible that subconsciously I have always wanted to come back here to the familiar scenes that are embedded in my memory? Generations of my ancestors have lived here, after all. Certainly I could not in my wildest dreams have imagined that Alex would happen to buy my childhood home, but the events of

yesterday and the pictures in these newspapers have proved to me
that I'm tired of running.

I sipped the coffee slowly. I want to clear my name. I want to
somehow learn the reason that my mother became deathly afraid of
Ted Cartwright. What happened yesterday has given me the cover to
investigate that need, I thought. As the new owner of the house, it
would not seem inappropriate for me to go to the courthouse and
make inquiries, saying that I would like to learn the truth of that
tragedy, devoid of the rumors and sensationalism. In attempting to
clear the stigma on the house, I might even find a way to clear my
own name.

"Excuse me, but aren't you Celia Nolan?"

I judged the woman who was standing at the table to be in her
early forties. I nodded.

"I'm Cynthia Granger. I just wanted to tell you how terrible the
townspeople feel about the vandalism to your house. We want to welcome you here. Mendham is a beautiful town. Do you ride?"

I skirted the answer. "I'm thinking of starting."

"Wonderful. I'll give you a chance to get settled, and then I'll drop
a note. I hope you and your husband will join us for dinner sometime."

I thanked her and, as she left the coffee shop, repeated her surname to myself: Granger. Granger. There had been a couple of
Granger kids in the upper classes of St. Joe's when I was there. I wondered if any of them belonged to Cynthia's husband's family.

I left the coffee shop and for the next hour drove around town, up
Mountainside Road to get a look at my grandparents' home, around
Horseshoe Bend, along Hilltop Road. I drove past the Pleasant Valley
Mill, the property better known as "the pig farm." Sure enough, there
was a sow grazing in the enclosure. Like every child in town, my par-

ents had taken me to observe the litter of piglets in the spring. I wanted to show it to Jack as well.

I did some quick food shopping and got back to St. Joe's well before twelve to be sure that Jack would spot me the minute his pre-K session ended. Then we went home. After Jack had gulped down a sandwich, he begged for a ride on Lizzie. Even though I refused to ride after my father died, the knowledge of how to saddle the pony seemed to be second nature as my hands moved to tighten the girth, to check the stirrups, to show Jack how to hold the reins properly.

"Where did you ever learn that?"

I whirled around. Alex was smiling at me. Neither one of us had heard the car pull in. I guess he'd left it in front of the house. If he had caught me going through his pockets, I could not have been more embarrassed or chagrined.

"Oh," I stammered, "I told you. My friend Gina loved to ride when we were kids. I used to go and watch her when she took lessons. Sometimes I'd help her saddle up."

Lies. Lie following lie.

"I don't remember you mentioning that at all," Alex said. "But who cares?" He picked up Jack and hugged me. "The client I was supposed to spend the better part of the afternoon with canceled. She's eighty-five and wanted to change her will again, but she wrenched her back. When I knew she wasn't coming, I beat it out fast."

Alex had opened the top button of his shirt and pulled down his tie. I kissed the nape of his neck and his arm tightened around me. I love the outdoorsy look he has, with his tanned skin and the sun-bleached highlights in his brown hair.

"Tell me about your first day at school," he teasingly demanded of Jack.

"First, can I have a ride on Lizzie?"

"Sure. And then you're going to tell me about your day."

"I'll tell you about how they asked us to talk about our most exciting day this summer, and I talked about moving here and the cops coming and everything and how today I went out to see Lizzie and there was a picture—"

"Why don't you tell Alex all about it after your ride, Jack?" I interrupted.

"Good idea," Alex said. He checked the saddle, but found nothing to adjust. I thought he looked at me quizzically, but didn't make any comment. "Jack just had a sandwich, but I'll start lunch for us," I said.

"How about having it on the patio?" Alex suggested. "It's too nice to be inside."

"That would be fun," I said hurriedly and headed into the house. I rushed upstairs. My father had redesigned the second floor to have two large corner rooms that could be used for any purpose. When I was little, one of them was his office, the other a playroom for me. I had directed the movers to place my desk in Daddy's office. The desk is a nondescript antique I purchased when I had my interior decorating business, and I chose it for one primary reason. One of the large file drawers has a concealed panel that is secured by a combination lock that looks like a decoration. The panel can only be opened if you know the combination.

I yanked the files out of the drawer, tapped out the code with my index finger, and the panel opened. The thick file about "Little Lizzie Borden" was there. I pulled it out, opened it, and grabbed the newspaper photo that had been taped to the post in the barn.

If Jack ended up telling Alex about it, Alex, of course, would ask to see it. If Jack then realized he had promised me not to talk about it to Alex, he'd probably blurt that out, too. "I forgot, I promised Mommy I wouldn't tell . . . "

And I would have to cover with yet more lies.

Putting the picture in the pocket of my slacks, I went downstairs. Knowing Alex loved it, I had bought smoked salmon at the supermarket. In these six months, he'd given Jack a taste for it, too. Now I fixed it on salad plates with capers and onions and slices of the hard boiled eggs I had prepared while Jack was having his sandwich. The wrought-iron patio set Alex had bought so that we could celebrate my birthday with champagne and tea sandwiches was now on the patio. I set out place mats and silver, then the salads and iced tea, along with heated French bread.

When I called out that everything was ready, Alex left the pony tethered to a post of the enclosure. She was still saddled, so that meant that he was planning to give Jack more time with the pony.

When they came to the patio, I could have cut with a knife the change in the emotional atmosphere. Alex looked serious, and Jack was on the verge of tears. There was a moment of silence, then, in a level tone, Alex asked, "Was there any reason you weren't planning to tell me about the picture you found in the barn, Ceil?"

"I didn't want to upset you," I said. "It's only one of the pictures of the Barton family that was in the newspaper."

"You don't think it upsets me to learn by chance that someone was trespassing here during the night? You don't think the police should know about that?"

There was only one answer that might be plausible: "Have you seen today's papers?" I asked Alex quietly. "Do you think I want any follow-up on it? For God's sake, give me a break."

"Ceil, Jack tells me he went out to see his pony before you woke up. Suppose he had come across someone in the barn? I'm beginning to wonder if there isn't some kind of nut loose around here."

Exactly the worry I had but could not share. "Jack wouldn't have been able to get out if you had reset the alarm," I said sharply.

"Mommy, why are you mad at Alex?" Jack asked.

"Why indeed, Jack?" Alex asked as he pushed back his chair and went into the house.

I didn't know whether to follow him and apologize, or to offer to show him the crumpled newspaper picture that was in my pocket. I simply didn't know what to do.

12

The morning after her new neighbors moved in, Marcella Williams was enjoying a second cup of coffee and devouring the newspapers when her phone rang. She picked it up and murmured, "Hello."

"By any chance, would a beautiful lady be free for lunch today?"

Ted Cartwright! Marcella felt her pulse begin to race.

"No beautiful ladies around here," she said coyly, "but I do know someone who would very much enjoy lunching with the distinguished Mr. Cartwright."

Three hours later, having carefully dressed for the date in tan slacks and a vivid, printed silk shirt, Marcella was sitting opposite Ted Cartwright in the pub of the Black Horse Tavern on West Main Street. In breathless detail she told him all about her new neighbors. "When they saw the vandalism, Alex Nolan was furious, and his wife, Celia, was *really* upset. I mean it's obvious isn't it? She *fainted*, for heaven's sake. I can understand that she probably was worn out from getting ready for the move. No matter how much help you have, there's always so much you have to do yourself."

"It still seems to be a pretty strong reaction," Cartwright observed skeptically.

"I agree, but on the other hand, it was a shocking sight. Ted, I tell you, that skull and crossbones on the door with Liza's initials in the eye sockets was just plain chilling, and you'd swear that red paint on the lawn and on the house was real blood. And that doll on the porch with the gun in its hand was scary, too."

Marcella bit her lip when she saw the expression on Cartwright's face. For God's sake, she told herself, it was *his* blood all over the place, as well as Audrey's, the night Liza shot them. "I'm sorry," she said, "I mean how stupid can anyone be?" Impulsively she reached across the table and squeezed his hand.

Smiling wryly, Cartwright reached for his glass and took a long sip of pinot noir. "I can skip hearing those details, Marcella," he said. "I saw the pictures in the newspapers and that was enough for me. Tell me more about your new neighbors."

"Very attractive," Marcella said emphatically. "She could be anywhere from twenty-eight to early thirties. I'd guess he's in his late thirties. The little boy, Jack, is really cute. Very concerned about his mother. He kept hanging on to her when she was lying on the couch. The poor kid was scared that she was dead."

Again Marcella had the feeling of stepping into dangerous territory. Twenty-four years ago, the cops had had to pry Liza away from her mother's body, while Ted was lying on the floor a few feet away. "I dropped over to Georgette Grove's office yesterday afternoon to see how she was feeling," Marcella said hastily. "I mean she was so upset about the vandalism, and I was a little concerned about her."

Marcella took the last bite of her Cobb salad and the final sip of her Chardonnay.

Seeing Ted's raised eyebrows and the amused smile on his face, she decided to acknowledge that she knew what he was thinking. "You know me too well," she laughed, "I wanted to see what was going on. I figured the cops would let Georgette know if they'd talked to any of the kids who might have pulled that stunt. Georgette wasn't there so I chatted with Robin, her secretary or receptionist or whatever she is."

"What did you find out?"

"Robin told me that the Nolans have only been married six months and that Alex bought the house as a surprise for Celia's birthday."

Cartwright again raised his eyebrows. "The only surprise a man gives a woman should be measured in carats," he said. "And I don't mean the kind that you find in the vegetable bin."

Marcella smiled across the table at him. The pub at the Black Horse Tavern had been a favorite lunch spot of people in the area for generations. She remembered a day when she and Victor and Audrey and Ted had had lunch here together. It was only a few months before Audrey and Ted had separated. It was obvious then that he was crazy about her, and she certainly acted as if she was in love with him, too. Whatever broke it up? she wondered. But that was twenty-four years ago, and as far as she knew, Ted's last girlfriend was history.

Ted was studying her, too. I know I look darn good, Marcella thought, and if I can judge a man's expression, he thinks so, too.

"Want to know what I'm thinking?" she challenged him.

"Of course."

"I'm thinking that a lot of men pushing sixty are starting to lose their looks. Their hair gets thin or disappears. They put on weight. They just go all-around blah. But you're even more attractive now than way back when we were neighbors. I love it that your hair has turned white. With those blue eyes of yours, it makes a great combination. You've always been a big man, without having an ounce of fat on you. I like that. Victor was such a wimpy-looking guy."

With a shrug she dismissed her husband of twenty-two years, along with the annoying fact that only months after their divorce ten years ago, Victor had remarried, was now the father of two children, and, according to her pipeline, was divinely happy.

"You flatter me and I don't mind a bit," Ted said. "Now how about a cup of coffee, and then, after I drop you off, I've got to get back to the office."

Ted had suggested that she meet him at the Black Horse, but she had asked him to pick her up. "I know I'll have a glass of wine, and I don't want to drive afterwards," she had explained. The fact was that she wanted the intimacy of being in a car with him and the opportunity to prolong the time they spent together.

Half an hour later, Ted was pulling into her driveway. He parked, got out of the car and walked around to open the door for her. As she stood up, a car passed slowly along the road. They both recognized the driver, the Morris County prosecutor, Jeff MacKingsley.

"What's that all about?" Cartwright asked sharply. "The prosecutor doesn't usually get involved with simple vandalism."

"I can't imagine. Yesterday, Sergeant Earley certainly acted as if he was running the show. I wonder if anything else happened. I'll try to find out. I was planning to make some cinnamon rolls tomorrow morning and take them up to the Nolans," Marcella told him. "I'll give you a call if I hear anything." She looked at him, trying to decide if it was too soon to invite him to dinner. I don't want to scare him away, she thought. Then something in Ted Cartwright's expression took her breath away. He was staring at the prosecutor's car as it disappeared around the bend, and it was as if a mask had dropped. The expression on his face was somber and worried. Why should seeing Jeff MacKingsley's car around here bother him? she wondered. Then it occurred to her that maybe the only reason Ted had invited her to lunch was to pump information from her about what was going on next door.

Well, two can play at that game, she thought. "Ted, this has been so pleasant," she said. "Why don't you come over for dinner Friday night? I don't know whether you remember, but I'm a great cook."

The mask was back. His expression affable, Ted kissed her on the cheek. "I remember, Marcella," he said. "Is seven o'clock good for you?"

13

Jeff MacKingsley spent the better part of the day at Roxiticus Golf Club, participating in a golf outing that benefited the Morris County Historical Society. An excellent golfer with a six handicap, it was the kind of event that on a normal day he thoroughly enjoyed. Today, despite the perfect weather and the good friends in his foursome, he could not keep his mind on his game. The stories in the morning newspapers about the vandalism at One Old Mill Lane had gotten under his skin.

The picture of Celia Nolan fainting as she tried to run from the media particularly distressed and irritated him. If this had been a bias crime, we'd be combing the town to find out who did it, he kept thinking. Unlike the last episode this is no Halloween prank. This is *vicious*.

By the end of the morning he had lost to all of his three golfing companions. The result was that he paid for a round of Bloody Marys at the bar before the festive luncheon.

The club was decorated with sketches and paintings borrowed from the museum at George Washington's headquarters at Morristown. Jeff, a history buff, never failed to appreciate the fact that so much of the surrounding countryside had been fought over during the Revolutionary War.

But today during the luncheon he glanced unseeingly at the historical artifacts. Before coffee was served he called his office and was assured by Anna that it was a quiet day. She did not let him end the call until she commented on the newspapers she had read that morning: "The pictures they took of Little Lizzie's Place show that somebody really did a job on it this time," she said, with a certain amount of relish in her voice. "I'm going to drive by and take a look at it on my way home."

Jeff did not let her in on the fact that he was planning to do the exact same thing. He only hoped that he would not bump into his omnipresent secretary, but then consoled himself with the realization that he'd be there around three o'clock, and Anna wouldn't dream of leaving her desk until five.

The luncheon finally over, and with a last apology for his dismal game, Jeff escaped to his car, and less than ten minutes later was turning onto Old Mill Lane. As he drove he was remembering the night twenty-four years ago when he'd been at his desk exceptionally late catching up on school assignments, and on impulse had turned on the radio that was his prize possession. It was equipped with the police shortwave band the squad cars used. That was when he heard the intense report. "Male calling for help at One Old Mill Lane. Says he's been shot and his wife murdered. Neighbors reporting sounds of gunshots."

It had been about one in the morning, Jeff remembered. Mom and Dad were asleep. I got on my bicycle and rode over there and stood with some of the Bartons' neighbors on the road. God, it was a lousy, cold night, October 28th, twenty-four years ago. Within minutes, the media was swarming around the place. I saw the stretcher with Ted Cartwright being carried out of the house, two EMTs holding IVs that were attached to him. Then they brought out the body bag with Audrey Barton's corpse and put it in the meat wagon. I even remember what I was thinking—seeing her ride in the horse show and how she took first prize in jumping.

He had stayed at the scene until he saw the squad car with Liza

Barton inside speeding away. Even then I wondered what was going through her mind, Jeff recalled.

He still wondered that same thing. From what he understood, after she had thanked Clyde Earley for the blanket he wrapped around her, she didn't say another word for months.

As he passed the house at 3 Old Mill Lane, he saw a man and a woman standing in the driveway. The next-door neighbor, he thought, the one who had so much to say to the reporters. And that's Ted Cartwright with her. Wonder why he's around here?

Jeff was tempted to stop and talk to them, but he decided against it. It was obvious from the way she'd talked to the media that Marcella Williams was a gossip. I don't need her spreading the word that I have some kind of personal interest in this case, Jeff thought.

He slowed the car down almost to a crawl. Here it was, the Barton house. Little Lizzie's Place. A commercial-type van was in the driveway, and a man dressed in overalls was ringing the doorbell.

At first blush, the nineteenth-century, two-story mansion, with its unusual combination of a frame structure and a limestone foundation, did not seem damaged. But after Jeff stopped the car and got out, he could see where a base coat had been applied to many vandalized shingles, and splashes of red were still visible on the foundation. The newly laid sod also stood out from the rest of the lawn, and Jeff grimaced as he realized just how large the lettering of the painted message must have been.

He watched as the door opened and a woman appeared. She looked to be fairly tall and very slender. It had to be Celia Nolan, the new owner. She spoke to the workman for a moment, then closed the door, and the workman returned to the van and began to pull out a drop cloth and tools.

Jeff had not intended to do more than drive past the vandalized house, but on a sudden impulse decided to walk up the driveway and see for himself the remaining damage before it was repaired. That, of course, meant that he would have to speak to the new owners. He hated to disturb them, but there was no way the Morris County prosecutor could be walking around on their property without an explanation.

The workman turned out to be a mason who had been hired by the real estate agent to polish the limestone. Skinny, in his late sixties, with weathered skin and a prominent Adam's apple, he introduced himself as Jimmy Walker.

"Like the mayor of New York in the 1920s," he said with a hearty laugh. "They even wrote a song about him."

Jimmy Walker was a talker. "Last Halloween, Mrs. Harriman, she was the owner then, had me here, too. Boy, was she mad. The stuff the kids used that night came right off, but I guess the doll with the gun in its hand sitting in a chair on the porch really spooked her. When she opened the door in the morning that was the first thing she saw."

Jeff turned to go up to the porch, but Walker kept talking. "Guess the women who own this house all get nervous living here. I seen the newspaper this morning. We get the *Daily Record* delivered. It's good to get the local paper. You know what's going on. They had a big story about this house. Did you read it?"

I wonder if he gets paid by the hour, Jeff thought. If so, the Nolans are being ripped off. I bet if he doesn't catch somebody's ear, he talks to himself.

"I have the newspapers," he said shortly as he walked up the final step to the porch. He had seen the picture of the skull and crossbones in the papers, but even so, to be standing in front of it was entirely different. Someone had dug into the beautiful mahogany doors, someone talented enough to have carved the skull with excellent symmetry, to have placed the letters *L* and *B* exactly in the middle of the eye sockets.

But why? He pushed the doorbell and heard the faint sound of chimes echoing inside the house.

14

I tried to calm myself down after Alex left and to calm Jack as well. I could see that the events of the past few days were overwhelming him—the move from the only home he'd ever known, the police and reporters here, the pony, my fainting, the first day of pre-K, and now the tension between Alex and me.

I suggested that instead of having another ride on Lizzie—how I hated that name!—he should curl up on the couch in the den and I would read to him. "Lizzie wants a nap, too," I added, and maybe that did it. He helped me take off her saddle, and then willingly selected one of his favorite books. Within minutes he was asleep. I covered him with a light blanket, then sat watching him as he slept.

Minute by minute, I went over the mistakes I had made today. A normal wife, finding that picture in the barn, would have called her husband and told him about it. A normal mother would not have attempted a conspiracy with a four-year-old to keep his father or stepfather in ignorance. No wonder Alex had been both angry and disgusted. And what could I say to him by way of explanation that would make sense?

The sound of the telephone ringing in the kitchen did not cause even a stir in Jack. He was in the deep sleep that tired four-year-olds can achieve so easily. I ran from the den to the kitchen. Let it be Alex, I prayed.

But it was Georgette Grove. Her voice hesitant, she said that if I decided that I did not want to live in this house, she had several others in the area that she wanted to show me. "If you saw one of them you liked, I would forego my sales commission," she offered. "And I will make every effort to sell your house also without commission."

It was a very generous offer. Of course it did assume that we could afford to buy a second house without first having the money that Alex had put in this one, but then I am sure Georgette realized that as Laurence Foster's widow, I had my own resources. I told Georgette that I'd be very interested in looking at other houses with her and was surprised at the relief I could hear in her voice.

When I hung up the phone, I felt more hopeful. When Alex came back, I would tell him about the conversation with Georgette, and that if she found a suitable house, I would insist on laying out the money to purchase it myself. Alex is generous to a fault, but after growing up with adoptive parents who had to watch their money carefully, and then living with a wealthy husband who never wasted money, I could understand why Alex might not want to buy another house until this one was sold.

I was too restless to read, so I just wandered through the first-floor rooms. Yesterday the movers had arranged the furniture marked for the living room before I came downstairs, and the placement was all wrong. I am not into *feng shui*, but I am, after all, an interior designer. Before I was even aware of what I was doing, I was shoving the couch across the room and rearranging the chairs and tables and area carpets so that the room, though still stark, no longer looked like a furniture store. Fortunately the movers had happened to place the antique highboy that had been Larry's favorite piece of furniture against the appropriate wall. That I could never have moved.

After Alex left without having lunch, I hadn't bothered to eat, either. I'd covered both plates and put them in the refrigerator, but now I realized I had the beginning of a headache. I wasn't hungry, but I knew a cup of tea would help stave it off.

The doorbell rang before I could take my first step toward the kitchen, and I stopped in my tracks. Suppose it was a reporter? But then I remembered that before she hung up, Georgette Grove had told me that a mason was on his way to repair the limestone. I looked out the window and with relief saw the commercial vehicle parked in the driveway.

I opened the door, spoke to the man who introduced himself as Jimmy Walker—"The same name as a mayor of New York in the 1920s. They even wrote a song about him." I told him that he was expected and closed the door, but not before I had to see from inches away the damage that was on the open side of the double door.

For a moment after I closed the door, I kept my hand on the handle. With every fiber of my being I wanted to open it again and shout out to Jimmy Walker and the whole world that I was Liza Barton, the ten-year-old child who was terrified for her mother's life, and to tell them that there had been a split second when Ted Cartwright had looked at me and seen the pistol in my hand and *then decided to throw my mother at me, knowing the gun might go off.*

That split second had made the difference between Mother's life and her death. I leaned my head against the door. Even though the house was pleasantly cool, I could feel perspiration on my forehead. Was that interval something I actually remembered, or merely something I wanted to remember? I stood there, transfixed. Till this moment, my memory had been of Ted turning and yelling "Sure," then throwing Mother in a single motion.

The door chimes sounded again. The mason had a question, I was sure. I waited for half a minute, the time it would take to answer if I'd been in the next room, and then opened the door to find a man in his late thirties with an air of authority about him. He introduced himself as Jeffrey MacKingsley, the prosecutor of Morris County, and, almost witless with worry, I invited him in.

"I would have phoned if I had planned to stop by, but I was in the vicinity and decided to express my personal regrets at the unfortunate incident yesterday," he said following me into the living room.

As I mumbled, "Thank you, Mr. MacKingsley," his eyes were darting around the living room and I was glad that I had rearranged the furniture. The slipper chairs were facing each other on either side of the couch. The love seat was in front of the fireplace. The area carpets are all mellow with age, and their muted but rich colors were caught in the rays of the afternoon sun. The highboy with its fine lacquering and intricate carving is a beautiful example of eighteenth-century craftsmanship. The room needed more furniture, and, despite the fact that there were no window treatments or paintings or bric-a-brac in place, it still suggested that I was a normal owner with good taste settling into a new home.

That realization calmed me, and I was able to smile when Jeffrey MacKingsley said, "This is a lovely room, and I only hope that you will be able to get past what happened yesterday and enjoy it and this home. I can assure you that my office and the local police department will work together to find the culprit, or culprits. There won't be any more incidents, Mrs. Nolan, if we can help it."

"I hope not." Then I hesitated. Suppose Alex walked in now and brought up the photo I had found in the barn. "Actually . . ." I hesitated. I didn't know what to say.

The prosecutor's expression changed. "Has there been another incident, Mrs. Nolan?"

I reached in the pocket of my slacks and pulled out the newspaper photo. "This was taped to a post in the barn. My little boy found it when he went out to see his pony this morning." Choking at the deception, I asked, "Do you know who these people are?"

MacKingsley took the picture from me. I noticed that he was careful to hold it by its edge. He examined it, then looked at me. "Yes, I do," he said. I felt that he was attempting to sound matter-of-fact. "This is a picture of the family who restored this house."

"The Barton family!" I hated myself for managing to sound genuinely surprised.

"Yes," he said. He was watching for my reaction.

"I guess I suspected that," I said. I know my voice was nervous and strained.

"Mrs. Nolan, we might be able to lift some fingerprints from this picture," MacKingsley said. "Who else has handled it?"

"No one else. My husband had already left this morning when I found it. It was taped to the post too high up for Jack to reach it."

"I see. I want to take it and have it examined for fingerprints. Do you by any chance have a plastic bag that I could drop it in?"

"Of course." I was grateful to be able to move. I did not want this man to be studying me face-to-face any longer.

He followed me into the kitchen and I took a sandwich bag out of the drawer and handed it to him.

He dropped the picture into it. "I won't take any more of your time, Mrs. Nolan," he said. "But I have to ask you this: Were you or your husband planning to let the police know that you'd had another trespasser on your property?"

"This seemed so trivial," I hedged.

"I agree that it doesn't compare with what happened yesterday. However, the fact remains that someone was trespassing on your property again. There may be fingerprints we can get off this picture, and that may prove helpful in finding who is responsible for all this. We'll need your fingerprints for comparison purposes. I know that you have had a lot of stress, and I don't want you to have to come down to the office. I'll arrange for a Mendham police officer to come over in a few minutes with a fingerprint kit. He can take them right here."

A frightening possibility occurred to me. Would they just use my fingerprints to distinguish them from any others on the picture, or would they also run them through the system? Some kid in town had admitted the vandalism last Halloween. Suppose the police decided to check the juvenile files. Mine might be on record there.

"Mrs. Nolan, if you find any evidence of someone being on this property, *please* give us a call. I'm also going to ask the police to ride past the house regularly."

"I think that's a very good idea."

I had not heard Alex come in, and I guess MacKingsley hadn't either, because we both turned abruptly to find Alex standing in the doorway of the kitchen. I introduced the two men, and MacKingsley repeated to him that he would check the picture I'd found in the barn for fingerprints.

To my relief, Alex did not ask to see it. Surely MacKingsley would have found it odd if he had known that I hadn't shown it to my husband. He left immediately after that, then Alex and I looked at each other. He put his arms around me. "Peace, Ceil," he said. "I'm sorry I blew up. It's just that you've got to let me in on things. I am your husband, remember? Don't treat me as a stranger who has no business knowing what's going on."

He took up my offer to get out the salmon that he had left on the lunch table. We ate together on the patio and I told him about the offer Georgette Grove had made. "Certainly, start looking," he agreed. "And if we end up with two houses for awhile, so be it." Then he added, "Who knows, we may end up needing both of them."

I knew he meant it as a joke, but neither one of us smiled, and the old truism rushed through my mind. "Many a true word is spoken in jest." The doorbell rang. I opened the door, and the Mendham police officer with the fingerprint kit stepped inside. As I rolled the tips of my fingers in the ink, I thought of having done this before—the night I killed my mother.

15

When she arrived at the office, Georgette Grove sensed the tension in the air between Henry and Robin. Henry's habitual timid Casper Milquetoast expression was now one of petulance, and his thin lips were set in a stubborn line.

Robin's eyes were sending angry darts at him, and her body language suggested that she was ready to spring out of her chair and throw him a punch.

"What's up?" Georgette asked brusquely, hoping that she would signal to the two of them that she was not in a mood for petty co-worker hissy fits.

"It's very simple," Robin snapped. "Henry is in one of his doom-and-gloom moods, and I told him you had enough on your plate without him hanging out the crepe and wringing his hands."

"If you call the potential of a law suit that would finish this agency, 'doom and gloom,' you ought not to come into the real estate business," Henry snapped back. "Georgette, I assume you've read the newspapers? I ask you to remember that I have a stake in this agency, too."

"A twenty percent stake," Georgette said levelly, "which, if my arithmetic hasn't failed me, means that I own eighty percent."

"I also own twenty percent of the property on Route 24 and I want my money from it," Henry continued. "We have an offer. Either sell it or buy me out."

"Henry, you know perfectly well that the people who want to buy that property are fronting for Ted Cartwright. If he gets his hands on it, he'll have enough land to press for commercial zoning. Long ago, we agreed that we'd eventually deed that property to the state."

"Or that you would buy me out," Henry insisted stubbornly. "Georgette, let me tell you something. That house on Old Mill Lane is cursed. You're the only real estate agent in town who would accept the exclusive listing on it. You've wasted this firm's money advertising it. When Alex Nolan asked to see it, you should have told him the truth about it right then and there. The morning I showed that place to Celia Nolan, there was something positively chilling in the atmosphere of the room where the murder took place. She felt it and it upset her. As I also told you, the damn place smelled like a funeral parlor."

"Her husband ordered the flowers. I didn't," Georgette replied hotly.

"I saw the picture in the newspaper of that poor girl collapsing, and *you* are responsible for it. I hope you realize that."

"All right, Henry, you've had your say," Robin said, suddenly speaking up, her tone even and firm. "Why don't you calm down?" She looked at Georgette. "I was hoping to spare you from getting hit with this the minute you walked in."

Georgette looked gratefully at Robin. I was her age when I opened this agency, she thought. She's got what it takes to make people want the houses she shows them. Henry doesn't give a damn anymore whether or not he makes a sale. He wants to retire so much that he can taste it. "Look, Henry," she said, "there is a potential solution. Alex Nolan did publicly admit that he cut me off when I tried to tell him about the background of the house. The Nolans want to live in the area. I'm going to go through every listing I can find and line up some houses to show Celia Nolan. If I find something she likes, I'll waive the commission. Alex Nolan didn't even want to press a complaint against whoever vandalized the house. I have a feeling they'll both be amenable to settling this matter quietly."

Henry Paley shrugged and, without answering, turned and walked down the hall to his office.

"I swear he'll be disappointed if you manage to pull that rabbit out of the hat," Robin commented.

"I'm afraid you're right," Georgette agreed, "but I *am* going to pull it out."

It was an unexpectedly busy morning with a young drop-in couple who seemed seriously interested in buying a home in the Mendham area. Georgette spent several hours driving them to view places in their price range, then calling the owners and getting permission to go through the ones they liked. They left after promising to come back with their parents to look at a house they seemed to have fallen in love with.

Georgette had a quick sandwich and coffee at her desk, and for the next two hours went through the multiple-broker listing of residences for sale and studied it carefully in the hope that one of them would jump out as an attractive prospect for Celia Nolan.

She finally culled the list down to four possibilities. She would push the two she had an exclusive on, but show Celia the others if necessary. She was friends with the agent who had those two listings, and could count on making some kind of arrangement about her share of the commission.

Her fingers crossed, she called the Nolans' number and was relieved and delighted that Celia seemed totally amenable to looking at other houses in the area. Next, she made phone calls to the owners of the houses she had selected and asked to see them immediately.

At four o'clock she was on her way. "I'll be back," she told Robin. "Wish me luck."

Three of the houses she eliminated from consideration. All were charming in their own way, but not, she was sure, what Celia Nolan would be interested in. The one she had saved for last seemed, from the description, to be a real possibility. It was a farmhouse that had been restored, and was vacant now because the owner had been transferred by his employer on short notice. She remembered that she had heard that the house showed well because it had just been redecorated. It was near the town line of Peapack, in the same area in which Jackie Kennedy once had a home. *I never did get to see this one because it received an immediate offer last month, but then the sale fell through,* Georgette reflected.

A beautiful piece of property, she thought as she drove up to the entrance. *It has twelve acres, so there's plenty of room for the pony.* She stopped to open the gate of the split-rail fence. *This kind of fence is so in harmony with the surroundings,* she decided as she pushed the gate back. *Some of those gaudy gates and fences they're putting on the McMansions are an insult to the eye.*

She got back in the car, then drove up the long driveway and parked at the house's front door. She opened the lockbox and was glad to see that the key was there, meaning that no one else was showing the house. *Of course, nobody is around,* she thought, *otherwise there'd be a car here.* She let herself in and walked through the rooms. The house was immaculate. Every room had been repainted recently. The kitchen was state-of-the-art, while retaining the look of an old-fashioned country kitchen.

It's in move-in condition, she thought. *Even though it's more expensive than Old Mill Lane, my guess is that if Celia Nolan likes it, the price wouldn't be a problem.*

With growing hope, she inspected the house from attic to basement. In the finished basement, a storage closet near the stairs was locked and the key for it was missing. I know Henry showed this house the other day, Georgette thought with growing irritation. I wonder if he absentmindedly pocketed the key. Last week he couldn't find his key to the office, and then later was searching everywhere for his car key. It doesn't have to be his fault, of course; right now I'm ready to blame him for everything, she admitted to herself.

There was a splotch of red on the floor outside the closet. Georgette knelt down to examine it. It was paint—she was sure of that. The dining room was a rich, deep shade of red. This was probably the storage closet for leftover cans of paint, she decided.

She went back upstairs, closed and locked the door, and returned the house key to the lockbox. As soon as she reached the office, she called Celia Nolan and raved about the farmhouse.

"It does sound worth taking a look at."

Celia sounds low-key, Georgette thought, but at least she's willing to see it. "It won't last on the market, Mrs. Nolan," she assured her. "If ten o'clock tomorrow morning is all right with you, I'll be happy to pick you up."

"No, that's all right. I'd rather drive myself. I always like to have my own car. That way I can be sure I'll be on time to pick up Jack at school."

"I understand. Well, let me give you the address," Georgette said. She listened as Celia repeated it after her, then was about to give directions, but Celia interrupted.

"There's another call coming in. I'll meet you there tomorrow at ten o'clock sharp."

Georgette snapped shut her cell phone and shrugged. When Celia Nolan has time to think, she'll probably call back for directions.

That house isn't the easiest place to find. She waited expectantly for her phone to ring, but it did not. She probably has a navigation system in her car, she decided.

"Georgette, I want to apologize." Henry Paley was standing at the door to her office.

Georgette looked up.

Before she could answer, Paley continued: "That is not to say I didn't mean every word, but I apologize for the way I said it."

"Accepted," Georgette told him, then added, "Henry, I'm taking Celia Nolan to see the farmhouse on Holland Road. I know you were there last week. Do you remember if the key to the storage closet in the basement was there?"

"I believe it was."

"Did you look in the closet?"

"No. The couple I took out were obviously not interested in the house. It was too pricey for them. We stayed only a few minutes. Well, I'll be on my way. Goodnight, Georgette."

Georgette sat for long minutes after he left. I always said I could smell a liar, she thought, but what in the name of God has Henry got to lie about? And why, after he viewed it, didn't he tip me off to the fact the house is sure to move fast?

16

After she had viewed the vandalism on Old Mill Lane, Dru Perry went straight back to the *Star-Ledger* office and wrote up the story. She was pleased to see that her picture of Celia Nolan fainting had been picked to run with it.

"Trying to put me out of business?" Charlie, the newspaper's photographer who had rushed to the scene, asked jokingly.

"No. Just lucky enough to be there and catch the moment." That was when Dru had told Ken Sharkey, her editor, that she wanted to do a feature story on the Barton case. "It's absolutely perfect for my 'Story Behind the Story' series," she said.

"Any idea where Barton is now?" Sharkey asked.

"No, not a clue."

"What will make it a real story is if you can track Liza Barton down and get her version of what happened in that house that night."

"I intend to try."

"Go ahead with it. Knowing you, you'll find something juicy." Ken Sharkey's quick smile was a dismissal.

"By the way, Ken. I'm going to work at home tomorrow."

"Okay with me."

When she had moved from Washington five years earlier, Dru had found the perfect home. A small house on Chestnut Street in

Montclair, it was a reasonable commute to the *Star-Ledger* in Newark. Unlike people who bought condos and town houses to avoid landscaping and snow-plowing problems, Dru loved tending her own lawn and having a small garden.

Another plus was that the train station was down the block, so she could be in midtown Manhattan in twenty minutes without the hassle of driving and parking. Dru, a film and theatre buff, went there three or four evenings a week.

Early in the morning, comfortably dressed in a sweatshirt and jeans, coffeepot plugged in beside her, she settled at her desk in the office she had created in what would have been a second bedroom for most people. The wall in front of her desk was covered with a corkboard. When she was writing a feature story, she tacked all the information she downloaded from the Internet on it. By the time she had completed a "Story Behind the Story" feature for the *Sunday Star-Ledger,* the wall was a jumble of pictures, clippings, and scrawled notes that made sense only to her.

She had downloaded everything available about the Liza Barton case. Twenty-four years ago, it had stayed in the news for weeks. Then, as with all sensational stories, it had quieted down until the trial. When the verdict was released, the story hit the headlines again. Psychiatrists, psychologists, and pseudo–mental health experts had been invited to comment on Liza's acquittal.

"Rent-a-Psychiatrist," Dru mumbled aloud as she read the quotes attributed to several medical professionals who agreed that they were gravely concerned by the verdict and believed that Liza Barton was one of those children capable of planning and executing a cold-blooded murder.

She found one interview particularly grating. "Let me give you an example," that psychiatrist had said. "Last year I treated a nine-year-old who smothered her baby sister. 'I wanted her to be dead,' she told me, 'but I didn't want her to stay dead.' That is the difference between my patient and Liza Barton. My patient simply didn't understand the finality of death. What she wanted was to stop the infant's crying. From every indication I see, Liza Barton wanted her mother dead. She thought her mother was betraying her deceased father when she remarried. The neighbors attested to the fact that Liza was always antagonistic to her stepfather. I wouldn't be surprised if she was intelligent enough to be able to fake that so-called trauma when she didn't say a word for months."

It's people like that windbag who helped perpetuate the "Little Lizzie" myth, Dru thought.

When she began to put together a feature article for her series, Dru always listed on the board any name she came across that had been mentioned as being connected in any way with the story. Now two columns on the board were already full. The list began with Liza, Audrey Barton, and Ted Cartwright. The next name Dru added after that was Liza's father, Will Barton. He had died in a riding accident. How idyllic had his marriage to Audrey been? She intended to find out.

A name that jumped out at her as being of special interest was that of Diane Wesley. Described in the newspapers as "a model and former girlfriend of Cartwright," at the time of the trial, she had posed for the photographers and willingly discussed her testimony even though she was under a gag order from the judge. She told reporters that she had dinner with Ted Cartwright the evening of the tragedy, and that he told her he'd been seeing his wife secretly, and that the child's hatred of him was the cause of the rift.

Diane's testimony could have helped convict Liza except for the fact that a former friend of hers went to court and said that Diane had complained that Ted had been physically abusive to her during their relationship. If so, then why was she so willing to back up his story at the trial? Dru wondered. I'd love to interview her now.

Benjamin Fletcher, the lawyer who had been appointed to defend Liza Barton, was another one who set Dru's antenna quivering. When she looked him up, she found that he had gotten a law degree when he was forty-six, had worked as a public defender for only two years, then quit to open a one-man office handling divorces, wills, and house closings. He was still in practice in Chester, a town not far from Mendham. Dru calculated his age now to be seventy-five. He'd be a good starting point, she decided. The court probably won't open any juvenile files. But it's obvious Fletcher never specialized in juvenile defense. So why was someone who was relatively inexperienced appointed to defend a child on a murder charge? she wondered.

More questions than answers, Dru thought. She leaned back in her swivel chair, took off her glasses, and began twirling them—a sign her friends compared to a fox picking up a scent.

17

Marcella hasn't changed a bit, Ted Cartwright thought bitterly as he sipped a scotch in his office in Morristown. Still the same nosey gossip and still potentially dangerous. He picked up the glass paperweight from his desk and hurled it across the room. With satisfaction he watched as it slammed into the center of the leather chair in the corner of his office. I never miss, he thought, as he visualized the faces of the people he wished were sitting in that chair when the paperweight landed.

What was Jeff MacKingsley doing on Old Mill Lane today? The question had been repeating itself in his mind ever since he saw MacKingsley drive past Marcella's house. Prosecutors don't personally investigate vandalism, so there had to be another reason.

The phone rang—his direct line. His sharp bark of "Ted Cartwright" was greeted by a familiar voice.

"Ted, I saw the newspapers. You take a good picture and tell a good story. I can vouch for how broken-hearted a husband you were. I can prove it, too. And, as you've probably guessed, I'm calling because I'm a little short of cash."

18

When Georgette phoned to suggest seeing other houses, I was quick to respond. Once we are out of this house and living in a different one, we will simply be the new people in town. We will have regained our anonymity. That thought kept me going all through the afternoon.

Alex had asked the movers to put his desk, his computer, and boxes of books in the library, a large room facing the back of the house. On my birthday, when he and the agent, Henry Paley, led me from room to room, Alex had enthusiastically announced that he would take the library as his home office, and pointed out that it would also accommodate his grand piano. I was nervous about asking him if he had canceled delivery of the piano from the storage house, scheduled for next week.

After our late lunch, with its strained atmosphere, Alex escaped to the library and began unpacking his books, at least those he intended to make accessible. When Jack woke up, I brought him upstairs. Luckily, he's a child who can amuse himself. In the joy of late parenthood, Larry swamped him with gifts, but it was clear from the beginning that blocks were his favorite toys. Jack loved to build with them, creating houses and bridges and the occasional skyscraper. I remember Larry commenting, "Well your father was an architect, Celia. Must be in his genes."

The genes of an architect are acceptable, I thought as I watched my son sitting cross-legged on the floor in the corner of my old playroom. While he played, I busied myself going through the files I had meant to clean out before we moved.

By five o'clock, Jack had tired of the blocks, so we went downstairs. Tentatively I looked into the library. Alex had papers scattered over the surface of his desk. He often brings home the file of a case he is working on, but I could also see a pile of newspapers on the floor beside him. He looked up and smiled when we came in. "Hey, you two, I was getting lonesome down here. Jack, we never did get very far with your pony ride did we? How about we try it now?"

Of course that was all Jack needed to hear. He rushed for the back door. Alex got up, came to me, and cradled my face in his hands. It is a loving gesture that never fails to make me feel protected.

"Ceil, I reread those newspapers. I think I'm beginning to understand how you feel about living here. Maybe this house *is* cursed. At least, a lot of people apparently think it is. Personally, I don't believe in that stuff, but my first and only goal is your happiness. Do you believe that?"

"Yes, I do." I said over the lump in my throat, thinking that Alex didn't need another weeping session.

The phone in the kitchen rang. I hurried to answer it, and Alex followed me on his way to the back yard. It was Georgette Grove telling me about a wonderful farmhouse that she wanted me to see. I agreed to meet her, then got off quickly because I heard the "call waiting" click. I switched to the other call as Alex started out the back door. He must have heard me gasp, because he turned quickly, but then I shook my head and hung up the phone. "The beginning of a sales pitch," I lied.

I had forgotten to ask the phone company to keep our phone number unlisted. What I had heard was a husky voice, obviously disguised, whispering, "May I speak to Little Lizzie, please?"

*   *   *

The three of us went out for dinner that evening, but all I could think of was the call. Had someone recognized me, I wondered anxiously, or was it the kind of prank kids play? I did my best to act festive with Alex and Jack, but I knew I wasn't fooling Alex. When we got home, I pleaded a headache and went to bed early.

Sometime in the middle of the night, Alex woke me up.

"Ceil, you're crying in your sleep," he said.

And I was. It was the same as after I fainted. I simply could not stop crying. Alex held me, and after awhile I fell asleep with my head on his shoulder. In the morning he waited to have breakfast with Jack and me. Then, when Jack ran back upstairs to get dressed, he said to me quietly, "Ceil, you've *got* to see a doctor, either the one you go to in New York, or someone out here. That fainting spell and these crying sessions may mean something is physically wrong with you. And if it isn't physical, then you must make an appointment with a psychologist or a psychiatrist. My cousin suffered from clinical depression, and that started with crying sessions."

"I'm not depressed," I protested. "It's just . . ."

I heard my voice trail off. When my adoptive parents took me to California I saw a psychologist, Dr. Moran, for seven years, stopping only when I left to attend the Fashion Institute. Dr. Moran wanted me to continue to be treated in New York, but I said no to that suggestion. I didn't want to rake over my past with a new shrink. Instead, from time to time, I phoned Dr. Moran, something I still do.

"To please you, I will get a checkup," I promised, "and we might as well find someone out here, but I promise you there's nothing wrong with me."

"Let's be *sure* of that, Ceil. I'll ask around at the club and get some names. And now I'd better get out of here. Good luck with your house hunting."

There is something that seems so normal about a husband who is in a bit of a hurry, kissing his wife and rushing out to the car. I stood at the window, watching Alex go, his well-tailored jacket accentuating the width of his shoulders. He gave a last quick wave and blew me a kiss as he drove away.

I tidied up the kitchen, went upstairs, showered, dressed, and made the beds, realizing as I did it that I would have to start looking for a housekeeper and a babysitter for Jack. After I dropped Jack off at pre-K, I picked up the papers and stopped again at the diner for coffee. I skimmed the papers quickly, finding thankfully that there was nothing about the vandalism except a brief item stating that the police were continuing their investigation. Finishing my coffee, I headed out to keep my appointment with Georgette Grove.

I knew exactly where Holland Road is located. My grandmother had a cousin who had lived on that road, and when I was little I used to visit there. I remembered that it's in a beautiful section. On one side of the road, you look down into the valley; on the other, the properties are built along the hill. The moment I saw the house and property where I was meeting Georgette, I thought, oh God, this could be the answer. I knew immediately that at least from the outside appearance, it was a house Alex would like, and in a location that would please him.

The gate of the split-rail fence was open and I could see Georgette's silver BMW sedan in front of the house. I glanced at my watch. It was only quarter to ten. I parked behind the BMW and went up on the porch and rang the bell. I waited, then rang it again. Perhaps she's in the basement or attic, and can't hear me, I thought. Not quite sure what to do, I turned the doorknob and found it unlocked. Pushing the door open, I went into the house and called Georgette's name as I walked from room to room.

The house is bigger than the one in Old Mill Lane. In addition to the family room and library, it has a second smaller dining room and a study. I checked all of them, even knocking on the doors of the three powder rooms, and opening them when there was no response.

Georgette was nowhere on the downstairs floor. I stood at the bottom of the front staircase and called out her name, but there was only silence from the second floor. The day had begun sunny, but had clouded over, and suddenly the house seemed very dark. I began to feel uneasy, but then told myself that it was ridiculous to worry. Georgette had to be there somewhere.

I remembered that in the kitchen I had noticed that the door to the lower level of the house was open a few inches, so I decided to look for her down there first. I walked back to the kitchen, pulled that door open wide, and switched on the light. I could see from the oak paneling along the stairway that this area of the house was no ordinary basement. I called Georgette's name again and started down the stairs, growing more uneasy with every step. My instinct now told me something was terribly wrong. Had Georgette had an accident? I wondered.

I turned on the switch at the foot of the stairs and the recreation room blazed with overhead lights. The back wall was completely glass, with sliding doors that led out to a patio. I walked over to them, thinking Georgette might have gone outside, but I found them locked. Then I realized there was a faint but pungent odor in the room, a smell I recognized as turpentine.

It became stronger as I crossed the room and went down a

hall, past another bathroom. As I turned a corner, I stumbled over a foot.

Georgette was lying on the floor, her eyes open, drying blood caked on her forehead. A can of turpentine was at her side, the contents seeping onto the carpet. She was still holding a rag in her hand. The gun that had killed her was lying precisely in the center of a splotch of red paint on the floor.

I remember screaming.

I remember running out of the house and into my car.

I remember driving home.

I remember dialing 911 at some point, but I could not get a word out when the operator answered.

I was sitting in my house, still clutching the phone when the police arrived, and the next thing I remember was waking up in the hospital and hearing Sergeant Earley ask me why I had dialed 911.

19

Jarrett Alberti, a locksmith, was the second person to find the body of Georgette Grove. He had an appointment to meet Georgette at the farmhouse on Holland Road at eleven thirty. When he got there, he parked behind Georgette's car, saw that the front door was open, and, like Celia Nolan, went inside looking for her. Not knowing that he was duplicating Celia's grim search, he went through the rooms calling out Georgette's name.

In the kitchen, he could see that the lights to the lower level were on, so he went downstairs. He caught the odor of turpentine and followed it until, like Celia an hour earlier, he turned the corner and found Georgette's body.

An ex-marine, the stocky twenty-eight-year-old was familiar with death on the battlefield, having served two tours in Iraq before being discharged for a wound that had shattered his ankle. This death was different though—Georgette Grove was a lifetime friend of his family.

He stood still for a full minute, taking in the scene. Then, in a disciplined response, he turned around, walked outside, dialed 911, and waited on the porch until the police arrived.

An hour later he observed in a detached way that the place was swarming with activity. Yellow tape was being put in place to keep the media and the neighbors away. The coroner was with the body, and the forensic team was searching the house and grounds for evidence. Jarrett had already assured them that he had touched neither the body nor anything around it.

Prosecutor Jeff MacKingsley and Lola Spaulding, a detective from the police department, were questioning him on the porch. "I'm a locksmith," Jarrett explained. "Last night Georgette called me at home."

"What time did she call you?" MacKingsley asked.

"About nine o'clock."

"Isn't that pretty late to make a business call?"

"Georgette was my mom's best friend. She used to call herself my surrogate aunt. She always called me if a house she was trying to sell needed locks fixed or replaced." Jarrett thought of how Georgette had sat with him at his mother's bedside when his mother was dying.

"What did she say she wanted done?"

"She said that the key was missing for a storage closet in this house. She wanted me to get over here by nine o'clock to replace the lock. I told her I couldn't get here until ten, and she said in that case to make it eleven thirty."

"Why was that?" Jeff asked.

"She said that she didn't want me working on the lock while her client was here, and that she surely would be gone by eleven thirty."

"Georgette referred to the client as 'she.' "

"Yes," Jarrett confirmed. He hesitated, then added, "I told Georgette that it would be a lot easier for my schedule to come at just about ten, but she said absolutely not. She didn't want the client around when the closet was opened. I thought that was kind of funny, so I jokingly asked her if she thought there was gold hidden in it. I said, 'You can trust me, Georgette, I won't steal it.' "

"And . . ."

The shock Jarrett had been feeling ever since he found the body was fading. In its place a sense of loss was settling in. Georgette Grove had been part of his life for all his twenty-eight years, and now somebody had shot her, killing her.

"And Georgette said that she knew she could trust me, which was more than she could say about certain other people in her life."

"She didn't elaborate on that statement?"

"No."

"Do you know where she was when she called you?"

"Yes. She told me she was still in her office."

"Jarrett, when the body is removed, can you open the door to the storage closet for us?"

"That's what I came here to do, isn't it?" Jarrett replied. "If it's all right with you, I'll wait in my van until you need me." He was not ashamed that he was becoming upset.

Forty minutes later he watched as the body bag was carried out and placed in the coroner's mortuary ambulance. Detective Spaulding came over to his van. "We're ready for you downstairs," she said.

Removing the lock to the storage closet was a simple operation. Without being asked, Jarrett pushed open the door. He didn't know what he expected to find, but he believed that whatever was in this closet was responsible for his friend's death.

The light went on automatically. He found himself staring at shelves with neatly aligned paint cans, most of them sealed and labeled with the name of the room for which they were intended.

"There's nothing but paint cans in here," he exclaimed. "Nobody shot Georgette because of paint cans, did they?"

Jeff MacKingsley did not answer him. He was looking at the cans on the bottom shelf. They were the only ones that were not sealed. Three of them were empty. The fourth was half full. The lid was missing. The splotch on the floor that Georgette Grove had been trying to clean up probably came from this one, Jeff thought. All the open cans were labeled "dining room." All had contained red paint. It doesn't take a genius to figure out that this was where the vandals got the paint they used on the Nolans' house, he thought. Is *that* why Georgette Grove was murdered? Would it be worth killing her to keep her quiet?

"Is it okay if I take off now?" Jarrett asked.

"Of course. We will need to get a formal statement from you, but that can be done later. Thanks for all your help, Jarrett."

Jarrett nodded and walked down the hall, taking care to avoid the chalked outline of where Georgette's body had fallen. As he did, Clyde Earley came down the stairs, his expression grim. He crossed the recreation room and went up to MacKingsley.

"I just came from the hospital," Earley said. "We took Celia Nolan there in an ambulance. At ten after ten she dialed 911, then didn't say anything, just was gasping into the phone. They alerted us, so we went to her house. She was in shock. No response to our questions. We took her to the hospital. In the emergency room, she started to come out of it. She was here this morning. She says she found the body and drove home."

"She found the body and drove home!" Jeff exclaimed.

"She says she remembers seeing the body, running out of the house, then getting in her car and driving home. She remembers trying to call us. She doesn't remember anything else until she started to come out of shock in the hospital."

"How is she now?" Jeff asked.

"Sedated, but okay. They reached the husband. He's on his way to the hospital, and she insists she's going home with him. There was a scene at the school when she didn't pick up her son. The kid got hysterical. He saw her faint the other day, and apparently is scared she's going to die. One of the teachers brought him to the hospital. He's with her now."

"We have to talk to her," Jeff said. "She must have been the client Georgette Grove was expecting to meet."

"Well, I don't think she'll be in the mood to buy this place now," Earley commented. "Looks like she has her hands full living in *one* crime scene."

"Did she say what time she got here?"

"Quarter of ten. She was early."

Then we lost over an hour from the time she saw the body until Jarrett Alberti called us, Jeff thought.

"Jeff, we found something in the victim's shoulder bag that might be interesting." With gloved hands, Detective Spaulding was holding a newspaper clipping. She brought it over for him to see. It was the picture of Celia Nolan fainting that had appeared in the newspaper the day before. "It looks as if it was put in Georgette's bag after she was killed," Spaulding said. "We've already checked it for fingerprints and there aren't any on it."

20

I think what really calmed me down was the absolute panic I saw in Jack's face. When he came into the emergency room cubicle where they had settled me, he was still sobbing. He usually goes willingly into Alex's arms, but after his scare when I wasn't there to pick him up at school, he would only cling to me.

We rode home in the back seat of the car, Jack's hand in mine. Alex was heartsick for both of us. "God, Ceil," he said. "I can't even imagine what a horrible experience that was for you. What's going *on* in this town?"

What indeed? I thought.

It was nearly quarter to two, and we were all hungry. Alex opened a can of soup for us and made Jack his favorite, a peanut butter and jelly sandwich. The hot soup helped me shake off the grogginess caused by the sedative the doctor had injected into my arm.

We had barely finished eating when reporters started ringing the doorbell. I glanced out the window and noticed that one of them was an older woman with wild gray hair. I remembered that she had been running toward me just as I had fainted on the day we moved in.

Alex went outside. For the second time in forty-eight hours, he made a statement to the press: "After the vandalism that we found when we moved into this house on Tuesday, we decided it would be better for us to choose a different home in the area. Georgette Grove arranged to meet my wife in a house being offered for sale on Holland Road. When Celia arrived, she found Ms. Grove's body and rushed home to notify the police."

When he was finished, I could see that he was being bombarded with questions. "What did they ask you?" was my question to him when he came back inside.

"I guess the ones you'd expect: Why didn't you call the police immediately? Weren't you carrying a cell phone? I pointed out that for all you knew the killer might still have been in the house, and you did the smartest thing possible—you got out of there."

A few minutes later, Jeffrey MacKingsley called and asked to come over and speak to me. Alex wanted to put him off, but I immediately agreed to see him. Every instinct told me that it was important I give the appearance of being a cooperative witness.

MacKingsley arrived with a man I'd guess to be in his early fifties. Chubby-faced, with thinning hair and a serious demeanor, he was introduced as Detective Paul Walsh. MacKingsley told me that Detective Walsh would be in charge of the investigation into Georgette Grove's death.

With Alex sitting on the couch beside me, I responded to their questions. I explained that we wanted to stay in the area, but the history of this house and the vandalism was too upsetting for us to remain here. I told them that Georgette had offered to forego her commission if she found a suitable house for us, and that she said she would make every effort to resell this one, also foregoing her commission.

"You were not aware of the background of this house before you saw it for the first time last month?" Detective Walsh asked.

I felt my palms begin to sweat. I chose my answer carefully. "I was not aware of the reputation of this house before I saw it last month."

"Mrs. Nolan, do you know about the law in New Jersey that mandates that a real estate broker must inform a prospective buyer if a house has a stigma on it, meaning if a crime has been committed here, or a suicide, or even if a house is reputed to be haunted."

I did not have to feign my astonishment. "I absolutely did not know that," I said. "Then Georgette really wasn't being all that generous when she offered to forego her commission?"

"She *did* try to tell me that the house had a history, but I cut her off," Alex explained. "As I told her, when I was a kid, my family used to rent a rundown house on Cape Cod that the natives swore was haunted."

"Nevertheless, from what I read in yesterday's papers, you bought this house as a gift for your wife. It's in her name only, so Ms. Grove had a responsibility to disclose the history to her," MacKingsley informed us.

"No wonder Georgette was so upset about the vandalism," I said. "When we arrived here Tuesday morning, she was trying to drag the hose out of the garage to wash the paint away." I felt a flash of anger. I should have been spared the horror of moving back into this house. Then I thought of Georgette Grove as I had seen her in that split second before I ran, the blood crusting her forehead, the rag in her hand. She'd been trying to get rid of that splash of red paint on the floor.

Red paint is like blood. First it spills, then it thickens and hardens . . .

"Mrs. Nolan, did you ever meet Georgette Grove before you moved into this house?"

The red paint on the floor near Georgette's body . . .

"Celia," Alex murmured, and I realized Detective Walsh had repeated his question. Had I ever met Georgette Grove when I was a child? My mother might easily have known her, but I had no memory of her.

"No," I said.

"Then you only saw her the day you moved in, and that was for a brief time?"

"That's right," Alex said, and I caught the edge in his voice. "Georgette didn't stay long on Tuesday. She wanted to get back to her office and arrange for the house and the lawn to be restored. When I got home yesterday, Celia told me that Georgette had phoned to say she wanted to show her other houses, and late yesterday afternoon I was here when she called back to make the appointment for this morning."

Walsh was taking notes. "Mrs. Nolan, if I may, let's go through this step by step. You had an appointment to meet Ms. Grove this morning."

There's no reason for me not to be absolutely cooperative, I warned myself. Don't look as if you're fumbling for answers, just describe exactly what happened. "Georgette offered to pick me up, but I told her I wanted to have my own car so I could be sure to be on time to pick Jack up after school at Saint Joe's. I dropped him off about quarter of nine, went into the diner in the shopping center for a cup of coffee, then drove to meet Georgette."

"She had given you directions to Holland Road?" Walsh asked.

"No. I mean YES, of course she did!"

I caught a flicker of surprise on both their faces. I was contradicting myself. I could feel them trying to read my thoughts, weighing and measuring my responses.

"Did you have any trouble finding the house?" Walsh asked. "Holland Road isn't that clearly marked."

"I drove slowly," I said. Then I described finding the gate open, seeing Georgette's car, walking through the entry floor, calling her name, going downstairs, smelling the turpentine, finding the body.

"Did you touch anything, Mrs. Nolan?" This time the question came from MacKingsley.

In my mind I retraced my steps. Was it only a few hours ago that I had been in that house? "I turned the handle on the front door," I said. "I don't think I touched anything else until I pushed open the door leading to the lower level. In the recreation room I went over to the glass doors that lead to the patio. I thought that Georgette might have gone outside. But they were locked, so I guess I might have touched them too, because how else would I have known they were locked? Then I walked down that hall because of the turpentine odor, and I found Georgette."

"Do you own a pistol, Mrs. Nolan?" Walsh asked suddenly.

The question came out of the blue. I knew it was intended to startle me. "No, of course not," I protested.

"Have you ever fired a pistol?"

I looked at my inquisitor. Behind his round glasses, his eyes were a muddy shade of brown. The expression in them was intense now, probing. What kind of question was that to ask of an innocent person who had been unfortunate enough to discover the victim of a deadly crime? I knew Walsh had picked up something in what I had said, or not said, that alerted his investigative instincts.

Of course, once again I lied. "No, I have not."

Finally Walsh pulled out a newspaper clipping that was in a plastic bag. It was the photograph of me in the process of fainting.

"Would you have any idea why this photograph would be in Ms. Grove's shoulder bag?" he asked me.

I was grateful that Alex answered for me. "Why in the name of God would my wife know what Georgette Grove was carrying in her shoulder bag?" He stood up. Without waiting for an answer, he said, "I am sure you can understand that this has been another stressful day for our family."

Both men got up immediately. "We may need to talk to you again, Mrs. Nolan," the prosecutor said. "You're not planning any trips are you?"

Only to the ends of the earth, I wanted to say, but instead, with bitterness I could not hide, I said, "No, Mr. MacKingsley, I'll be right here, at home."

21

Zach Willet's leathery face, hard-muscled body, and callused hands gave mute testimony to the fact that he was a lifelong outdoorsman. Now sixty-two, Zach had worked at the Washington Valley Riding Club from the time he was twelve years old. He started by mucking out the stables on weekends, then, at age sixteen, quit school to work at the club full time.

"I know everything I need to know," he had told the teacher who protested that he had a good mind and should continue his education. "I understand horses and they understand me."

A pervasive lack of ambition had kept him from progressing beyond the role of all-around handyman at Washington Valley. He liked grooming and exercising horses and was content just to do that. He could take care of any minor ailments his equine friends suffered from, and he could skillfully clean and repair tack. On the side he ran a tidy business reselling the artifacts of the horsey set. He dealt with two types of customers: people who were replacing tack and people whose enthusiasm for riding had waned and were glad to unload the pricey trappings of the expensive sport.

When the regular instructors were booked, Zach would sometimes give riding lessons, but that wasn't one of his favorite activities. It annoyed him to see people who had no business on a horse nervously pulling at the reins and then being scared out of their wits when the horse protested by throwing back its head.

Thirty years ago, Ted Cartwright had kept his horses at Washington Valley. A couple of years later, he had moved them to the nearby but more prestigious Peapack stables.

Early Thursday afternoon, the word of Georgette Grove's death spread through the club. Zach had known and liked Georgette. From time to time she had recommended him to people looking to board a horse. "Introduce yourself to Zach at Washington Valley. Take care of him, and he'll treat your horse like a baby," she'd tell them.

"Why would anybody want to kill a nice lady like Georgette Grove?" was the question everyone was asking.

Zach did his best thinking when he was out riding. Frowning thoughtfully, he saddled up one of the horses he was paid to exercise and took off on the trail that led up the hills behind the club. When he was near the top, he veered off onto a trail in which very few riders ever ventured. The descent was too steep for anyone but an experienced rider, but that was not the reason Zach usually avoided it. What passed for his conscience did not need reminding of what had happened there so many years ago.

If you can do that to one human being who's in your way, you can do it to another, he reasoned, as he kept the horse to a walk. No question, I heard enough around town to know that Georgette was in his way. He needs that land she owned on Route 24 for the commercial buildings he wants to put up. Bet the cops get on his tail fast. If he did it, wonder if he'd be stupid enough to use the same gun?

Zach thought of the bent cartridge he had hidden in his apartment on the upstairs floor of a two-family house in Chester. Last night, when Ted Cartwright had slipped him the envelope in Sammy's Bar, there was no mistaking the threat Ted had whispered: "Be careful, Zach. Don't push your luck."

Ted's the one pushing his luck, Zach thought, as he stared down into the valley. At the precise spot where the trail turned sharply, he tightened his fingers on the reins and the horse stopped. Zach fished in his vest pocket for his cell phone, pulled it out, pointed it, and clicked. A picture is worth a thousand words, he thought with a satisfied smile, as he pressed his knees against the horse's body, and it began to pick its way obediently along the treacherous path.

22

Because she had been covering a trial in the Morris County courthouse, Dru Perry did not learn immediately about Georgette Grove's death. When the judge declared a lunch break, she checked messages on her cell phone and promptly called Ken Sharkey, her editor. Five minutes later, she was on her way to the crime scene on Holland Road in Peapack.

She was there when Jeff MacKingsley held a brief press conference in which he confirmed that Georgette Grove, a lifetime resident of Mendham and a well-known real estate agent, had been found shot to death on the lower level of the farmhouse at which she had arranged to meet a potential buyer.

The bombshell news was that Celia Nolan, and not the locksmith, had been the first one to find the body and it raised a barrage of questions. Dru was furious at herself when another reporter asked about the law stating that a real estate agent must disclose to a potential buyer if the house has a stigma on it. I should have known about that law, Dru thought. How did I miss it?

The facts that Jeff MacKingsley shared were bare fundamentals: Celia Nolan had arrived at quarter of ten for the ten o'clock meeting. She found the door unlocked and went inside, calling Georgette's name. When she found the body, she ran back to her car, drove home, and dialed 911, but then went into shock and could not speak.

Jeff then told them about the locksmith who called the police shortly after eleven thirty. "Our investigation is continuing," he emphasized. "It is possible that Georgette Grove was followed into the house, or that someone was already there, waiting for her. The gun that killed her was found near the body."

Sensing there was nothing more to be learned on Holland Road, Dru next headed to the Nolan home. Here again, her timing was good. She arrived only a few minutes before Alex Nolan made his brief statement.

"Did you know about the law regarding a stigmatized house?" Dru called out, but Nolan was already on his way back inside the house.

On a hunch, Dru did not leave with the rest of the media, but instead waited in her car a few hundred feet past the Nolans' home. She was there when Prosecutor MacKingsley and Detective Walsh drove up the road, parked behind the Nolans' car, rang the bell, and were admitted into the house.

She immediately got out of her car, went up the driveway, and waited. The two men stayed inside a scant twenty minutes, but when they came out both were grim faced and closemouthed. "Dru, I'm holding a press conference at five," MacKingsley told her firmly. "I'll answer what questions I can at that time. I assume I'll see you there."

"You bet you will," she called after him, as he and Detective Walsh sped away.

Her next stop was the Grove Real Estate Agency on East Main Street. She drove there, half-expecting to find it closed, but when she parked the car and walked over to it, she could see that there were three people in the reception area, even though the CLOSED sign was on the door.

To her astonishment, one of them was Marcella Williams. *Of course* she'd be here, Dru thought. She wants to get the dirt firsthand. But Marcella could be useful, she conceded a moment later, when she unlocked the door, invited her in, and introduced her to Georgette Grove's associates.

Both the man and the woman looked annoyed, and were obviously about to refuse her request for an interview, even though she put it as innocently as possible, saying, "I want to write a fitting tribute to Georgette Grove, who was a pillar of this community."

Marcella intervened on her behalf. "You really should talk to Dru," she told Robin Carpenter and Henry Paley. "In her story in the *Star-Ledger* yesterday, she wrote very sympathetically about Georgette, how distressed she was at the vandalism, and even told how Georgette had dragged the hose out trying to clean it up before the Nolans arrived."

That was before I knew that Georgette may have been in violation of the law, selling that house to the Nolans and not telling them about the stigma, Dru thought. "Georgette Grove was important to Mendham," she said. "I think she deserves to be remembered for all her community activities."

As she spoke she was studying both Carpenter and Paley.

Despite the fact that Carpenter's blue eyes were swollen and her face blotched from recent tears, there was no mistaking the fact that she was beautiful, Dru decided. She's a natural blond, but those highlights came from the hairdresser. Lovely face. Big, wide-set eyes. If that nose is her own, she was born lucky. Come-hither lips. Wonder if she gets injections to keep them puffed up. Great body. Could easily have been a model, although since she's only about five four, she's not tall enough to have ever made the big money in fashion. She also knows how to dress, Dru thought, noting Robin's well-tailored, cream-colored gabardine pant suit and the lowcut neckline of her frilly pink and cream print blouse.

If she's trying to be sexy, though, she's wasting her efforts here, Dru decided as she concentrated on Henry Paley. The thin, nervous-looking, sixtyish real estate agent appeared to be more worried than grieved, a thought she tucked away for later consideration.

They told her they were just about to have coffee and invited her to join them. Cup in hand, Dru followed Robin across the room to the couch and chairs that were grouped around a television set.

"When I came to work here last year, Georgette told me that she had redesigned this reception area so that she could have a friendly visit with potential clients and then show them the videos of houses she thought might be right for them," Robin explained sadly.

"Did she have a video of the house on Holland Road?" Dru asked, hoping the question didn't come across as too abrupt.

"No," Henry Paley said. "That house was sold the minute it came on the market. We never even got a chance to look at it. But the sale fell through, and it went into multiple listing only last week."

"Did you inspect it?" Dru asked, mentally crossing her fingers that they would be able to answer some questions about the house where Georgette Grove had been murdered.

"I did last week," Paley replied. "In fact, I took potential buyers to see it, but then they admitted it was way out of their price range."

"I was there covering the story for my newspaper a couple of hours ago," Dru said. "We were only outside, of course, but it's obviously a beautiful home. I can't help wondering why Georgette Grove was so quick to show it to Celia Nolan. Did Celia tell her that she wouldn't stay in the house on Old Mill Lane, or did it have anything to do with the real estate law about a stigmatized house? If the Nolans had sued Georgette, wouldn't she have had to refund their money?"

Dru did not miss the way Henry Paley's lips tightened. "The Nolans wanted to stay in the area," Henry said, his voice frosty. "Georgette told me that she phoned Mrs. Nolan and offered to show her other houses, foregoing her commission."

Dru decided to take a chance on asking another thin-ice question. "But after Georgette Grove betrayed them in a way by not giving full disclosure, wouldn't it have been reasonable for them to demand their money back and go to a different broker?"

"I heard Georgette, right here in this room, try to tell Alex Nolan about the history of the house, and he brushed it off," Robin said heatedly. "Whether or not she should have insisted on telling Mrs. Nolan about it is something else, of course. I've got to be honest. If I were in Celia Nolan's shoes, I'd have been damn mad about the vandalism, but I wouldn't have passed out. Georgette was worried that her legal position was vulnerable. That's why she was so anxious to find another house for Celia Nolan. And that urgency cost her her life."

"What do you think happened to her?" Dru asked.

"I think somebody found a way to get into that house and was surprised when Georgette showed up, or else somebody followed her in with the idea of robbing her, then panicked."

"Did Georgette come into the office this morning?"

"No, and we didn't expect her. When Henry and I were leaving yesterday, she told us she was planning to go directly to the farmhouse."

"Did Georgette stay after you left because she was meeting someone here?"

"This was Georgette's second home. She often stayed late."

Dru had gotten more information than she had dared to expect. She could tell that Henry Paley was about to object to her questions, and Robin Carpenter's answer gave her the escape route she needed.

"You say this was her second home. Let's talk about the kind of person Georgette was. I know she's been a leader in community affairs."

"She kept a scrapbook," Robin said. "Why don't I get it for you?"

Fifteen minutes later, her notebook filled with jottings, Dru was ready to leave. Marcella Williams got up to go with her. Outside the office, when Dru started to say goodbye, Marcella said, "I'll walk you to your car."

"It's terrible isn't it?" she began. "I mean I still can't believe Georgette is dead. I don't think most people in town even know about it yet. The prosecutor and a detective were just leaving when I got to the office. I guess they'd been questioning Robin and Henry. I went over because I wanted to see if there was anything I could do, you know, make phone calls to notify people or something.

"That was nice of you," Dru said drily.

"I mean it's not as if Georgette was popular with *everybody*. She had very strong feelings about what should and shouldn't be built around town. You remember Ronald Reagan's great remark that if the environmentalists had it their way, they'd be building bird cages in the White House. Some people think that if Georgette had her way, we'd be driving over cobblestone roads and reading by gaslight in Mendham."

What is Marcella getting at? Dru wondered.

"Robin told me that Henry cried like a baby when he heard about Georgette, and I believe it," Marcella continued. "From what I understand, ever since his wife died a few years back, he's had a thing for Georgette, but she apparently wasn't interested. I also heard that since he's been getting ready to retire, his attitude has really changed. He's told a lot of people that he'd like to close the agency and sell the office. You were just there. Originally it was a pleasant family home but now, because that block is a commercial zone, it's really gone up in value. In addition to that, Henry bought property on Route 24 with Georgette as an investment years ago. He's been wanting to sell it, but she wanted to deed it to the state."

"What will happen to it now?" Dru asked.

"Your guess is as good as mine. Georgette has a couple of cousins in Pennsylvania she was close to, so I bet she remembered them in her will." Marcella's laugh was sardonic. "One thing I'm sure of. If she left that land to her cousins, the state can whistle for that property. They'll sell it in a heartbeat."

Dru had left her car in the parking lot next to Robinson's, the nineteenth-century pharmacy that was one of the landmarks of the town. When they reached the car, she said goodbye to Marcella and agreed to keep in touch. As she drove away, she glanced at the pharmacy and reflected that the sight of the quaint building had probably given great pleasure to Georgette Grove.

Dru also reflected on the fact that Marcella Williams had gone out of her way to tell her that Henry Paley would profit by Georgette Grove's death. Does she have a personal grudge against Henry, Dru wondered—or is she trying to protect someone else?

23

Charley Hatch lived in one of the smallest houses in Mendham, a nineteenth-century, four-room cottage. He had bought it after his divorce. The attraction of the property was that it had a barn that housed all his landscaping and snowplowing equipment. Forty-four years old and mildly attractive with dark blond hair and an olive complexion, Charley made a good living out of the residents of Mendham, but had a deep-seated resentment toward his wealthy clients.

He cut their lawns and trimmed their hedges from spring until fall, and then plowed their driveways in the winter, and always he wondered why their positions weren't reversed, why he hadn't been the one to be born into money and privilege.

A handful of his oldest customers trusted him with a key, and paid him to check their homes after a heavy rain or snowstorm when they were away. If he was in the mood, he sometimes took his sleeping bag to one of those houses and spent the night watching television in the family room and helping himself to whatever he liked from their liquor cabinets. Doing this gave him a satisfying feeling of one-upmanship—the same feeling he had when he agreed to vandalize the house on Old Mill Lane.

On Thursday evening, Charley was settled in his imitation leather recliner, his feet on the ottoman, when his cell phone rang. He glanced at his watch as he took his phone from his pocket and was surprised to see that it was eleven thirty. I slept through the news, he thought. He'd wanted to see it, knowing there probably would be a big story about the Grove murder. He recognized the number of his caller and mumbled a greeting.

The familiar voice, now crisp and angry, snapped, "Charley, you were a fool to leave those empty paint cans in the closet. Why didn't you get rid of them?"

"Are you crazy?" he answered heatedly. "With all that publicity, don't you think cans of red paint might be noticed in the trash? Listen, you got what you wanted. I did a great job."

"Nobody asked you to carve the skull and crossbones in the front door. I warned you the other night to hide any of those carvings of yours that you have around. Have you done it yet?"

"I don't think—" he began.

"That's *right*. You *don't* think! You're bound to be questioned by the police. They'll find out you do the landscaping there."

Without answering, Charley snapped shut his cell phone, breaking the connection. Now fully awake, he pressed his feet against the recliner's ottoman, forcing it to retract, and stood up. With growing anxiety, he looked around the cluttered room and counted six of his carved figures in plain view on the mantel and table tops. Cursing quietly, he picked them up, went into the kitchen, got a roll of plastic, wrapped them, and carefully stacked them in a garbage bag. For a moment he stood uncertainly, then carried the bag out to the barn, hiding it on a shelf behind fifty-pound bags of rock salt.

Sullenly, he went back into the house, opened his cell phone, and dialed. "Just so you can sleep tonight, I put my stuff away."

"Good."

"What did you get me into anyhow?" he asked, his voice rising. "Why would the police want to talk to me? I hardly even knew that real estate woman."

This time, it was the caller who had disturbed Charley's nap who broke the connection.

24

"*The hour of death is nigh. 'Tis time to drop the mask . . .*"

I don't know why that quote kept running through my head the rest of the day, but it did. Alex had to cancel appointments when he rushed home, so after the prosecutor and detective left, he went into his office and began to make phone calls. I took Jack outside and let him have a long ride on the pony. I didn't go through the farce of asking Alex to help me with the saddle. He had seen that I was perfectly capable of tacking up the pony myself.

After a few times of walking around the enclosure next to him, I gave in to Jack's pleadings and let him hold the reins without me. "Just sit on the fence and watch me, Mom," he begged. "I'm big."

Hadn't I asked my mother something like that when I was Jack's age? She started me on a pony when I was only three. It's funny how a flash of memory like that will come over me. I always tried not to think about my early life, even the happy times, because it hurt too much to remember it. But now I'm in the house where I lived for the first ten years of my life, and it feels as if the memories are crashing around me.

Dr. Moran, my psychologist, told me that suppressed memories never stay suppressed. But there's still something that I've tried to remember about that night, and it always seems as though I can't dig deep enough in my mind to find it. When I woke up, I thought the television was on, but it wasn't. It was my mother's voice I heard first, and I am sure she called my father's name or spoke of him. *What did she say to Ted?*

Then, as though I'd pushed a remote and changed channels, Georgette Grove's face loomed in my mind. I could see her expression as it was the first moment I laid eyes on her. She had been distressed and on the verge of tears. I now realize that much of her distress had been for herself, not for me. She didn't want to lose her sale. That was why she had rushed to make an appointment with me to see the house this morning.

Did that appointment cost Georgette her life? Did someone follow her in, or was someone already hiding in the house? She couldn't have suspected anything. She must have been on her knees working away on the stain when she was shot.

That moment, as Jack rode by, smiling joyfully, starting to wave to me then quickly putting his hand back on the rein, I made the connection. Was that paint on the floor of that house from the same batch of paint that someone had used on this house?

It was. I was *sure* of it. I was sure also that the police would not only come to that conclusion, they would be able to prove it. Then they would not only be questioning me because I found Georgette's body, but because her death may have been tied somehow to the vandalism of this house.

Whoever killed Georgette had carefully placed the pistol on that splotch of paint. The paint was supposed to be tied to her death. And tied to me, I thought.

The hour of death is nigh. 'Tis time to drop the mask.

The hour of death has come, I thought—Georgette's death. But unfortunately I can't drop the mask. I can't inquire about getting a transcript of my trial. I can't get a copy of Mother's autopsy report.

How can I possibly be seen walking around the Morris County court-house looking for that information?

If they find out who am I, will they think that I had a gun with me, that when I got to that house and saw Georgette cleaning up the paint that I connected her with the vandalism and shot her?

Beware! Little Lizzie's Place . . .

Lizzie Borden had an axe . . .

"Mom, isn't Lizzie a great pony?" Jack called.

"Don't call her Lizzie," I screamed. "You can't call her Lizzie! I won't have it!"

Frightened, Jack began to cry. I rushed over to him, encircled his waist with my arms and tried to comfort him. Then Jack pulled away. I helped him down from the pony. "You scared me, Mom," he said, and ran into the house.

25

On Friday morning, the day after Georgette Grove was murdered, Jeff MacKingsley called a meeting in his office for the team of detectives assigned to solve her homicide. Joining Paul Walsh were two veteran investigators, Mort Shelley and Angelo Ortiz. It was apparent to all three that their boss was deeply concerned.

After the barest of greetings, Jeff went straight to the point.

"The red paint used to vandalize the Nolan home came from Tannon Hardware in Mendham and was custom mixed for the Carrolls, the people who own the house on Holland Road. It shouldn't have taken a phone call from me to Mrs. Carroll in San Diego to find *that* out."

Ortiz responded, his tone defensive: "I looked into that. Rick Kling, with the Mendham police, was assigned to check out the paint stores there. The kid on duty at Tannon Hardware was new and didn't know anything about checking records on paint sales. Sam Tannon was on a business trip until yesterday. Rick was planning to see him, but then we found the empty cans in the Holland Road house.

"We knew Tuesday afternoon that whoever vandalized the Nolan home used Benjamin Moore paint," Jeff replied firmly. "Since Tannon Hardware is the only store in the area with the franchise to sell that brand of paint, it would seem to me that Detective Kling might have decided it was worth a phone call to Sam Tannon, wherever he was, to see if he would remember a purchase that involved mixing the Moore red color with burnt umber. I spoke to Mr. Tannon an hour ago. Of course he remembered the sale. He worked with the interior designer, mixing all the paints for the Carroll's home."

"Kling realizes that he dropped the ball," Ortiz concluded. "If we had known that the red paint was part of the overage on that redecoration, we would have been on Holland Road on Wednesday."

The weight of what he was saying hung in the air. "That doesn't mean we could have saved Georgette Grove's life," Jeff acknowledged. "She may have been the victim of a random robbery attempt, but if Detective Kling had followed through, we would have opened that storage closet and confiscated the remaining paint on Wednesday. It looked pretty stupid to acknowledge at the press conference that we couldn't trace the source of the red paint immediately when in fact it was purchased right here in Mendham."

"Jeff, in my opinion the importance of the paint is not *when* we found it, but that it was used on Little Lizzie's Place. I think that the murder weapon was centered on the splash of paint to emphasize that fact, which brings us back to Celia Nolan, a lady I think needs a whole lot of investigating." Paul Walsh's dry tone bordered on insolence.

"That gun was deliberately placed on the red paint," Jeff shot back. "That was obvious." He paused. His voice more emphatic, he said, "I do not agree with your theory that Mrs. Nolan is concealing something. I think the woman has had one shock after another in the past three days, and naturally she is nervous and distressed. Clyde Earley was in the squad car that rushed to the house after she dialed 911, and he said that she couldn't have faked the state of shock she was in. She couldn't even speak until she got to the hospital."

"We have her fingerprints on that picture she found in the barn and gave to you. I want to run them through the database file," Walsh said stubbornly. "I wouldn't be surprised if that lady has a past she might not want us to find out about."

"Go ahead," Jeff snapped. "But if you're going to be in charge of this investigation, I want you concentrating on finding a killer, not wasting your time on Celia Nolan."

"Jeff, don't you think it's funny that she talks about her kid being at St. *Joe's?*" Walsh persisted.

"What's that supposed to mean?"

"She said it like someone accustomed to saying it that way. I would think that someone new to the town and to the school would call it 'St. Joseph's'. I also think she was lying when she said Georgette Grove gave her directions to Holland Road. If you remember, Nolan contradicted herself when I asked her that question. First she said 'No,' then in a heartbeat said, 'Yes, of course.' She knew she had blundered. Incidentally, I checked the time she called 911 from her home. It was ten after ten."

"Your point is . . . ?"

"My point is that according to her testimony, she went into the house on Holland Road at quarter of ten, and walked around the main floor calling Georgette's name. That's a big house, Jeff. Mrs. Nolan told us that she debated about going upstairs, but remembered the door in the kitchen to the lower level was open, went back to the kitchen, went downstairs, checked the doors to the patio and found them locked, then walked down the hallway, turned the corner, and found the body. She then ran back to her car, got in, and drove home."

Paul Walsh knew he was as much as telling his boss that he had missed the salient facts of a crime scene, but he forged ahead doggedly. "I went back last night and clocked the trip between Holland and Old Mill Road. Getting to Holland, and leaving it, can be confusing. I made a wrong turn on my way to Old Mill, went back, and started again. Normal driving, by which I mean about ten over the speed limit, it took me nineteen minutes from Holland Road to Old Mill Lane. So let's do the arithmetic."

Paul Walsh glanced at Shelley and Ortiz, as if to confirm that they were following his reasoning. "If Celia Nolan was correct about getting to the house on Holland Road at quarter of ten, and if she had to leave that house by nine minutes of ten to drive back home without flooring the gas pedal, it means that she was in the house only four to six minutes."

"Which is possible," Jeff said quietly. "Fast, but possible."

"That would also assume she drove straight as an arrow, and knew exactly when to turn on unfamiliar and confusing roads while she was in a state of severe shock."

"I would suggest you make your point," Jeff said grimly.

"My point is that she either got there much earlier and was waiting for Georgette, or that she has been at that house before and was sure of the roads she would take back and forth."

"Again, your point?"

"I believe Nolan when she said she didn't know about the real estate law that could have gotten her out of the sale. Her generous husband bought the house for her, and she wanted no part of it, but didn't dare tell him. She somehow learned about the vandalism the kids pulled last Halloween and decided to go it one better. She got someone to mess up the house for her, arrives, and pulls the fainting act, and now she has her way out. She's leaving the house she never wanted, and her nice new husband understands. Then somehow Georgette caught onto her act. She was carrying a picture of Celia Nolan doing her swan dive in her purse. I say she was going to show it to Nolan and tell her she wasn't going to get away with it."

"Then why weren't there any fingerprints on the picture, including Georgette's?" Ortiz asked.

"Nolan may have handled it but been afraid to take it with her in case other people had seen Georgette with it. Instead, she wiped it clean of any fingerprints and put it in Georgette's bag."

"You've missed your calling, Paul," Jeff snapped. "You should have been a trial attorney. You sound persuasive on the surface, but it's full of holes. Celia Nolan is a wealthy woman. She could have bought another house with a snap of her fingers, *and* sweet-talked her husband into going along with it. It's obvious he's crazy about her. Go ahead and check her prints in the database and then let's move on. What's happening, Mort?"

Mort Shelley pulled a notebook from his pocket. We're putting together a list of the people who might have had access to that house and then we're interviewing them. People like other real estate agents who have keys to the lockbox, and people who do any kind of service, like housecleaning or landscaping. We're investigating to see if Georgette Grove had any enemies, if she owed any money, if there's a boyfriend in the picture. We still haven't been able to trace the doll that was left on the porch of the Nolan house. It was expensive in its day, but my guess is it was picked up at a garage sale at some point and has probably been in someone's attic for years."

"How about the gun the doll was holding? It looked real enough to scare me if I was facing it," Jeff said.

"We checked out the company that makes them. It's not in business anymore. It got a lot of bad publicity because the gun is too realistic. The guy who owned the company destroyed all the records after seven years. That's a dead end."

"All right. Keep me posted." Jeff stood up, signifying the meeting was over. As they were leaving he called out to Anna, his secretary, to hold any calls for an hour.

Ten minutes later, she buzzed him on the intercom. "Jeff, there's a woman on the phone who claims she was in the Black Horse Tavern last night and heard Ted Cartwright threatening Georgette Grove. I knew you'd want to talk to her."

"Put her on," Jeff said.

26

After she left Marcella Williams, Dru Perry went directly to the *Star-Ledger* offices to write her story about the homicide on Holland Road. She then cleared it with her editor, Ken Sharkey, that she would work at home in the morning to put together a feature story on Georgette Grove for the weekend edition of the newspaper.

That was why, with a mug of coffee in her hand, and still dressed in her pajamas and robe, she was at her desk at home on Friday morning, watching local Channel 12, on which the news anchor was interviewing Grove's cousin, Thomas Madison, who had come from Pennsylvania when he received the news of Georgette's death. Madison, a soft-spoken man in his early fifties, expressed his family's grief at their loss and his outrage at her coldblooded murder. He announced the funeral arrangements he had made—Georgette would be cremated when her body was released by the coroner, and her ashes placed in the family plot in Morris County Cemetery. A memorial service would be held at 10 A.M. on Monday at Hilltop Presbyterian, the church she had attended all her life.

A memorial service so soon, Dru thought. That says to me cousin Thomas just wants to get things over with and go back home. As she pressed the remote button and snapped off the television, she decided to attend the service.

She turned on her computer and began to search the Internet for references to Georgette Grove. What she loved about the Internet was that when she combed it for research, she often stumbled across valuable information that she had not expected to find.

"Pay dirt," she said aloud an hour later, as she came across a school picture of Georgette Grove and Henry Paley when they were seniors in Mendham High. The photo caption said that they each had won a long distance race in the annual county competition. They were holding their trophies. Henry's skinny arm was around Georgette, and while she smiled directly into the camera, his fatuous smile was only for her.

Boy, he looks lovesick, Dru thought—he must have been sweet on Georgette even then.

She decided to try to find more information on Henry Paley. The pertinent facts that turned up were that he had worked as a real estate agent after college, married Constance Liller at age twenty-five, and joined the newly formed Grove Real Estate Agency when he was forty. An obituary notice showed that Constance Liller Paley had been dead for six years.

Then, if one could believe Marcella Williams, he tried to romance Georgette again, Dru mused. But she had wanted no part of it, and lately they had been quarreling because he wanted to cash out his interest in the business and the Route 24 property. I don't see Henry as a murderer she thought, but love and money are the two main reasons people kill or get killed. Interesting.

She leaned back in her creaking desk chair and looked up at the ceiling. When they had talked yesterday, did Henry Paley talk about his whereabouts when Georgette was killed? I don't think so, she decided. Her shoulder bag was on the floor beside her desk. Dru fished in it, pulled out her notebook, and jotted down the questions and facts that were jumping into her mind.

Where was Henry Paley the morning of the murder? Did he go to the office at the usual time or did he have any appointments with clients? Lockboxes have a computerized record. It should show how often Henry visited Holland Road. Was he aware of the paint cans in that storage closet? He wanted the agency to close. Would he deliberately sabotage the Old Mill property to embarrass Georgette, or to kill the sale to the Nolans?

Dru closed her notebook, dropped it in her bag, and switched back to researching Georgette Grove on the Internet. In the next two hours she was able to form a clear picture of an independent woman who, judging from her many awards, was not only community minded but a dynamic force in preserving the quality of life, as she saw it, in Mendham.

Lots of people who applied for variances to the zoning board must have wanted to strangle her, Dru thought, as she came upon reference after reference to Georgette Grove eloquently and successfully arguing against loosening or bending the existing zoning guidelines.

Or maybe one of them wanted to shoot her, she amended. The record showed that Georgette had stepped on a lot of toes, especially during the last few years, but maybe her pro-community actions had affected nobody more directly than Henry Paley. She picked up the phone and dialed the agency, half-expecting it to be closed.

Henry Paley answered her call.

"Henry, I'm so glad to reach you. I didn't know if you'd open the agency today. I'm working on the article I'm writing about Georgette, and I was thinking how nice it would be to include some of those wonderful pictures in your scrapbook. I'd like to drive over and borrow your scrapbook, or at least make a copy of some of the pictures."

After some encouragement, Paley reluctantly agreed to allow her to photograph the pages. "I don't want the book to leave the office," he said, "and I don't want anything taken out of it."

"Henry, I want you to stand beside me when I'm doing it. Thanks very much. I'll see you around noon. I won't take too much of your time."

When she replaced the receiver, Dru stood up and pushed back her bangs. Got to get them cut, she thought. I'm starting to look like a sheep dog. She went down the hallway to her bedroom and began to dress. As she did, a question came to mind, an intuitive question that was partly hunch, the kind that made her a good investigative reporter. Does Henry still run or jog, and, if so, how would that fact fit into this whole scenario?

It was something else to check out.

27

Martin and Kathleen Kellogg of Santa Barbara, California, were the distant cousins who adopted me. At the time of Mother's death, they had been living in Saudi Arabia where he was with an engineering firm. They did not learn anything about what had happened until the company relocated them back to Santa Barbara. By then the trial was over and I was living in the juvenile shelter here in New Jersey while the Division of Youth and Family Services, DYFS for short, decided where to place me.

In a way, it was good that they hadn't had any contact with me until that time. Childless themselves, they learned of what had happened, then, quietly and without a hint of publicity, came to Morris County and petitioned to adopt me. They were interviewed and checked out. The court readily approved them as being suitable to become the guardians and adoptive parents of a minor who had not spoken more than a few words in over a year.

At that time, the Kelloggs were in their early fifties, not too old to parent an eleven-year-old. However distant the connection, Martin was a blood relative. More important, though, they were genuinely compassionate. The first time I met Kathleen, she said that she hoped I would like her and, in time, come to love her. She said, "I al-

ways wanted to have a little girl. Now I want to give you back the rest
of your childhood, Liza."

I went with them willingly. Of course, no one can give you back
something that has been destroyed. I was no longer a child—I was an
acquitted killer. They desperately wanted me to get beyond the "Little Lizzie" horror, and so coached me in the story we told to anyone
who had known them before they returned to Santa Barbara.

I was the daughter of a widowed friend who, when she learned she
was terminally ill with cancer, asked them to adopt me. They chose
my new name, Celia, because my grandmother had been Cecelia.
They were wise enough to understand that I needed some link to the
past, even though it would be secret.

I lived with them for only seven years. During all that time, I saw
Dr. Moran once a week. I trusted him from the beginning. I think he,
rather than Martin, became a real father figure for me. When I could
not speak, he had me draw pictures for him. Over and over, I drew the
same ones. Mother's sitting room, a ferocious apelike figure, his back
to me, his arms holding a woman against the wall. I drew the picture
of a gun poised in midair with bullets flying from it, but the gun was
not held by any hand. I drew a picture that was the reverse of the
Pietà. Mine depicted the child holding the dead figure of the mother.

I had lost a year of grammar school but made it up quickly and
went to a local high school in Santa Barbara. In both places I was
known as being "quiet but nice." I had friends, but never let anyone
get close to me. For someone who lives a lie, truth must always be
avoided, and I was constantly having to guard my tongue. I also had
to fiercely conceal my emotions. I remember in a sophomore English class, the surprise test was for the students to write an essay about
the most memorable day of their lives.

That terrible night flashed vividly before my eyes. It was as if I
were watching a movie. I tried to pick up my pen but my fingers re-

fused to grasp it. I tried to breathe, but I couldn't pull air into my lungs. And then I fainted.

The cover story we used was that I had almost drowned as a small child, and had occasional flashbacks. I told Dr. Moran that what had happened that night had never been so clear, that for a split second I had remembered what Mother had been screaming at Ted. And then it was gone again.

The same year I moved to New York to attend the Fashion Institute, Martin reached compulsory retirement at his company, and they gladly moved to Naples, Florida, where he took a position with an engineering firm. He has since fully retired, and now, past eighty, has become what Kathleen calls "forgetful," but which I fear is the beginning stages of Alzheimer's.

When we married, Alex and I had a quiet wedding in the Lady Chapel of St. Patrick's Cathedral, just the two of us and Jack, Richard Ackerman, the elderly lawyer who is the senior partner of Alex's law firm, and Joan Donlan who was my right hand when I had the interior design business and who is the closest I have to an intimate friend.

Shortly after that, Alex and Jack and I flew down to Naples to visit Martin and Kathleen for a few days. Thank God we stayed at a hotel, because Martin often became disoriented. One day when we were lingering over lunch on the patio, he called me "Liza." Fortunately, Alex was not within earshot because he had headed to the beach for a swim, but Jack heard. It puzzled him so much that it became embedded in his memory, and from time to time he still asks me, "Why did Grandpa call you Liza, Mom?"

Once, at the apartment in New York, Alex was in the room when Jack asked that question, but his reaction was to explain to Jack that sometimes people who are old begin to forget and mix up people's names. "Remember, your grandpa called me 'Larry' a couple of times. He mixed me up with your first daddy."

After my outburst over the pony's name, I had followed Jack into the house. He had run to Alex and was sitting on his lap, tearfully telling him that Mommy scared him. "She scares me too, sometimes, Jack," Alex said, and I know he meant it to be a joke, but the underlying truth was undeniable. My fainting spell, my crying episodes, even the state of shock I'd been in after finding Georgette's body—all those things had frightened him. And the fear might as well have been stamped on Alex's forehead: he obviously thought I was having some sort of breakdown.

He listened to Jack's story about how I had yelled at him, saying he couldn't call the pony Lizzie, and then he tried to explain: "You know, Jack, a long time ago a little girl named Lizzie lived in this house and she did some very bad things. Nobody liked her and they made her go away. We think about that bad girl when we hear that name. What's something you hate more than anything else?"

"When the doctor gives me a booster shot."

"Well think about it this way. When we hear the name Lizzie, it reminds Mommy and me of that bad girl. Would you want to call your pony 'Booster Shot?' "

Jack began to laugh. "Nooooooooo."

"So now you know how Mommy feels. Let's think about another name for that pretty pony."

"Mommy said we should call her 'Star' because she has a star on her forehead."

"I think that's a great name, and we should make it official. Mommy, don't we have some birthday wrapping paper?"

"Yes, I think so." I was so grateful to Alex for calming Jack down, but oh, dear God, the explanation he gave him!

"Why don't you make a big star and we'll put it on the door of the barn so everyone will know a pony named 'Star' lives there?"

Jack loved the idea. I drew the outline of a star on a section of glittery wrapping paper and he cut it out. We made a ceremony of pasting it on the door of the barn, and then I recited for them the poem I remembered from childhood:

> "*Star light, star bright,*
> *First star I see tonight,*
> *I wish I may, I wish I might,*
> *Have the wish I wish tonight.*"

By then it was six o'clock, and the evening shadows were beginning to settle in.

"What is *your* wish, Mommy?" Jack asked.

"I wish that the three of us will be together forever."

"What do you wish, Alex?" Jack asked.

"I wish that you'll start to call me 'Daddy' soon, and that by this time next year you'll have a little brother or sister."

That night, when Alex tried to draw me close to him, he sensed my resistance and immediately released me. "Ceil, why don't you take a sleeping pill?" he suggested. "You need to relax. I'm not sleepy. I'll go downstairs and read for awhile."

When I take a sleeping pill, I usually break it in half, but after the day I had just gone through, I swallowed a whole one and for the next eight hours slept soundly. When I awakened, it was almost eight o'clock, and Alex was gone. I pulled on a robe and rushed downstairs. Jack was up and dressed and at the table, having breakfast with Alex.

Alex jumped up and came over to me. "That was some sleep," he said. "I don't think you stirred all night." He kissed me with that gesture I love, cupping my face in his hands. "I've got to be off. You okay?"

"I'm good." And I was. As the remnants of sleep left me, I felt physically stronger than I've felt since the morning we first pulled up to this driveway. I knew what I was going to do. After I dropped Jack at school, I would go to one of the other real estate agents in town and try to find a house that we could rent or buy immediately. I didn't care how suitable it was. Getting out of this house would be the first step toward regaining something approaching normality.

At least it seemed like the best thing to do. Later that morning, however, when I went to the Mark W. Grannon Agency and Mark Grannon himself took me around, I learned something about Georgette Grove that took my breath away. "Georgette was the one who got the exclusive listing on your house," he told me as we drove along Hardscrabble Road. "None of the rest of us wanted to touch it. But Georgette always had a guilty feeling about the place. She and Audrey Barton had been good friends at one time. They went to Mendham High at the same time, although Georgette was a couple of years older than Audrey."

I listened, hoping Grannon could not sense the tension rushing through my body.

"Audrey was a great rider, you know. A real horsewoman. Her husband, Will, though, was deathly afraid of them and embarrassed about it. He wanted to be able to ride with Audrey. It was Georgette who suggested that he ask Zach at Washington Valley Riding Club to give him lessons, something they agreed to keep secret from Audrey, which they did. Audrey knew nothing about it until the police came to tell her Will was dead. She and Georgette never spoke again."

Zach!

The name hit me like a thunderbolt. It was one of the words my mother had screamed at Ted the night I killed her.

Zach: It was part of the puzzle!

28

On Friday afternoon, Ted Cartwright's secretary informed him that a Detective Paul Walsh from the Morris County Prosecutor's Office was in the waiting room and needed to ask him a few questions.

In a way, Ted had been expecting the visit, but now that it actually had happened he felt perspiration form on the palms of his hands. Impatiently, he wiped them dry on his jacket, pulled open his desk drawer, and took a quick look in the mirror that he always kept there. I look fine, he thought. In a split second he decided that showing cordiality might be construed as a sign of weakness.

"I wasn't aware that Mr. Walsh had made an appointment to see me," he spat into the intercom. "However, send him in."

Paul Walsh's suit-off-the-rack, slightly rumpled look immediately triggered Cartwright's contempt, which put him somewhat at ease. The round frame of Walsh's glasses reminded Cartwright of the color of his tan riding boots. He decided to be condescendingly cordial to his visitor.

"I really don't like unexpected drop-ins," he said. "And I'm going to be on a conference call in ten minutes, so we'd better get to the point, Mr. Walsh. It is Mr. Walsh, isn't it?"

"That's right," Walsh replied, his firm, steely tone of voice out of sync with his mild-mannered appearance. He handed Cartwright his card and, uninvited, sat down in the chair facing Cartwright's desk.

Feeling that he had somehow lost control, Cartwright sat down again himself. "What can I do for you?" This time his tone was brusque.

"I am, as I would presume you have guessed, investigating the murder yesterday morning of Georgette Grove. I assume you've heard about it."

"You would have to be deaf, dumb, and blind not to have heard about it," Cartwright snapped.

"You knew Ms. Grove?"

"Of course, I knew her. We both lived in this area all our lives."

"Were you friends?"

He's heard about Wednesday night, Cartwright thought. Hoping to disarm Walsh, he said, "We had been friendly enough." He paused, choosing his words carefully. "In recent years, Georgette became very confrontational. When she was on the zoning board, she made it extremely difficult for anybody trying to get any kind of variance. Even when she wasn't appointed to another term, she still never missed a meeting, and continued to be an obstructionist. For that reason, I, along with a number of other people, ended any semblance of friendship with her."

"When was the last time you saw her?"

"On Wednesday night, at the Black Horse Tavern."

"What time was that, Mr. Cartwright?"

"Somewhere between nine fifteen and nine thirty. She was alone, having dinner."

"Did you approach her?'

"We made eye contact. She beckoned to me and I went over to greet her and was astonished when she all but accused me of being the one responsible for the vandalism of the house on Old Mill Lane."

"The house in which you lived at one time."

"That's correct."

"What did you tell her?"

"I told her that she was turning into a crackpot and demanded to know why she would think that I had anything to do with it. She said that I was working with Henry Paley to put her out of business so that she'd have to sell the property on Route 24. She said she'd see me in hell before she sold it."

"What was your response?"

"I told her I was not working with Henry Paley. I told her that while I would certainly *like* to develop that property by putting in tasteful, commercial offices, I had plenty of other projects I was working on. And that was the end of it."

"I see. Where were you yesterday morning between eight and ten o'clock, Mr. Cartwright?"

"At eight o'clock I was riding my horse on a trail at the Peapack Riding Club. I rode until nine o'clock, showered at the club, and drove here, arriving at about nine thirty."

"The house on Holland Road in which Ms. Grove was shot has wooded property behind it, all part of the acreage attached to the house. Isn't there a riding path on that property that connects to a Peapack trail?"

Cartwright stood up. "Get out of here," he ordered angrily. "And don't come back. If I have to talk further with you or anyone from your office, I'll do it in the presence of my lawyer."

Paul Walsh stood and walked to the door. As he turned the handle, he said quietly, "You will be seeing me again, Mr. Cartwright. And if you're speaking to your friend Mr. Paley, you can tell him that he'll be seeing me as well."

29

At four o'clock on Friday afternoon, Charley Hatch pulled his van into the dirt driveway behind his barn, then unhitched the trailer he'd used to haul his riding mower and other landscaping equipment. Some nights he didn't bother to do that but tonight he was going out again, meeting some pals for dinner at a bar where they would watch the Yankee game. He was looking forward to it.

It had been a long day. The sprinkler system at one of the places he serviced had broken down and the grass was parched. Not that the sprinkler failure was his fault, but the owner was due home from vacation soon and would be furious if the grounds weren't up to snuff. It was one of Charley's easier jobs, and he didn't want to lose it, so he had spent extra time getting the sprinkler guy out to fix the system, then hung around until he was sure the grass was getting properly soaked.

Still upset by his phone conversation with Ted Cartwright the previous night, he'd used the time while he was waiting for the sprinkler guy to carefully examine the clothes he had worn on Monday night when he was on Old Mill Lane. He was wearing the same jeans as he had then, and found three drops of red paint on the right knee and traces of it in the back of the van. The jeans were old but very comfortable, and he didn't want to dump them. He'd have to see if he could get the paint off with turpentine.

He had to be especially careful since the Grove woman had been shot while she was trying to clean up the paint he'd spilled putting the cans away Monday night.

Still in a foul mood, Charley finished putting away the trailer and went into the house, heading straight to the refrigerator. He pulled out a beer, flipped off the top, and began to drink. A glance out the front window made him withdraw the bottle from his lips. A squad car was turning into his driveway. The cops. He knew they would be coming to ask questions eventually, because he took care of the place on Holland Road where the real estate agent had been murdered.

Charley glanced down. The three drops of red paint on the right knee on his jeans suddenly looked as if they were billboard size. He rushed into his bedroom, pulled off his sneakers, and was dismayed to see that the sole of his left one was smeared with red paint. He grabbed a pair of corduroy pants from the floor of his closet, put them on, shoved his feet into well-worn loafers, and was able to answer the door after the second ring.

Sergeant Clyde Earley was standing there. "Mind if I come in, Charley?" he asked. "Just want to ask you a few questions."

"Sure, sure, come on in, Sergeant." Charley stood aside and watched as Earley's eyes swept the room. "Sit down. I just got home. Opened a beer for myself first thing. It's hot out there. Funny how the other day you could feel the cool in the air, but then all of a sudden, bang, it's back to summer. How about a beer?"

"Thanks, but I'm on duty, Charley." Earley selected a straight chair, one of two at the butcher block table at which Charley ate his meals.

Charley sat on the edge of the worn club chair that had been part of the decor of the living room in the house he had shared with his wife before their divorce.

"Terrible thing, what happened on Holland Road yesterday," Earley began.

"I should say so. It gives you the creeps, doesn't it?" Charley took a sip of his beer, then was sorry he had. Earley's face was flushed. He had removed his uniform hat and his sandy hair was damp. Bet he'd love a slug of this brew, Charley thought. He probably doesn't like me sitting in front of him and drinking it. Casually, he put the bottle on the floor.

"You just get home from work, Charley?"

"That's right."

"Any reason you changed into corduroy pants and leather shoes? You didn't work in them, did you?"

"Trouble with a sprinkler system. My jeans and sneakers were soaked. I'd just taken them off and was heading for the shower when I saw your car, so I pulled these on."

"I see. Well, I'm sorry to keep you from your shower, but I just need to get a few facts. You do the landscaping for 10 Holland Road, right?"

"Yeah. I started when the Carrolls bought the place eight, nine years ago. When Mr. Carroll got transferred, they asked me to keep up the place until it's sold."

"What do you mean by 'keeping up the place,' Charley?"

"The grounds, you know—mow the lawn, trim the bushes, sweep the porch and the walk."

"Have you got a key to the house?"

"Yes. I go in every couple of days to dry mop and make sure everything is shipshape. Sometimes the realtors bring people in when it's raining, and they track in mud. I check it out, you know what I mean?"

"When was the last time you were in the house?"

"Monday. I always go in after the weekend. That's when the house gets the most traffic."

"What did you do at the house this past Monday?"

"Same as usual. I made it my first stop because I figured that if any broker was coming in, it should look nice."

"Did you know there was red paint in the storage room?"

"Sure, I did. There were a lot of paint cans there, not just red, but all different colors. I guess when the house was painted, the decorator ordered a lot more colors than they needed."

"Then you didn't know that the red paint from that storage room was stolen and used to vandalize the house on Old Mill Lane?"

"I read about Little Lizzie's Place being messed up, but I didn't know that the paint came from the Holland Road house. Who would do such a thing, Sarge?"

"I was hoping you'd have some suggestions, Charley."

Charley shrugged. "You better talk to all those real estate agents who keep marching in and out of that house. Maybe one of them had a grudge against Georgette Grove or against the people who were moving into Lizzie's Place."

"That's an interesting theory, Charley. A couple more questions, and then I'll let you head for that shower. The key to the storage room where that paint was kept is missing. Did you know that?"

"I know it was there last week. I didn't notice that it wasn't there on Monday."

Earley smiled. "I didn't say it was missing on Monday. I don't know that it was."

"Well that was the last time I was there," Charley said defensively. "That's what I meant."

"Last question, Charley. Is there any chance that anyone, a real estate agent, maybe, might have been careless and left a door unlocked after they were done showing the house?"

"Sure, it can happen, and it *has* happened. I've found the door from the kitchen to the backyard unlocked. Same thing with the sliding glass doors to the patio from the rec room. Some of these agents are so all-fired to make a sale that they get careless. They make a big thing of locking the front door and closing the lockbox, but in the meantime the Pope's army could be marching in by another entrance."

"Are you certain you always lock the doors after you've been in the house, Charley?"

"Listen, Sergeant, I make my living taking care of people's homes and property. You think any one of them would give me a second chance if I messed up that way? I'll answer that for you. Not one of them would. They'd climb over my dead body if I didn't do everything just right."

Clyde Earley got up to go. "Looks like somebody climbed over Georgette Grove's dead body, Charley. Let me know if you think of anything that will help. The way I look at it, maybe the same person who did that job on Little Lizzie's Place got scared because Ms. Grove was on to him, so he just had to kill her. That's the real shame. The most time somebody would get for vandalizing the Old Mill Lane place would be a year or so, and if that person didn't have a record, it probably would be probation and some community service. But if that vandal killed Grove to keep her quiet, then he could get the death penalty. Well, I'll see you, Charley." Earley stood, then let himself out.

Charley held his breath until the squad car drove away, then pulled out his cell phone and, in a panic, began to dial. Instead of a ring, a computerized voice announced that the number he was calling was out of service.

30

At five o'clock, Thomas Madison entered the Grove Real Estate office. At the motel in which he had stayed overnight he had changed from the dark blue suit he wore when he had been interviewed on Channel 12 into slacks and a light sweater, which made him look younger than his fifty-two years. His lean frame was not the only genetic heritage he shared with his late cousin. Like Georgette, he was very clear about what he wanted.

Henry and Robin were just about to lock up when he arrived. "I'm glad I caught you," Madison said. "I originally thought I'd stay for the weekend, but there really isn't any point, so I'll go home and come back Sunday night. We'll all be here for the service—I mean by that, my wife, my sisters, and their husbands."

"We'll be open tomorrow," Henry told him. "As fate would have it, we seem to be about to close several sales. Have you been to Georgette's house yet?"

"No. The police haven't finished going through it. I don't know what they're looking for."

"I would imagine any personal correspondence that might give them a lead to her killer," Robin said. "They went through her desk here as well."

"It's a lousy business," Madison said. "I mean, they asked me if I wanted to see the body. In all honesty, I didn't want to, but it seemed wrong to say so. I did go to the morgue. I tell you I almost got sick. That bullet hit her right between the eyes."

He noticed that Robin winced. "I'm sorry," he said. "It's just . . ." He shrugged, a gesture that conveyed his dismay at the circumstances. "I've really got to get home," he said. "I'm the coach of my kid's soccer team, and we have a game tomorrow." For a moment a smile played on his lips. "We have the best team in our division in all of Philadelphia, if I do say so myself."

Henry smiled politely. He had absolutely no interest in whether Georgette's cousin had the best or the worst soccer team in Philadelphia, or in the United States for that matter. What he *did* care about was immediately nailing down business details with Georgette's heir. "Tom," he said, "from what I understand, you and your two sisters will share in Georgette's estate."

"That's right. I dropped in on Orin Haskell, her lawyer, this morning. He's right down the block here, as you know. He has a copy of the will. He's submitting it for probate, but that's the way it reads." Madison shrugged again. "My sisters are already arguing about who gets what. Georgette had some nice family pieces that go way back. Our great-grandmothers were sisters."

He looked at Henry. "I know that you own twenty percent of both this place and some property on Route 24. I'll tell you this—we have absolutely *no* interest in continuing the business. My suggestion is that we get three appraisals, then you buy us out, or if you're not interested in keeping the business going, we close the office and sell everything, including Georgette's house, which, of course, was completely in her name."

"You do know that Georgette intended to deed the property on Route 24 to the state," Robin said, ignoring Henry's angry glance.

"I know all about that. But fortunately she never got around to it, or maybe she couldn't because you didn't go along with it, Henry. Frankly we'd all like to kiss your feet for not letting her play Lady Bountiful to the state of New Jersey. I've got three kids, my sisters each have two, and whatever we get from the sale of Georgette's real estate will go a long way toward paying to educate them."

"I'll start getting appraisals immediately," Henry promised.

"The sooner, the better. I'll be on my way." Madison turned to leave, then stopped. "The family will be having lunch after the church service. We'd like to have you join us. I mean, you two were Georgette's other family."

Henry waited until the door closed behind Madison. "*Are* we her other family?" he asked dryly.

"I was very fond of Georgette," Robin said quietly. "As were you at one time, or so I gather," she added.

"Were you so fond of her that you don't mind the fact that when she stayed late Wednesday night she went through your desk?" Henry asked.

"I wasn't going to say anything about it. You mean she went through your desk as well?"

"She not only went through it, she removed a file that belonged to me. Did she take anything from yours?"

"Not that I've noticed. There's nothing in my desk that would be of any interest to her, unless she preferred my hair spray or perfume to hers."

"You're *sure* of that, Robin?"

They were still standing in the reception room. Henry was not a tall man, and Robin's three-inch heels put her at eye level with him. For a long moment they looked directly at each other. "Want to play, *I've Got a Secret?*" he asked.

31

The weekend went unexpectedly well. Both days were very warm. Alex went for an early morning ride on Saturday, and, when he returned, I suggested we go to Spring Lake. A client of mine had been married there in July. We had attended her wedding and stayed at the Breakers Hotel. Because we'd been there together, it was one place that I didn't have to worry too much about letting slip the fact that I was familiar with it.

"Now that Labor Day's over, I bet we can get a reservation," I said.

Alex liked the idea. Jack loved it. Alex called over to the club and was able to hire one of the kids who worked weekends at the stable to come over Saturday evening and Sunday morning to take care of Star.

It worked out just as I had hoped. We got two connecting ocean-front rooms at the Breakers. We stayed on the beach all Saturday afternoon. After dinner, we took a long stroll on the boardwalk, and the breeze carried the salty scent of the ocean. Oh, how the ocean calms my soul. I was even able to think about being here before, when I was a child, like Jack, my hand in my mother's, as his was now in mine.

In the morning, we went to early Mass at St. Catherine's, the beautiful church that never fails to comfort me. I prayed that I would find a way to clear my name, to change the impression the world has of Liza Barton. I prayed that we could someday be like the other young families I saw around me. I wanted the life they were leading.

In the pew directly ahead of us, there was a couple with two little boys I judged to be about four and three, and a baby girl less than a year old. At first the boys were well behaved, but then they started to fidget. The three-year-old began poking his older brother, who responded by leaning heavily against him. Their father noticed and separated them with a warning glance. Then the baby, obviously on the verge of being able to walk, began struggling to get down from her mother's arms.

I wanted to be able to give Alex the family he wanted, with all the blessed aggravations that are part of that life.

Of course, Alex and Jack had noticed the kids in front of us. When we were walking back to the car after Mass, Alex asked Jack what he would do if a little brother started poking him.

"I'd give him a punch," Jack said matter-of-factly.

"Jack, you wouldn't! That's not the way a big brother acts," I told him.

"I'd give him a punch, too," Alex confirmed. They grinned at each other. I made myself push aside the thought that if Alex somehow learned the truth about my past before I could present a compelling defense, he might simply move out and disappear from our lives.

We spent the rest of the day on the beach, went to Rod's Olde Irish Tavern in Sea Girt for an early dinner, then, happily tired, started back to Mendham. On the way, I told Alex that I was going to sign up for riding lessons at the Washington Valley Riding Club.

"Why not at Peapack?" he asked.

"Because there's a guy named Zach at Washington Valley who is supposed to be a wonderful teacher."

"Who told you about him?"

"Georgette did," I said, my throat choking on the lie. "I called over there Friday afternoon and talked to him. He said he wasn't especially busy, and agreed to take me on. I kind of sweet-talked him into it, I guess. I told him my husband was a wonderful rider and that I was embarrassed to be starting out at a place where his friends could see how inexperienced I was."

Lie after lie after lie. The truth, of course, was that riding a horse is like learning to ride a bicycle. Once you've learned it, you simply don't forget. I was afraid that it was my experience, not my inexperience, that would trip me up.

And of course, taking lessons from Zach would be the most natural way for me to be around a man whose name had been on my mother's lips seconds before she died.

32

Detective Paul Walsh was one of the first to arrive at Hilltop Presbyterian Church for Georgette Grove's memorial service on Monday morning. To be certain that he didn't miss seeing anyone who showed up, he chose a seat in the last pew. During the night, hidden cameras had been set up both inside the church and on the grounds outside. The tapes from them would be scrutinized later. Georgette's killer would not be the first to arrive at the victim's send-off, but it was likely that he—or she—would put in an appearance.

Walsh had absolutely dismissed the possibility that Georgette Grove had been murdered by a stranger who had followed her into the house with the intention of robbing her. So far as he was concerned, the presence of Celia Nolan's picture in Georgette's shoulder bag eliminated that consideration. It was obvious that the picture had been wiped clean of fingerprints for a reason.

The more he thought about it, the more convinced he was that Celia Nolan was an unbalanced woman, and that she had carried a gun with her to Holland Road. He could visualize her looking for Georgette, going from room to room, the pistol in her hand. You can bet she wasn't calling Georgette's name, Walsh thought. She found her on her knees with the turpentine-soaked rag in her hand, shot her, then put the picture from the newspaper in Georgette's shoulder bag. It was her way of explaining the reason for killing her. Even placing the pistol precisely in the center of the splash of paint was, in his opinion, another sign of an unbalanced mind.

The search of Georgette's house over the weekend had proven fruitful. One of the Mendham cops had found a file hidden in the closet of her bedroom that contained an exchange of E-mails between Henry Paley and Ted Cartwright. In one of them, Cartwright promised Paley a bonus if he could force Georgette to sell the property on Route 24. In several of Paley's E-mails to Cartwright, he had written that the agency was in a shaky financial situation and that he was doing everything possible to keep it that way by not actively pursuing clients.

Nice guy, Walsh thought; he was actively trying to put his partner out of business. I wouldn't be surprised if Paley didn't hire someone to mess up Little Lizzie's Place, too. MacKingsley's mind-set is that Paley was the killer, having panicked because Georgette somehow got her hands on his Cartwright file, but Walsh wasn't so sure.

It was common knowledge that Jeff MacKingsley intended to make a run for the governor's office in two years, and a lot of people thought he would make it. This kind of high-profile case was just what he wanted. Well, solving this case would also be a nice feather in my cap, too, Paul Walsh thought. He wanted to retire soon and land a plush job doing security for some big corporation.

At ten minutes of ten, the organ began to play, and suddenly the church began to fill with people. Walsh recognized some members of the local media who, like him, stayed in the back pews. Dru Perry was easy to pick out with her mane of gray hair. Although too persistent for his taste, he thought she was a good newspaperwoman. He wondered if, like Samson, she got her strength from her hair.

He watched as Marcella Williams, the neighbor on Old Mill

Lane, sat in the fourth pew. Doesn't want to miss a trick, Walsh thought. It's a wonder she didn't go up and sit on the altar.

At five of ten, the family arrived. Walsh remembered that there were three of them: a brother, Thomas Madison, and his two sisters. Must be the sisters' husbands and Madison's wife with them, he figured. They went down the aisle and took seats in the front pew.

The relatives had been eliminated as persons of interest to those investigating Georgette Grove's murder. A quiet check had confirmed that they were well-respected, solid citizens in the Philadelphia area. Walsh loved the expression "persons of interest." Translated, it meant, we think you're guilty and we're breaking our necks to prove it.

Henry Paley, looking suitably mournful, and Robin Carpenter were the next to come down the aisle and take front seats. Robin had chosen to wear a black and white dress that was molded to her body. Henry's black tie was his only concession to the outward appearance of funeral dress, and it seemed ill-suited to his beige sports jacket and brown slacks. I bet that tie gets changed the minute he hears the last "Amen," Walsh decided.

Talk about people of interest, he thought when, just as the minister stepped before the altar, Celia and Alex Nolan entered the church and took seats across the aisle and only a few rows ahead of him. Celia was wearing an obviously expensive suit, light gray with a faint yellow pin stripe. Dark glasses shielded her eyes. Her long, dark hair was twisted loosely into a knot at the back of her head. When she turned to whisper something to her husband, Walsh had a full view of her profile.

Classy looking, he admitted to himself—a killer with the face of an angel.

He watched as Alex Nolan, in a protective gesture, patted his wife's back, as if to relax or comfort her.

Don't do that, Walsh thought. I'd love to see her explode again.

A soloist began to sing "The Lord Is My Shepherd," and the congregation in the crowded church rose.

The pastor, in his eulogy, spoke of a woman who gave selflessly for the good of others: "Time after time, over the years, people who wanted to live in this beautiful community have told me how Georgette somehow managed to find them a house they could afford. We all know of her selfless efforts to preserve the tranquil beauty of our community. . . ."

At the end of the ceremony, Walsh stayed in his pew, observing the expressions of the people as they filed out of the church. He was glad to see that a number of them were dabbing at their eyes, and that one of the relatives was clearly upset. In these few days since Georgette Grove's death, he had gotten the feeling that while she was admired, there weren't many people who were close to her. In her last moment of life, she had looked up at someone who had hated her enough to kill her. He wanted to believe that somehow Georgette was aware of the affection of those who had come here today to mourn her.

When Celia Nolan passed him, Walsh could see that she was very pale, and was holding tightly onto her husband's hand. For a split second, their eyes locked. Read my thoughts, Walsh signaled. Be afraid of me. Sense that I can't wait to cuff you, lady.

As he left the church, he found Robin Carpenter waiting for him just outside. "Detective Walsh," she said hesitantly, "when we were sitting inside at the service, I kept thinking about Georgette, of course, and then of something she happened to say to me on Wednesday evening. It was about six o'clock, and before I left the office I went in to say goodnight to her. She had her scrapbook on her desk and she was looking at it so intently. She never even heard me push open the door, so she didn't know I was there. The door wasn't fully closed, you see. And while I was standing there, I heard her say something that maybe I should share with you."

Walsh waited.

"Georgette was talking to herself, but what she said was something like, 'Dear God, I'll never tell anyone I recognized her.' "

Walsh knew he was onto something. What it was, he couldn't be sure, but every instinct told him that Carpenter's information was important. "Where is that scrapbook?" he demanded.

"Henry lent it to Dru Perry for the story she wrote about Georgette that ran in the *Star-Ledger* yesterday. He wasn't planning to lend it to her, but she persuaded him. She's returning it this afternoon."

"I'll be over to get it. Thank you, Ms. Carpenter."

Deep in thought, Paul Walsh walked to his car. This information has to do with Celia Nolan, he thought. I *know* it does.

33

Sue Wortman was the young woman who had taken care of the pony while we were in Spring Lake. She was in the barn with him when we got home Sunday evening. She explained she had stopped by to be sure Star was all right, just in case we were delayed.

Sue is a striking girl with golden-red hair, pale skin, and blue-green eyes. The oldest of four siblings, she has a way with children, and Jack took to her immediately. He explained to her why his pony used to be called Lizzie, but that wasn't a good name, so now she was Star. Sue told Jack that was a much nicer name for a pony, and that she would bet Jack that he was going to become a champion rider on a pony named Star.

On the way home from Spring Lake Alex had suggested that we ought to attend Georgette's service. "She gave me a lot of time showing houses before I bought this one," he said.

No thanks to her for finding this one, I thought, but I did agree with him. That was why, when Sue told me she was available for babysitting, I hired her on the spot. I had planned to go to the Washington Valley Riding Club while Jack was in school, but with Sue to take care of Jack, I was able to change my riding lesson with Zach from 10 A.M. to 2 P.M. on Monday.

Four hours wasn't much, but in a way I was glad to have that extra time before meeting Zach. All Sunday night, I had disturbing dreams. In all of them I was afraid. In one, I was drowning and too weak to fight. In another, Jack was missing. Then he was near me in the water, and I couldn't reach him. In another dream, people without faces were pointing their index fingers at me, except that those fingers were shaped like guns. They were chanting, *"J'accuse! J'accuse!"* I, with my high school French, was dreaming in the language.

I woke Monday morning feeling as if I had been in a battle. My eyes were heavy and tired. My shoulders and neck were tense and aching. I took a long, hot shower, letting the water splash over my head and face and body, as though I could wash away the bad dreams and the constant fear of exposure that haunted my waking hours.

I had assumed we would drive to the memorial service in separate cars because Alex was going to work afterward, but he said he'd drop me back home when it was over. Sitting there in that church, all I could think of was Georgette as I saw her for the first time, trying to drag the hose in her effort to wash away the paint. I thought of the distress I saw on her face, her frantic apologies. Then my mind jumped to that moment in the house on Holland Road when I turned the corner and almost tripped over her body. As I sat in that church, I could smell the turpentine that had spilled on the floor.

Of course, Alex sensed my distress. "This was a lousy idea, Ceil," he whispered. "I'm sorry."

On the way out of church, my hand in his, we passed Detective Walsh. He and I looked at each other and I swear the hatred in his face was palpable. His disdain and contempt for me was apparent, and I knew he *wanted* me to see it. He was the Grand Inquisitor. He was all the voices of my nightmare: *J'accuse! J'accuse!*

Alex and I walked back to the car. I knew by now that he was concerned about the time. I said I was sorry I hadn't driven my car, that I knew he was running late. Unfortunately, Marcella Williams had walked up behind us in the parking lot and overheard our conversation. "Why should you waste time dropping off Celia?" she insisted. "I'm going straight home, and it will give us a chance to visit. I've been wanting to stop by and see how you are doing, but I never want to intrude."

Alex and I exchanged glances. Mine reflected dismay, I know, but as I climbed into Marcella's car, I comforted myself that it would only be a ten-minute ride.

I guess my training as an interior designer, which allows me to glance at a room and immediately take in both its good and bad points, extends to my immediate impressions of the appearance of the people I meet. I had known Marcella Williams when I was a child, and I'd met her again the day Alex and I moved in, but that day I was distraught. Today, as I reluctantly sat next to her and clipped on my seat belt, I found myself studying her.

Marcella is a good-looking woman, in a brittle kind of way. She has dark blond hair that's been brightened with skillfully applied streaks, good features, and an excellent figure. But I could also tell that she's had a lot of cosmetic surgery. Her mouth is pulled at the sides. The result, of course, of a facelift. I suspect Botox is the reason for the smoothness of her forehead and cheeks. What so many women don't understand is that smile lines around our eyes, and the little creases we all have at the sides of our lips, give us character and define us. But because she lacked the touches of time on her face, Marcella's eyes and mouth seemed to jump out at me. Her eyes, intelligent, piercing, questioning; her mouth slightly open, showing her sharp, too-white teeth. She was wearing a Chanel suit, a mixture of cream and light-green fabric edged with a deeper shade of green. It occurred to me that she had come to the service dressed to be seen and admired.

"I'm so glad to have the chance to be with you, Celia," she said warmly, as she steered her BMW convertible out of the parking lot. "That was a nice turnout, wasn't it? I think it was so good of you to come. You hardly knew Georgette. She sold that house to your husband without telling him the background, then you had the horror of being the one to find her body. Even with all that, you came to pay your respects."

"Georgette gave Alex a great deal of time when he was house hunting. He felt we should be there."

"I wish some other people felt that way. I could give you a list of longtime residents of Mendham who should have been there, but who at one time or another had fallen out with Georgette. Oh, well."

Marcella was driving along Main Street. "I understand that you were already looking for a different house, and that was why you went to Holland Road. I'd love to keep you for a neighbor, but I can certainly understand. I'm very good friends with Ted Cartwright. He's the stepfather Liza Barton shot after she killed her mother. I guess by now you know the full story of that tragedy?"

"Yes, I do."

"You wonder where that kid is now. Of course she isn't really a kid anymore. She'd be in her early thirties, I guess. It would be interesting to know what happened to her. Ted said he doesn't give a damn. He hopes she fell off the earth."

Was she toying with me? "I can understand that he wants to put everything behind him," I said.

"In all these years, he never remarried. Oh, he's had girlfriends, of course. Plenty of them. Ted's no hermit, far from it. But he sure was crazy about Audrey. When she dropped him for Will Barton, it just about broke his heart."

My mother dropped Ted for my father! I'd never known that.

Mother was twenty-four when she married Daddy. I tried to sound casual when I asked, "What do you mean by saying she dropped him? Was Audrey serious about Cartwright before she married Barton?"

"Oh, my dear, was she ever. Big engagement ring, plans for a wedding. The whole nine yards. She certainly seemed just as much in love as he was, but then she was maid of honor at a college friend's wedding in Connecticut. Will Barton was the best man. And as they say, the rest is history."

Why didn't I ever know that? I wondered. But, looking back, I could see why Mother would not have told me. With my intense loyalty to my father's memory. I would have resented the marriage even more had I felt Ted had been an intimate part of my mother's life, and was simply resuming the role after being sidetracked for a few years.

But why was Mother suddenly afraid of him, and why had he thrown her at me while I was pointing a gun?

We were turning down Old Mill Lane. "How about stopping at my house for a cup of coffee?" Marcella asked.

I managed to get out of that one by saying I had some phone calls to make before I picked up Jack. Uttering the vaguest of promises to get together soon, I finally was able to get out of her car. With a sigh of relief I let myself in the kitchen door, then closed and locked it.

The message light was blinking on the phone. I picked up the receiver, pushed the PLAY button and listened.

It was that same shadowy voice I had heard the other day. This time it whispered, "More about Little Lizzie . . .

"And when the dreadful deed was done,

"She gave her father forty-one.

"Thursday got another gun,

"Shot Georgette and began to run."

34

Jeff MacKingsley called a two o'clock meeting of the detectives assigned to the investigation of Georgette Grove's death. Paul Walsh, Mort Shelley, and Angelo Ortiz were present and ready to give their reports.

Shelley went first: "The personal codes of eight local brokers were programmed into the lockbox on Holland Road. Two of those eight were Georgette Grove and Henry Paley. There's a computer record of which broker's code was punched in and the time it was punched. Paley told us he'd been out there once. The fact is, he was there three times. The last time was Sunday afternoon, a week ago. The paint in that storage room was used on the Nolan house sometime Monday night."

He glanced down at his notes. "I've checked with the other brokers who showed the house last week. They all swear they did not leave the kitchen or patio doors unlocked. But they did agree that somebody showing a house *could* leave a door unlocked—it's been known to happen. The alarm system is programmed for fire and carbon monoxide, not for entry or exit, the reason being that several times someone punched in the wrong code to disarm the alarm system, and the cops came rushing over. The owners decided that since the house was empty, and with Charley Hatch keeping an eye on things, it was more of a nuisance than a protection."

"Do any of the brokers you spoke to remember seeing the key in the door of the storage closet?" Jeff asked.

"One of them from the Mark Grannon Agency showed the house on Sunday morning. He said the key was there. He remembers because he opened the storage closet door. The cans of paint that were inside were all unopened. He put the key back in the door and locked the closet."

"Let's go step-by-step," Jeff suggested. "We know the key to the storage closet was there on Sunday morning. Paley showed the house on Sunday afternoon and claims he didn't notice if the key was there. Wednesday in the Black Horse Tavern, Georgette publicly accused Ted Cartwright of conniving with Henry to force her to sell her property in Route 24. Now that we found Henry's file in her closet, we know why she made that accusation. She had proof that they were working together."

"I gather that everybody in the tavern got that message," Mort Shelley commented.

"That's right," Jeff agreed. "Follow this reasoning. I don't see Henry Paley actually painting that lawn or carving that skull and crossbones on the door, but I *can* see that either he or Cartwright might pay someone else to do it. I can also understand why Henry might panic if Georgette had proof that he was connected to the vandalism. I can't see a judge letting him off with just a slap on the wrist on that one, especially since his purpose was to destroy his partner. I think he'd get some jail time."

Jeff linked his fingers together and leaned back in his chair. "Henry knew the paint was there. He wanted to get his money out of the office property. He also wanted his money out of the Route 24 parcel. Cartwright had promised him a hefty bonus if he forced the sale. If Georgette Grove knew all that, from what I hear of her, she was the kind of woman who'd have hung onto that property even if she was starving rather than let Henry get his hands on it. I say that Paley and Cartwright are our primary suspects in Grove's death, so let's keep the heat on both of them. Cartwright will never crack, but I bet we can put the squeeze on Paley."

"Jeff, respectfully, you're barking up the wrong tree." This time Paul Walsh's voice was devoid of its usual hint of sarcasm. "Georgette's death has everything to do with the pretty lady on Old Mill Lane."

"You were going to run Celia Nolan's fingerprints through the database," Jeff said. Even though his voice was quiet there was no mistaking the anger that was building in him. "I trust you did it, and what did you find?"

"Oh, she's clean," Walsh admitted freely. "She never committed a crime for which she's been caught. But there's something fishy there. Celia Nolan is scared. She's defensive, and she's hiding something. When I was leaving the service for Grove, Robin Carpenter stopped me outside the church."

"That is one good-looking lady," Ortiz injected.

A glance from Jeff MacKingsley silenced him.

"As we know, Georgette worked late in her office on Wednesday night," Walsh continued. "My bet is that she was suspicious of Henry Paley, went through his desk, and found that file. Then, when she was having dinner at the Black Horse, she spotted Ted Cartwright and verbally attacked him. But I think those facts pale in significance when compared to what Georgette's other associate, Robin, told me this morning."

He paused, wanting to emphasize his point. "She told me that on Wednesday evening, she went back to say goodnight to Georgette. The door to Georgette's office was slightly ajar, and Robin pushed it open. Georgette was looking at her scrapbook, and, not realizing she was being overheard, said, *"Dear God, I'll never tell anyone I recognized her."*

"Who was she talking about?" Jeff asked.

"My guess is that a picture of Celia Nolan may be in that book."

"Have you got the scrapbook?"

"No. Henry lent it to Dru Perry from the *Star-Ledger* for an article she is writing. According to Carpenter, she promised to return it by four o'clock this afternoon. I'm going to pick it up later. I didn't call Perry, because I didn't want her to realize we were interested in the book."

"Once again, Paul, I think it's necessary for you to keep an open mind, or else you're going to miss the obvious just because it doesn't fit in with your theory," Jeff snapped. "We had this conversation on Friday. Let's move on. What about fingerprints?"

"They're all in the usual spots in the Holland Road house," Mort Shelley reported. "They're on doorknobs, light switches, kitchen drawers—you know, where you'd expect to find them. We've run all of them through the database and we came up with zip. No criminal records on any of the people who left them there."

"How about the gun?"

"What you expected, Jeff," Shelley told him. "Saturday night special, impossible to trace."

Angelo Ortiz was next: "Clyde Earley talked to the landscaper, Charley Hatch, Friday afternoon. He felt that Hatch was nervous— not nervous the way people are when a cop starts asking questions, but nervous, defensive, like he's got something to hide."

"Is Earley checking Hatch out?" Jeff asked.

"Yes. I talked to him this morning. He hadn't uncovered anything that would show any reason for Hatch to have a grudge against Georgette Grove. He gets paid by the owners of the houses, not by the real estate agent. But Earley's got one of his hunches. He's still sniffing around Hatch."

"Well, tell him not to pull any of his 'in plain view' tricks," Jeff said. "Remember, we lost a drug case a couple of years ago because the judge didn't believe Earley's story that the cocaine the guy was transporting was plainly visible on the front seat of the car."

"Earley has wonderful eyesight," Mort Shelley said mildly. "As I remember, he adjusted his story to tell the judge he spotted some traces of the drug on the door of the glove compartment."

"Warn him, Angelo," Jeff ordered. "The trouble with Clyde is that ever since he got publicity on the Barton case twenty-four years ago, he's been trying to find a way back into the spotlight again." He stood up. "Okay, that's it."

*   *   *

Ten miles away, Sergeant Clyde Earley was standing outside Charley Hatch's barn. He'd already established that Charley wasn't home, having seen his landscaping van in front of one of the houses on Kahdena Road. I'm just paying a little visit to go over Charley's schedule at the Holland Road house, Earley told himself. Sorry that he's not here.

The trash barrels by the barn were full. Wouldn't hurt to take a look, would it? Clyde thought. The lid's practically off this one anyhow. I know I can't get a search warrant at this point, because I don't have probable cause on Charley Hatch, so I guess I'll just have to make do without one. I like it the way it used to be when the courts considered garbage abandoned property, and no warrant was needed. Now they've changed their minds. No wonder so many crooks are getting away with murder!

His conscience satisfied, Clyde Earley knocked the lid off the first barrel. It was stuffed with two black trash bags, each of them securely tied and knotted at the top. With a yank of his strong hands, Clyde opened the first one. It contained the unappetizing remains of Charley Hatch's most recent meals. With a muttered expletive, Clyde threw it back in the barrel, picked up the other bag and opened it. This one was stuffed with shabby clothes that suggested Charley had cleaned out his closet.

Clyde shook the contents onto the ground. The last items to fall out were sneakers, jeans, and a bag of carved figurines. With a satisfied smile, he examined the jeans and sneakers closely and found what he was looking for: drops of red paint on the jeans, a smear of red paint on the sole of the left-foot sneaker. Charley must have jumped into those corduroy pants when he saw me coming, Clyde thought. I wouldn't have suspected anything if he'd been smart enough to just wrap a towel around himself.

The figurines were a half-dozen statuettes of animals and birds, all intricately carved, all about six inches tall. These are good, Clyde thought; if Charley did them, he's been hiding his talent. Why would he get rid of these? Doesn't take a genius to figure that one out, he decided. He doesn't want them around because he didn't just do a paint job on Lizzie's place—he got creative and carved the skull and crossbones on the door. That's the way I'll get him. Somebody has to know about his little hobby.

Thoroughly satisfied with his detective work, Sergeant Clyde Earley carefully placed the figurines, the sneakers, and the jeans in the squad car.

The sanitation department would have picked these up tomorrow morning if I hadn't been here, he thought virtuously. At least now we know who messed up Little Lizzie's Place. Next thing to prove is why he did it, and find out who he was working for.

Now that he had what he wanted, Earley was eager to get away. He stuffed the rest of the clothing Hatch had discarded back in the trash bag, retied it, but deliberately left it on the ground. Let him sweat blood when he sees someone's been here and taken the evidence he thought he was getting rid of. Wish I could be a little bird and see his expression, he thought.

Earley got back in the squad car and turned the key in the engine. I don't think I have to worry about Charley Hatch reporting a theft, he told himself. That ludicrous possibility made him snicker out loud as he drove away.

35

My first instinct was to erase that horrible message, but I didn't do it. Instead I took the answering tape out of the machine and brought it up to my office. I pulled out the file drawer of my desk and tapped in the combination that opened the hidden panel. As if my fingers were burning from touching it, I dropped the tape in the file, along with all the other material that has been written over the years about Little Lizzie Borden. When the panel was safely secured again, I sat at my desk, holding my hands down on my knees to keep them from trembling.

I simply could not believe what I had heard. Someone who knew I was Liza Barton was accusing me of murdering Georgette Grove. I've spent twenty-four years wondering when someone would point a finger at me and shout my real name, but even that fear could not compare with *this* attack. How could anyone think I would kill a woman whom I've met only once in my life, and for less than an hour?

Detective Walsh. His name sprang into my mind. *"Have you ever fired a gun?"* It was the kind of question you ask a person you view as a suspect, not something you'd say to an innocent woman who has just had the shock of discovering a murder victim. Was it possible that Walsh was the one who had left that phone message, and was now playing a cat-and-mouse game with me?

But even if he knows I'm Liza Barton—and *how* would he know?—why would he think I would kill Georgette Grove? Did Walsh imagine that I was angry enough at Georgette to kill her because she had sold Alex this house? Could Walsh *possibly* believe my mind is so twisted that being brought back to this house, plus the cruel reminders of the tragedy, would send me over the edge? That possibility made me sick with fear.

Even if Walsh is not the one who knows I am Liza Barton, he's still suspicious of me. I've already lied to him. And if he comes around again, I'll be forced into a continuing series of lies.

I thought about last week. Last week at this time I was in my Fifth Avenue apartment. All was right with my world. It felt like one hundred years ago.

It was time to pick up Jack. As always, his need for me is the focus of my life. I got up, went into my bathroom and washed my face, splashing it with cold water, trying to shock myself into some kind of reality. For some incongruous reason, I remembered Henry Paley pointing out the advantage of having his-and-her bathrooms in the master bedroom suite. At the time, I'd wanted to be able to tell him that my father had figured that one out.

I changed from the suit I had worn to the church service into jeans and a cotton sweater. As I got in the car, I reminded myself that I had to buy a new tape for the answering machine. Otherwise Alex would surely ask why the one that had been there this morning was missing.

I collected Jack at St. Joe's and suggested we have lunch at the coffee shop. I realized that a new fear factor had been added to being in the house—from now on I was going to panic whenever the phone there rang.

I managed to persuade Jack to eat a grilled cheese sandwich instead of his inevitable choice of peanut butter and jelly. He was filled with stories about pre-K, including the fact that a girl had tried to kiss him.

"Did you let her kiss you?" I asked.

"No, it's stupid."

"You let *me* kiss you," I teased.

"That's different."

"Then you'll never let a girl in your class kiss you?"

"Oh, sure. I let Maggie kiss me. I'm going to marry her someday."

His fourth day in class, and his future is already settled. But for now, in this diner, over a grilled cheese sandwich, he is perfectly content with me.

And I with him, of course. It's funny how my love for Jack was the root cause of my marrying Alex. I had met Alex for the first time at Larry's funeral two years ago. Larry had been one of those men whose business associates become their primary family. I'd met a few of his relatives, but only when, as Larry put it, "We can't get out of the damn family get-together."

Even standing at my husband's casket, I couldn't help being aware that Alex Nolan was a very attractive man. I didn't see him again until he came up and introduced himself to me at a charity dinner a year ago. We had lunch the next week, and went to dinner and the theatre a few nights later. From the beginning, it was obvious that he was interested in me, but I had no intention of getting involved with anyone at that time. I had genuinely loved Larry, but the realization of just how disturbed he had been about my past had unsettled me terribly.

Larry was the man who had told me that the happiest part of his life began the day he met me. Larry was the man who put his arms around me and said, "My God, you poor kid," when I showed him the sensational stories of Little Lizzie. Larry was the man who shouted with joy the day I told him I was pregnant, and who did not leave me for one single minute of my long and difficult delivery.

Larry was the man who, in his will, left me one third of his wealth, and made me residual heir of Jack's estate.

Larry was also the man who on his deathbed, his weakened hand clutching mine, his eyes opaque with the nearness of impending death, begged me not to disgrace his son by revealing my past.

Alex and I began to date with the understanding that this was going nowhere, that this was all platonic, a word that today I'm sure many people find amusing. "I'll be platonic as long as you want, Ceil," he would joke, "but don't for a minute believe I *think* platonic." Then he'd turn to Jack. "Hey, guy, we've got to work on your mother. How can I make her like me?"

We'd been in that mode for four months when one night everything changed. Jack's babysitter was late. By the time she got to the apartment, it was ten of eight, and I was expected at an eight o'clock dinner party on the West Side. The doorman was getting a cab for someone else. I saw another cab coming down Fifth and rushed out to hail it. I didn't see the limo that was just pulling out from the curb.

I woke up in the hospital two hours later, battered and bruised, and with a concussion, but basically okay. Alex was sitting by my bedside. He answered my question before I asked: "Jack's fine. Your babysitter called me when the police tried to reach someone at the apartment. They couldn't get in touch with your mother and father in Florida."

He ran his hand across my cheek. "Ceil, you could have been killed!" Then he answered my next unasked question. "The babysitter will wait till I get there. I'll stay at your place with Jack tonight. If he wakes up, you know he'll be comfortable with me."

Alex and I were married two months later. The difference, of course, is that while we were simply seeing each other without commitment, I owed him nothing. Now that I am his wife—no, *before* I became his wife, I owed him the truth.

All these thoughts and memories were leaping through my mind as I watched Jack finish the last crumb of his sandwich, a hint of a smile on his lips. Was he thinking about Maggie, the four-year-old he was planning to marry?

It's strange how, in the midst of having my life dissolve into chaos, I can still find moments of peace and normalcy, like having lunch with Jack. When I signaled for the check, he told me that he had been invited for a play date the next day, and would I call his friend Billy's mom. He fished in his pocket and gave me the number.

"Isn't Billy the little boy who was crying the first day?" I asked.

"That was another Billy. He's still crying."

We started to drive home, but then I remembered I hadn't bought the new answering machine tape. We backtracked, and as a result, it was twenty of two by the time we got to the house. Sue was already there, and I rushed upstairs to trade my sneakers for boots that would work well enough for my first riding lesson.

It's funny that it didn't occur to me to cancel the lesson. I was distraught at the dual threat that somebody knew I was Liza Barton, and that Detective Walsh, even if he was not aware of my other identity, was suspicious of me.

But every instinct in my being said that by getting to know Zach, I might learn why my mother had screamed his name that night she and Ted fought.

On the way to the Washington Valley Riding Club, I was flooded with vivid memories of my mother. I remember her impeccably outfitted in her beautifully tailored black jacket and cream-colored breeches, her smooth blond hair in a chignon, mostly hidden under her riding helmet, as my father and I watched her take the jumps at Peapack.

"Doesn't Mommy look like a princess?" I remember my father

asking as she cantered by. Yes, she did. I wondered now if by then he had begun to take riding lessons.

I left the car in the parking lot of the club, went inside, and told the receptionist I had an appointment with Zach Willet. I caught her disapproval of my makeshift riding gear and made a silent promise to myself that I would be more suitably dressed in the future.

Zach Willet came into the reception room to fetch me. I judged him to be about sixty. His lined face suggested long exposure to the elements, and the broken capillaries in his cheeks and nose made me suspect that he liked his liquor. His eyebrows were bushy, and drew attention to his eyes. They were an odd shade of hazel, more green than brown, almost faded in color, as though they, too, had known long years under bright sunshine.

As he looked me over, I detected a hint of insolence in his manner. I was sure I knew what he was thinking: I was one of those people who thought it would be glamorous to learn how to ride a horse, and I probably would end up being a nervous wreck and quitting after a couple of lessons.

Introductions over, he said, "Come on back. I tacked up a horse that's used to beginners." As we walked back to the stables, he asked, "Ever ridden before, and I don't mean one pony ride when you were a kid?"

I had my answer ready for him, but now it sounded stupid: "My friend had a pony when I was little. She'd let me have rides on it."

"Uh-huh." Clearly he was unimpressed.

There were two horses saddled and tied to the hitching post. The large mare was obviously his. A smaller, docile-looking gelding was there for me. I listened attentively to Zach's first instructions about riding: "Remember, you always mount a horse from the left side. Here, I'll boost you up. Get your foot in the stirrup, then point your heel down. That way it won't slip. Hold the reins between these fingers and, remember, don't ever yank on them. You'll hurt his mouth. His name is Biscuit, short for Sea Biscuit. That was the original owner's idea of a joke."

It had been a long time since I had sat on a horse, but I immediately felt at home. I held the reins in one hand and patted Biscuit's neck, then turned to Zach for approval. He nodded, and we started to walk the horses side by side around the ring.

I was with him for an hour, and while he was far from gregarious, I did get him to talk. He told me about working at the club from the time he was twelve, how being around horses was a lot more satisfying than being around most of the people he knew. He told me that horses were herd animals and liked each other's company, that often they will calm down a racehorse by putting a familiar stablemate near it before a race.

I remembered to make the mistakes new riders do, like letting the reins slide, letting out a squeal when Biscuit unexpectedly picked up the pace.

Of course Zach was curious about me. When he realized that I lived on Old Mill Lane, he immediately connected me with Little Lizzie's Place. "Then you're the one who found Georgette's body!"

"Yes, I am."

"Lousy experience for you. Georgette was a nice lady. I read that your husband bought that house as a birthday present. Some present! Ted Cartwright, the stepfather the kid shot that night, used to keep his horses here," Zach went on. "We're old friends. Wait till I tell him I'm giving you lessons. Have you seen any ghosts yet in that house?"

I made myself smile. "Not a single one, and I don't expect to either." Then, trying to sound casual, I said, "Didn't I hear that Liza — or Lizzie as everyone calls her — didn't I hear that her father died as a result of a riding accident somewhere around here?"

"That's right. Next time you come, I'll show you the spot. Well, not the exact spot. That's on a trail only the real experts take. Nobody can understand why Will Barton went on it. He knew better. I was supposed to be with him that day."

"Were you?" I tried to sound casually interested. "What happened?"

"He'd had about ten lessons and could tack up his own horse. My horse had picked up a stone in its hoof and I was trying to get it out. Will said he'd start walking his horse on the trail. I think he was excited about going alone, but I tell you, that man was scared of horses and the horses knew it. Makes them nervous and jittery. But Will was bound and determined to go ahead. Anyhow, I was about five minutes behind him, and I started to get worried that I wasn't catching up with him. Never occurred to me to look for him on that trail. As I said, Will knew enough not to go on it, or so I thought.

"But I couldn't find him anywhere, and by the time I got back to the stable, the word was all over the place. He and the horse had gone over the cliff. Will was dead, and the horse had broken legs. He was finished, too."

"Why do you think he went on the trail?"

"Got confused."

"Weren't there signs to warn him?"

"Sure there were, but I bet the horse got frisky, and Will was so nervous he didn't notice them. Then when the horse chose that path and Will saw what he was up against, my bet is that he yanked on the reins and the horse reared. The dirt and rocks are loose over there. Anyhow, they both went over, and in a way I've blamed myself all these years. I should have made Will Barton wait for me."

So that was how it happened, I thought. The sequence of events began with a stone in the hoof of a horse. Knowing that story, Mother might have blamed Zach Willet for not being with my father when he rode from the stable, but why would she have screamed his name at Ted?

Unless Ted Cartwright had brought my father to Zach to take the riding lessons that had caused his death.

"We'll turn back to the stable," Willet told me. "You're okay. Stick to it and you'll make a good rider."

The answer came before I asked the question. "You know," Willet said, "you told me Georgette Grove suggested me as a teacher. She was also the one who brought Will Barton here to take lessons from me. And now you're living in his house. That's a real coincidence, or fate, or something."

On the way home, I was appalled by the thought that if Detective Walsh knows, or manages to learn that I am Liza Barton, he would have one more reason to think I hated Georgette Grove. By suggesting Zach Willet to my father as a riding teacher, she had directly contributed to his death.

I *can't* answer any more of Walsh's questions, I thought. I can't be trapped by the lies I tell him. I've got to hire a criminal lawyer.

But how would I explain that to my lawyer husband?

36

Dru Perry wrote a brief story about Georgette Grove's memorial service, turned it in to her boss at the *Star-Ledger*, and then went back to work on the "Story Behind the Story" feature. It was her favorite kind of reporting, and by now she was thoroughly intrigued with the prospect of taking a fresh look at the Liza Barton/Little Lizzie Borden case.

She had left a message on the answering machine of Benjamin Fletcher, the lawyer who had defended Liza at her trial. He finally called her back on her cell phone as she was walking up the steps of the Hilltop Church on her way to the service. They had arranged that she would come to his office in Chester at four o'clock.

She intended to ask him about Diane Wesley, Ted Cartwright's one-time girlfriend, who, as the trial began, had called the press and given an interview. She said that she'd been at dinner with Ted the night before the tragedy, and he had told her that Liza's hatred of him was the reason for the separation.

Dru had also found an interview that had come out in one of the trashy tabloids, on the second anniversary of the tragedy. In that one, a scantily clad Julie Brett, another of Ted's girlfriends, revealed that she had been subpoenaed by the defense to refute Ted's claim that he had never physically abused a woman. "I got on the witness stand in court," she had told the reporter, "and I made it clear to them that when Ted Cartwright gets drunk, he's a mean, vicious guy. He starts talking about people he hates and works himself into a fury. Then he'll get it out of his system by throwing something or by taking a swing at the nearest person. Believe me, if I'd had a gun the night he roughed me up, he wouldn't be here right now."

Too bad she didn't tell the media that at the time of the trial, Dru thought wryly, but the judge probably had a gag order on her at the time.

Benjamin Fletcher, Diane Wesley, and Julie Brett—she wanted to talk to all three of them. After that, she intended to find people who had been friends of Audrey Barton at the Peapack Riding Club both before and after she married Will Barton.

From all the reports I've read, that marriage was very happy, Dru thought, but I've heard that song before. She thought about her close friends who had split after forty-two years of marriage. Afterward, Natalie, the wife, had confided to her, "Dru, I knew as I was walking down the aisle that I was making a mistake. It's taken me all this time to have the courage to do something about it."

At one thirty, Dru picked up a ham and cheese sandwich and a container of black coffee from the cafeteria. Having noticed that Ken Sharkey was in line ahead of her, she carried the bag with her lunch back to his desk. "Would my editor be pleased if I have lunch with him?" she asked.

"What? Oh, sure, Dru."

From Ken's expression, Dru was not convinced that he welcomed her company, but she liked to bounce ideas off Ken, and this seemed like a good time to do it. "Paul Walsh was at the service today," she began.

Ken shrugged. "I'm not surprised. He's heading up the investigation into the Grove homicide."

"Am I wrong, or do I detect a little friction between him and Jeff?" Dru asked.

Sharkey, a beanpole of a man whose quizzical expression seemed permanently etched on his features, frowned. "Of course you detected it, because it's there. Walsh is jealous of Jeff. He'd like to be the one shooting for the gubernatorial spot. Failing that, he's eligible to retire soon and wouldn't mind a nice, plush job as head of security somewhere. Obviously it would help if he grabbed some notoriety by solving a big case, and now he's got one. But whatever is going on behind the scenes, the rumors are that he and MacKingsley are close to being on the outs, and that the split is becoming fairly open."

"I'll have to have a talk with Jeff's secretary," Dru said. "She doesn't mean to gossip, but she has a way of saying things that allow me to read between the lines." She took several healthy bites of her sandwich and sipped her coffee, then continued to think out loud: "Ken, I've been keeping in touch with Marcella Williams, or maybe it's more accurate to say that she's been keeping in touch with me. She's the one who lives in the house next to the Nolans on Old Mill Lane, and had so much to say to the media when the vandalism was discovered. She told me that she saw Jeff MacKingsley drive past her place last Wednesday. Then, being Marcella, she walked up the road and saw his car parked in the Nolans' driveway. Isn't it kind of unusual for the Morris County prosecutor to get involved in a vandalism case? I mean, that was before Georgette was murdered."

"Dru, figure it out," Sharkey said. "Jeff's ambitious, and soon he's going to be beating the drums about how safe he's kept Morris County for the four years he's been prosecutor. That latest vandalism case made front-page news. That's why he was there. From what I understand, people are starting to believe that some nut who's fixated on the story of Little Lizzie defaced the house, then murdered Georgette because she was involved with it. Jeff's naturally taking a special interest in seeing that both cases are solved quickly. I hope that happens. If he does get to run for governor, I'll vote for him."

Sharkey finished his sandwich. "I don't like Paul Walsh. He's contemptuous of the media, but at the same time he'll use us to float stories about imminent arrests, just to squeeze people he thinks are hiding something. Remember the Hartford case? When Jim Hartford's wife disappeared, Walsh did everything except accuse him of being an axe murderer. Turns out the poor woman must have pulled her car off the road because she didn't feel well. Autopsy showed she died of a massive heart attack. But until someone finally spotted that car, Hartford wasn't just dealing with his wife of forty years being missing; he was reading every day in the paper that the police suspected she had been the victim of foul play, and that he was 'a person of interest,' meaning, they thought he had killed her."

Sharkey folded up the paper his sandwich had been wrapped in and tossed it into the basket at his feet. "Walsh is a smart guy, but he doesn't play fair with anyone—not with innocent people, not with the media, and not even with his own team. If I were Jeff MacKingsley, I'd have sent him packing long ago."

Dru stood up. "Well, I'm going to send myself packing," she said. "I've got some calls to make, then, at four o'clock, I have an appointment with Benjamin Fletcher, the lawyer who defended Liza Barton at her trial."

Sharkey's face registered surprise. "That was twenty-four years ago, and from what I remember, Fletcher was in his fifties then. Is he still practicing law?"

"He's seventy-five now, and he's still practicing law, but he's no Clarence Darrow. His Web site doesn't offer his services as an expert in criminal defense."

"Keep me posted," Sharkey told her.

Dru smiled to herself as she walked across the news room. I wonder if Ken has ever said, "See you later," or "Take it easy," or "Have fun," or even "Good-bye" to anyone. I bet when he leaves his house in the morning, he kisses his wife, then says to her, "Keep me posted."

*   *   *

Two hours later, Dru was sitting in Benjamin Fletcher's cubbyhole office, staring at him across a desk that was a jumble of files and family pictures. She didn't know what she had expected, but it wasn't that he'd be a giant of a man, six feet three or four, and at least a hundred pounds overweight. His few remaining strands of hair were damp with perspiration, and his forehead glistened as if he were ready to break into a sweat.

His jacket was hung over the back of his chair, and he had opened the top button of his shirt and pulled down his tie. Rimless glasses magnified his already wide gray-green eyes. "Do you have any idea how many times over the years some reporter has called me about the Barton case?" he asked Dru. "Don't know what you people think you're going to find to write about that hasn't been written before. Liza thought her mother was in danger. She got her father's pistol. She told Cartwright to let go of her mother, and the rest is history."

"I guess we all know the basic facts of the case," Dru agreed. "But I'd like to talk about your relationship with Liza."

"I was her lawyer."

"I mean, she didn't have close relatives. Did she bond with you? In those months after you were appointed by the court to defend her, how much did you see of her? Is it true that she never spoke to anyone?"

"From the time she thanked that cop for putting a blanket around her in the squad car, she didn't say a single word for at least two months. Even after that, the psychiatrists couldn't get much out of her, and what she did tell them didn't help her case any. She mentioned her father's riding teacher and got all upset. They asked her about her stepfather, and she said, 'I hate him.'"

"Isn't that understandable, since she blamed him for her mother's death?"

Fletcher pulled a wrinkled handkerchief out of his pocket and rubbed his face with it. "New medicine I'm on causes me to perspire as if I'm in a steam bath," he said matter-of-factly. "Goes with the territory. Since I turned seventy, I've been a walking drugstore. But listen, I'm still around, which is more than I can say about a lot of people my age."

His easygoing manner vanished. "Ms. Perry, I'm going to tell you something. That little girl was very, very smart. She never intended to kill her mother. Far as I'm concerned, that's a given. But Ted Cartwright, the stepfather, is something else. I was always surprised that the press didn't dig a little more into Audrey Barton's relationship with him. Oh, sure they knew she'd been engaged to him, then broke it off when she married Will Barton, and that the old flame got rekindled after she was widowed. What they all missed was what went on during that marriage. Barton was an intellectual, a fine architect, but not a particularly successful one. There wasn't much money in that house, and what there was came from Audrey. She came from money. From the time she was a child, Audrey rode every day. She still was riding every day after she married Barton, and guess who was in that Peapack club riding with her? Ted Cartwright. And her husband never went with her because he was terrified of horses."

"Are you saying that Audrey was having an affair with him while she was married?" Dru asked quickly.

"No, I'm not saying that, because I don't know if it's true. I *am* saying that she saw him at the club practically every day, that they'd often go on the trails together or take the jumps together. At the time, Ted was expanding his construction business and starting to make lots of money."

"You're suggesting that Audrey may have regretted her marriage to Will Barton?"

"I'm not suggesting it. I'm *saying* it. I heard that from a half-dozen people at the club when I was preparing for the trial. If it was such an open secret, wouldn't a smart kid like Liza have caught on to it, too?"

Fletcher picked up the unlit cigar from the ashtray at his elbow, put it between his lips and took it out again. "Trying to break the habit," he remarked, then continued his explanation to Dru. "From the time Audrey buried her husband, she was seeing Ted Cartwright. She waited a couple of years to marry him because the kid resented him from the get-go."

"Then why did Audrey file for divorce? Why was she so afraid of him?"

"We'll never know for sure, but my guess is that life with the three of them under the same roof was unbearable, and obviously Audrey couldn't dump her child. But don't forget one more point that kept coming up." Benjamin Fletcher looked sharply at Dru, challenging her scholarship on the Barton case.

"I understand there was a question about the alarm system," Dru suggested.

"That's right, the alarm, Ms. Perry. One of the things we managed to get out of Liza was that her mother set the alarm that night before the two of them went upstairs. But when the cops came, the alarm was turned off. Cartwright didn't break in. If he'd disconnected the alarm from the outside, there'd be a record of a malfunction. I believed him when he said Audrey had called him and invited him over to discuss a reconciliation. And now, Ms. Perry, I have to tell you I'm planning to leave a little early today."

"Just one more thing, Mr. Fletcher. I read an article that was printed in one of those trashy tabloids about two years after the trial. It was an interview with Julie Brett. She testified at the trial that Ted Cartwright physically abused her."

Fletcher chuckled. "She sure did, but the abuse she got from Cartwright was that he dropped her for another woman. Don't get me wrong. That guy has an explosive temper and has been known to swing a punch, but not at Julie."

"You mean she was lying?"

"Now I didn't say that, did I? I think the real truth is that they'd had an argument. He was on his way out. She grabbed him and he shoved her. But in sympathy for Liza, Julie dressed up her story a little. She's got a good heart. That's off the record, of course."

Dru looked at Fletcher. The elderly lawyer had a satisfied smile on his face. Clearly he was amused by his memory of Julie Brett. Then his face became stern. "Ms. Perry, Julie made a big impression on the judge. Trust me, if it wasn't for her, Liza Barton would have been confined in a juvenile detention center until she was twenty-one."

"What about Diane Wesley, another of Cartwright's girlfriends?" Dru asked quickly. "She told the media that Ted had dinner with her the night before the tragedy, during which he blamed Liza for the problem he was having with Audrey."

"She told that to the press, but she didn't get to say it in court. But anyhow, she was just another voice confirming that Liza caused the rift." Fletcher stood up and extended his hand. "Nice to meet you, Ms. Perry. When you write up your article, have some kind words for this former underpaid public defender. That little girl got one hell of a good defense from me."

Dru shook his hand. "Many thanks for your time, Mr. Fletcher. Have you any idea where Liza is now?"

"No. I wonder about her from time to time. I just hope she got the psychiatric help she needed. If she didn't, I wouldn't put it past her to sneak back around here someday and blow Ted's brains out. Good luck to you, Ms. Perry."

37

Late Monday afternoon, Charley Hatch sat in his living room, drinking a beer and waiting nervously for the call he'd been told to expect. He was going over in his mind how he would explain that there was a problem.

It's not my fault, he thought. After that cop, Earley, left on Friday afternoon, I tried to call the usual number, but it had been disconnected, and I couldn't figure out what was going on. Then, a minute later, my phone rings. I'm told to go out and buy one of those cell phones with minutes on it so nobody can trace it.

Then, in an effort to show that I was being careful, I mentioned that I'd noticed some spots of paint on my jeans and sneakers, and had managed to change them before I let the cop in. I thought that would show that I'm on the ball, but instead I'm told to get rid of the jeans and sneakers, and to make sure there's no paint spots on the truck. Then I have to listen to more bull about how dumb I was to do the carving in that door.

So over the weekend I left the jeans and sneakers bundled with my carvings on a shelf in the garage, and then, trying to be extra careful, I decided I'd better get rid of them for good. I even took the trouble to pull out some old clothes I've been meaning to throw out, and dumped them, along with the jeans and sneakers and my nice carvings, in a big trash bag. Then I tied up the bag real tight and put it in the barrel. I even cleaned out the refrigerator so that the bag on top of the one with the clothes was gloppy with things like old Chinese food, and slices of dried up pizza, and coffee grinds, and those oranges that had turned green.

My garbage is supposed to be picked up every Tuesday and Friday. I thought putting it in the garbage bin Sunday night would be okay. How am I supposed to know that some jerk is going to rummage through my stinking garbage? I'll bet it was that nosy cop, Sergeant Earley, who did it and found my jeans and sneakers and carvings. Anyway, now they're gone. I admit I was a dope to put on those heavy corduroy pants on a hot day. Earley noticed it; he even said something about it.

Charley's regular cell phone rang. His throat suddenly tight, he took a deep breath, then answered. "Hello."

"Did you buy the other phone?"

"You told me to buy it. I bought it."

"Give me the number."

"973-555-0347."

"I'll call you on it."

Charley took a long swig of beer, draining the bottle. When his new phone rang, he picked it up. Instead of giving his carefully rehearsed explanation, he nervously blurted out, "I threw my sneakers, jeans, and my carved figures in the garbage. Someone fished them out. I think it was that cop who came to see me Friday."

The long silence that followed was worse than the angry tirade he'd been subjected to because of the skull and crossbones he'd carved into the door of the house on Old Mill Lane.

When his caller spoke, the voice was calm and even. "Why did you put that stuff in the garbage?"

"It was supposed to be picked up tomorrow. I was too nervous having the stuff in the barn," Charley said defensively.

"I didn't ask for the garbage pick-up schedule. Putting those items in your own trash bin more than a day before collection was idiotic. You should have just thrown them in a Dumpster behind some store, and that would have been the end of it. Listen and try to keep straight what I'm telling you. I don't know who shot Georgette Grove, but if the cops have evidence that shows that you did the job on the Nolan house, they'll blame you for it."

"Blame *us* for it," Charley corrected.

"Don't threaten me, Charley. I'm pretty sure that cop had no right to go through your garbage and remove anything from it without a search warrant, so even if they found something incriminating, they can't use it against you. They can, however, try to wear you down. So get a lawyer, and refuse to answer any questions."

"A lawyer! Who's going to pay for a lawyer?"

"You know damn well, I'll pay for it."

There was a pause, then his caller said, "Charley, you'll never have to worry about money again if you can get through this without messing it up."

"That's the kind of news I like to hear." Charley snapped the phone shut. Vastly relieved, he went to the refrigerator and got another beer. If they couldn't use the jeans and sneakers against him, what did they have? My little statues may show that I'm really talented, he thought, but that doesn't make me the only person in the world who could have carved the skull and crossbones in that door.

He carried his beer outside, walked around to the barn, and looked at his landscaping equipment—the power mower and hedge cutter and rakes and shovels, all of them representing hours and days and months and years of boring hard work.

Pretty soon I'll be paying someone to mow my lawn, he promised himself.

38

On Monday night Zach had a hamburger and a couple of drinks at Marty's Bar and debated in his mind about calling Ted Cartwright. The picture he had mailed him must have arrived at his office by now. Straight to him, Zach thought. No chance of a secretary deciding it wasn't important enough to put that one through to the big boss.

In the lower left corner of the envelope Zach had written, "Personal, Please."

It tickled Zach to add that little touch. It was so la-de-da. A couple of years ago, one of the women who owed him for a riding lesson had sent a check to him at the club and written that on the envelope. Ever since that day, Zach had been marking everything he mailed, "Personal, Please," even the telephone bill.

The cops had to be questioning Ted Cartwright about Georgette Grove, he figured. Everyone in town knew how furious he was that she was always blocking his building plans. The case against him would be a lot stronger if a certain Zach Willet had an attack of conscience and decided to share a certain memory with the police.

But that would happen only after he got immunity from prosecution, or whatever it was they call it, he warned himself.

I'm the little minnow who can lead them to the shark, Zach thought, savoring the power he held.

He decided against having a third scotch and got into his car to drive home. *Home!* He used to really like his place. It wasn't big, but it was big enough for him. Three rooms and a back porch, where on nice days, when he wasn't working, he could settle down with the papers and his portable TV. But last year, Old Lady Potters died, and her daughter moved into the downstairs apartment. She had four kids, and one of them had a set of drums. The racket was driving Zach nuts. Sometimes he suspected she paid the kid to play them. She wanted to take over his apartment, but Zach's lease had two years to go, so she couldn't get rid of him yet.

Ted's building town houses in Madison, Zach thought. His name is all over the construction site. They're about finished and they look real nice. Must be seventy or eighty of them. I wouldn't mind having a little more room. And a place to park, he added to himself, as he drove down his street and found every spot taken. It was clear the landlady's kids were having a gang of their friends over.

Zach finally parked a block and a half away, and sullenly walked back to the house. It was a warm evening, and when he went up the steps to the porch, kids were everywhere. A few of them said, "Hi, Zach," a greeting he ignored. He was sure he caught a whiff of pot as he unlocked the door that led to the second floor apartment and climbed the stairs with a deliberately heavy foot. He had looked forward to sitting outside on his back porch and settling down with a cigar, but there were more kids in the backyard, all shouting at each other.

The fact that one of the neighbors was sure to call the cops soon did little to soothe Zach. He felt unsettled and put upon. He got out his cell phone and put it on the table, trying to decide whether or not to make the call. He'd hit Ted up only a week or so ago, so normally he wouldn't try again so soon. But that was before Georgette took a bullet in the head. Ted must be real nervous now, Zach told himself, feeling reassured.

The sudden beat of the drums came from downstairs, making Zach jump. Muttering a curse, he dialed Ted's cell phone.

"The customer you are trying to reach is unavailable. . . . If you wish to leave a message . . ."

Zach waited impatiently until the computerized voice had finished, then said, "Sorry to miss you Ted. Know how upset you must be about Georgette's death. I bet you're taking it real hard. Hope you can hear me. The racket downstairs is driving me nuts. I really need another place to live, like one of those town houses you're building. I hope you got that nice picture I sent you."

He was about to hang up when a thought occurred to him. "By the way, I have a new lady taking riding lessons. She's Celia Nolan, the one who lives in your old house. She was asking all about Will Barton's accident. Thought you'd want to know."

39

All Monday evening, I struggled to tell Alex that I wanted to hire a criminal defense lawyer, but the words kept dying in my throat. The pleasant weekend at Spring Lake had relaxed some of the tension between us, and I was coward enough to want that good feeling to last a little while longer.

On the way home from the riding lesson, I had of necessity gone food shopping. Kathleen, my adoptive mother, is the kind of cook who can concoct a feast out of whatever she finds in the refrigerator. I can't compete with her, but I do enjoy cooking, and I actually find it calming.

Jack and his babysitter, Sue, had gotten along splendidly while I was gone. She had taken him for a long walk on his pony, and he excitedly told me about the kids he'd met on the next street, one of whom was in his class. "The Billy who doesn't cry. And remember, Mom, you have to call his mother to say I can go over for a play date tomorrow after school."

Jack helped me mix the flour and butter and milk for biscuits, and turn the salad spinner to dry the lettuce, and make a mustard sauce to coat the salmon, and by himself he put the asparagus in the poacher.

When Alex got home at six thirty, we all sat together in the living room. Alex and I had a glass of wine and Jack a soft drink. Then we

194

had dinner in the dining room, our first meal there. Alex told me about his aging client who finally did make it in to change her will. "This time the grandniece gets the house in the Hamptons, which is going to start the third world war in the family," he said. "I really think that old gal gets her jollies torturing her relatives. But if she doesn't mind running up billable time, I'm happy to help her play her game."

Alex had changed into a sport shirt and chinos. As usual, I found myself thinking what an absolutely great-looking guy he is. I love the shape of his hands and his long, sensitive fingers. If I were asked to sketch how I envision a surgeon's hands, I would sketch his. Still, I know how strong they are. If he's in the kitchen when I'm struggling to open a jar, all I have to do is to hand it to him. With one easy motion of his hands, the lid begins to turn.

It was a pleasant dinner, a normal family dinner. Then, when Alex said he had to go to Chicago tomorrow afternoon to take a deposition in a case he was handling, and would be there for at least one night, possibly two, I almost was relieved. If any more of those terrible calls came in, he wouldn't be around to answer the phone and hear them. I wanted to call Dr. Moran, who had treated me when I was young. He's retired now, but I have his number. I needed his advice. I spoke to him last when I decided to marry Alex. He warned me that I was taking a terrible risk by not being truthful about my past. "Larry had no right to demand that of you, Celia," he had said.

Now, if I called Dr. Moran and didn't reach him, I wouldn't have to worry about leaving a message for him to call me back. I could ask his advice also on how to tell Alex that I felt I needed a lawyer.

All this I was thinking while I was getting Jack ready for bed. I read him a story, then left him to read one himself before it was time to turn off the light.

The room that once was mine, and is now Jack's, at least for now, is big, but there is really only one place for the bed—the long wall between the windows. When the movers went to set up the bed there, I had asked them to try positioning it on the opposite wall, but it was out of place.

As a child, I had white furniture, perfect for a little girl's room, and a blue and white bed coverlet and window treatments. Jack's furniture is more suitable for a boy, maple and sturdy. On his bed is a patchwork quilt that I made while I was expecting him. The colors are vivid, red and yellow and green and blue. When I tuck it around him after he has fallen asleep, I think of the joy with which I stitched it, how at that time I really thought I could go through life as Celia Kellogg Foster.

Before I went downstairs, I lingered in the doorway, looking back into the room, remembering myself at that age, in this room, reading my book, secure and happy, unaware of what the future had in store for me.

What did the future hold for Jack? I wondered. In my wildest dreams, could I have imagined myself at his age, thinking that in a few years I would be the instrument, if not the cause, of my own mother's death? It was an accident, but still, I have killed, and I know what it is like to experience the moment in which a life ends. My mother's eyes began to stare. Her body sagged. She gasped, making a small gurgling sound. And then, while the gun continued to go off, while Ted was crawling, trying to reach me, she slid down onto the carpet, her hand resting on my foot.

These were crazy, dark thoughts. But as I start down the stairs, I am filled with the sense that Jack needs to be protected. He loves to answer the phone. He runs for it at the first ring. Suppose he heard that shadowy voice talking about Little Lizzie. Because of the pony episode, he has been told that Lizzie was a very bad girl. I know he sensed the evil that is implied in that statement. The vandalism, the excitement of the police arriving, and the media and the ambulance—all that has got to have made an impression on him. He seems to be all right, but I have to wonder what is going on in that intelligent little mind?

Trying to recapture the warmth we had shared at the dinner table, I gave myself a mental shake, hoping to clear my head of all the darkness. Then I went into the kitchen. Alex had volunteered to clear the table and to put the dishes in the dishwasher, while I put Jack to bed.

"Just in time," he said with a smile. "Espresso's ready. Let's have it in the living room." We sat opposite each other in the fireside chairs. By then, I had a feeling he was picking the right moment to bring up something "What time did you tell Jack he has to turn out the light?" Alex asked.

"Eight thirty. But you know the routine. He'll be asleep before that."

"I'm still getting used to the way a kid begs for more time, then falls asleep the minute his head hits the pillow." Then Alex looked at me, and I knew something was up. "Ceil, my piano is being delivered on Saturday," he said.

He raised a hand before I could protest. "Ceil, I miss having the piano. It's been six months since I gave up my apartment and put it in storage. You may find a different house tomorrow, or it could be a year from tomorrow. Even if you do find one, the odds are that it's not going to be available immediately."

"You want to stay here in this house, don't you?" I asked.

"Yes, I do, Ceil. I know that with your talent, if you decorated it, this would be a showplace, as well as a very comfortable home. We can put up a security fence to be sure we never have a vandalism episode again."

"But it will still be 'Little Lizzie's Place' in people's minds," I protested.

"Ceil, I know a way to put a stop to that. I've been going through some of the books written about the history of this area. A lot of the owners of the larger country homes used to name their houses. This house was originally called Knollcrest. Let's call it that again, and have a sign made to put at the gate. Then, when we're ready, we could have a cocktail party, have a picture of the house on the invitation, and welcome people to Knollcrest. I believe the name would begin to stick. How about it?"

The look on my face must have conveyed my answer. "Well, never mind," Alex said. "It was probably a lousy idea." Then as he stood up, he added, "But I *am* going to have the piano delivered on Saturday."

*   *   *

The next morning Alex gave me a hurried kiss on his way out. "I'm going for a ride. I'll shower and dress at the club. I'll call you tonight from Chicago."

I don't know if he suspected that I had been awake most of the night. He came to bed about an hour after me, moving very quietly, assuming, I guess, that I was asleep, and settling on his side of the bed without even the perfunctory kiss that was becoming our nightly routine.

After I dropped Jack at school, I went to the coffee shop again. Cynthia Granger, the woman who had chatted with me last week, was seated at a nearby table with another lady. When she saw me come in, she got up and asked me to join them. It wasn't what I wanted to do, but I did instinctively like Cynthia, and thought that it might be a chance to get a sense of what the local people were saying about Georgette's death—and the fact that I had been the one to find her body.

After expressing concern for me at the shock I had experienced on Holland Road, Cynthia told me the general feeling in the community was that Ted Cartwright was involved in Georgette's death.

"Ted's always been considered a Mafia-type," Cynthia explained to me. "Not that I mean he's *in* the Mafia, but with all his surface charm, you sense that underneath you're dealing with one very tough cookie. I understand that somebody from the prosecutor's office was in Ted's office Friday afternoon."

For what turned out to be a very short interval, I felt as if everything might be all right. If the prosecutor thought Ted Cartwright was connected to Georgette's death, I might have been wrong about Detective Walsh zeroing in on me. Maybe, after all, in their eyes, I was only the victim of the vandalism, the lady from New York who had the incredibly bad luck to buy a stigmatized house, and then to find a murder victim.

Lee Woods, the woman seated with Cynthia, had moved to Mendham last year from Manhattan. It turned out that she had a friend, Jean Simons, whose apartment I had decorated before I married Larry, and she was effusive in her praise of it. "Then you're Celia Kellogg," she said. "I loved what you did for Jean, and she's been loving it ever since. Talk about coincidence. I was redoing our apartment and asked her for your name. I called your number, but your assistant said that you recently had a baby and wouldn't be taking on any new clients. Is that still true?"

"It won't be much longer," I said. "Sooner or later, I do plan to hang out my shingle around here."

It felt so good to be Celia Kellogg, the interior designer again. Cynthia and Lee even had a suggestion for a housekeeper whose longtime employer was moving to North Carolina. Gratefully, I took her name. But as we got up to leave, I had a sudden sense of being watched. I turned around and saw the man who was sitting at a nearby table.

It was Detective Paul Walsh.

40

At three o'clock on Tuesday afternoon, feeling irritable and unsettled, Jeff MacKingsley told his secretary, Anna, to hold his calls. Paul Walsh had come back to the office at noon and reported that he had followed Celia Nolan around all morning. "I really jolted her when she saw me in the coffee shop," he said. "And then I followed her over to Bedminster, where she went into that place where they sell riding clothes. She didn't realize I'd followed her there. When she came out of the store with a bunch of boxes, I thought she'd have a heart attack on seeing me parked behind her. I knew she was picking up the kid, so I let it go for today. But tomorrow, I'll be showing up in her space again."

He looked at me as if he's defying me to take him off the case, Jeff thought, and I won't do that, at least not yet. As far as I'm concerned, the investigations into Georgette Grove's death and the vandalism on Old Mill Lane are going nowhere fast.

Even the so-called "threat" Ted Cartwright had been heard to make to Georgette Grove in the Black Horse Tavern was more a response to her verbal attack on him than what most people would consider a warning of some kind. That doesn't mean I think Cartwright is in the clear, though, Jeff thought. Far from it.

He reached for his ever-present spiral notebook and turned to a fresh page. He always thought more clearly in the early stages of an investigation when he was sorting out the facts for himself.

Who had a motive in killing Georgette? Two people, and Ted was one of them. Henry Paley was the other. Ted wrote their names in the notebook and underlined them. Cartwright had been riding Wednesday morning and conceivably could have turned onto the trail that went through the woods behind the house on Holland Road. He could have been waiting for Georgette and followed her into the house. After all, she had left the door unlocked for Celia Nolan.

The problem with that scenario, as Jeff saw it, was that one would have to assume that Cartwright knew that Georgette was showing the house that morning. Of course, his buddy Henry Paley could have tipped him off, but how could Cartwright be sure that Celia Nolan wouldn't have driven over with Georgette instead of meeting her there? If Nolan and Grove had shown up together, would Ted Cartwright have killed both of them? Unlikely, Jeff decided.

Henry Paley is the one who makes the most sense for both crimes, he thought, as he circled Henry's name on his notebook. He admitted that he knew Georgette was scheduled to meet Nolan at the Holland Road house. He could have been waiting for Georgette to show up, then followed her in, killed her, and made his escape before Celia Nolan arrived. Money was his motive in wanting to kill Georgette, and another motive surely would be fear of disclosure. If she was able to tie him to the vandalism, he was facing a jail term, and he knew it.

Henry is the one with motive *and* opportunity, Jeff concluded. Let's say he had the Nolan house vandalized to embarrass Georgette, hoping the Nolans would sue her, which would have finished her financially. He was aware that she had failed to apprise Celia Nolan of the stigma on the house. But then, when she saw that splash of red paint on the floor in the Holland Road house, she started asking questions. Jeff underlined Henry's name again.

Henry Paley admits to being in the vicinity of Holland Road on Thursday morning, he reflected. He was at a nine o'clock open house for realtors. The other realtors Angelo talked to remember seeing him there at about nine fifteen. Celia Nolan arrived at the Holland Road house at quarter of ten. That means Henry had somewhere between fifteen and twenty minutes to leave the open house, cut through those woods, shoot Georgette, go back to where he left his car, and take off.

But if Henry is the killer, then who did he hire to vandalize the Nolan house? I don't think he did it all by himself, Jeff thought. Those paint cans were heavy. The paint that was splashed on the house went higher than he could have thrown it. Also, there was nothing amateurish about the carving in the door.

In Jeff's opinion, the most puzzling unknown was the picture of Celia Nolan found in Georgette's bag. What was the point of putting it there? Why had it been wiped clean of fingerprints? I could see where Georgette might have cut it out of the newspaper, he thought. Maybe she was beating up on herself because of the reaction Celia Nolan had to the vandalism. But Georgette certainly wouldn't have wiped it clean of fingerprints. That was a deliberate act, done by someone else.

What about the picture that Celia Nolan had found the day after the vandalism, the old one of the Barton family, the picture she was planning to hide? Granted she didn't want any more publicity, but even so, she should have been worried at the possibility that some deranged person had been on their property. Or maybe she simply hadn't thought it through. She'd found the picture only that morning, and her husband didn't even know about it yet.

Two pictures: one of the Barton family, one of Celia Nolan. One taped to a post in plain sight. The other deliberately cleaned of fingerprints—which anyone who ever watched a cops-and-robbers TV show would recognize as something investigators would consider significant.

He looked down at his pad and realized the page was full of doodles, and that there were only three words on it: "Ted," "Henry," and "pictures." The telephone rang. He had told Anna to hold calls unless they were urgent. He picked up the phone. "Yes, Anna."

"Sergeant Earley is on the phone. He says it's very important. He sounds like the cat that swallowed the canary."

"Put him through." Jeff heard a click and said, "Hello, Clyde, what's up?"

"Jeff, I got to thinking about who would be likely to do that job on Little Lizzie's Place."

Does he expect me to play twenty questions? Jeff thought. "Get to the point, Clyde."

"I *am* getting to the point. And I thought, who besides the realtors could have had easy access to that red paint, you know, Benjamin Moore, red mixed with burnt umber?"

He's onto something, Jeff thought, but I'm not going to let him drag it out. He knew Clyde was waiting for him to get excited, but he said nothing.

After a pause which did not get the reaction he had anticipated, Earley, his voice now crisper, continued: "I started to think about that landscaper, Charley Hatch. He had round-the-clock access to the Holland Road house. It was his job to keep the inside dusted and mopped up. He would have known about the paint cans being in the storage closet."

Jeff was no longer impatient with Clyde's narrative. "Go on," he said.

"Anyhow, I had a little talk with him Friday afternoon, and when he let me in, I got the feeling that Charley was real nervous. Remember how hot it was Friday afternoon, Jeff?"

"I remember. Why do you think Charley Hatch was nervous?"

Now that he had the prosecutor's attention, Sergeant Clyde Earley was not about to be rushed. "First thing I noticed was that Charley was wearing real heavy corduroy pants, and I thought that was peculiar. He was wearing what he would consider dress shoes, too, a pair of scuffed loafers. He tried to explain them away by saying that he'd just started to strip to shower, then saw me coming and grabbed the corduroys and stuck his feet in the loafers. Frankly, I didn't buy it. I got real curious about where his regular work pants and shoes might be."

Jeff tightened his grip on the phone. The pants and shoes Hatch was wearing might have had paint stains, he thought.

"So this morning I waited by Charley Hatch's place until the guy who picks up the garbage came. I knew this would be the first collection since I visited him last Friday afternoon, and I thought that he might be just dumb enough to leave evidence like this in his own bin. The garbage truck finally showed up a half an hour ago. I waited for the guy to collect Charley's garbage, and then I followed him till he was off Charley's property. He was just about to throw the bags in the back of the truck. I think, as of then, we can consider the property to be legally abandoned. I asked the waste engineer, as he calls himself, to open Charley's trash bags. He opened them, and lo and behold, in the second one beneath some old sweaters and sweatshirts, we found a pair of jeans with red spots, sneakers with red paint on the left foot, and nice little carved figures with the initials CH on the bottom. Apparently, Charley Hatch loves to do wood carvings. I've got all of these items in my office."

At the other end of the call, at his desk in the Mendham police station, Clyde Earley smiled to himself. He did not think it necessary to inform the prosecutor that, at 4:00 A.M. today, while it was still pitch dark outside, he had returned to Charley's property and had put these items back into their original bag, with all of the old clothes that still sat in the bin awaiting today's pickup. The plan had worked perfectly when he had retrieved the evidence in full view of a wonderfully reliable witness — Mr. Waste Engineer.

"The garbageman witnessed you opening the bag, and he knew it came from Charley's?" Jeff asked, his voice conveying the excitement Earley felt he deserved to hear.

"Absolutely," Clyde replied. "Like I said, he had carried the bags to the truck that was parked on the street, and it was right in front of Charley's place. I also made it a point to specifically hold up a couple of the carvings so that he could see the CH initials on them."

"Clyde, as you know, this is a real breakthrough," Jeff said. "That's great police work. Where is Charley now?"

"Out landscaping somewhere."

"We'll send the clothes to the State lab, and I'm sure that they'll match the paint on the clothes to the paint from the vandalism," Jeff said. "But that could take a day or two, and I'm not going to wait. I think that we have enough probable cause. I'm going to file a complaint against him for criminal mischief, and we'll pick him up. Clyde, I can't thank you enough."

"My guess is that someone paid Charley to mess up the Old Mill Lane house, Jeff. He doesn't come through as the kind of guy who would do something like that on his own."

"That's my guess, too." Jeff hung up the phone and went on the intercom. "Come in please, Anna. I've got a complaint to dictate."

She had barely settled in the chair across from his desk when the phone rang again. "Take a message," Jeff said. "I want to get this arrest warrant out ASAP."

The call was from Clyde Earley. "We just heard from the 911 dispatcher. A hysterical woman on Sheep Hill Drive reported that she found her landscaper, Charley Hatch, lying on the ground at the north end of her property. He was shot in the face, and she thinks he's dead."

41

At twelve thirty on Tuesday afternoon, Henry Paley walked from his office to the Black Horse Tavern to meet Ted Cartwright who had called and insisted they have lunch together. When he arrived, he glanced around the dining room, half-expecting to see either Detective Shelley or Ortiz at a table there. Over the weekend, both of them had separately stopped by the office to ask again about what Georgette had said to him that last evening. They'd been particularly interested to know if he had happened to figure out what Georgette meant when Robin overheard her say, "I'll never tell anyone that I recognized her."

I told them both that I have no idea who she recognized, Henry thought, and they both acted as if they didn't believe me.

As usual, most of the tables were occupied, but to his relief, Henry did not see either Shelley or Ortiz seated at any of them. Ted Cartwright was already at a corner table. He had chosen to sit facing the wall, but his white hair made him easy to spot. He's probably halfway through his first scotch, Henry thought as he made his way across the room.

"Do you think this meeting is a good idea, Ted?" he asked as he pulled out a chair and sat down.

"Hello, Henry. To answer your question, yes, I happen to think it's an excellent idea," Cartwright said. "As the owner of twenty percent of the Route 24 property, you had every right to be in contact with someone interested in buying it. I could wish that you hadn't put our bonus arrangement on paper for Georgette—and then the prosecutor—to find, but there's nothing that can be done about that now."

"You sound a lot less upset about those notes that I kept than you did the other day," Henry commented, then realized that the waiter was standing at his side. "A glass of Merlot, please," he said.

"Bring another one of these while you're at it," Cartwright told the waiter. Then, as the man reached for his glass, he added irritably, "I'm not finished with this one yet. Leave it alone."

He's drinking fast even for him, Henry thought. He's not as calm as he wants me to think he is.

Cartwright looked across the table at Henry. "I do feel somewhat better, and I'll tell you why. I've hired a lawyer, and the reason for this lunch is not only to let people see we have nothing to hide, but to tell you you'd better hire a lawyer, too. The prosecutor's office wants to solve this case, and one approach they're going to take is to try to prove that we agreed to get rid of Georgette, and that one of us actually shot her, or hired someone else to do it."

Henry stared at Cartwright, but said nothing until the waiter returned with the drinks. Then he took a sip of the Merlot and said reflectively, "I had not even considered that the prosecutor would be looking at me as a possible suspect in Georgette's death. Not, to be perfectly honest, that I am burdened with grief about it. At one time I was quite fond of her, but the older Georgette got, the more set in her ways she became, as you well know. However, it simply isn't in my nature to hurt anyone. I have never even held a gun in my hand."

"Are you practicing for your defense?" Cartwright asked. "If so, you're wasting it on me. I know your type, Henry. You're a sneak. Were you behind what happened to the house on Old Mill Lane? It's just the sort of trick I'd expect of you."

"Shall we order?" Henry suggested. "I have an appointment to take some people house hunting this afternoon. It's quite interesting that Georgette's death gave our agency a shot in the arm. We've suddenly had quite a few drop-ins who are interested in buying a home in this area."

The two men did not speak again until the steak sandwiches they both ordered were served. Then, in a conversational tone, Henry said, "Ted, now that I've persuaded Georgette's nephew to sell the Route 24 property, I'd appreciate the bonus check you offered me. I believe the sum we agreed on is one hundred thousand dollars."

Cartwright stopped the fork he was holding in midair. "You have *got* to be kidding," he said.

"No, I am not kidding. We made a deal, and I expect you to uphold your end of it."

"The deal was that you would persuade Georgette to sell that property instead of deeding it to the state."

"The deal was, and is, that the property is for sale. Somehow, I anticipated that you might not wish to pay the bonus you owe me. Over the weekend I have been in touch with Georgette's nephew, Thomas Madison. I pointed out to him that while your offer was reasonable, other offers for that property have also been made over the past few years. I suggested to Tom that I go over those offers, contact the people who made them and see if they would like to begin negotiations with us."

"You're bluffing," Cartwright said, anger rising in his face.

"I really am *not* bluffing, Ted. But you are. You're scared to death that you'll be arrested for Georgette's murder. You were horseback riding near the house on Holland Road. You're a proud member of the National Rifle Association and have a pistol permit. You had a quarrel with Georgette in this very room the night before her death. Now, shall I pursue those other interested parties in the Route 24 property, or shall I expect your check within forty-eight hours?"

Without waiting for an answer, Henry stood up. "I really must get back to the office, Ted. Thanks for lunch. Oh, by the way, why not satisfy my curiosity? Are you still seeing Robin, or was she only last year's diversion for you?"

42

Lorraine Smith was the woman whose hysterical 911 call about Charley Hatch had brought not only the police, but an ambulance, the medical examiner, the media, and the team from the Morris County prosecutor's office, including the prosecutor himself, Jeffrey MacKingsley.

Fifty years old and the mother of eighteen-year-old twins, Lorraine gradually regained her composure sufficiently to join the investigative team in the breakfast room of her Federal-style home on Sheep Hill Road. "Charley got here about one o'clock," she told Jeff, Paul Walsh, Angelo Ortiz, and Mort Shelley. "He comes every Tuesday to do the lawn."

"Did you talk to him at all?" Jeff asked.

"Today I did. Normally I might not run into him for a month at a time. I mean, he just arrives, unloads his equipment, and gets to work. In a couple of weeks he'll be, I mean, he *would have been*, taking out the impatiens and the other annuals and putting in the fall flowers, and normally I'd go over everything with him then. But when he's just doing the lawn, I don't necessarily talk to him."

Lorraine knew she was talking rapidly and excessively. She took a sip of coffee and resolved to calm down and just answer the questions the prosecutor was asking.

"Why did you go out to speak to him today?"

"Because I was annoyed at him for being late. Charley's supposed to come at nine o'clock in the morning, and I had friends over for lunch today. We were on the patio and had to listen to the roar of his power mower. I finally went outside and told him to come back and finish tomorrow."

"What did he say?"

"He kind of laughed and said something like, 'You know, Mrs. Smith, it's okay for me to be tired and sleep in once in a while. You better take advantage of my services while you still have the chance.' "

"Then what happened?"

"His cell phone rang." Lorraine Smith paused. "Or I should say, one of his cell phones rang."

"He had *two* of them?" Paul Walsh asked quickly.

"I was surprised, too. He took one phone out of his breast pocket, but then, when the ringing kept going, he rushed to get the other one out of his back pocket."

"Did you happen to hear the name of the person who called him?"

"No. In fact he obviously did not want to talk in front of me. He told the person who called him to wait a minute, then said, 'I'll load my stuff and get out of here now, Mrs. Smith.' "

"That was at one thirty?"

"Twenty-five of two at the latest. Then I went back inside. My friends and I finished lunch, and they left at about two fifteen. They were parked in the circular driveway in the front of the house, so I didn't realize that Charlie's pickup truck was still in the back by the garage. When I saw it, I went looking to see where he was."

"How long was that after your friends left, Mrs. Smith?" Angelo Ortiz asked.

"Only a few minutes. I could see he wasn't in the backyard, so I walked around the fenced area where the pool and tennis court are. Just past them is that row of boxwoods that we planted for privacy, because on that side, our property ends at Valley Road. Charley was lying on his back in the little space between two of them. His eyes were open and staring, and there was a lot of blood on the right side of his face." Smith rubbed her hand over her forehead as if to erase the memory.

"Mrs. Smith, when you dialed 911, you said you *thought* he was dead. Was there any reason why you thought he might still be alive when you found him?"

"I don't think I knew what I was saying."

"That's understandable. Let's go back to one thing, Mrs. Smith. You say that Charley Hatch made some reference to your taking advantage of his services while you still had the chance. Have you any idea what he meant by that?"

"Charley was a very touchy guy. He did a good job, but I never had the feeling that he enjoyed what he did. You know how some landscapers love working with growing things? To Charley it was a job, and I think the fact that I was annoyed with him meant he was going to quit working for us."

"I see." Jeff stood up. "We'll ask you to sign a statement later, but thank you for being so helpful. It makes our job easier."

"Mom, what's going on? Are you okay?"

Two identical teenage girls who, like their mother, had auburn hair and slim athletic bodies rushed into the room. Lorraine Smith jumped up as they ran to embrace her. Both were traumatized. "When we saw the police cars and all the people here, we thought something happened to you," one of them said.

"She may have been lucky that she wasn't talking to Charley

Hatch when he was hit," Mort Shelley commented to Jeff as they walked through the foyer to the front door. "What do you think?"

"I think that whoever paid Charley Hatch to mess up the house on Old Mill Lane got nervous and was afraid that if we started putting the screws on Charley, he'd tell us who he was working for."

Detective Lola Spaulding from the forensic unit had been gathering evidence. She met the four men as they came out of the house. "Jeff, his wallet is in the truck. Doesn't look touched. No sign of a cell phone. But we did find something in his pocket that I think you'll find interesting. It hasn't been tested for fingerprints yet."

The photograph she was offering him, like the one that had been in Georgette Grove's shoulder bag had been cut out of a newspaper. It showed a stunningly attractive woman in her early thirties. She was wearing riding breeches and a hunt coat and holding a silver trophy.

"This was in Charley Hatch's vest pocket," Lola said. "Any idea who it is?"

"Yes," Jeff said. "This is Liza Barton's mother, Audrey, and this is one of the pictures the newspapers used last week when they carried the story of the vandalism."

He gave the picture back to Spaulding and walked to the yellow crime scene tape that had been strung up to hold the media back. Audrey Barton lived in the house on Old Mill Lane, he thought. The key to what is going on has to do with that house. The psycho who killed two people is leaving those pictures, and is either playing a game with us, or is begging to be stopped.

What are you trying to tell us? Jeff mentally asked the killer as light bulbs began to flash at his approach. And how can we stop you before you kill again?

43

On the way home from shopping in Bedminster, I kept looking out the rear view mirror to see if Detective Walsh was still following me. I decided he wasn't, because I couldn't see any trace of that black Chevrolet sedan. I picked up Jack at school, brought him home, washed his face and hands, and drove him around the corner for his play date with the Billy who didn't cry.

I met Billy's mother, Carolyn Browne, and liked her immediately. She was about my age, with curly dark hair, brown eyes, and a warm, cheerful manner. "Billy and Jack have gotten thick as thieves this past week," she told me. "I'm glad he has a friend living so near. There are no other children his age on this street."

Carolyn invited me to have a cup of coffee with her while she gave the boys lunch, but I begged off, saying that I had phone calls to make. Unlike yesterday, when I'd given Marcella Williams that excuse, this time I was being honest. I had to talk to Dr. Moran. It was about ten o'clock in California, a good time to reach him. And I also wanted to call Kathleen. Now that Martin was failing mentally, she was the only one other than Dr. Moran in whom I could confide. Unlike Dr. Moran, who thought I should have told Alex the truth about myself, Kathleen adamantly believed I should leave the past buried.

Jack gave me a hurried kiss before I left, and, after promising to be back at four o'clock, I went home. As soon as I was inside the house, I ran to the answering machine. When Jack and I stopped at the house after I picked him up, I'd noticed the light was blinking, but I was afraid to play the message while he was in earshot, for fear it was one of the Lizzie Borden calls.

The message was from Detective Walsh. He said he was looking forward to going over my statement with me. He thought that possibly I had been wrong about the time I found Georgette's body, saying it was impossible that someone who didn't know the route from the house on Holland Road to my house could have made the trip so quickly. "I understand how traumatized you were, Mrs. Nolan," he said, his voice smooth but sarcastic, "but by now I imagine you could sort the time element out a little better. I'd like to hear from you."

I pushed the delete button, but erasing Walsh's voice from my answering machine could not erase the implication of what he was saying. He was implying that I had lied about either the time I got to Holland Road, or about not knowing exactly how to get back from there.

Now I was even more anxious to talk to Dr. Moran. He had told me to call him anytime, day or night, but I hadn't called him since the wedding. I hadn't wanted to admit to him that he was right— I should not have married Alex without being completely honest with him.

I started to pick up the receiver in the kitchen, then put it down and got my cell phone out of my pocketbook. In the apartment, the household bills had gone directly to my accountant, but Alex had said that when we moved he would have them sent to his office. I could imagine him glancing at the phone bill and casually asking who I had called in California. My cell phone bill still went to my accountant.

Dr. Moran answered on the second ring. "Celia," he said, his voice as warm and reassuring as always, "you've been on my mind a lot lately. How is everything going?"

"Not that great, Doctor." I told him about Alex buying this house, about the vandalism, about Georgette's death, the bizarre phone calls, and the threatening way Detective Walsh was treating me.

His voice became increasingly grave as he asked questions of me. "Celia, you should trust Alex, and tell him the truth now," he said.

"I can't, not now, not yet, not until I can show him that what they say about me isn't true."

"Celia, if that detective is trying to tie you to the real estate agent's death, there's a chance that they'll dig into your past and find out who you are. I think you should get a lawyer and protect yourself."

"The only lawyers I know are like Alex, in the financial sector."

"Is the lawyer still practicing who defended you when you were a child?"

"I don't know."

"Do you remember his name? If not, I'm sure I have it in your file."

"It was Benjamin Fletcher. I didn't like him."

"But he got you acquitted. From what I understand, he did a very good job in light of the way your stepfather was testifying. Have you got a business telephone directory nearby?"

"Yes, I have."

"Get it and look him up."

The telephone books were in the cabinet under the phone. I pulled out the yellow pages directory and turned to the section on lawyers. "He's listed here," I told Dr. Moran. "He practices in Chester. That's only twenty minutes away from here."

"Ceil, I think you should consult him. Anything you tell him will be protected by attorney-client privilege. At the very least, he could recommend a suitable lawyer to you."

"I'll call him, Doctor, I promise."

"And keep in touch with me?"

"Yes, I will."

I called Kathleen next. She has always understood that calling her "Mother" or "Mom" was difficult for me. She did not, could not replace my mother, but she is very dear to me. We talk every few weeks on the phone. She had been upset when she heard about the house, but then agreed that I could probably get Alex to move to a different one. "As for Mendham," she said, "your maternal ancestors came from that area, Celia. One of them fought in the Revolutionary War in Washington's army. Your roots are there, even if you can't let that fact be known."

When Kathleen answered, I could hear Martin in the background. "It's Celia," she called to him. I heard his response, and it chilled my blood.

"Her name is Liza," he called back. "She made up the other name."

"Kathleen," my voice was now a whisper. "Does he *tell* that to people?"

"He's gotten so much worse," she whispered back. "I never know *what* he's going to say. I'm at the end of my rope. I took him to a nursing home that is really wonderful and only a mile away, but he sensed that I was looking at it with the possibility of putting him there. First he started shouting at me, then when we got home, he cried like a baby. For a little while he was perfectly lucid, and begged me to keep him home."

I could hear the despair in her voice. "Oh, Kathleen," I said. Then I insisted that she immediately find a live-in aide and told her that I would gladly take care of the expense. I think that by the time the conversation ended, I had cheered her a little. Of course, I didn't talk to her about what was going on in my life. It was clear she had enough on her plate without having to listen to my problems. But suppose Martin blurted out my story to someone who would have read about Little Lizzie Borden, and that person talked to friends or wrote about it on an Internet chat room.

I could hear the conversation. "There's an old guy who lives near us. He has an adopted daughter. He's in the early stage of Alzheimer's now, but he claims she's Little Lizzie Borden, the kid who shot her mother years ago."

I took the only action open to me. I dialed Benjamin Fletcher's phone number. He answered himself. I told him I was Celia Nolan. I said that he had been recommended to me and I would like to make an appointment to speak with him.

"Who recommended me, Celia?" He asked with a laugh that sounded almost as if he didn't believe me.

"I'd rather discuss it when I see you."

"That's fine with me. How's tomorrow for you?"

"I'd prefer between nine and ten, when my little boy is in school."

"You got it. Nine o'clock. You have my address?"

"If it's the one in the book, I do."

"That's it. See you then."

The phone clicked in my ear. I put the receiver down, wondering if I had made a mistake. Upon hearing his voice, even though it had become somewhat husky with age, I could see him clearly in my mind—that hulking giant of a man whose size had made me shrink from him when he visited me at the juvenile detention center.

For a few moments I stood irresolutely in the center of the kitchen. During another sleepless night I had decided that I had to do something to make this house more livable until we could move. I had decided that I owed that much to Alex. Except for the piano, he had sold his apartment furnished, because he'd said that when we bought a house he'd be delighted to have his wife, a fabulous interior designer, start from scratch.

I had decided to go out and buy some sectionals for the library and a few extra pieces for the living room, and to have some draperies made. At least I'd try to pull together the downstairs floor. I knew Alex was right: even if we found another house, it might be months before we could move into it.

But I did not feel like going shopping. I was sure that if I did, I would look in the rear view mirror and see Detective Walsh's car. I did remember to phone the housekeeper who had been so well recommended by Cynthia Granger. We agreed that she would come to meet me next week.

That was when I made the decision that was to throw me into an even deeper nightmare. I called the Washington Valley Riding Club, reached Zach, and asked if he was free for another lesson at two o'clock.

He agreed, and I rushed upstairs to change into the breeches and boots and a long-sleeved shirt that I'd just bought. As I pulled the riding jacket out of the closet, I thought how similar it was to the ones my mother had worn years ago. In a detached way, I thought about how Zach Willet had been the last human being my father spoke to before he died. In one way I loved my father for trying to overcome his fear of horses so that he could share my mother's passion for them; in another, I realized I was angry at him for riding off alone without Zach. We would never know why he did that, and what really happened.

And that was the unanswered question. My mother *must* have demanded to know the exact circumstances of my father's death. She could hardly blame Zach Willet for the fact that my father rode off without him, or that he got on the dangerous trail. So then why did she hurl Zach's name at Ted Cartwright less than a minute before she died?

I had a premonition that if I spent enough time with Zach, whatever else my mother screamed at Ted that night might come back to me.

I drove to the club, arriving there at ten of two, and was rewarded by Zach's grunt of approval at my appropriate new outfit. We went out on the trail, and I thought of how my mother enjoyed riding on an afternoon like this. In thinking of her, the riding expertise I had gained as a child was returning, becoming second nature to me again. Zach was much quieter today, but obviously was in a good mood. On the way back to the stable, he apologized for not saying much, but added that I was doing just fine, and he was tired since he'd lost sleep last night because the kids downstairs were having a party.

When I sympathized that it must be a problem to have noisy neighbors, he smiled and said that at least he wouldn't be stuck with them much longer because he was planning to move to a new town house. Then, as we hit the open field, with the clubhouse in the distance, he said, "Let's go," and began to canter. Biscuit immediately followed him, and we raced across the grass until we pulled up at the barn.

We slid off the horses, and Zach's eyes were wary when he faced me. "You've done a lot of riding," he said flatly. "Why didn't you tell me?"

"I told you my friend had a pony."

"Uh-huh. Well unless you want to waste your money, why don't we figure out exactly how good you are, and start your lessons from there."

"That would be fine, Zach," I said quickly.

"Ted, you admitted that Zach . . ."

Suddenly, I was hearing my mother's voice—those were a few of the words I had heard her screaming when I woke up that night.

What had Ted admitted to her? Trying not to let my face give me away, I mumbled to Zach that I would call him, and then I went straight to the car.

As I drove down Sheep Hill Road, I could see that something must have happened at the corner house. When I had passed a little over an hour before there had been no sign of activity around it. Now there were squad cars and media trucks parked in the driveway, and I could see police milling around the grounds. It was a sight that I wanted to avoid, and I stepped on the gas, then tried to take a right turn onto Valley Road. It was closed to traffic and I could see a mortuary van and people gathered at a break in the hedge. I kept going straight, not caring where the road took me, because all I wanted to do was to get away from the sight of police cars and all the trappings of death.

It was quarter of four when I got home. I was anxious to shower and change, but I didn't want to be late picking up Jack. Still dressed in my riding outfit, I walked over to the next street, thanked Carolyn, asked Billy if he'd come over soon and have a ride on Jack's pony, and then strolled home hand in hand with Jack.

We were barely inside and having a soda together in the kitchen when the bell rang. My heart in my throat, I went to answer it. Even before I opened the door, I knew that I would be looking at Detective Paul Walsh.

I was right. But this time he was accompanied not only by the prosecutor, but also by two other men who were introduced to me as Detectives Ortiz and Shelley.

There was something about the way they all stared at me as I stood there in my riding clothes that made me know that my appearance had startled them. As I would later learn, all four of them were mentally comparing me with the newspaper picture of my mother that they had found in Charley Hatch's breast pocket.

44

Dru Perry went to the Morris County courthouse late Tuesday morning to search through old records. At first, she thought she was wasting her time. Liza Barton's adoption records were sealed. The record of Liza's trial in Juvenile Court was sealed. She'd expected that, but wanted to see if there was any point in the *Star-Ledger* testing the public's "right to know" law.

"Forget it," she was told matter-of-factly by a clerk. "Juvenile and adoption cases don't come under that law."

Then, as she was leaving the courthouse, a grandmotherly-type woman who introduced herself as Ellen O'Brien caught her at the door. "You're Dru Perry. I have to tell you I love when your "Story Behind the Story" series is in the *Star-Ledger*. Are you going to do one of them again soon?"

"I'd like to do one on the Liza Barton case," Dru admitted. "I thought I'd do some research here, but I'm hitting a stone wall."

"That case would make a great story for you," O'Brien enthused. "I've been at this courthouse thirty years, and I've seen a lot of cases, but nothing like that one."

Thirty years, Dru thought. That means she worked here when

that case was going on. She noticed it was twelve o'clock. "By any chance, are you on your way to lunch, Ellen?" she asked.

"Yes, I am. I'm just popping into the cafeteria. The food there really isn't bad at all."

"Then, unless you have other plans, is it all right if I join you?"

Fifteen minutes later, over a Cobb salad, Ellen O'Brien was willingly sharing her recollections about what happened from the time Liza Barton was taken into custody. "You can imagine how curious we all were about her," she said. "My son was a teenager then, and you know how kids are. If I yelled at him for anything, he'd say, 'Hey, Mom, be careful or you'll end up like that Audrey Barton.' "

Ellen glanced across the table at Dru, obviously expecting her to get a chuckle out of her son's gallows humor. Not getting that response, she continued lamely, "Anyhow, the night she shot her mother and stepfather, Liza was taken to the local police station. That would be in Mendham, of course. They photographed and fingerprinted her there. She was cool as a cucumber. Never once asked about her mother or stepfather. I know with absolute certainty that no one had told her that her mother was dead. Then she was taken to the juvenile detention center and examined by a state psychiatrist."

O'Brien broke off a piece of roll and buttered it. "I always say I won't have bread at a meal, but it tastes so good, doesn't it? The so-called food experts write about diets, but they change their minds more than the weatherman, don't they? When I was a kid, I had an egg every morning. My mother thought she was giving me a good start for the day. No, that's not the way it is, the experts suddenly decide. Eggs give you cholesterol. Eat them and you'll keel over with a heart attack. Now eggs are kind of back in again. Then they tell us a low carbohydrate diet will keep you alive till you're one hundred, so forget the pasta and bread. On the other hand, someone else says we need carbs, so eat more of them. Eat a lot of fish, but don't forget fish has a lot of mercury, so don't eat it if you're pregnant. A body doesn't know what to do."

While heartily agreeing, Dru tried to get the conversation back on track. "From the accounts I read, I understand that Liza didn't say a word for the first several months she was in custody."

"That's right, except my friend, who was a friend of one of the aides in the detention center and got this straight from her, said that Liza used to say the name 'Zach' sometimes. And then she'd start shaking her head and moving her body. Do you know what 'keening' is?"

"Yes, it's a lament for the dead, a kind of wailing," Dru said. "It's a word you see particularly in Irish history."

"That's exactly right. I'm Irish and it's a word I remember my grandmother using. Anyhow, my friend says she overheard the psychiatrist describe Liza's emotions that way whenever she said that name."

Important, Dru thought. Very important. She made a single notation in her book: "Zach."

"She was examined by state psychiatrists," O'Brien continued. "Now if they had decided she was no danger to herself or others, they could have sent her to the juvenile shelter. But that didn't happen. She was kept in the detention center. It leaked out that she was profoundly depressed and on a suicide watch for months."

"Her trial took place six months after her mother's death," Dru said. "What would have been going on at the detention center?"

"Psychiatric counseling. A social worker would have arranged for some schooling. Then when Liza was acquitted, DYFS—you certainly know that stands for the Division of Youth and Family Services—tried to find a suitable home for her. She had been moved to the juvenile shelter while they were trying to figure out what to do with her. I mean a kid who shot two people, killing one of them, is not exactly the kind of person most people want sleeping under their roof. Then some relatives showed up and adopted her."

"Has anybody any idea who they were?"

"It was very hush-hush. I gather whoever they are, they felt Liza's chance for a normal life meant burying the past. The court agreed with them."

"I think anyone in the tristate area at least would have known her the minute they looked at her face," Dru said. "I bet whoever these people are, they weren't local."

"From what I understand, there weren't any very close relatives. Audrey and Will Barton were both only children. It's almost ironic. Audrey's ancestors settled here before the Revolutionary War. Liza's mother's maiden name was Sutton. You see that name over and over again in the Morris Country archives. But the family has died out around here. So God knows how far distant the cousin might have been who took her in. Your guess is as good as mine. I've always felt kind of sorry for Liza. On the other hand, remember that movie *The Bad Seed*. It was about a kid without a conscience. Have I got it wrong, or did she kill her mother, too?"

Ellen O'Brien took a final sip of her iced tea and looked at her watch. "The State of New Jersey calls," she announced. "I can't tell you what a pleasure it has been talking to you, Dru. You said you were doing a story on the case. Maybe it's better if you don't mention my name. You know what I mean. They'd just as soon we don't pass on any information we pick up around here."

"That's perfectly understandable," Dru agreed. "I can't thank you enough. You've been a great help, Ellen."

"I didn't tell you anything that anyone else in the office couldn't have told you," O'Brien protested modestly.

"Yes, you did. When you talked about the Suttons, you gave me an idea. Now if you'll point me to where the marriage records are kept, I'll get back to work."

I'll trace Liza's ancestry back at least three generations, Dru thought. My hunch is that it's more likely she was adopted by a member of her mother's family than her father's. I'll collect the names of the people the Sutton family members married and trace their descendents to see if one of them has a thirty-four-year-old daughter. It's worth a shot, she thought.

My story depends on tracking down Liza Barton, Dru concluded as she paid the check. Something else that I'm going to do right now is get a computerized image of what she might look like today. And I'm going to find out who Zach is and why, when she couldn't say any other word, Liza was keening over his name.

45

I knew that I had to take a stand. I could not have these four men come into my house and question me about the death of a woman I had met only once. These people from the prosecutor's office did not know I was Liza Barton, and I want to keep it that way. They were trying to tie me to Georgette's death only because I had not dialed 911 from Holland Road, and because I had driven home so quickly.

Jack had followed me out to answer the doorbell, and now he slipped his hand in mine. I'm not sure if he was seeking reassurance from me, or trying to give me reassurance. My anger at what all this might be doing to him gave me the backbone to go on the attack.

I directed my first question to Jeffrey MacKingsley. "Mr. Mac-Kingsley, will you please explain to me why Detective Walsh was following me around this morning?"

"Mrs. Nolan, I apologize for any inconvenience," MacKingsley said. "Would you mind if we stepped in to speak with you for a few minutes? Let me explain what it's about. The other day, you showed me a photograph of the Barton family that was taped to the post in the barn. There were no fingerprints on it except yours, which, as you can understand, is unusual. You took it off the post and gave it to me, but someone had to have handled it first. We have not released this information publicly, but in Georgette Grove's shoulder bag we found a newspaper clipping with a picture of you taken just as you fainted. That also had no fingerprints on it. Today we found a picture of Audrey Barton at another crime scene."

I almost blurted out, "A picture of my mother at a crime scene!" My nerves were just that raw. Instead I asked, "What has that got to do with me?" trying to sound as calm as possible.

I was still standing in the doorway, and MacKingsley saw that I had no intention of either answering his questions or inviting them in. When he had begun speaking, his manner had been courteous and apologetic. Now, whatever warmth I had felt from him was gone. "Mrs. Nolan, the landscaper for the house on Holland Road was shot to death a few hours ago. We have proof that he was the person who vandalized this property. He had a picture of Audrey Barton in his pocket, and I doubt that he put it there himself. What I am trying to say is that Georgette Grove's murder, and this homicide, are some-how connected to this house."

"Did you know Charley Hatch, Mrs. Nolan?" Walsh asked me, point blank.

"No, I did not." I looked at him. "Why were you in the coffee shop this morning, and why did you follow me to Bedminster?"

"Mrs. Nolan," Walsh said, "I believe you either left the Holland Road house where you discovered the body of Georgette Grove much earlier than you have admitted, or that you are so familiar with these roads you could make a number of rather confusing turns and still make that phone call to 911 at the time it was received."

Before I could respond, MacKingsley said, "Mrs. Nolan, Georgette Grove sold this house to your husband. Charley Hatch vandalized it. You live in it. Georgette had your picture. Charley Hatch had Audrey Barton's picture. You found a picture of the Barton family. There's an obvious connection and we are trying to solve two homicides. That is why we are here."

"Are you *sure* you never met Charley Hatch, Mrs. Nolan?" Walsh asked.

"I have never even *heard* of the man." My anger put steel in my voice.

"Mom." Jack tugged at my hand. I knew he was frightened by the tone of my voice, and by the insinuating attitude of Detective Walsh.

"It's all right, Jack. These nice people just want us to know how happy they are that we moved into this town." I ignored Walsh and the other two and looked straight at Jeff MacKingsley. "I arrived here last week to find this house vandalized. I had an appointment to meet Georgette Grove, a woman I had seen only once before in my life, and found her dead. I think the doctor at the hospital can testify to the state of shock I was in when I reached the emergency room. I do not know what is going on, but I suggest that you concentrate on trying to find whoever is guilty of these crimes, and have the decency to leave me and my family alone."

I began to close the door. Walsh put his foot forward to block it from closing. "One more question, Mrs. Nolan. Where were you between one thirty and two o'clock this afternoon?"

That one seemed easy to answer: "I had a two o'clock appointment for a riding lesson at the Washington Valley Riding Club. I arrived there at five of two. Why don't you clock the distance from here to there, Mr. Walsh? That way you can figure out all by yourself what time I left this house."

I slammed the door against his shoe and he withdrew it, but as I turned the lock, a horrible possibility occurred to me. The police activity at the corner house on Sheep Hill and Valley Roads—could that have anything to do with the death of the landscaper who had vandalized this house? And if so, by answering that last question I had placed myself directly in the area where he died.

46

On Tuesday afternoon at four o'clock, Henry Paley returned to the realty office.

"How did it go?" Robin asked.

"I think we have a sale. As you know, this is the third time the Muellers have looked at the house, and the second time his parents came with them. His father is obviously the one with the checkbook. The owner was there, too, pulled me aside, and asked me about shaving my commission."

"Knowing you, I'm sure that went over like a lead balloon," Robin commented.

Henry smiled at her. "That's exactly the way it went over, but I would call it a test balloon. I bet the senior Mr. Mueller talked to him, seeing a reduced commission as a way of lowering the price. He's the kind of guy who probably bargains to get a penny off a quart of milk."

He walked over and stood at her desk. "Robin, did I tell you that you're looking quite provocative today? I don't think Georgette would have approved of that rather revealing sweater, but then she wouldn't have approved of your boyfriend if she'd known about him, would she?"

"Henry, I'm not very comfortable with this subject," Robin said matter-of-factly.

"I'm sure you're not. Simply thinking out loud, of course, but I wonder if at the end Georgette wasn't on to you. But maybe not. She certainly never got wind of the fact that you and Cartwright were see- ing each other last year. If she had, you'd have been out on your ear."

"I knew Ted Cartwright before I started to work here. I do not have a personal relationship with him. The fact that I knew him never un- dermined my loyalty to Georgette."

"Robin, you're the one who fielded phone call inquiries about available properties. You're the one who handled the drop-ins. I admit that I haven't worked hard for a while, but you're something else. Was Ted paying you to turn away potential business?"

"You mean something like the bonus he was paying you to get Georgette to sell the Route 24 property?" Robin asked sarcastically. "Of course not."

The door that fronted East Main Street opened. Startled, they both looked up to see a grim-faced Sergeant Clyde Earley come into the office.

Clyde Earley had been in the first squad car that went screeching up the driveway of Lorraine Smith's home on Sheep Hill Road. After her frantic description of finding Charley Hatch's body, he had or- dered the officer who accompanied him to stay with Mrs. Smith while he ran across the lawn and around the pool area. It was there that he found himself standing over the lifeless form of the land- scaper.

At that moment, Clyde had permitted himself a feeling of gen- uine regret. He had no intention of admitting that he had deliber- ately tormented Charley Hatch by leaving the retied bag of garbage on the ground so that when he got home from work yesterday,

Charley couldn't help but become aware that his jeans and sneakers and carvings were missing. But as he looked down at the dead man's bloody face, Clyde saw the inevitability of what had happened. Charley must have panicked and called whoever had paid him to vandalize the house. Whoever that is then decided that Charley was an unacceptable risk, Clyde thought. Poor Charley. He didn't seem like a bad guy. I wouldn't be surprised if that wasn't the first time he ever did anything illegal. He must have gotten paid well for it.

Careful not to disturb the grass around Charley's body, Earley took in the scene. His power mower is over behind the house, he noted. My bet is that he walked over here to meet someone. But how was the meeting set up? I'm sure Jeff will have Charley's phone records checked out right away. His bank account, too. Or they may find a wad of cash hidden in his closet somewhere.

That house on Old Mill Lane sure does have a curse on it, Clyde thought. Charley vandalized it, and now he's dead. Georgette sold it, and now she's dead. That Nolan woman looked like she was having a nervous breakdown over it. Where does it stop?

More squad cars arrived. Clyde had taken charge of closing Sheep Hill Road, of having the crime scene roped off, of stationing a cop at the gate to make sure no unauthorized vehicles tried to enter the grounds. "And that means the media," he'd instructed firmly.

Clyde liked being in charge. It irritated him that the minute the prosecutor's people arrived, the local police were shunted aside. Jeff MacKingsley was more considerate than most of the others in keeping him in the loop, but even so, there was no question that in the pecking order, the locals lost out.

When Jeff did arrive, his greeting to Clyde had been brusque. No more telling me about my great police work in finding Charley's stuff with the paint on it, Clyde thought.

After the body was removed, and the forensic team had taken

over, Clyde started back to the precinct, but then changed his mind and parked in front of Grove Realty on East Main Street. He could see Robin Carpenter sitting at her desk and Henry Paley talking to her. He wanted to be the one to tell them about Charley Hatch's death and to ask if for any reason either one of them had been in touch with him.

It wouldn't surprise me if Charley had been reporting to Paley, Clyde thought grimly as he opened the door. I don't like that guy. "I'm glad to catch both of you together," he said. "You know Charley Hatch, the landscaper who took care of the Holland Road property?"

"I've seen him around," Paley answered.

"This afternoon, sometime between one thirty and two o'clock, he was shot to death while he was working at Sheep Hill Road."

Robin jumped up, her face turning pale. "Charley! That can't be!"

Both men stared at her. "Charley was my half brother," she wailed. "He *can't* be dead."

47

At five o'clock on Tuesday afternoon, Zach Willet drove to the neighboring town of Madison and parked in front of the sales office of the Cartwright Town Houses Corporation. He went inside, where he found a sales clerk, a woman in her thirties, tidying up in preparation for closing down for the day. He noted the nameplate on her desk: AMY STACK.

"Hi, Amy," Zach said as he looked around the room. "I can see you're getting ready to skedaddle out of here, so I won't take but two minutes of your time."

On the walls were sketches of different models of the town houses, and the artist's conception of how they might look when furnished. Zach walked from one to the other, examining them closely. Brochures on the table listed the prices and sizes and particular features of the various units. He picked up one of the brochures and read aloud some of the selling features of the most expensive model. "Four-story town house, four bedrooms, master bedroom suite, state-of-the-art kitchen, three fireplaces, four baths, washer and dryer, double garage, private patio and yard, all services." Zach smiled appreciatively. "Looks as though you just can't go wrong with that one," he said. He dropped the brochure back on the table, walked over to the biggest picture, and pointed to it. "Now, Amy, I know you're probably rushing to meet your husband or your boyfriend, but how about indulging a nice fellow like me and show me that fancy homestead."

"I'll be glad to take you over, Mr. . . . ." Amy hesitated. "I don't think you introduced yourself."

"That's right. I didn't. I'm Zach Willet, and unless you borrowed somebody else's nameplate, you're Amy Stack."

"You've got it." Amy opened the top drawer of her desk and fished inside for her key ring. "That's 8 Pawnee Avenue. I have to warn you that is our top-of-the-line town house. It's fully loaded with every conceivable extra, and naturally that is reflected in the cost. It's also the furnished model."

"Sounds better and better," Zach said genially. "Let's take a look at it."

On the way through the development, Amy Stack pointed out that the landscaping was almost finished, and was scheduled to be featured in a national gardening magazine, and that the driveways were heated to prevent ice from forming in the winter. "Mr. Cartwright has thought of everything," she said proudly. "He's one of those hands-on builders who is involved in every detail, every step of the way."

"Ted's a good friend of mine," Zach said expansively. "Has been for forty years, since we were both kids riding bareback at the stable." He looked around. Some of the handsome red brick town houses were already occupied. "Expensive cars in the driveways," he commented. "Nice class of neighbors. I can see that."

"Absolutely," Amy assured him. "The nicest people you'd ever want to meet." She walked a few steps more, then said, "Here we are at number 8. As you can see, it's a corner unit, and it really is the crown jewel of the development."

Zach's smile broadened as Amy turned the key, opened the door, and led him into the family room on the entry level. "Raised-hearth fireplace, wet bar—what's not to like?" he asked rhetorically.

"Some people use the room on the other side for a gym, and, of course, there's a full bath with a hot tub right beside it. It's such a convenient arrangement," Amy said, her voice crackling with professional enthusiasm.

Zach insisted on riding the elevator to each of the floors. Like a child opening presents, he took obvious pleasure in every detail of the house. "Plate-warmer drawer! My, oh my, Amy. I remember my momma putting the plates on top of the burners on the stove to keep them warm. She always ended up with blistered fingers.

"Two guest bedrooms," he joked. "I don't have close family, but with those two bedrooms, I'd better look up those cousins of mine in Ohio and have them out for a weekend."

They rode back down in the elevator, went outside, and, as Amy locked the front door, Zach said, "I'll take it. As is. Furnished."

"That's wonderful," Amy Stack exclaimed. "Are you prepared to make a deposit now?"

"Didn't Ted Cartwright tell you that he's giving me this unit?" Zach asked, his tone astonished. "I saved his life once, and now that I have to get out of where I've been living, he told me to come over and choose my space. Ted never forgets a favor. You must be proud to be in his employ."

48

Alex called shortly after the prosecutor and his entourage left. He was at the airport in Chicago. "I'm going to have to go back tomorrow for a couple of days more," he said. "But I miss you guys and just want to get back for the night. Why don't you see if Sue is available to babysit, so you and I can go out for a late dinner at The Grand Cafe?"

The Grand Cafe in Morristown is another one of the restaurants from the past. Mother and Daddy went there frequently, and on weekends, they'd often take me with them. I knew I'd enjoy going there with Alex. "Sounds great," I told him. "Jack had a play date, so he'll be ready for bed early, and I'll call Sue right away."

I was still in my riding clothes. I phoned Sue. She was free to come over. I made the reservation at the restaurant. I gave Jack a ride on Star, then settled him in front of the television with a Muppet tape and went upstairs. For the week we had been here, I'd been showering in the morning. But now, in the bathroom that my father had designed for my mother, I luxuriated in her deep English tub, trying to wash away the bewildering events of the day. So many things had happened: Detective Walsh following me. The fact that I must have passed the place where the landscaper was shot at right around the time of the shooting. The prosecutor, previously so courteous, becoming cold and formal when I refused to let him and his associates in. My appointment with Benjamin Fletcher tomorrow.

How much should I tell Alex? Or should I just say nothing, and try to have a stress-free evening with him? He has to go back to Chicago tomorrow morning. Maybe in the next few days they would solve these two crimes and the prosecutor's office would lose interest in me. I tried hard to believe that's what would happen, because it was the only thing I could believe and stay sane.

When I got out of the tub, I put on a robe, fed Jack, bathed him, and put him to bed. Then I went back to the master bedroom to get changed. A memory suddenly came to me, and it was not a pleasant one. I had gone to this bedroom to say goodnight to my mother before she and Ted went out to dinner. I thought he was downstairs, and I knew she was dressing. The door was open, and I saw she was untying her robe. Then, before I could speak, Ted came out of his bathroom pulling on a tie. He reached his arms behind her and slid the robe off her shoulders. She turned to him, and the kiss she gave him was as ardent as the ones he showered on her.

That was only days before she threw him out.

What happened? What caused her to change so dramatically? From the time she started dating him until the day they separated, she was always pleading with me to be friends with Ted. "I know how much you loved Daddy, Liza, and how much you miss him, but it's okay to love Ted in a different way. Daddy would be happy to know that Ted is taking care of us."

I remember my answer: "All Daddy wanted to do was to live with us forever and ever."

How different it is with Jack. Of course, he can barely remember his father, but he truly loves Alex.

I have a dark green silk shantung pant suit that's dressy without being fussy. I decided to wear it tonight. While living in New York, Alex and I had gotten in the habit of going out a couple of times a week for a late dinner. The babysitter would come in as I was reading Jack his story, then Alex and I would go to Neary's, our favorite Irish pub, or, if we were in the mood for pasta, to Il Tennille. Sometimes we'd go with friends, but more often it would be just the two of us.

The feeling of being a newlywed certainly has been erased since we moved in here last week, I thought, as I touched my eyelids with mascara and applied blush to my lips. I had washed my hair, and decided to let it hang loose, knowing that Alex likes it that way. I clipped on my favorite emerald and gold earrings, given to me by Larry on our first wedding anniversary. Larry—how sad it is that the memory of those few contented years I had with him is forever marred by the fact that he extracted that promise from me on his deathbed.

I hadn't heard Alex come in, and didn't know he was there until I felt his arms around me. He laughed at my startled gasp, then turned me to him. His lips found mine and I responded, eager for his embrace.

"I've missed you," he said. "Those stupid depositions are turning out to be endless. I simply had to get home, even if only overnight."

I smoothed his hair back. "I'm so glad you did."

Jack came running in. "You didn't say hello to me."

"I thought you were asleep," Alex said as he laughed and scooped him up, so that now his strong arms were hugging both of us. It felt so good. It felt so right, and for a few hours, I was able to pretend that it was.

Several people stopped by our table at The Grand Cafe. They turned out to be friends of Alex's from the Peapack Riding Club. All of them offered their regrets about the vandalism and my experience of having found Georgette's body. Alex's response was that we were thinking of giving the house its old name again, "Knollcrest," and he promised each visitor, "When Ceil does her magic on it we'll have the mother of all cocktail parties."

When we were alone at our table, Alex smiled and said, "You can't blame me for hoping."

That was when I told him about the prosecutor coming to the house, and about Detective Walsh following me and telling me that there was something suspicious about the fact I made it home so quickly from Holland Road.

I watched as the muscles in Alex's face tightened, and a dark red flush stained his cheekbones. "Do you mean to tell me that those people have nothing better to do than worry about the fact that you managed to get home quickly in a catatonic state?"

"It gets worse," I said, and told him about the murder of the landscaper, and the fact that I must have passed the property about the time he was killed. "Alex, I don't know what to do." I was practically whispering now. "They say it all has to do with our house, but I swear to you, they're looking at me as though I was responsible for Georgette's death."

"Oh, Ceil, that's ridiculous," Alex protested, but then he saw that once again I was on the verge of breaking down. "Honey," he said, "I'll get a later plane to Chicago tomorrow. I'm going over to Morristown tomorrow morning and talk to that prosecutor. He has one hell of a nerve to let one of his detectives follow you around. He also has one hell of a nerve to show up at your doorstep and ask you where you were when that landscaper was killed. I'll straighten the bunch of them out fast."

On the one hand, I felt gratitude. My husband wants to fight my battles, I thought. On the other hand, what will Alex think when, the next time Walsh or Jeff MacKingsley shows up, I refuse to answer their questions on the grounds that I might incriminate myself? I have already lied to them about firing a gun, and about Georgette giving me directions to Holland Road.

I cannot answer even the simplest of questions, like, "Mrs. Nolan, were you ever in Mendham before your birthday last month? Were you ever on Holland Road before last Thursday?" To answer those questions would lead to so many others.

"Ceil, you have nothing to be concerned about. This is ridiculous," Alex said. He reached across the table to take my hand, but I pulled it away, fishing in my purse for my handkerchief.

"Maybe this isn't the best time for me to stop by, Celia. You seem to be upset."

I looked up at Marcella Williams. Her voice was kindly and soothing, but her eyes, alive with curiosity, betrayed her excitement at happening upon us when we both were visibly upset.

The man standing at her side was Ted Cartwright.

49

At four thirty on Tuesday afternoon, Jeff MacKingsley had barely returned to his office when Sergeant Earley phoned to tell him that he'd just learned that Robin Carpenter was Charley Hatch's half sister. "I've called a press conference for five o'clock," Jeff told him. "Ask her to come to my office at six. Or better yet, maybe you'd better drive her over."

As he had expected, the press conference was confrontational. "There have been two homicides in Morris County in less than one week, both at million-dollar-plus homes. Were the deaths connected?" the *Record* reporter asked.

"Charley Hatch had been the landscaper at the Holland Road house. The man who collected his garbage claims that this afternoon Sergeant Earley confiscated a bag he'd collected from Hatch's trash barrel and took jeans and sneakers and figurines out of it? Was Charley Hatch a suspect in Georgette Grove's death?" That was the question from the *New York Post* reporter.

"Did these homicides have anything to do with the vandalizing of Little Lizzie's Place on Old Mill Lane, and does the prosecutor's office have any leads?" the *Asbury Park Press* stringer demanded.

Jeff cleared his throat. Choosing his words carefully, he said, "Charley Hatch, a landscaper, was shot sometime between one forty and two ten this afternoon. We believe his assailant was known to him, and possibly had arranged to meet him. No one reported hearing the shot, which was not unusual since there was a power mower in use on a neighboring property on Valley Road." He had not intended to say anything more, but then changed his mind, realizing that he could not stop without giving some additional information to the media. "We believe the deaths of Charley Hatch and Georgette Grove were connected, and also may be linked to the vandalism on Old Mill Lane. We are pursuing several leads, and will keep you informed."

He made his way back to his office, aware that his frustration and irritation were landing squarely on Clyde Earley. I'll bet anything that he didn't wait to go through Charley Hatch's garbage until it was off the premises, he fumed. I'll bet Charley knew it had been disturbed and panicked. If Earley was suspicious, he should have waited until the garbage got to the dump to go through it. Then we could have put a tap on Charley's phone and found out who he was working for. That way, we wouldn't have the guy who picked up the garbage blabbing about it to everybody.

And where does that sexy receptionist from Grove's office, who claims to be Charley Hatch's half sister, fit into the picture? he wondered.

At six o'clock, Robin Carpenter, escorted by Sergeant Earley, arrived at Jeff's office. Walsh, Ortiz and Shelley sat in on the meeting, and Jeff was sure that all of them were aware that Robin was the kind of woman who could get whatever she wanted from a man. Funny, Jeff thought. She kept herself fairly low-key last week when we talked to her, after Grove's body was found. Now she's openly playing to the field. And to my staff, he thought, noticing that Ortiz could not keep his eyes off her.

"Ms. Carpenter, I'd like to extend my sympathy at your brother's death. I'm sure this has been quite a shock for you."

"Thank you, Mr. MacKingsley, but I don't want to give the wrong impression. I am very sorry about Charley, but I must explain that I never even knew he existed until a year ago."

Jeff listened intently as Robin explained that at age seventeen her mother had given birth to a baby. In a private adoption, she had signed him over to a childless couple to raise. "My mother's been dead for ten years. Then one day last year, Charley showed up on my father's doorstep and introduced himself. He had his birth certificate and pictures of himself in my mother's arms, so there was no doubt he was who he said he was.

"My father's remarried, so he wasn't at all interested in Charley. In all honesty, he may be my half brother, but the little I got to know him, I didn't much care for him. I mean he was always whining. He complained that he had to pay too much to his wife when they were divorced. He said he hated landscaping, but that once he got into that business, he was kind of stuck with it. He couldn't stand most of the people he worked for. He just wasn't the kind of person anyone would seek out to try to make a friend."

"Did you have much contact with him?" Jeff asked.

"Quite frankly, I didn't want any. Occasionally he'd call and ask me to have a cup of coffee with him. The divorce was fairly recent, and he was at loose ends."

"Ms. Carpenter, we have reason to believe Charley Hatch was the person who vandalized the house on Old Mill Lane."

"That's absolutely impossible," Robin protested. "Why would Charley do that?"

"That's exactly what we want to know," Jeff replied. "Did Charley ever come into your office to see you?"

"No, never."

"Did Georgette know he was related to you?"

"No. There was no reason to talk about him."

"Would Georgette or Henry have had any contact with him?"

"Possibly. I mean sometimes the people who are selling houses are away, and of course the houses and properties must be maintained. Charley was a landscaper and also had a snowplowing service in the winter. If Georgette had an exclusive listing on a property, she'd be the one making sure that it was being kept up, so it's entirely possible that she knew Charley if he was working on one of those properties. But his name never came up in the year I worked with her."

"Then that would be true of Henry Paley as well?" Jeff asked. "He might have known Charley before last week."

"Of course."

"When was the last time you spoke to your half brother, Ms. Carpenter?"

"It was at least three months ago."

"Where were you between one forty and two ten this afternoon?"

"In the office. You see, Henry was having lunch with Ted Cartwright. When he came back a little after one o'clock, I ran across the street to get a sandwich and bring it back in. Henry had an appointment at one thirty to take a client out."

"Did he keep that appointment?"

Robin hesitated, then said, "Yes he did, but Mr. Mueller, the potential buyer, phoned to say he was delayed, and couldn't meet Henry until two thirty."

"Then Henry was in the office with you until that time?"

Robin Carpenter hesitated. Her eyes moistened, and she bit her lip to keep it from quivering. "I can't believe that Charley is dead. Is that why . . . ? " Her voice trailed off.

Jeff waited, then slowly and deliberately said, "Ms. Carpenter, if you have any information that would assist this investigation, it is your obligation to reveal it. What did you just start to say?"

Robin's composure broke. "Henry has been trying to blackmail me," she burst out. "Before I went to work for Georgette, I dated Ted Cartwright a few times. Of course, when I realized how much she despised him, I didn't mention it. Henry's been trying to twist everything around to make it sound as if I was undermining Georgette. That wasn't true, but what is true is that Henry Paley was not in the office today from the time he left at one fifteen until nearly four o'clock. In fact, he had just gotten back minutes before Sergeant Earley came in and told us Charley was dead."

"His appointment to show a house had been changed from one thirty to two thirty?" Jeff confirmed.

"Yes."

"Thank you, Ms. Carpenter. I know this has been very trying for you. If you wait just a few minutes until your statement is ready to sign, Sergeant Earley will drive you home."

"Thank you."

Jeff looked at his assistants, each of whom had been quietly taking notes. "Any one of you have a question for Ms. Carpenter?"

"Just one," Paul Walsh said. "Ms. Carpenter, what is the number of your cell phone?"

50

At quarter of three, Dru Perry received a call from her editor, Ken Sharkey, telling her about the report that had come over the police band. Charley Hatch, the landscaper of the Holland Road house where Georgette Grove had been murdered, had been shot to death. Ken was dispatching someone else to cover the story at the location, but he wanted Dru to attend the press conference MacKingsley was sure to call.

Dru assured Ken she would wait around for the press conference, but she did not share with him the stunning information she had just uncovered. She had been busy tracing back three generations of Liza Barton's maternal ancestors. Liza's mother and grandmother had been only children. Her great-grandmother had three sisters. One of them never married. Another married a man names James Kennedy and died without issue. The third great-great aunt married a man named William Kellogg.

Celia Foster Nolan's maiden name is Kellogg. One of the New York reporters referred to that fact when he wrote about the vandalism, Dru remembered. I just wrote that she was the widow of the financier Laurence Foster. I think it was the guy from the *Post* who gave the background about her—that she had met Foster when she was decorating his apartment, that she had her own design business, Celia Kellogg Interiors.

Dru went down to the courthouse cafeteria and ordered a cup of tea. The cafeteria was almost deserted, which suited her well. She needed time to think, and was only just beginning to realize the ramifications of what she had learned.

As she held the tea cup with both hands, she stared ahead unseeingly. Maybe the fact that her name is Kellogg is merely the wildest of coincidences, Dru thought. But no, I don't believe in that kind of coincidence. Celia Nolan is *exactly* the right age to be the grown-up Liza Barton. Is it really a coincidence that Alex Nolan just happened to buy that house as a surprise? It's a one-in-a-million chance, but it *could* happen. But if he bought it as a surprise, it has to mean that Celia never told him about her true background. My God, I can only imagine how shocked she must have been when he drove her up to the house on her birthday, and she had to pretend to be thrilled.

And as if that wasn't bad enough, the day she moved in she was greeted by that writing on the lawn, and the paint on the house, and that doll with the gun, and the skull and crossbones carved into the door. No wonder she fainted when she saw all the media charging at her.

Did it cause her to become unbalanced? Dru wondered. Celia Nolan had been the one who found Georgette's body. Is it possible she was in such a frenzy about being in the house and all that terrible publicity that she would kill Georgette?

It was a possibility Dru did not relish considering.

Later, at the press conference she was uncharacteristically silent. The fact that Sergeant Earley had confiscated the murdered landscaper's jeans and sneakers and carvings meant only one thing to her. They were looking to tie Charley Hatch to the vandalism.

Dru found herself hoping that Celia Nolan had an ironclad alibi for the thirty minutes between one forty and two ten that afternoon, and then feeling with increasing certainty that she would not have any alibi at all.

It had been a long day, but after the press conference, Dru went back to the office. On the Internet she found a number of articles about Celia Kellogg. One of them was an interview in *Architectural Digest* that had taken place seven years earlier. When the established designer she had been working for retired, Celia had gone out on her own, and the magazine was calling her one of the most innovative and talented of the new crop of designers.

It gave her background as the daughter of Martin and Kathleen Kellogg. She didn't let on that she was their adopted daughter, Dru noticed. She had been raised in Santa Barbara. Reading further, Dru found the information she wanted. Shortly after Celia moved east to go to the Fashion Institute of Technology, the Kelloggs had relocated to Naples, Florida.

It was an easy matter to get their telephone number from the directory. Dru copied it in her notebook. *It's not time to call them yet,* she decided. *They're sure to deny that their adopted daughter is Liza Barton. The next thing to do is to get Liza's picture computer aged, then I have to decide if I should share my suspicions with Jeff Mac-Kingsley. Because, if I'm right, Little Lizzie Borden is not only back, but she's very possibly unhinged and on a killing spree. Her own lawyer said he wouldn't be surprised if she came back someday and blew Ted Cartwright's brains out.*

And I've got to find out who Zach is. If his name sent her into spasms of grief when she was in detention, maybe she has a grudge against him, too.

51

Even as Ted Cartwright was being introduced to me I was sure that seeing me was triggering something inside him. He could not take his eyes off my face, and I am certain that in looking at it, he was seeing my mother. I knew that for some reason tonight I looked very much like her.

"It's very nice to meet you, Mrs. Nolan," he said.

His voice was jarring—hearty, resonant, commanding, confident, the same voice that rose to an ugly jeer as he shoved my mother at me.

Over the twenty-four years since then, I have heard his voice in my mind at times when I would have done anything to forget it, and at other times when I wanted desperately to reconstruct those last words he and my mother shouted at each other before I reached them.

And all these years my last words to him have echoed in my soul: "Let go of my mother!"

I looked up at him. I did not touch his extended hand, but neither did I want to raise questions by being overtly rude. I murmured, "How are you?" and turned back to Alex. Alex, unaware of what was going on, did what most people do when there is an awkward silence. He covered it with polite conversation, telling me that Ted is also a member of the Peapack Club, and that they'd run into each other occasionally.

Of course, Marcella Williams could not leave without trying to find out why I had been dabbing at my eyes. "Celia, is there anything at all I can do to help you?" she asked.

"Perhaps minding your own business would be a start," I said.

Marcella's sympathetic smile froze on her face. Before she could say anything, Ted took her arm and pulled her away.

I looked at Alex and saw the distress in his face.

"Ceil, what was *that* all about? There was absolutely no reason to be so rude."

"I think there was," I said. "We were having a private conversation. That woman saw that I'm upset, yet couldn't *wait* to find out what is upsetting me. As for Mr. Cartwright, you saw as well as I did that long interview he so happily gave the newspapers, raking up that lurid story about the house you want us to live in."

"Ceil, I read what he said," Alex protested. "He answered a few questions a reporter asked him, that's all. I barely know Cartwright, but he's very well thought of at the club. I think Marcella was genuinely trying to be helpful. My God, she drove you home yesterday when she learned I had a time problem."

"You told me Zach saw you!"

My mother's voice was shouting in my mind. I was sure that was part of what she had said that night. Hearing Ted's voice again had verified the flash of memory I had this past week. Mother had spoken Zach's name, and now I had a few words more: *"You told me Zach saw you!"*

What did Zach see Ted do?

And then I said aloud, "Oh, no."

"Ceil, what is it? You look pale as a ghost."

A possible answer to the meaning of my mother's words occurred to me. The day my father died, he had ridden ahead of Zach, and then taken the wrong trail. At least that was the story Zach had told me and everyone else. But Zach had also bragged to me that he was a longtime friend of Ted Cartwright. Had Ted Cartwright also been riding those trails that day? Did he have anything to do with my father's accident? Had Zach seen it?

"Ceil, what is it?" Alex insisted.

I had literally felt the blood drain from my face, and quickly searched my mind for a plausible explanation. At least I could tell Alex a half-truth. "Before Marcella barged over, I was about to tell you that I had been talking to my mother. She tells me that my dad is in bad shape."

"Is the Alzheimer's getting worse?"

I nodded.

"Oh, Ceil, I'm so sorry. Is there anything we can do?"

The "we" was so comforting to hear. "I've told Kathleen to hire a full-time aide immediately. I told her I'd take care of it."

"Let me do that."

I shook my head as I thanked him. "That's not necessary, but I love you for wanting to help."

"Ceil, you have to know that I'd give you the world on a platter if you'd take it." He reached over, took my hands, and entwined our fingers.

"I just want a tiny piece of the world," I said, "a nice, normal piece of it, with you and Jack."

"And Jill and Junior," Alex said, smiling.

Our check came. As we got up, Alex suggested that we stop by Marcella and Ted's table and say goodnight. "It wouldn't hurt to smooth things over," he urged. "Marcella is our neighbor and she meant well. When we start going to affairs at the Peapack Club, you'll be bumping into Ted, like it or not."

I was on the verge of an angry reply, but then something occurred to me. If Ted had recognized me, he might be worried that I would remember what my mother had shouted at him. If he had *not* recognized me, but I had stirred something in his subconscious, there might be a way I could force a reaction from him.

"I think that's a good idea," I said.

I was pretty sure Marcella and Ted had been looking over at us, but when we turned in their direction, they looked at each other and acted as if they were deep in conversation. I walked over to their table. Ted was holding an espresso cup that looked lost in his powerful right hand. His left hand was on the table, the long, thick fingers splayed out over the white surface. I had felt the strength of those hands when he had flung my mother against me like a weightless toy.

I smiled at Marcella even as I realized how thoroughly I despised her. I had a clear memory of how she had always flirted with Ted after he married my mother, then rushed to support his version of my mother's death with her own recollections of me. "Marcella, I'm so sorry," I said. "I got very bad news about my father today. He's quite ill." I looked at Ted. "I've been taking riding lessons from a man who claims he's a great friend of yours. His name is Zach. He's a wonderful teacher. I'm so glad to have lucked onto him."

Later, when we were home and getting ready for bed, Alex said, "Ceil, you looked so beautiful tonight, but I'll be perfectly honest. The way you went so pale, I thought you were going to faint. I know you haven't been sleeping well lately. Is it this Detective Walsh guy who's upsetting you, as well as your Dad being sick?"

"Detective Walsh hasn't helped," I said.

"I'll be on the prosecutor's doorstep at nine o'clock. I'll go straight to the airport from there, but I'll call and tell you how it went."

"Okay."

"As you well know, I'm not much for sleeping pills, but I do think you'd do yourself a favor to take one now. A decent night's sleep makes the whole world look different."

"I think that's a good idea," I agreed. Then I added, "I'm not being much of a wife to you these days."

Alex kissed me. "There are thousands of days ahead of us." He kissed me again. "And nights."

The sleeping pill worked. It was nearly eight o'clock when I woke up. My first awareness was that sometime during my dreams I had heard the first part of what my mother screamed at Ted that night.

"You admitted it when you were drunk."

52

Jeff MacKingsley was at his desk promptly at eight thirty on Wednesday morning. He had a sense that it was going to be a long day and not a good one. Both his Scottish and his Irish grandmothers had cautioned him that everything comes in threes, especially death.

First Georgette Grove, then Charley Hatch. The superstitious part of Jeff's Celtic nature warned him that the specter of violent death was still hovering over Morris County, waiting to claim a third victim.

Unlike Paul Walsh, who remained fixated on the belief that Celia Nolan had murdered Georgette for her own unbalanced reasons, and that she had both motive and opportunity to kill Charley Hatch, Jeff believed that Celia Nolan was a victim of circumstance.

That was why, when Anna came into his office to tell him a Mr. Alex Nolan was at her desk, insisting that he had to see the prosecutor, Jeff's immediate instinct was to welcome the opportunity to have a talk with Celia Nolan's husband. On the other hand, he did not want to have a meeting after which he might be misquoted. "Is Mort Shelley in his office?" he asked Anna.

"He just went by with a container of coffee."

"Tell him to put it down and come in here at once. Ask Mr. Nolan to wait five minutes, then send him in."

"Fine."

As Anna turned to go, Jeff added, "If Walsh stops at your desk, I don't want him to know that Alex Nolan is here. Understood?"

Anna's response was to raise her eyebrows and put her finger to her lips. Jeff knew that Walsh was no favorite of hers. Barely a minute later, Mort Shelley came in.

"Sorry to tear you away from your coffee, but Celia Nolan's husband is here, and I need a witness to the conversation," Jeff told him. "Don't take notes in front of him. I get the feeling that this is *not* going to be a friendly chat."

It was clear from the moment Alex Nolan entered the room that he was both angry and spoiling for a fight. He barely acknowledged Jeff's greeting and the introduction to Shelley, and then demanded, "Why is one of your detectives following my wife around?"

Jeff admitted to himself that if he had been Celia Nolan's husband, he would have reacted exactly the same way. Even given his total focus on Celia Nolan, Walsh had been grandstanding by openly following her when she was shopping. He thought making her aware of his scrutiny would rattle her enough to make her confess to killing Georgette. Instead it had produced hostility, and now Nolan's lawyer husband was on the attack.

"Mr. Nolan, please sit down and let me explain something," Jeff said. "Your new home was vandalized. The agent who sold it to you was murdered. We have evidence that seems to prove that the man who was shot yesterday committed the vandalism. I'm going to lay my cards on the table. You know, of course, the history of your house— that Liza Barton fatally shot her mother and wounded her stepfather in it twenty-four years ago. There was a picture of the Barton family taped to a post in your barn the day after you moved in."

"The one of them on the beach?" Alex asked.

"Yes. There were no fingerprints on it except those of your wife, which was to be expected since she was the one who took it down and gave it to me."

"That's impossible," Alex Nolan protested. "Whoever put it up must have left fingerprints."

"That's exactly the point. That picture had been wiped clean of fingerprints. Georgette Grove had a picture in her shoulder bag of your wife in the process of fainting. It had been cut out of the *Star-Ledger*. It also had no fingerprints on it. Finally, Charley Hatch, the landscaper who was shot yesterday in the yard of a house very close to the Washington Valley Riding Club where your wife was taking a riding lesson, had a picture of Audrey Barton in the pocket of his vest. Like the others, it had no fingerprints on it."

"I still fail to see what that has to do with my wife," Alex Nolan said flatly.

"It may not have anything to do with your wife, but it has everything to do with your house, and we have to find the connection. I assure you that we are pursuing this investigation on a very broad scale, and we have a number of people we are questioning."

"Celia seems to feel that a great deal is being made of the fact that she got home quickly after finding Georgette Grove's body. Mr. MacKingsley, I'm sure you are aware of the feats of physical strength that people have been known to perform when under great stress. I remember an incident of a man lifting a car to rescue his child who was trapped under it. My wife is a young woman who was absolutely shocked by the vandalism. Two days later she found the body of a woman she barely knew in a house she had never set foot in. For all she knew, the person who shot Georgette Grove was still in that house. Don't you think it is possible that, in a catatonic state, and with a terrible sense of being in danger, her subconscious mind retraced her route?"

"I take your point," Jeff said candidly. "But the fact remains, two people are dead, and we are questioning anyone who might contribute any information at all to help us solve these crimes. We know Mrs. Nolan had to have driven past the house on Sheep Hill Road where Charley Hatch was shot. We know that she was on that road within the time frame of his death. We have checked at the riding club. She arrived there at approximately eight minutes of two. She may have seen another car when she came down that road. She may have seen someone walking on it. She told us yesterday that she's never met Charley Hatch. Don't you think it's reasonable that we question her for any impressions she may have subconsciously registered?"

"I am sure that Celia would want to cooperate in any way with your investigation," Alex Nolan said. "Obviously she has nothing to hide. My God, she was never even in this town until her birthday last month, and the second time was last week when we moved in. But I insist that you call off this Detective Walsh. I will *not* have her harassed and distressed. Last night when we were out for dinner, Celia broke down. Of course, I blame myself for being so shortsighted as to buy a house without showing it to her."

"It *is* a rather curious thing to do in this day and age," Jeff commented.

Alex Nolan's narrow hint of a smile had no mirth in it. "Maybe idealistic rather than curious," he said. "Celia has gone through a lot in the last several years. Her first husband was terminally ill for almost a year before he died. Eight months ago she was hit by a limousine and suffered a severe concussion. Her father has Alzheimer's, and she just heard yesterday that he's declining rapidly. She was perfectly happy to move out of the city into this area, but kept delaying house hunting. She wanted me to do it. When I saw the one I bought, I thought it was exactly what she would enjoy. It's everything we were looking for—a fine, spacious older house, with large rooms, in good condition and with a lot of property."

Jeff noticed that Nolan's eyes softened when he spoke about his wife.

"Ceil told me about a beautiful house she had visited years ago, and it sounded just like this one. Should I have brought her out to see it before I bought it? Of course. Should I have listened to the history of the house? Of course. But I'm not here to second guess myself, or to explain why we're in the house. I'm here to make sure my wife is not bullied by people on your staff."

He got up and extended his hand. "Mr. MacKingsley, do I have your word that Detective Walsh will stay away from my wife?"

Jeff got up. "Yes, you do," he said. "I do need to ask her about driving past the house on Sheep Hill Road where Charley Hatch died, but I will do it myself."

"Do you consider my wife to be a suspect in either of these homicides?"

"Based upon the evidence we have now, I do not."

"In that case, I will advise my wife to talk with you."

"Thank you. That will be very helpful. I'll try to arrange a meeting for later today. Will you be around, Mr. Nolan?"

"Not for the next few days. I've been taking depositions in Chicago on a case I'm involved in pertaining to a will. I just came home last evening, and I'm going straight back to Chicago now."

The door had barely closed behind Nolan when Anna came in. "That is one good-looking guy," she said. "All the girls under the age of fifty were asking if he's single. I told them to forget it. He seemed a lot calmer when he left than when he came in."

"I think he was," Jeff agreed, even as he wondered if he had played it fair with Celia Nolan's husband. He looked at Mort Shelley. "What do you think, Mort?"

"I agree with you. I don't consider her a suspect, but I think there's something she hasn't told us yet. I swear, when she opened the door yesterday dressed in those riding clothes, I thought for a minute that she had posed for the picture we found in Charley Hatch's pocket."

"I had the same reaction, but, of course, when you compare that picture of Audrey Barton with Mrs. Nolan, the difference is obvious. Nolan is much taller, her hair is darker, the shape of her face is different. She just happened to be wearing exactly the same kind of outfit that Barton was wearing in the picture—the riding coat, breeches, and boots. Even the way she wore her hair was similar."

The difference was obvious, Jeff told himself, but there was still something about Celia Nolan that reminded him of Audrey Barton. And it was more than the fact that they were both beautiful women in riding clothes.

53

On Wednesday morning, Ted Cartwright made a stop at the Cartwright Town Houses Corporation in Madison. At ten thirty, he opened the door into the reception area that led to his office. There, a smiling Amy Stack greeted him by chirping, "How are things at the North Pole, Santa Claus?"

"Amy," Cartwright said irritably, "I don't know what that's supposed to mean, and I'm not interested in finding out. I've got a busy day lined up and I had to take time to come over here and talk to Chris Brown again. He doesn't seem to be able to get it into his head that I'm not paying any more overtime to that crew of his."

"I'm sorry, Mr. Cartwright," Amy said apologetically. "It's just that I can't help thinking how few people would be so generous, even to someone who saved their life."

Cartwright had been about to pass her desk to go into his office, but stopped suddenly. "What are you talking about?"

Amy looked up at him and swallowed nervously. She liked working for Ted Cartwright, but she was always mentally moving on tiptoe, trying to do everything exactly the way he wanted it. Sometimes he could be relaxed and funny, but she sensed she should have known better than to try to joke with him this morning without first testing his mood. He usually was happy with her work, but the few times she had ever done anything wrong, his biting sarcasm had rattled her.

Now he was demanding an explanation for teasing him about Mr. Willet.

"I'm so sorry," she said. She sensed that whatever she told Mr. Cartwright, he was not going to be happy. Maybe he wouldn't have wanted Mr. Willet to talk to her about why he was being given the town house. "Mr. Willet didn't tell me that it was a secret you were giving him the model town house because he saved your life years ago."

"He saved my life and I am giving him the model town house! Are you telling me that is what Zach Willet told you?"

"Yes, and if it isn't true, we may have already lost a sale. The couple from Basking Ridge, who were looking at it, the Matthews, called a little while ago, and I told them it was sold."

Cartwright continued to stare down at Amy, his normally ruddy complexion draining of all color, his eyes boring into her face.

"Mr. Willet phoned a little while ago. He said that he intended to move in over the weekend," she went on, gaining courage from the fact that none of this was her fault. "I told him that since that unit is our furnished model, maybe he could wait a few months until we're sold out, but he said that wouldn't be possible."

Ted Cartwright had been leaning forward, looking down at Amy. He straightened up and stood for a moment in perfect silence. "I'll talk to Mr. Willet," he said quietly.

In the year she'd been sales agent for the Cartwright Town Houses Corporation, Amy had suffered through her boss's rages about construction delays and cost overruns. In none of his outbursts had she seen his usually blustery red face become pale with anger.

But then Cartwright unexpectedly smiled. "Amy, I have to tell you that for a few minutes, I was just as taken in as you were. All this is

Zach's idea of a joke. A lousy joke, I admit. We have been friends for many years. Last week we made a bet on the Yankee–Red Sox game. He's a passionate Red Sox fan. I'm for the Yankees. Our bet was a hundred bucks, but Zach threw in that if the difference in the score was over ten runs, I owed him a town house." Ted Cartwright chuckled. "I laughed it off, but I guess Zach decided to test the waters. I'm sorry he wasted your time."

"He *did* waste it," Amy agreed resentfully. Taking Zach Willet around last evening had made her late for her date with her new boyfriend, and she'd had to listen to his complaints that they'd have to rush through dinner to make the movie. "I should have known from the way he dressed that he couldn't afford that unit. But I'll be honest, Mr. Cartwright, it does make me mad that we may have lost the other sale because of him."

"Get back to the Matthews right away," Cartwright ordered. "If they only called this morning, it may not be too late. Charm them for me, and there'll be a bonus in it for you. As for Zach Willet, let's keep that story between us, shall we? Falling for it makes the two of us look like fools."

"Will do," Amy agreed, immensely cheered at the possibility of a bonus. "But, Mr. Cartwright, when you talk to Mr. Willet, tell him for me that he's not funny, and he shouldn't play practical jokes on a good friend like you."

"No, he shouldn't, Amy," Ted Cartwright said softly. "No, he absolutely shouldn't."

54

It was another quick good-bye between Alex and me. He was going directly from the prosecutor's office to the airport. His promise to "straighten the bunch of them out" caused me to both hope and fear. If they stopped asking me questions, I'd be all right. But if they *didn't*, and I refused to answer, I knew I'd become their prime suspect. As I kissed Alex, I whispered, "Make them leave me alone."

His grim, "You bet I will," was reassuring. Besides that, I had the appointment with Benjamin Fletcher. If I told him I was Liza, he would be bound to secrecy by attorney-client privilege. But he might be the best person to guide me through the investigation—if he knew the truth. I told myself I would have to wait until I saw him face-to-face to make that decision.

I dropped Jack off at school at eight fifteen. There was no way I was going to go into the coffee shop this morning, especially with the possibility that Detective Walsh would be sitting there, waiting for me. Instead, I went behind the church into the cemetery grounds. I've been wanting to visit my mother's and father's graves, but was afraid that I might be noticed, and would arouse curiosity. But no one was around, so I was able to stand at the foot of the graves where they lie side by side.

The tombstone is very simple, with a leaf design in the form of a frame on the polished marble, with the words "Love Is Eternal" carved above the base. My parents' names and the dates they were born and died are inscribed on it. Generations of my family are buried in other parts of the cemetery, but when my father died, my mother bought this plot and had this stone erected. I remember his funeral clearly. I was seven years old, and wearing a white dress and carrying a long-stemmed rose that I was told to place on the casket. I understood that my father was dead, but I was beyond tears. I was too busy shutting out the prayers of the priest and the murmured responses of the people who were gathered there.

In my mind I was trying to reach out to my father, to hear his voice, to figuratively grasp his hand and make him stay with us. My mother was composed throughout the funeral mass, and also at the grave, until that final moment when, the last one to place a flower on the casket, she cried out, "I want my husband. I want my husband!" and collapsed to her knees in heartbreaking sobs.

Is it possible that my memory is accurate, and that Ted Cartwright started forward to support her, then thought better of it?

I believe that love is eternal. And as I stood there, I prayed for and to both of my parents. Help me, please help me. Let me get through this. *Guide* me. I don't know what to do.

Benjamin Fletcher's office is in Chester, a town a twenty-minute ride from Mendham. My appointment with him was for nine o'clock. I drove directly there from the cemetery, parked, and managed to find a delicatessen around the corner from his office where I could get hot coffee and nibble at a piece of bagel.

There was the tang of fall in the clear, crisp air. I was wearing a cable stitch cardigan sweater with a wide shawl in a shade that was somewhere between burnt-orange and cinnamon. The sweater felt warm against my body, which had been feeling chilled these past few days even when the sun was strong. I felt that the cheerful color of the

sweater brightened my face, which I knew looked drawn and troubled.

At one minute of nine I was climbing the steps to Benjamin
Fletcher's second-floor office. I walked into a small anteroom which
held a shabby desk that I guess accommodated a secretary if and
when he had one. The walls were badly in need of painting. The
wooden floors were dull and scarred. Two small armchairs covered in
vinyl were pushed against the wall opposite the desk. The small table
between them held a haphazard pile of dog-eared magazines.

"That's got to be Celia Nolan," a voice from the inner office
yelled.

Just hearing that voice made my palms begin to sweat. I was sure I
had made a mistake coming here. I wanted to turn and run down the
stairs. But I was too late. That giant of a man was filling the doorway,
his hand extended, his smile as mirthless and wide as it had been that
first day years ago when I'd met him and he'd said, "So this is the little
girl who's in lots of trouble?"

Why hadn't I remembered that?

He was walking toward me, taking my hand, saying, "Always glad
to help a pretty lady in trouble. Come on in."

There was nothing I could do except follow him into the cluttered
room that was his private office. He settled himself behind his desk,
his wide hips jutting out past the arm rests, beads of perspiration on
his face even though the window was open. I believe the shirt he was
wearing was fresh when he dressed that morning, but with the sleeves
rolled up and the top two buttons opened, he looked like what I suspect he was, a retired lawyer who kept his shingle out because it gave
him a place to go.

But he was not stupid. I could tell that the minute I reluctantly
took the seat he offered me and he began to talk. "Celia Nolan of

One Old Mill Lane in Mendham," he said. "That's a very exciting address you have."

When I made the appointment, I had given him my name and phone number, nothing else. "Yes, it is," I agreed. "That's why I'm here."

"I read all about you. Your husband bought that house for you as a surprise. Some surprise, I might add. That man of yours doesn't understand much about the way women think. Then you arrived to find it all messed up, and a couple of days later you happen upon the body of the lady who sold it to you. That's a lot going on in your life. Now how did you hear about me and why are you here?"

Before I could even attempt to answer, he raised his hand. "We're putting the cart before the horse. I charge three fifty an hour plus expenses and require a ten thousand dollar retainer before you get to say, 'Help me counselor for I have sinned.'"

Without speaking, I pulled out my checkbook and I wrote the check. Benjamin Fletcher did not know it, but by looking up information about me, he had made it easier for me to get him to give me the protection I needed without having to tell him that I am Liza.

Threading my way through what I wanted him to know and what I didn't want to tell him, I said, "I'm glad you looked me up. Then you'll understand how it feels to have the prosecutor's office practically accuse me of murdering Georgette Grove."

Fletcher's eyelids had seemed to be permanently settled halfway down over his eyes, but now they lifted. "Why would they even begin to think that?"

I told him about the three pictures found without fingerprints, about how I had managed to drive home quickly after I found Georgette, and that I might have driven past the house on Sheep Hill Road around the time the landscaper was killed. "I never met Georgette

Grove until the day I moved into the house," I protested. "I never heard of the landscaper until the prosecutor asked me about him, but I know they think I'm involved in some way, and it's all because of that house."

"Surely you must know the history of it by now," Fletcher said.

"Of course. My point is that because of those three pictures, the prosecutor's office feels all this has to do with the house or the Barton family." I don't know how I managed to say my surname so matter-of-factly, and all the while looking right at him.

And then he said something that chilled me to the bone. "I always thought that kid, Liza, would come back here someday and shoot her stepfather, Ted Cartwright. But it's crazy that those birds in the prosecutor's office are bothering you, a stranger who had the hard luck to get that house as a birthday present. Celia, I promise you, we'll take care of them, because you know what will happen? I'll tell you. You start answering their questions, and they'll trip you up and turn you around and confuse you so much that in a day or so *you'll* believe you killed those people simply because you didn't like the house."

"Do you mean I shouldn't answer questions?" I asked.

"That's exactly what I mean. I know that Paul Walsh. He's out to make a name for himself. You ever read the philosophers?"

"I took several philosophy courses in college."

"I don't suppose you read St. Thomas More? He was a lawyer, the Lord Chancellor of England. He wrote a book called *Utopia*. In it he wrote, 'There are no lawyers in heaven,' and though Walsh is a detective, More meant it for him, too. That guy's out to feather his own nest and nobody better get in his way."

"You're making me feel a bit better," I said.

"At my age, you say it like it is. For instance, Monday afternoon, this lady from the *Star-Ledger*, Dru Perry, came to see me. She writes a feature called 'The Story Behind the Story.' Thanks to all the publicity about your house, she's doing a feature piece on the Barton case. I filled her in as best I could. I suspect she's something of a bleeding heart for Liza, but I told her she was wasting her sympathy. Liza knew what she was doing when she kept firing that pistol at Ted Cartwright. He'd been romancing her mother before, during, and after the time she was married to Will Barton."

The biblical phrase, "I will vomit you from my mouth," ran through my mind, and I felt a powerful urge to reach over Benjamin Fletcher's desk, grab the check I had just written out, and tear it up. But I knew I needed him. Instead, I said, "Mr. Fletcher, I am the wife of an attorney. I do know something about attorney-client privilege, and if I'm going to hire you, let's make something clear. I want no part of a lawyer who will spread gossip about his client's family, even if it *is* nearly a quarter of a century later."

"The truth isn't gossip, Celia," he said, "but I hear you. Now if Jeff MacKingsley or Paulie Walsh or any one else in that crowd tries to question you, send them to me. I'll take good care of you. And listen, don't think I was being too hard on Little Lizzie. She never meant to kill her Momma, and that skunk Ted Cartwright deserved what she gave him."

55

Lena Santini, the divorced wife of the late Charley Hatch, agreed to speak to Detective Angelo Ortiz at eleven o'clock in Charley's home in Mendham. A small, thin woman of about forty-five, with flaming red hair that had not been granted to her naturally, she seemed genuinely sorry about the death of her former husband. "I can't believe anyone would shoot him. Doesn't make sense. Why would they? He never hurt anybody."

"I'm sad for Charley, not for myself," she explained. "I can't pretend that there was ever much between us. We got married ten years ago. I'd been married before, but it hadn't worked. That guy was a drinker. It could have been good between Charley and me. I'm a waitress, and I make pretty decent money, and I like my job."

They were sitting in the living room. Lena took a puff of her cigarette. "Look at this place," she said with a dismissive wave of her hand. "It's so messy it makes my skin crawl. That's the way it was when I was living with Charley. I used to say that it doesn't take a nanosecond to put your underwear and socks in the hamper, but no, he always dropped them on the floor. Guess who picked them up? I'd say, 'Charley, all you have to do when you have a snack is to rinse off the plate and glass and knife or whatever and put it in the dishwasher.' It never happened. Charley left stuff on the table or on the rug near where he'd been sitting. And he'd complain. Let me tell you, he was a prize winner in the complaint department. I bet if he won ten million bucks in the lottery, he'd have been mad because the week before it had been worth ten times that. I finally couldn't take it any more, and we split a year ago."

Lena's face softened. "But you know, he was really talented with his hands. Those figures he carved were beautiful. I used to tell him that he should start a little business selling them, but of course he wouldn't listen. He only felt like carving them once in a while. Oh well, God rest him. I hope he likes heaven." A brief smile appeared and then disappeared on her lips. "Wouldn't it be a joke if St. Peter makes Charley head landscaper up there?"

Ortiz, perched on the edge of Charley's lounge chair, had been listening sympathetically. Now he decided it was time to move into the questioning. "Did you see much of Charley in this year since you've been divorced?"

"Not much. We sold the house we had, and split the money we'd saved. I got the furniture and he got the car. It was even steven. Every once in a while he'd give me a call and we'd have coffee for old times' sake. He dated a little, I think."

"Do you know if he was close to his half sister, Robin Carpenter?"

"That one!" Lena raised her eyes to the ceiling. "That was another thing. The people who adopted Charley were real nice folks. Very good to him. The father died about eight years ago. When the mother was dying, she gave Charley pictures of him as a baby, and told him his real name. I'm telling you, no one could have been more excited. I guess he hoped his birth family would turn out to be worth a lot of money. Boy, was he disappointed. His birth mother was dead and her husband wanted no part of him. But he met his half sister Robin, and ever since then she's been playing him like a fiddle."

Ortiz tensed and straightened up, but then, not wanting to alert

Santini to be careful of what she told him, relaxed his posture again. "Then they saw each other regularly?"

"Did they ever! 'Charley, can you drive me into the city? Charley, would you mind taking my car to be serviced?' "

"Did she pay him?"

"No, but she made him feel important. You've met her, I guess. She's the kind that guys look at, liking what they see." Lena looked over at Ortiz. "You're a good-looking guy. Has she shined up to you yet?"

"No," the detective answered honestly.

"Give her time. Anyhow, she used to take Charley out for dinner in New York sometimes. That made him feel special. She didn't want anyone around here to know he was her half brother, and she didn't want to be seen with him around here either, because she's got a rich boyfriend. Oh, and get this. Charley told her that he sometimes stayed in the houses of people who were away. I mean, he had the keys to those houses because he was a caretaker for them and knew the security codes so he could go in and out of them. So Robin had the nerve to ask him to let her use those houses when she was with her boyfriend. Can you *imagine* that?"

"Ms. Santini, have you heard about the vandalism on Old Mill Lane in Mendham last week?"

"At Little Lizzie's Place? Sure, everybody knows about it."

"We have reason to believe that Charley was the one who committed that act of vandalism."

"You've got to be kidding," Santini said, astonished. "Charley would never do that. It doesn't make sense."

"Would he do it if he was paid to do it?"

"Who would ask him to do a crazy thing like that?" Lena Santini crushed the butt of the cigarette she was holding into the ashtray and slid a new cigarette out of the open pack in front of her on the table.

"Come to think of it, the only person I know who could get Charley to do a stupid trick like that is Robin."

"Robin Carpenter told us that she has not been in touch with Charley for three months."

"Then why did she have dinner with him in New York recently at Patsy's Restaurant on West 56th Street?"

"Do you happen to remember the exact date?"

"It was Saturday of Labor Day weekend. I remember because it was Charley's birthday, and I called and offered to buy him dinner. He told me Robin was taking him out to Patsy's."

Lena's eyes suddenly glistened. "If that's all you want to ask me, I have to go. Charley left this place to me, you know. Not that it's worth much, what with the mortgage so high. This morning I asked you to meet me here because I wanted to get a couple of Charley's carvings to put in the casket with him, but they're all gone."

"We have them," Ortiz told her. "Unfortunately, since these items are evidence, we have to keep them."

56

D etective Mort Shelley walked into the Grove Real Estate Agency with the late Georgette Grove's scrapbook under his arm. He and everyone else on the investigative team, including Jeff, had gone through every page of the book, and found not one newspaper clipping in it that might be tied to Georgette having suddenly recognized someone. The scrapbook covered many years, and most of the pictures were of Georgette at civic affairs, or receiving an honor, or smiling with minor celebrities to whom she had sold property in the area.

"She may have had the scrapbook on her desk, but whoever she recognized isn't in it," was Jeff's conclusion.

But it's serving its purpose, Shelley thought. Returning it gives me a good reason to have another chat with Robin and Henry. Robin was at her desk, and looked up immediately on hearing the door open. Her professional welcoming smile vanished, however, when she saw who her visitor was.

"Just returning the scrapbook, like I promised," Mort said mildly. "Thanks for lending it to me."

"I hope it was useful," Robin said. She had papers on her desk and dropped her eyes to them, her body language making it clear that she was too busy to be interrupted.

With the air of a man who has nothing to do and plenty of time to do it in, Mort sat down on the sectional sofa that faced Robin's desk.

Clearly annoyed, she looked up at him. "If you have a question, I'll be glad to answer it."

Mort hoisted his ample body to his feet. "That couch is comfortable, but too deep for my taste. Can hardly get out of it. Maybe I'd better pull up a chair by you."

"Mr, uhmm . . . I'm sorry. I know we've been introduced, but I've forgotten your name."

"Shelley. Like the poet. Mort Shelley."

"Mr. Shelley, I went to the prosecutor's office yesterday to tell Mr. MacKingsley everything I knew that might be helpful to your investigation. I can't add a single word to what I said earlier, and while this agency is still functioning I have a job to do."

"And so do I, Ms. Carpenter, and so do I. It's half-past twelve. Have you had lunch yet?"

"No. I'll wait till Henry returns. He's out with a client."

"Henry's a busy man, isn't he?"

"Yes, I guess he is."

"Now suppose he didn't come back till, let's say, four o'clock? Would you have something sent in? I mean, you wouldn't wait to have lunch till four o'clock would you?"

"No. I'd put the sign with the clock on the door and run across the street and grab something."

"Isn't that what you did yesterday, Ms. Carpenter?"

"I already told you that I brought my lunch in yesterday because Henry was going to take a client out."

"Yes, but you *didn't* tell us that you put that little clock on the door sometime before two o'clock did you? According to that sweet, elderly lady in the curtain shop down the street, she happened to notice that sign on the door when she passed here at 2:05."

"What are you talking about? Oh, I see what you're getting at. With all that's been going on, I had a dreadful headache. I ran to the drugstore to get some aspirin. I was in and out in a few minutes."

"Uh-huh. On another subject, my partner, Detective Ortiz, was talking to your ex-half-sister-in-law, if that's the proper way to put it, a little while ago."

"Lena?"

"That's right, Lena. Now you told us you hadn't talked to Charley in three months or so. Lena says you had dinner with him at Patsy's in New York less than two weeks ago. Who's right?"

"I am. About three months ago he just happened to phone when my car wouldn't start. He offered to get it started, then run it over to the dealer. I was meeting a friend in New York at Patsy's, and he drove me in. That night he said he wanted me to take him there for his birthday, and I jokingly said, 'It's a date.' Then, when he left a message to remind me about it, I left a return message on his phone saying it wouldn't work out. The poor guy thought I was serious about going."

"Are you involved with any one particular man at this time?"

"No, I am not. I presume you're inferring that the 'one particular man' is Ted Cartwright. As I told all of you yesterday, he is just a friend. We dated a few times. Period."

"One last question, Ms. Carpenter. Your half brother's former wife tells us that you asked Charley to allow you and your rich boyfriend to stay overnight in some of the houses he was looking after for people who were away. Is that true?"

Robin Carpenter stood up. "That does it, Mr. Shelley. Tell Mr. MacKingsley that if he or any of his lackeys want to ask me any more questions, they can contact my lawyer. You'll have his name to-morrow."

57

On Wednesday morning, Dru Perry phoned into the newspaper office and spoke to Ken Sharkey. "I'm onto something big," she told him. "Get someone else to cover the courthouse."

"Sure. Want to talk about it?"

"Not on the phone."

"Okay. Keep me posted."

Dru had a friend, Kit Logan, whose son Bob was a New Jersey State Trooper, working in the computer lab. She called Kit, exchanged pleasantries, promised to get together very soon, then asked for Bob's home phone. "I'm going to ask him to do me a favor, Kit, and I don't want to call him at headquarters."

Bob lived in Morristown. She caught him on his way to work. "Sure, I can use the computer to age a picture for you, Dru," he promised. "If you drop it in my mailbox today, I'll have it for you tomorrow night. It goes without saying, get the clearest picture you can find."

Dru mulled over that problem as she spread marmalade on whole wheat toast and sipped coffee. The photographs the newspapers had reprinted after the vandalism had been mostly of Liza with her mother and father. There'd been one of the three of them on the beach at Spring Lake, another at the Peapack Riding Club when Audrey won a trophy, and another at some kind of party at the golf club. None of them, however, had been particularly clear. Audrey was married to Ted a little over a year, Dru thought. I'll bet the local paper, the *Daily Record*, covered the wedding.

She considered how to go about getting access to other photos, then got up and popped another piece of bread in the toaster. "Why not?" she asked herself out loud. There's somebody else who might just have some pictures of Liza. When I talked to Marcella Williams last week, she said something about how sour Liza looked at her mother's wedding to Ted Cartwright. I'll make her house my first stop today. Maybe I'd better call to be sure I don't miss her. She'll wait for me if she knows I'm coming. Otherwise she might get on her broom and fly away, off to dig up dirt on someone else.

Dru caught her reflection in the glass door of the dish cabinet. Seeing it, she stuck out her tongue and began to pant. With these bangs I really do look like a sheep dog, she thought. Well, I haven't got time to waste at the salon, so I'll cut them myself. Who cares if they're uneven? One thing about hair is that it grows back. *Some* people's hair grows back, she added with a silent chuckle as she thought of her editor, Ken Sharkey.

The toast sprang up. As usual, it was brown on only one side. She spun it around and dropped it back in. Something else, I've got to get a new toaster, she decided as she pushed down the lever. This one is getting to be a pain in the neck.

The second slice of toast in front of her, Dru continued to mentally lay out her day. I've got to find out who Zach is. Maybe I'll stop at the police station and see if Clyde Earley is around. Not that I'm going to tell him who I think Celia Nolan really is, but maybe I can start talking about her and see what happens. Clyde loves the sound of his own voice. It would be interesting to see if he has even a clue that Celia Nolan is possibly or even probably Liza Barton.

Possibly or probably—those were the key words. The Kelloggs *might* be distant cousins, and *might* have an adopted daughter Celia's age, but that still wasn't conclusive proof that Celia was Liza. There was something else, Dru thought. Clyde Earley responded to Ted Cartwright's 911 call the night of the shooting. He might know if there was a guy named Zach in the picture. Whoever he is, Zach has to have been significant at that time, otherwise why would Liza have been so traumatized when she spoke his name?

Her mind made up, Dru quickly did the little tidying up that her coffee and toast breakfast required, went upstairs, tossed the quilt over her bed in some attempt to restore it to order, went into the bathroom and showered. Wrapped in a terrycloth robe that almost concealed her generous proportions, she opened the window, tested the air, and decided that a running suit was just about perfect for the temperature. The running suit that's never been run in, she thought. Well, nobody's perfect, she told herself by way of consolation.

At nine o'clock she phoned Marcella Williams. Bet anything by now she's been on the treadmill for an hour, Dru thought, as the phone rang for the third time. Maybe she's in the shower.

Marcella picked up the receiver just as the answering machine clicked on. "Hold on," she said above the recorded message.

She sounds irritated, Dru thought. Maybe I *did* catch her in the shower.

The recorded message stopped. "Mrs. Williams, this is Dru Perry of the *Star-Ledger*. I do hope I'm not calling too early."

"Oh, not at all, Ms. Perry. I've been on the treadmill for an hour, and was stepping out of the shower when the phone rang."

The thought of Marcella Williams with a towel wrapped around her and dripping on her carpet made Dru feel good about the timing of her call. "I write a feature called 'The Story Behind the Story' for the Sunday edition of the *Star-Ledger*," she explained.

"I know that feature. I always look forward to reading it," Marcella interrupted.

"I'm preparing one on Liza Barton, and I know you knew the family intimately. I wonder if I could come and interview you about the Bartons and, of course, Liza particularly."

"I'd be delighted to be interviewed by a fine writer like you."

"Do you happen to have any pictures of the Bartons?"

"Yes, of course, I do. We were great friends, you know. And when Audrey married Ted, the reception was in the garden of her home. I took a slew of pictures of all of them, but I have to warn you, there isn't a single one where you'll see Liza smiling."

This is my lucky day, Dru thought. "Would eleven o'clock be convenient for you?"

"Perfect. I do have a lunch date at 12:30."

"An hour will be more than enough. And Mrs. Williams . . ."

"Oh, please, call me Marcella, Dru."

"How nice. Marcella, will you just think and try to remember if Audrey or Will Barton or Ted Cartwright had a friend named Zach."

"Oh, I know who Zach is. He's the riding instructor Will Barton had at Washington Valley stables. That last day, the day he died, Will rode out ahead of him and got on the wrong trail. That's why he had that fatal accident. Dru, I'm standing here dripping. I'll see you at eleven."

Dru heard the click of the phone, but stood for a long minute before the mechanical voice reminded her to either make another call or hang up. The fatal accident, she thought. Zach was Will Barton's riding teacher. Was it Zach's fault that Will Barton died? Had he been careless to let Barton ride off without him?

A final possibility occurred to Dru as she started down the stairs. Suppose Barton's death was *not* an accident and, if it wasn't, when did Liza learn the truth about it?

58

At one o'clock, Ted Cartwright rounded the corner of the Washington Valley Club House and headed to the stable. "Is Zach around?" he asked Manny Pagan, one of the grooms.

Manny was brushing a skittish mare that had been given a too-strenuous workout by its insensitive owner. "Easy, easy, girl," he was muttering soothingly.

"Are you deaf? I asked if Zach is around?" Cartwright shouted.

An annoyed Manny was about to snap, "Find him yourself," but when he looked up, he realized that Cartwright, whom he knew by sight, was trembling with fury. Instead, he said, "I'm pretty sure he's eating his lunch at the picnic table over there," and pointed to a grove of trees about a hundred yards away.

Ted Cartwright covered the ground with rapid strides in seconds. Zach was eating the second half of a baloney sandwich when he arrived. Ted sat down opposite him. "Who the hell do you think you are?" he asked, his voice now a menacing whisper.

Zach took another bite of the sandwich and a swig of soda before he replied. "Now that's no way for a friend to talk to a friend," he said mildly.

"What makes you think you can go over to my town houses and tell my sales rep that I am giving you the model unit?"

"Did she tell you that I called, and that I'm planning to move in over the weekend?" Zach asked. "I tell you, Ted, that place where I'm living has turned out to be sheer hell. The landlady's kids are having parties every night, playing the drums till I think my ears are gonna bust, and here you have that nice place in the middle of all those other nice places, and I just know you want me to have it."

"I'll call the police if you try to set one *foot* inside it."

"Now why do I think that won't happen?" Zach asked, as he looked pensively past Cartwright.

"Zach, you've been bleeding me for over twenty years now. You've got to stop or you won't be around to bleed me any more."

"Ted, that constitutes a threat, and I'm sure you don't mean it. Maybe *I* should be going to the police. The way I look at it, I've been keeping you out of prison for all these years. Of course, if I'd spoken up back then, you'd probably have served your time by now and would be starting all over—without your road and bridge construction company and your town-house developments and your business complexes and your string of gyms. You could be giving speeches to school kids as part of the Scared Straight program."

"There is also a penalty for blackmail." Cartwright spat out the words.

"Ted, that town house is a drop in the bucket to you, but it would be a comfort to me. These old bones are developing aches and pains. Much as I love taking care of my horses, they're a lot of work. And then there's the matter of my conscience. Suppose I were to wander down to the Mendham police station and say that I knew about an accident that wasn't an accident at all, and tell them that I have proof, but before I say another word, I'll have to be guaranteed immunity from prosecution. I think I mentioned this before."

Ted Cartwright stood up. The veins in his temples were bulging. His hands were gripping the edge of the picnic table as if that was the only way he could keep them from flailing at the man he was facing. "Be careful, Zach. Be very careful." His words were clipped, and sharp as a dagger.

"I am being careful," Zach assured him cheerfully. "That's why, if anything happens to me, the proof of what I'm saying will be found immediately. Well, gotta get back. I have a nice lady coming in for a riding lesson. She lives in your old house—you know, the one where you were shot? She's kind of intriguing. Claims she had a ride on a pony only once in a while, but she's fibbing. She's a pretty good horsewoman. And what's more, for some reason, she's real interested in that accident you and I know about."

"Have you been talking to her about it?"

"Oh, sure. Everything but the good stuff. Think it over, Ted. Maybe you'll even want your sales rep, Amy, to have the refrigerator stocked for me when I move in on Saturday. That would be a nice welcoming gesture, don't you think?"

59

At two o'clock on Wednesday afternoon, Paul Walsh, Angelo Ortiz, and Mort Shelley gathered in Jeff MacKingsley's office to review their findings in what the media was now calling the "Little Lizzie Homicides." They had all brought paper bags with sandwiches and coffee or a soft drink.

At Jeff's request, Ortiz started with his report. He gave them a quick rundown of his interview with Lena Santini, Charley Hatch's ex-wife, and what she had told him about Robin Carpenter's relationship with Charley.

"You mean Carpenter's story yesterday was a bold-faced lie?" Jeff asked. "How stupid does she think we are?"

"I saw Carpenter this morning," Mort Shelley said. "She sticks by her statement that she hasn't spoken to Charley in three months. She explained away the so-called birthday date by saying it was his idea and she left a message for him that it wouldn't happen. She absolutely denies being in Patsy's that night."

"Let's get pictures of Robin Carpenter and Charley Hatch and show them to the maitre d', the bartender, and all the waiters at Patsy's," Jeff said. "I think we have enough to get a judge to let us access her phone records. We'll subpoena her credit card charges, and her E-ZPass statement. We've already got the judge's order to get Charley

Hatch's phone records. We should be receiving them later today. We'd better take a look at his credit cards and E-ZPass as well. Either Carpenter or the ex-wife is lying. Let's find out which it is."

"I don't see Lena Santini as a liar," Ortiz objected. "She was quoting what Charley told her about Robin Carpenter. By the way, she even asked if she could put a couple of those carved figures of his in the coffin. I told her we couldn't release them."

"Too bad she didn't ask for that skull and crossbones Charley carved in the Nolans' front door," Mort Shelley observed dryly. "That was good craftsmanship. I was surprised to see that it was still there yesterday."

"Yes, we had plenty of time to stare at those doors when Celia Nolan wouldn't let us in," Paul Walsh said mildly. "I understand that you're planning to see her today, Jeff."

"I'm not seeing her today," Jeff said shortly. "When I called her she referred me to her lawyer, Benjamin Fletcher."

"Benjamin Fletcher!" Mort Shelley exclaimed. "He was Little Lizzie's lawyer! Why on earth would Celia Nolan go to him?"

"He got her off once before, didn't he?" Walsh asked quietly.

"Got who off?"

"Liza Barton, who else?" Walsh asked.

Jeff, Mort, and Angelo stared at him. Enjoying the astonishment on their faces, Paul Walsh smiled. "I lay odds with you that the deranged ten-year-old who shot her mother and stepfather has now resurfaced as Celia Nolan, a woman who flipped when she found herself back in home sweet home."

"You're absolutely crazy," Jeff snapped. "And you're the reason she ran to get a lawyer. She'd have cooperated with us if you hadn't been in her face about the time it took her to drive home from Holland Road."

"I have taken the time to look up Celia Nolan's background. She is adopted. She is thirty-four years old, exactly Liza Barton's present age. We all felt the impact of seeing her in those riding clothes yesterday, and I'll tell you why. I'll admit she's taller than Audrey Barton. And her hair is darker than Audrey Barton's, but I suggest that is because of her visits to the salon—I happened to notice that her roots are growing in blond. So I'm making a flat statement: Audrey Barton was Celia Nolan's mother."

Jeff sat silently for a minute, not wanting to believe what he was beginning to believe—that perhaps Paul Walsh was on to something.

"After I saw Celia Nolan in riding clothes, I made a few inquiries. She's taking lessons at the Washington Valley Riding Club. Her teacher is Zach Willet, who happens to be the teacher who was giving Will Barton riding lessons at the time of his death, the result of a fall with his horse," Walsh continued, barely able to conceal his satisfaction at the impact he was making on his colleagues.

"If Celia Nolan *is* Liza Barton, do you think she holds Zach Willet responsible for her father's death?" Mort asked quietly.

"Let me put it this way: if I were Zach Willet, I wouldn't want to be alone with that lady for long," Walsh answered.

"Your theory, Paul—and it is still a theory—completely overlooks the fact that the house was vandalized by Charley Hatch," Jeff told him. "Are you suggesting that Celia Nolan knew Charley Hatch?"

"No, I am not, and I accept the fact that she never met Georgette before a week ago Tuesday when she moved into the house. I *do* say that she became unbalanced when she saw the writing on the lawn and the doll with the gun and the skull and crossbones and the splattered paint. She wanted revenge on the people who put her in that position. She was the one who found Georgette's body. If she is Liza Barton, there's an explanation for why she knew her way home. Her grandmother lived only a few streets away from Holland Road. She admits that she was driving past the house where Hatch was working in the exact time frame when he was killed. Even those pictures we found are a way of begging us to recognize her."

"That still doesn't fly so far as blaming Celia Nolan for killing Hatch. How would she have found out that he was the one who vandalized the house?" Ortiz asked Walsh.

"The garbageman was talking about Clyde Earley taking Hatch's sneakers and jeans and carvings out of the trash bag," Walsh responded.

Jeff began to feel solid ground for his instinctive reaction to Walsh's theory. "Are you suggesting that Celia Nolan, even if she is Liza Barton, happened to hear the gossip of a garbageman, figured out where Charley Hatch, whom she'd never met, was working, somehow got him to be standing at the break of the hedge in the road, shot him and then went off to have a riding lesson?"

"She put herself on that road at the right time," Walsh insisted stubbornly.

"Yes, she did. And if you hadn't pushed her against the wall she might be talking to me right now and telling me something that would be helpful to us about seeing another car on the road or a person on foot. Paul, you want to pin everything on Celia Nolan, and I agree that it will make a great story: 'Little Lizzie Strikes Again.' I'm telling you that someone else hired Charley Hatch. I don't for a minute believe Earley's story. It's too pat, too convenient. I bet Clyde went through that garbage when it was on Hatch's property. I wouldn't be surprised if he took it and Hatch knew it was gone. Then Earley could come back and put it in the trash barrel again and wait to have a convenient witness see him open it after it's been abandoned. If Hatch panicked, whoever hired him may have panicked as well. And my guess is that Georgette Grove learned who ordered the vandalism and paid for it with her life."

"Jeff, you'd have made a great defense lawyer for Celia Nolan. She is very attractive, isn't she? I've noticed the way you look at her."

When he saw the prosecutor's icy stare, Walsh realized he had gone too far. "Sorry," he mumbled. "But I stand by my theory."

"When this case is over, I am sure you'll be happier reassigned to another division in the office," Jeff said. "You're a smart man, Paul, and you could be a good detective, except for one thing—you get a theory, and you're like a dog with a bone. You don't keep an open mind and never have, and frankly, I'm sick and tired of it *and* of you. Here is what we're going to do now.

"We should be getting Charley Hatch's phone records later today. Mort, you prepare an affidavit for the judge to get the phone records of not only Robin Carpenter, but also of Henry Paley and Ted Cartwright—both their personal and business phones. I want to know about all incoming and outgoing calls any of them made or received over the past two months. I think we have sufficient grounds to ask for them. I also want Carpenter's and Hatch's credit card bills and E-ZPass statements. And I am going to petition the Family Court to allow us to unseal the adoption records of Liza Barton."

Jeff looked at Paul Walsh. "I will lay you odds that even if Celia Nolan *is* Liza Barton, she is a victim of what is going on. I have always believed that as a child, Liza was the victim of Ted Cartwright's misdeeds, and I believe that now, for whatever reason, someone is trying to trap Celia Nolan into being accused of commiting these murders."

60

When I left Benjamin Fletcher's office, I drove around aimlessly for a while trying to decide if I should have told him I was Liza Barton, or if I even should have gone to see him at all. His horrible statement that my mother had been having an affair with Ted while she was married to my father infuriated me, even while I recognized the bitter truth that she had certainly been in love with Ted when she married him.

I told myself that the plus of hiring Fletcher was that it was obviously he despised Paul Walsh, and would be a tiger in keeping him from harassing me. Hiring Fletcher also would ease my explanation to Alex of my refusal to cooperate with the prosecutor's office. I reasonably could say that everything that has happened seems to be connected to the Liza Barton case, and therefore I went straight to Liza Barton's lawyer for help. It seemed like a natural thing to do.

I knew that eventually I would have to tell Alex the truth about myself—and risk losing him—but I didn't want to do it yet. If I could only remember exactly what my mother shouted at Ted that night, I felt sure I would have the key to why he threw her at me, and perhaps even the answer to whether or not I shot him deliberately.

In all the pictures I drew for Dr. Moran when I was a child, the gun is in midair. No hand is touching it. I know the impact of my mother's body caused it to go off in my hand the first time. I only wish I could somehow prove that when I shot Ted I was in a catatonic state.

Zach was the key to answering all these questions. All these years, I have never considered that my father's death was anything but an accident. But now, as I try to piece together my mother's final words, I can't find the missing ones:

"You told me when you were drunk . . . Zach saw you . . ."

What did Ted tell my mother? And what did Zach see?

It was only ten o'clock. I called the office of the *Daily Record* and was told that all back issues of the newspaper were on microfilm in the county library on Randolph Street. At ten thirty I was in the reference room of the library, requesting the microfilm of the newspapers that included May 9th, the day my father died, twenty-seven years ago.

Of course, the minute I started to read the May 9th edition, I realized that any account of my father's death would be printed the next day. I glanced through the columns anyhow, and noticed that an antique-gun marksmanship contest was scheduled that day at Jockey Hollow at noon. Twenty antique-gun collectors were competing, including the prominent Morris County collector, Ted Cartwright.

I looked at the picture of Ted. He was in his late thirties then, his hair still dark, a swaggering, devil-may-care look about him. He was staring at the camera, holding in his hand the gun he planned to use in the contest.

I hurriedly moved the microfilm to the next day. On the front page I found the story about my father: "Will Barton, Award-winning Architect, Dies in Riding Accident."

The picture of my father was exactly as I remember him—the thoughtful eyes that always held a hint of a smile, the aristocratic nose and mouth, the full head of dark blond hair. If he had lived, he would be in his sixties now. I found myself playing the dangerous game of wondering what my life would have been like if he were still alive, if that horrible night had never happened.

The newspaper account of his accident was the same as the one Zach Willet had told me. Other people heard my father tell Zach that he'd start walking his horse on the trail instead of waiting for Zach to get the stone out of his own horse's hoof. No one had seen my father go on the trail, which was clearly marked, DANGER. DO NOT ENTER. The consensus of opinion was that something may have frightened the horse, and that "Barton, an inexperienced rider, was unable to control him."

Then I read the sentence that seemed to explode before my eyes: "A groom, Herbert West, who was exercising a horse on a nearby trail, reported hearing a loud noise that sounded like a gunshot at the time that Mr. Barton would have been near the fork in the road that led to the treacherous slope."

"A loud noise that sounded like a gunshot."

I moved the microfilm until I came to the sports pages of that day's edition. Ted Cartwright was holding a trophy in one hand and an old Colt .22 target auto pistol in the other. He had won the marksmanship contest, and the article said he was going to celebrate by having lunch at the Peapack Club with friends, and then was going for a long horseback ride. "I've been so busy practicing my marksmanship that I haven't had a decent ride for weeks," he told the reporter.

My father died at three o'clock—plenty of time for Ted to have had lunch and gone out for a ride, traveling along the trail that leads to the Washington Valley trails. Was it possible he came upon my father, the man who had taken my mother from him, perhaps saw him struggling to control the horse he was riding?

It was possible, but it was all conjecture. There was only one way I could learn the truth, and that was from Zach Willet.

I printed out the articles—the one about my father's accident and the one about Ted winning the marksmanship contest. It was time to pick up Jack. I left the library, got in my car, and drove to St. Joe's.

Today I could tell by Jack's woebegone face that the morning hadn't gone well. He didn't want to talk about what had happened, but by the time we got home, and were sitting in the kitchen having lunch, he was starting to open up.

"One of the kids in my class said that I live in a house where a kid shot her mother. Is that right, Mom?" he asked.

My mind leaped ahead to the day when he might find out that *I* was the kid who shot her mother. I took a deep breath and said, "From what I understand, Jack, that little girl lived in this house with her mother and father, and she was very, very happy. Then her father died, and one night someone tried to hurt her mother, and so she tried to save her."

"If someone tried to hurt you, I'd save you," Jack promised.

"I know you would, sweetheart. So if your friend asks about that little girl again, say that she was very brave. She couldn't save her mother, but that was what she was trying so hard to do."

"Mommy, don't cry."

"I don't want to, Jack," I said. "I just feel so sorry for that little girl."

"I'm sorry for her, too," Jack decided.

I told him that if it was okay with him, Sue was going to come over and stay with him, and I'd go for another riding lesson. I saw a shadow of doubt across his face, so I hurried on: "Sue is teaching *you* to ride, and I'm taking lessons so that I can keep up with you."

That explanation helped, but then Jack finished his sandwich, pushed back his chair, came around, and lifted his arms to me. "Can I sit on your lap for a little while?" he asked.

"You bet." I picked him up and hugged him. "Who thinks you're a perfect little boy?" I asked him.

This was a game we played. I saw a hint of a smile. "You do," he said.

"Who loves you to pieces?"

"You do, Mommy."

"You're so smart," I marveled. "I can't believe how smart you are."

Now he was laughing. "I love you, Mommy."

As I held him, I thought of the night the limo hit me, and how, in that scary moment before I lost consciousness, all I could think was, What will happen to Jack if I die? When I woke up in the hospital, it was my first thought as well. Kathleen and Martin were his guardians, but Kathleen was seventy-four, and Martin was a full-time responsibility. Even if she remained healthy for another ten years, Jack would only be fourteen when she reached eighty-four. That was why it had been such a vast relief to see Alex there, to know he was going home to my apartment to be with Jack. In these six months, I have felt so secure knowing that Alex is Jack's guardian. But suppose Alex leaves us when he finds out about me? What will that do to Jack?

My little boy fell asleep in my arms, just a nap for about twenty minutes. I wondered if I gave him the same sense of security my father had given me that day the wave crashed us to shore. I prayed to my father that he would help me to learn the truth about his death. I thought of what Benjamin Fletcher had said about my mother and Ted Cartwright. I thought of my mother falling to her knees at my father's funeral, wailing, "I want my husband. I want my husband!"

You told me when you were drunk. You killed my husband. You told me Zach saw you do it.

That was what my mother had screamed that night! I was as certain of it as I was that my little boy was in my arms. The pieces had finally fallen into place. For a long time I sat there very quietly, absorbing the import of those words. It explained why my mother threw Ted out. It explained why she was afraid of him, and of what he might do to her to save himself.

Why didn't she go to the police? I wondered. Was it because she was afraid of how I might judge her if I learned that another man killed my father because he wanted her?

When Sue arrived, I left for my final riding lesson with Zach Willet.

61

Much as Dru Perry instinctively disliked Marcella Williams, she had to admit that Marcella was a golden source of information. She insisted that Dru have coffee with her, and even had miniature Danish pastries which Dru unsuccessfully tried to resist.

At Dru's hint that Audrey Barton might have been involved with Ted Cartwright during her marriage, Williams was adamant that she didn't believe it. "Audrey loved her husband," she said. "Will Barton was a very special guy. He had real class, and Audrey loved that. Ted's always been an exciting guy. He still is. Would Audrey have left Will for him? No. If she was free, would she marry him? Proof in the pudding—she did. But she never took his name. I think she kept the Barton name to appease Liza."

Marcella had a stack of pictures that she thought might interest Dru. "Will Barton and my ex liked each other," she explained. "That's the one place where I thought Will's judgment was lacking. Then after Will died and Ted started coming around all the time to see Audrey, the ex and I would stop at her house and have a cocktail with them. I think Audrey didn't want Liza to realize that she was becoming involved with Ted, so having us around took a little of the pressure off. I always liked to take pictures, and after Liza went on her shooting spree, I got them all together and gave some of them to the media."

I'll just bet you did, Dru thought. But as she went through the pictures, and studied the close-ups of Will and Audrey Barton, she could barely hide her emotions from Marcella's inquisitive eyes.

I'll still ask Bob to do the computer-aging she thought, but I think I know the result. Celia Nolan *is* Liza Barton. She's a combination of both her parents. She looks like both of them.

"Will you use all the pictures in your feature story?" Marcella asked.

"Depends on how much space they give me. Marcella, did you ever meet this Zach guy, the one who gave Will Barton riding lessons?"

"No. Why would I? Audrey was furious when she heard that Will had been taking lessons from him without her knowledge. Will tried to explain that he didn't want to take them at the Peapack club because he didn't want to look like a fool. He knew he wasn't any good, and probably never would be, but he wanted to try to learn to ride so that he could keep his wife company. My guess is he wasn't thrilled to see Audrey riding so often with Ted Cartwright."

"Do you know if Audrey blamed Zach for the accident?"

"She really couldn't. Everyone at the stable told her that Will insisted on starting out alone, despite Zach's asking him to wait."

Marcella's phone rang just as Dru got up to go. Marcella rushed to answer it, and when she did, it was clear that she had received disappointing news.

"That's the way it goes," she told Dru. "My lunch date was with Ted Cartwright, but he's been with his contractor all morning and now he has to see someone on an urgent matter. Maybe it's just as well. Sounds to me as though Ted is in one of his ugly moods, and I can assure you that is not the time to be around him."

After Dru left Marcella, she drove directly to the reference room in the county library. She submitted her request for the microfilm of the *Daily Record* which included the day after Will Barton's death. The reference librarian smiled. "That day is mighty popular this morning. I released that same segment to someone else an hour ago."

Celia Nolan, Dru thought. She's been talking to Zach Willet, and may suspect something about the accident. "I wonder if that could have been my friend, Celia Nolan," she asked. "We're both working on the same project."

"Why, yes it is," the librarian confirmed. "She did several print-outs from that issue of the paper."

Several, Dru thought, as she turned to the May 10th issue. I wonder why several.

Five minutes later, she was printing out the account of Will Barton's death. Then, to see if she had missed anything, she kept going through the paper until she found the sports section, and, like Celia Nolan, reasoned that Ted Cartwright might very well have been in the vicinity at the time of Will Barton's accident, and could have been carrying a gun.

Desperately troubled by what Celia's state of mind might be, Dru made one more stop, this one at the police station in Mendham. As she had hoped, Sergeant Clyde Earley was on duty, and was delighted to be interviewed by her.

With considerable embellishment, he gave her the step-by-step account of his visit to Charley Hatch, and his growing suspicion that Charley had changed to corduroy pants because, as he put it, "That fellow didn't want me to see him in those jeans with the red paint on them."

After he wound up his story with the discovery of the evidence in the trash bag with the garbageman as witness, Dru nudged him onto another subject. "It all seems to be connected to the Little Lizzie case, doesn't it?" she mused. "I bet that night is still clear in your mind."

"You bet it is, Dru. I can still see that little cool-as-a-cucumber kid sitting in my squad car, thanking me for the blanket I wrapped around her."

"You drove off with her, didn't you?"

"That's it."

"Did she say anything to you in the car?"

"Not a word."

"Where did you take her?"

"Right here. I booked her."

"You *booked* her!"

"What do you think I did? Give her a lollypop? I fingerprinted her and we took her picture."

"Do you still have her fingerprints?"

"Once a juvenile is cleared of any wrongdoing, we're supposed to destroy them."

"Did you destroy Liza's fingerprints, Clyde?"

He winked. "Off the record, no. I kept them in the file, sort of like souvenirs."

Dru thought of the way Celia Nolan had tried to run from the photographers that first day she'd met her. She felt sorry for her, but knew she had to finish her investigation. Two people were dead, and if Celia was indeed Liza Barton, she now knew that her father's death might not have been an accident. She might soon be in danger herself.

And if she is the killer, then she has to be stopped, Dru thought.

"Clyde, there's something you have to do," she said. "Get Liza's fingerprints to Jeff MacKingsley right away. I think Liza has come back to Mendham and may be taking revenge on the people who hurt her."

62

I sensed that there was something different about Zach Willet when I met him at the stable. He seemed somewhat tense, guarded. I knew he was trying to figure me out, but I didn't want him to become wary of me. I had to get him to talk. If he had witnessed my father's "accident," and was willing to testify to the truth of what had happened that day, I was sure that the only way to get him to do it was to make it worth his while.

He helped me tack the horse up, then we walked the horses toward the spot where the trails begin to snake through the woods. "Let's take the trail that leads to the fork where Will Barton had his accident," I said. "I'm curious to see it."

"You sure are interested in that accident," Zach commented.

"I've been reading up on it. It was interesting that a groom insisted he heard a shot. His name was Herbert West. Is he still around here?"

"He's a starter at the Monmouth Park Racetrack now."

"Zach, how far were you behind Will Barton that day? Three minutes? Five minutes?"

Zach and I were traveling side by side. A strong breeze had blown the clouds away, and now it was sunny and cool, a perfect afternoon for a ride. The leaves on the trees were showing the first sign of fall. Tints of yellow and orange and russet were beginning to streak through their summer green shading, and they made a canopy of color under the vivid blue of the sky. The smell of the damp soil under the horses' hooves reminded me of the times when I would ride on my pony with my mother at the Peapack club. Sometimes my father would drive over with us and read the newspaper or a book while we were on the trail.

"I'd say I was about five minutes behind him," Zach answered me. "And, young lady, I think we better have a showdown right here and now. Why all the questions about that accident?"

"Let's discuss it at the fork up ahead," I suggested. Making no further effort to conceal my ease on horseback, I pressed my legs against my horse's sides. He broke into a canter, and Zach followed me. It was six minutes later that we drew rein and halted at the fork.

"You see, Zach," I said. "I've been timing this. We left the stable at ten after two. It's two nineteen now, and part of the time we've been going at a pretty good pace. So you really couldn't have been only four or five minutes behind Will Barton, could you?"

I saw the way his mouth tightened.

"Zach, I'm going to level with you," I began.

Of course, I was only going to level with him up to a point. "My grandmother's sister was Will Barton's mother. She went to her grave sure that there was more to his death than was reported. There was that gunshot that Herbert West swore he heard. That would have scared a horse, wouldn't it? Especially if the horse had a nervous rider who might have been pulling on its mouth too much, or jerking the reins. Don't you agree? I mean, I wonder if when you were looking for Will Barton, you might have seen him galloping down that dangerous trail on a horse that was out of control, and you knew you couldn't stop it. And maybe you saw the man who fired the gun. And maybe that man was Ted Cartwright."

"I don't know what you're talking about," Zach said. But I could see the perspiration on his forehead, and the nervous way he clenched and unclenched his hands.

"Zach, you told me you're a good friend of Ted Cartwright. I can understand how reluctant you'd be to get him in trouble. But Will Barton should not have died. Our family is pretty comfortable. I've been authorized to pay one million dollars to you if you will go to the police and tell them what really happened. The only thing that you did wrong was to lie to the police about what happened. I really doubt that they could even charge you for this kind of offense after so many years. You'd be a hero, a man with a conscience trying to right a wrong."

"Did you say one million dollars?"

"Cash. Wired to your bank."

Zach's smile was merely a narrowing of his thin lips. "Is there a bonus if I tell the cops that I saw Cartwright charge his horse at Barton's, forcing it up that trail, and then that he fired the shot that panicked Barton's horse and made it bolt?"

I felt my heart begin to pound. I tried to keep my voice steady. "There'll be a ten percent bonus, an extra hundred thousand dollars. Is that the way it happened?"

"That's the way it happened all right. Cartwright had his old Colt pistol. That takes a special bullet. The second he fired it, he turned and went back out on the trail that connects to Peapack."

"What did you do?"

"I heard Barton yell when he went over the edge. I knew he didn't have a chance. I guess I was pretty shocked. I just rode around on the different trails as if I was looking for Barton. Eventually, somebody spotted the body down in the ravine. In the meantime, I had gotten a camera and had gone back to the fork in the trail. I wanted to protect myself. It was May 9th. I'd grabbed a copy of the morning newspaper that contained an article on Ted that included a picture of him holding the Colt .22 he was planning to use in a marksmanship contest. I put that picture next to the bullet he'd fired—which was sticking out of a tree trunk—and photographed it. I pried it out carefully with my hoof pick. I found the casing, too, right there on the bridle path. Then I walked onto the steep trail and took a picture of the scene below. You know police cars, ambulances, vets for the horse. Useless of course. The moment the poor guy went over the edge, it was all over."

"Will you show me those pictures? Do you still have the casing and the bullet?"

"I'll show you the photos. But I keep them until I get the money. And yes, I also have the bullet and the casing."

I don't know why I asked Zach Willet this next question, but I did: "Zach, is money the only reason you're telling me this?"

"Mostly," he said, "but there is another reason. I'm kind of sick of Ted Cartwright getting away with murder and then coming here and threatening me."

"When can I get this proof you're talking about?"

"Tonight, when I go home."

"If my babysitter is free, can I drive over to get it from you later, at about nine o'clock?"

"That's okay with me. I'll give you my address. Remember, you only get to see the pictures. The bullet, the casing, and the pictures I'll give to the cops—but only after I get the money and a promise of no prosecution."

We rode back to the stable in silence. I tried to imagine how my father must have felt when Ted charged at him, how he must have felt when the horse he could not control bolted, taking him to certain death. I was sure the feeling must be the same as I felt when Ted threw my mother at me, and then started lunging toward me.

Zach's cell phone rang as we were dismounting at the stable. He answered, then winked at me. "Hello," he said. "What's up? Oh, the town house is worth seven hundred thousand furnished, but you don't want me living in it, so you'll give me the money instead? You're too late. I've had a better offer. Goodbye."

"That felt real good," Zach told me as he scrawled his address on the back of an envelope. "See you around nine. The house number is kind of hard to read from the street, but you can tell it by the kids swarming around and the drums banging."

"I'll find it," I said.

I left knowing that if Ted Cartwright ever went to trial, his lawyer would argue to the jury that Zach's testimony had been bought and paid for. That would be true on one level, but how could they refute the physical evidence that Zach had kept for all these years? And how different was this from what the police do all the time—post rewards for people to come forward with evidence?

I was just offering a lot more than they do.

63

At four o'clock, Sergeant Clyde Earley and Dru Perry were waiting outside Jeff MacKingsley's office. "I don't know if he's going to like the fact that you're with me," Clyde groused.

"Listen, Clyde, I'm a newspaperwoman. This is my story. I'm going to protect my exclusive."

Anna was at her desk. She could see the discomfort on Clyde Earley's face, and she was enjoying it. Whenever he phoned Jeff, she referred to him as "Wyatt Earp" when she announced him. She knew that his predilection for ignoring the law when it suited him to do so drove Jeff crazy. From the memo she had typed, she knew that Jeff seriously questioned Clyde's story on how he discovered Charley Hatch's incriminating possessions, and was concerned about whether or not he would be able to use that evidence if it became necessary at a criminal trial.

"Hope you're bringing good news to the prosecutor," she told Clyde in a friendly tone. "He's in one horrible mood today."

As she watched Clyde's shoulders slump, her intercom went on. "Send them in," Jeff said.

"Let me talk first," Dru murmured to Clyde as he held the door to Jeff's office open for her.

"Dru, Clyde," Jeff acknowledged them. "What can I do for you?"

"Thank you. I will sit down," Dru said. "Jeff, you've made your point. You're busy, but you're going to be glad you're seeing us. What I have to tell you is very important, and I need to have your word that there'll be no leak to the press. I *am* the press in this story, and I'm bringing it to you because I think I have an obligation to do that. I'm worried that another life may be in danger."

Jeff leaned forward, his arms crossed on his desk. "Go on."

"I think Celia Nolan is Liza Barton, and thanks to Clyde, you may be able to prove it."

Seeing the grave look on Jeff's face, Dru realized two things right away: Jeff MacKingsley had been aware of the possibility, and he would not be happy to have it verified. She took out the pictures of Liza that she had taken from Marcella Williams. "I was going to have a couple of these computer-aged," she said. "But I don't think it's necessary. Jeff, look at them, and then think of Celia Nolan. She's a combination of her mother and father."

Jeff took the pictures and laid them out on his desk. "Where were you going to get them computer-aged?" he asked.

"A friend."

"A friend in the state police, I'll bet. I can do it faster."

"I want them or a copy of them back. And I want a copy of the computer-aged version," Dru insisted.

"Dru, you know how unusual it is to make a promise like that to a reporter? But I know you're coming to me because you're afraid someone else may be killed. Because of that, I owe this to you." He turned to Clyde. "Why are you here?"

"Well, you see—" Clyde began.

"Jeff," Dru interrupted. "Clyde is here because Celia Nolan already may have killed two people, and she may be gunning for the man who was at least partially responsible for her father's accident. Take a look at what I got from the library today."

As Jeff skimmed the articles, Dru said, "I went over to talk to Clyde. He was the one who booked Liza the night she killed her mother and shot Ted."

"I kept her fingerprints," Clyde Earley said bluntly. "I have them with me now."

"You kept her fingerprints," Jeff repeated. "I believe we have a law that says when a juvenile is acquitted of a crime, the record is expunged, including fingerprints."

"It was just as a kind of a personal souvenir," Clyde said defensively, "but it does mean you can find out real fast if Celia Nolan is Liza Barton."

"Jeff," Dru began, "if I'm right, and Celia is Liza, she may be out for revenge. I interviewed the lawyer who defended her twenty-four years ago, and he told me he wouldn't be surprised if someday she came back and blew Ted Cartwright's head off. And a court clerk who's been around forever told me that she had heard that when Liza was in the juvenile detention center, still in a state of shock, she would say the name 'Zach,' and then go into spasms of grief. Maybe these articles are showing us why that happened. I phoned the Washington Valley stables this afternoon and asked to speak to Zach. They told me he was giving a riding lesson to Celia Nolan."

"All right. Thank you, both," Jeff said. "Clyde, you know what I think of your habit of ignoring the law to suit your purposes, but I'm glad you had the guts to give me these prints. Dru, it's your story. You have my word."

When they were gone, Jeff sat for long minutes at his desk, studying the pictures of Liza Barton. She's Celia, he thought. We can make sure by checking her fingerprints against the ones on the picture that was in the barn. I know that in court I can never use the old fingerprints that Clyde kept, but at least I'll know who I'm dealing with. And hopefully this will be resolved before we find another body.

The picture that was taped in the barn.

Deep in thought, Jeff was now gazing blankly at the photos that were on his desk. Was this what he had been missing?

In Criminology 101 they tell us that the motive for most homicides is either love or money, he thought.

He turned on the intercom. "Is Mort Shelley around?"

"Yes, I can see he's at his desk. Clyde looked relieved when he went out," Anna said. "I guess you didn't hang him by the thumbs."

"Careful, I may hang *you* by the thumbs," Jeff said. "Send Mort in, please."

"You said 'please.' You must be in a better mood."

"Possibly I am."

When Mort Shelley came in, Jeff said, "Drop whatever you're doing. There's someone else I want checked out from top to bottom." He showed Mort the name he had written on his notepad.

Shelley's eyes widened. "You think?"

"I don't know what I think yet, but put as many of our people on it as you need. I want to know everything, including when this guy cut his first tooth and which one it was."

As Mort Shelley got up, Jeff handed him the copies of the newspaper stories Dru had given him. "Give these to Anna, please." He turned on the intercom. "Anna, there was a death at the Washington Valley Riding Club twenty-seven years ago. There must have been an investigation by either the Mendham police or us. I want the complete file on the incident if it still exists. You'll get the details from the papers Mort is giving you. Also call that club and see if you can get Zach Willet on the phone."

64

When I got home from the stable, the barn was empty, and Jack and Sue were gone. She was evidently taking him for a walk around the neighborhood on Star, and that was fine with me. I called my accountant and checked with him to be sure that I had at least one million one hundred thousand dollars at the ready in my cash account fund at the brokerage house.

Larry has been dead two years, but it still seems so odd to me to think in terms of such large amounts. Larry's investment counselor, Karl Winston, continues to advise me, and pretty much I go along with his suggestions about finances. He's conservative and so am I. But I could hear the question in his voice when I told him to be prepared to wire that sum of money to someone else's account.

"We can't take it as a charity deduction," I told him, "or charge it to expenses, but, believe me, it's money that must be spent."

"It's your money, Celia," he said. "You certainly can afford it. But I must warn you, wealthy as you are, a million one hundred thousand dollars is a very substantial sum."

"I would pay ten times that to accomplish what I am hoping to with that money, Karl," I said.

And it was true. If Zach Willet had the proof he claimed to have, evidence that Ted Cartwright was directly responsible for my father's death, and if Ted went on trial, I would happily take the witness stand and testify to those final words my mother screamed at Ted. And for the first time the world would hear *my* version of what happened that night. I would swear under oath that Ted meant to kill my mother by throwing her at me, and *would* have killed me that same evening if he'd had the chance. I would say that, because I know it is true. Ted loved my mother, but he loved himself more. He couldn't take the chance that someday she might decide to go to the police and tell them about his drunken revelation.

Alex phoned at dinner time. He was staying at the Ritz-Carlton in Chicago, his favorite hotel there. "Ceil, I miss you and Jack so much. I'm definitely going to be stuck here till Friday afternoon but I was thinking, do you want to go into New York this weekend? We could see a couple of plays? Maybe your old babysitter would mind Jack on Saturday night, and then Sunday we could go to a matinee that he'd enjoy? How about it?"

It sounded wonderful to me and I told him that. "I'll make a reservation at the Carlyle," I told him. Then I took a deep breath. "Alex, you've said you feel there's something wrong between us, and there is. I have something to tell you that may change the way you feel about me, and if it does I will respect your decision."

"Ceil, for God's sake. Nothing would ever change the way I feel about you."

"We'll see, but I have to take the chance. I love you."

When I replaced the receiver, my hand was trembling. I knew, though, I had made the right decision. I would tell Benjamin Fletcher the truth, too. I wonder if he would still be willing to represent me. If he did not, then I would find someone else.

I didn't know who killed Georgette or the landscaper, but the fact that I was Liza Barton was certainly not sufficient evidence to incriminate me in their deaths. It is all the furtive evasions that have made me look suspicious. Zach Willet is the instrument of my liberation.

Now I can tell Alex the truth about myself, speaking in the voice of someone who has been deeply wronged. I will ask him to forgive me for not trusting him with the truth but I will also ask of him the protection of a husband.

"Mommy, are you happy?" Jack asked when I was drying him after his bath.

"I'm always happy when I'm with you, Jack," I said. "But I think I'm getting happy in a lot of other ways, too." Then I told him that Sue was coming to babysit for a little while because I had a couple of errands to run.

Sue arrived at eight thirty.

Zach lived in Chester. I had looked up his street on the map and marked the way to get there. He lived in a neighborhood of smaller houses, many of them obviously converted into two family homes. I found his house—the number was 358—but I had to drive to the next block before I could find a parking space. There were street lights, but they were pretty well hidden by the heavy trees that lined the sidewalk. The evening had turned really cool, and I didn't see anyone else outside.

Zach had been right about one thing. You could identify his house by the sound of drums being played somewhere inside. I went up the stairs onto the porch. There were two doors, a center one and one to the side. I decided that the latter probably led to the upstairs apartment, so I went over to it. There was a name over the doorbell, and by squinting I was able to make out the letter Z. I rang the bell and waited, but there was no answer. I tried again and listened, but with the drums beating, I could not be sure if the bell was working.

I was uncertain of what to do. It was just nine o'clock. I decided that maybe he had gone out for dinner and wasn't home yet. I went down the steps of the porch and stood on the sidewalk looking up. The windows on the second floor, at least from the front of the house, were dark. I wouldn't let myself believe that Zach had changed his mind about meeting me. I could tell he wanted that money so much he could taste it. Then I wondered if perhaps Ted Cartwright had made him a better offer? If he had, then I would double mine, I decided.

I didn't want to stand there any longer, but I didn't want to give up on the hope that Zach would be along any minute. I decided to get my car and double-park in front of Zach's house and wait for him in it. There was almost no traffic, so I knew I really wouldn't be too much in the way of any passing vehicles.

I don't know what made me turn around and look at the car that was parked directly in front of the house. I could see Zach sitting in it. The driver's window was open and he seemed to be asleep. He must have decided to meet me outside, I thought, as I walked over to his car. "Hi, Zach," I said. "I was afraid you were standing me up."

When he didn't respond, I touched his shoulder, and he fell forward slumping against the steering wheel. My hand felt sticky. I looked down. It was covered with blood. I grabbed the door of his car to steady myself. Then I realized I had touched it and frantically wiped it with my handkerchief. Then I rushed back to my own car and drove home, trying to wipe the blood away by rubbing my hand on my slacks. I don't know what I was thinking during that drive. I just knew I had to escape.

When I walked in the house, Sue was watching television in the family room. Her back was to me. The light wasn't on in the hall. "Sue," I called. "I'm late phoning my mother. I'll be down in just a minute."

Upstairs, I rushed into the bathroom, stripped, and turned on the shower. I felt as though my whole body had been washed with Zach's blood. I threw my slacks into the shower and watched as the water turned red at my feet.

I don't think I was acting rationally. I only knew that I had to establish some kind of alibi. I dressed hurriedly and went back downstairs. "The person I was supposed to see wasn't home," I said.

I know Sue saw that I had changed clothes, but she was happy when I gave her the equivalent of three hours babysitting pay. After she left, I poured a stiff scotch into a cup and sat in the kitchen sipping it, wondering what I was going to do. Zach was dead, and I had no way of knowing if the evidence he had for me was gone.

I should not have run away. I knew it. But Georgette had sent my father to Zach for riding lessons. Zach had let my father ride out alone. Suppose they find out that I am Liza Barton? If I had called the police, how could I explain to them why I had once again come upon the body of a person who had contributed to my father's death?

I finished the scotch, went upstairs, undressed, got into bed, and realized I was facing a sleepless night of worry, even of despair. Knowing it was the wrong thing to do, I took a sleeping pill. Somewhere around eleven, I was aware that the phone was ringing. It was Alex. "Ceil, you must be in a dead sleep. I'm sorry I woke you up. I had to let you know that no matter what you say you have to tell me, it won't change one iota of the way I feel about you."

I was so sleepy, but also so glad to hear his voice, to hear his words. "I believe that's true," I whispered.

Then with a smile in his tone, Alex said, "I wouldn't even care if you told me you were Little Lizzie Borden. Goodnight, sweetheart."

65

The body of Zachary Eugene Willet was found by a sixteen-year-old drummer, Tony "Rap" Corrigan, at 6 A.M., as he was preparing to leave on his bicycle to do his morning paper route.

"I thought old Zach had tied one on," he explained excitedly to Jeff MacKingsley and Angelo Ortiz, who had rushed to the scene after the Chester police notified them of the 911 call. "But then, I could see all that dried blood. Yuck. I thought I'd throw up."

No one in the Corrigan family remembered seeing Zach park the car. "It had to be after dark," said Sandy Corrigan, Rap's mother, a trim woman of about forty. "I know because there was an SUV parked there when I got home from work last evening at about quarter past seven. I'm a nurse at Morristown Hospital. The girls were with me when I came in. They go to my mother's after school, and I pick them up on the way home."

The three girls, ten, eleven, and twelve, were sitting next to their mother. In response to Jeff's questions, it was clear that none of them had noticed anything unusual when they returned home. They had dashed past the SUV and spent the rest of the evening watching television.

"We do our homework with Nana," the twelve-year-old explained.

Sandy's husband, Steve, a fireman, had come home from work at ten o'clock. "I drove right into the garage without a glance at the street," he explained. "We had a real busy shift, a fire in a house that was about to be pulled down. We think some kids did it. Thank God I've got four good kids. We encourage them to have their friends here. Rap is a great drummer. He practices all the time."

"Zach was planning to move over the weekend," Sandy Corrigan volunteered. "He was always complaining about Rap's drums, and anyhow I told him that when his lease was up, we wouldn't renew it. We need the room. This was my mother-in-law's house. We moved in after she died. I felt kind of sorry for Zach. He was such a loner. But I have to tell you, I was delighted when he said he was leaving."

"Then he didn't have much company?" Jeff asked.

"Never," Sandy Corrigan said emphatically. "He'd get here around six or seven at night, and almost never went out. Weekends he'd stay upstairs if he wasn't going back to the riding club, but as often as not, he was there. That was more his home than this place."

"Did he tell you where he was moving?"

"Yes. He was taking the model unit at Cartwright Town Houses in Madison."

"Cartwright?" Jeff exclaimed.

"Yes, Ted Cartwright, the developer, is building them."

"What isn't he building?" her husband asked sourly.

"I would think that one of those town houses would be quite expensive," Jeff said casually, trying not to let his excitement show. Cartwright, again, he was thinking.

"Especially if it comes furnished," Sandy Corrigan agreed. "Zach claimed Mr. Cartwright was going to give it to him because he saved his life once."

"Two moving men came by to pack for Zach yesterday, Mr. MacKingsley," Rap volunteered. "I let them in at about three o'clock.

I told them one of them could probably have done the whole job in an hour. Zach didn't have much stuff up there. They didn't stay long, and only took out a couple of boxes that didn't weigh much."

"Did they give you their cards?" Jeff asked.

"Well, no. I mean they had uniforms on and a truck. Anyway, why would anyone come to pack for Zach who wasn't on the level?"

Jeff and Angelo looked at each other. "Can you describe these men?" Jeff asked.

"One of them was a big guy. He had dark glasses on, and had kind of funny looking blond hair. I think it was dyed. He was kind of old—I mean, more than fifty. The other guy was short, and maybe about thirty or so. To be honest, I didn't pay too much attention to them."

"I see. Well if anything comes back to you about them, I'm leaving my card with your mother." Jeff turned to Sandy Corrigan. "Have you got a key to Zach's apartment, Mrs. Corrigan?" he asked.

"Of course."

"May I have it please? Thank you all very much for your cooperation."

The forensic unit was dusting the handle of the door to Zach's apartment and the doorbell. "Oh, we've got a nice clean one here," Dennis from the lab commented. "We got a partial off the door of the car, too. That one someone tried to wipe off."

"I haven't had a chance to tell you," Jeff told Angelo as he turned the key in the door from the porch to the apartment and pushed it open. "I spoke to Zach Willet by phone at five o'clock last night."

They started up the stairs which creaked under the weight of their feet. "What kind of guy did he seem to be?" Ortiz asked.

"Cocky. Very sure of himself. When I asked if I could come over and have a talk with him, he told me that, as a matter of fact, he was thinking of arranging a meeting with me. He said he might have

some interesting things to tell me, but there'd be a few details we'd
have to work out. He said that between the three of us, he was sure we
could come to an understanding."

"The *three* of us?" Angelo asked.

"Yes, the three of us—Celia Nolan, Zach, and me."

There was a narrow hallway at the top of the stairs. "The old rail-
road flat layout," Jeff commented. "All the rooms off the hall." They
walked a few steps and looked into what was meant to be a living
room.

"What a mess," Angelo said.

The couch and chairs had been slit in every direction. Stuffing
oozed out from the faded upholstery. The rug had been rolled up
and flipped over. Shelves of knickknacks had been dumped onto a
blanket.

Silently, the men walked into the kitchen and the bedroom.
Everywhere it was the same—contents of drawers and dressers had
been tossed onto towels or blankets; the mattress on the bed had been
sliced open. In the bathroom, the medicine chest had been emptied
into the tub. Loose tiles were stacked on the floor.

"The self-proclaimed moving men," Jeff said quietly. "Looks more
like a wrecking crew."

They went back into the bedroom. Ten or twelve photo albums
were thrown together in a corner. It was obvious that pages had been
yanked from them. "I think the first album was sold the day the camera was invented," Ortiz observed. "I never could understand the fix-
ation with old photos. When old people die, the next generation
keeps the photos for sentimental reasons. The third generation keeps
a few pictures of the great-grandparents to prove that they had ancestors, and deep-sixes the rest."

"Along with the medals and prizes the grandparents treasured,"

Jeff said in agreement. "I wonder if those guys who were here found what they were looking for?"

"Time to talk to Mrs. Nolan?" Angelo asked.

"She's hiding behind her lawyer, but maybe she'll agree to answer some questions with him present."

They stopped again in the living room. "The kid downstairs said the moving men took out some boxes. What do you think was in them?"

"What could possibly be missing around here?" Jeff asked.

"Who knows?"

"Papers," Jeff said briefly. "Do you see a single bill or letter or any scrap of paper in this place? I say that whoever was here didn't find what he wanted. Maybe he's looking for safe-deposit-box or storage-room receipts."

"How's this for artwork?" Ortiz asked dryly, lifting a broken picture frame. "Looks as though this was the mirror over the couch, and Zach took the mirror out and made this monstrosity." In the center of the frame there was a large caricature of Zach Willet, which was surrounded by dozens of pictures with inscriptions that had been taped around it. Ortiz read the inscription under the caricature. "'To Zach, on the occasion of your twenty-fifth anniversary at Washington Valley.' I guess everybody was asked to give their pictures that night with a sentiment written on it. I'd also bet they sang, 'For He's a Jolly Good Fellow' to the poor guy."

"Let's take that with us," Jeff said. "We might find something interesting in it. And now, it's past eight o'clock, not too early to pay a little visit to Mrs. Nolan."

Or a little visit to Liza Barton, he corrected himself silently.

66

"Mommy, can I stay home with you today?" Jack asked.

The request was so unexpected that I was taken aback. But I soon had an explanation.

"You were crying. I can tell," he said matter-of-factly.

"No, Jack," I protested. "I just didn't sleep very well last night, and my eyes are tired."

"You were crying," he said simply.

"Want to bet?" I tried to sound as if we were playing a game. Jack loved games. "What kind of bet?" he asked.

"I'll tell you what. After I drop you off at school, I'll come back and take a nap, and if my eyes are nice and bright when I pick you up, you owe me a hundred trillion dollars."

"And if they're not nice and bright, you owe me a hundred trillion dollars." Jack began to laugh. We usually settled those bets with an ice cream cone or a trip to the movies.

The wager decided upon, Jack willingly let me drop him off at school. I managed to get home before I started to break down again. I felt so trapped and helpless. For all I knew, Zach had told other people I was meeting him. How could I explain that he told me he had proof that Ted Cartwright had killed my father? And where was that proof now? They were practically accusing me of murdering Geor-

gette Grove and that landscaper. I had touched Zach. Maybe my fingerprints were on his car.

I was dead tired, and decided that maybe I should do what I had
told Jack I would do, and that was to try to take a nap. I was halfway up
the stairs to the second floor when the bell rang. My hand froze on
the banister. My instinct was to keep going upstairs, but when the bell
rang again, I started back down. I was sure it was going to be someone
from the prosecutor's office. All I have to tell them is that I will not answer questions unless my attorney is present, I reminded myself.

When I opened the door, it was a relief to see that at least Detective Walsh was not there. The prosecutor, Jeff MacKingsley, was
standing on the porch with the younger detective with black hair
who'd been very polite to me.

I had left my dark glasses in the kitchen, and so could only imagine what they were thinking when they saw me with my red-rimmed,
swollen eyes. For a moment, I don't think I cared. I was tired of running, tired of fighting. I wondered if they had come to arrest me.

"Mrs. Nolan, I know you are represented by an attorney, and I assure you I am not going to ask you any questions about either the
Georgette Grove or Charley Hatch homicides," Jeff MacKingsley
said. "But I believe that you may have some information that could
help us regarding a crime that was just committed. I know you have
been taking riding lessons from Zach Willet. Zach was found shot to
death early this morning."

I did not say anything. I could not go through the charade of pre-
tending I was surprised. Let them think that my silence indicated
shock and distress—that is if they didn't decide it meant that they
were telling me something I already knew.

MacKingsley waited for some response from me, but when he
didn't get it, he said, "We know that you took a riding lesson with
Zach yesterday afternoon. Did he indicate to you that he had plans to

meet anyone? Anything you can remember is potentially very important."

"Was he planning to meet anyone?" I repeated, and I heard my
voice rising into near hysteria. I clasped my hand against my mouth.
"I have an attorney." I managed to lower the pitch of my voice. "I
won't speak to you without him being present."

"I understand. Mrs. Nolan, this is a simple question. The picture
of the Barton family that you found taped to your barn. Did you ever
show it to your husband?"

I thought of finding the picture in the barn, of hiding it in the secret drawer, then Jack telling Alex about it, and Alex being so upset
because I wasn't planning to tell him about it. That picture was one
more item in the string of occurrences that was driving a wedge between Alex and me.

At least MacKingsley's question was one I could answer without
fear. "My husband had already gone to work when I found it. He
came home as I was giving it to you. No, Mr. MacKingsley, he did not
see it."

The prosecutor nodded and thanked me, but then, as he turned to
go, he said in a tone that sounded strangely sympathetic, "Celia, I really think that everything is falling into place. I think that you are
going to be all right."

67

J eff MacKingsley was quiet on the drive back to the office, and Angelo Ortiz knew better than to intrude. It was clear to Angelo that his boss was deeply troubled, and he was sure he knew why. Celia Nolan seemed to be on the verge of a total breakdown.

The forensic group was waiting for them when they arrived. "We've got nice prints for you, Jeff," Dennis, the fingerprint expert from the lab announced with great satisfaction. "A nice index finger from the doorbell, and a thumbprint from the car."

"Were there any in Zach's apartment?" Jeff asked.

"Lots and lots and lots of Zach's. Nobody else. I understand there were some moving men in there. They sure did turn that place upside down. Funny—they must have had on gloves the whole time."

"You mean funny as in peculiar?" Jeff confirmed.

"You know I do, Boss. What moving man have you ever met who wears gloves?"

"Dennis, I have two sets of fingerprints I want you to check for me," Jeff said. He hesitated, then added firmly, "And check them against the ones you got off Zach's car and doorbell."

Inwardly, Jeff was having a struggle. If the fingerprints Clyde had kept of Liza Barton matched the ones on the picture that had been in the barn, it was conclusive proof that Liza Barton was Celia Nolan. If those fingerprints matched the ones Dennis had lifted from Zach Willet's car and doorbell, it was conclusive proof that Celia had been at the crime scene where Zach Willet had lost his life.

The juvenile prints are illegally retained evidence, Jeff reminded himself, which means I could never use it in court. But it doesn't matter, he told himself stubbornly. I do *not* believe that Celia Nolan had anything to do with Zach Willet's death.

Dennis got back to him in half an hour. "You've got yourself a match, Prosecutor," he said. "The three sets of prints belong to the same person."

"Thanks, Dennis."

Jeff sat quietly for almost twenty minutes, twirling a pencil as he weighed the pros and cons of the decision he was struggling to make. Then, with a decisive snap, he broke the pencil, sending splinters across his desk.

He reached for his phone, and without going through Anna, dialed information to get the number of Benjamin Fletcher, Attorney-at-Law.

68

Jimmy Franklin was a newly appointed detective, and unofficially under the guidance of his good friend, Angelo Ortiz. On Thursday morning, with his cell phone camera and following Angelo's instructions, he stopped at the Grove Real Estate office, ostensibly to inquire about the availability of a small starter house in the Mendham area.

Jimmy was twenty-six, but like Angelo, had a boyish look that was very appealing. Robin responded to him by explaining pleasantly that there were very few starter houses available in Mendham, but that she did have some in neighboring towns.

While she marked pages for him to study in the loose-leaf book that was filled with listings, Jimmy pretended to be on the phone. What he was doing was taking close-up pictures of Robin, which he then rushed to the office to download, after, of course, he had dutifully looked at the listings she thought might interest him.

The night before he had managed to get a picture of Charley Hatch from Charley's former wife, Lena, a picture that she assured him really did not do poor Charley justice.

He enlarged several of the pictures he took of Robin, as well as the one that did not do Charley justice, and took them with him when he drove into Manhattan, parking on West 56th Street near Patsy's Restaurant.

It was quarter of twelve when he arrived there. The enticing aroma that hinted of tomato sauce and garlic made Jimmy remember that he had only coffee and a bagel for breakfast that morning, and that had been at six A.M.

Business first, he thought, selecting a seat at the bar. The restaurant had not yet begun to fill with the luncheon crowd, and there was only one other customer there, sipping a beer on a corner stool. Jimmy brought out his pictures and laid them on the bar. "Cranberry juice," he ordered, as he flashed his badge. "Recognize either of these people?" he asked the bartender.

The bartender studied the pictures. "They look familiar, especially the woman, like they might have passed by the bar on their way to a table. But I can't be sure."

Jimmy had better luck with the maître d', who definitely recognized Robin. "She comes in here sometimes. She might have been with that guy. I think she was once, but that's not usually who she's with. Let me ask the waiters."

Jimmy watched as the maitre d' went from one waiter to the other. He disappeared upstairs to the second-floor dining room, and when he returned he had a waiter in tow and was wearing the satisfied look of a man who had completed his mission.

"Dominick will fill you in," he said. "He's been here forty years, and I swear he never forgets a face."

Dominick was holding the pictures. "She comes in once in a while. Good looking. The kind you notice when she's around, you know, a little sexy. That guy I saw only once. He was with her a couple of weeks ago, shortly before Labor Day, I'd say. Reason I remember, it was the guy's birthday. She ordered a slice of cheese cake and had us put a candle on it. Then she gave him an envelope. I could see she'd laid some nice change on him. He counted it at the table. Twenty hundred dollar bills."

"That's a nice birthday present," Jimmy agreed.

"The guy was a real class act. He counted them *out loud*: One hundred, two hundred, three hundred, and so on. When he got to two thousand, he put them in his pocket."

"Did she give him a birthday card?" Jimmy asked.

"Who needs a birthday card when you get that kind of cash?"

"I just wonder if that was all birthday cash, or did she have a little job for him to do, and she was paying him for it. You say she comes in here with some other guy. Do you know his name?"

"No."

"Can you describe him?"

"Sure."

Jimmy got out his notebook and began jotting down the description of Robin Carpenter's other dinner companion. Then, feeling inordinately pleased with the success of his morning, he decided it would be in the line of duty to have some of Patsy's linguini.

69

Paul Walsh was sufficiently sobered by his boss's threat of reassignment, and willingly accepted the job of checking out the validity of Zach's landlady's statement that he had been planning to move into a town house that Ted Cartwright was giving him.

At nine thirty on Thursday morning, Paul was talking to Amy Stack, who in indignant detail told how Zach Willet had the nerve to play a practical joke on her and Mr. Cartwright. "He sounded so convincing when he said that Mr. Cartwright was giving him the model unit. I feel like such a dope for believing him."

"What did Mr. Cartwright say when you told him about Zach claiming the town house?"

"At first, he didn't believe me, but then I thought he'd go into orbit. That's how mad he was. But then he started to laugh, and explained it was just a silly bet they had made, and said that Zach was acting as if he'd really won."

"But bet or no bet, it was not your impression that Mr. Cartwright had any intention of giving Zach Willet that town house?" Walsh asked.

"Even if he did save Mr. Cartwright's life years ago, Zach Willet had no chance in the world of ever setting foot in that condo," Amy said in the tone of a person taking an oath.

"Did Mr. Cartwright spend the day here yesterday?"

"No, he was in somewhere between nine and ten, but only stayed a short while. He said that he was coming back at four o'clock to meet with the contractor, but I guess he changed his mind."

"That certainly was his prerogative," Walsh said, with a hint of humor. "Thank you, Ms. Stack. You've been very helpful."

*   *   *

The news of Zach's death had spread through the Washington Valley Riding Club. The idea that someone had shot him seemed unthinkable to the people who worked in the stables. "He wouldn't harm a fly," a scrawny old-timer named Alonzo protested when Paul Walsh asked if Zach Willet had any enemies. "Zach kept to himself. Never got in an argument in the fifty years I've known him."

"Do you know if anybody had it in for him for any reason?"

No one could think of anything until Alonzo remembered that Manny Pagan had made some comment about Ted Cartwright getting into an argument with Zach yesterday. "Manny's exercising a horse in the ring. I'll get him," Alonzo offered.

Manny Pagan came over to the stable, leading his horse. "Mr. Cartwright practically shouted at me. I never saw a guy so mad in my life. I pointed out where Zach was eating lunch at the picnic table and saw Cartwright go charging over to him. I could see from here that he was arguing with Zach. I swear there was steam coming out of his ears when he passed me a few minutes later on his way back to his car."

"That was yesterday at lunchtime?"

"That's right."

Paul Walsh had learned what he had come to find out and was anxious to get out of there. He was allergic to horses and could feel his eyes beginning to water.

70

"Benjamin Fletcher, returning your call," Anna announced on the intercom.

Jeff MacKingsley drew a deep breath and picked up the receiver. "Hello, Ben," he said warmly. "How are you?"

"Hello, Jeff. Nice to hear from you, but I'm sure you're not interested in the state of my health, which could be better in case you actually are interested."

"Of course I'm interested in how you're doing, but you're right, that's not the reason I called. I need your help."

"I'm not so sure I'm feeling very helpful, Jeff. That viper you call a detective, Walsh, has been pretty busy intimidating my new client."

"Yes, I realize that and I'm sorry. I apologize."

"I heard about Walsh making a big fuss because he thinks my client moved fast when she didn't know if a killer might still be lurking around. I don't take kindly to that."

"Ben, I don't blame you. Listen to me. Do you know that your new client, Celia Nolan, is actually Liza Barton?"

Jeff heard the sharp intake of breath at the other end of the phone and knew that Benjamin Fletcher had not been aware that Celia and Liza were the same person.

"I have absolute proof," he said. "Fingerprints."

"You better not have fingerprints from the juvenile case," Benjamin Fletcher said sharply.

"Ben, for now, never mind where or how I got them. I need to talk to Celia. I won't ask her one word about the two homicides last week, but there's something else I do have to talk to her about. Do you remember the name Zach Willet?"

"Sure. He's the guy who was giving her father riding lessons. Even when she wouldn't say anything else in the detention center, she kept repeating his name. What about him?"

"Zach was shot while he was in his car sometime last evening. Celia must have had an appointment to meet him. Her fingerprints are on Zach's car door and on his doorbell. I don't for one single minute think that she had anything to do with Zach's death, but I need her help. I need to know why she was meeting him, and why Zach told me on the phone only yesterday that he might be coming in to see me with Celia. Will you let her talk to me? I'm worried that there may be other lives at risk—including hers."

"I'll talk to her, then make a decision. Of course, I must be present if she ends up agreeing to meet with you, and at any point, if I say stop, you stop. I'll call her now and try to get back to you later today," Fletcher said.

"Please," Jeff urged. "As soon as you can. Whatever time and place is convenient for her, I'll be there."

"Okay, Jeff, and I'll tell you another thing. With all those people you've got working for you, have someone protect her. Make sure nothing happens to that pretty lady."

"I won't let that happen," Jeff said grimly. "But you've got to let me talk to her."

71

Jack had won the bet. I agreed that my eyes still looked tired, but insisted that it was because I had a headache, and not because I was so stressed. Instead of paying him one hundred trillion dollars, I took him to lunch at the coffee shop and bought him an ice cream cone for dessert. I kept on my dark glasses and told Jack the light hurt my eyes because of the headache. Did he believe me? I don't know. I doubt it. He's a smart and perceptive kid.

After that, we drove into Morristown. Jack had outgrown all his last year's clothes, and really needed some new sweaters and slacks. Like most children, he didn't think much of shopping so I stayed with the list of essentials that I had jotted down. What frightened me was that I realized I was anticipating not being with Jack. In case I'm arrested, he'd have these clothes.

We arrived home to find there were two messages on the phone. I tricked Jack into carrying his new clothes upstairs and putting them in his bureau "all by yourself." As always, I was so afraid it was one of the Lizzie Borden messages awaiting me, but both were from Benjamin Fletcher, with instructions for me to call him immediately.

They are going to arrest me, I thought. They have my fingerprints. He's going to tell me I have to turn myself in. I misdialed twice before I finally reached him.

"It's Celia Nolan, returning your call, Mr. Fletcher," I said, trying to keep my voice calm.

"First thing a client has to learn to do is to trust her attorney, Liza," he told me.

Liza. With the exception of Dr. Moran in my early days of treatment, and the time Martin's mind was wandering, I have not been called Liza since I was ten years old. I had always envisioned someone throwing the name at me unexpectedly, and ripping away my carefully constructed persona. The matter-of-fact way in which Fletcher said my name helped to reduce the shock that he knew who I was.

"I wasn't sure whether or not to tell you yesterday," I said. "I'm still not sure if I can trust you."

"You can trust me, Liza."

"How did you know it was me? Did you recognize me yesterday?"

"Can't say that I did. Jeff MacKingsley told me about an hour ago."

"Jeff MacKingsley told you!"

"He wants to talk to you, Liza. But first, I must be absolutely certain that if I allow you to do this, it will be in your best interest. Don't worry, I'll be there with you, but I'll say it again, I am *very* concerned. He tells me that you left your fingerprints on a doorbell and on a car door where a dead body was found. And as I told you, he also knows you are Liza Barton."

"Does that mean I am going to be arrested?" I could barely make my lips form the words.

"Not if I can help it. This is all very unusual, but the prosecutor tells me that he believes you had nothing to do with it. However, he does think you can help him find out who did."

I closed my eyes as relief flooded every inch of my body. Jeff MacKingsley did not believe I was involved in Zach's death! Would he believe me when I told him that Zach had seen Ted Cartwright cause my father's death? If he did, maybe, just maybe, he had been right when he said that I'd be all right. I wondered if he had known I was Liza when he made that statement.

I told Benjamin Fletcher about Zach Willet. I told him about my suspicion that my father's death had not been an accident, that I had been taking riding lessons from Zach so that I could get to know him. I told Fletcher that yesterday I had promised Zach one million one hundred thousand dollars if he would tell the police what really happened when my father went over that cliff.

"How did Zach respond to that, Liza?"

"Zach swore that Ted Cartwright had charged my father's horse and forced it onto the dangerous trail, and then spooked it by firing a gun. Zach kept the bullet and the casing, and even took pictures of the bullet lodged in a tree. All these years, he's kept the evidence of Cartwright's guilt. He told me yesterday that Cartwright has been threatening him. In fact, while I was with him yesterday, Zach got a call on his cell phone. I'm sure it was from Ted Cartwright, because although Zach didn't refer to the caller by name, he just laughed and sarcastically told him that he didn't need to live in his condominium because he'd received a better offer."

"You're going to be giving Jeff MacKingsley some mighty powerful stuff, Liza. But tell me this: how did your fingerprints get on that car and doorbell?"

I told Fletcher about my appointment to see Zach, about him not answering the bell, and then seeing him in the car and panicking and rushing home.

"Does anyone else know you were there, Liza?"

"No, not even Alex. But I did call my investment adviser yesterday and asked him to be ready to wire the money I promised Zach to a private bank account. He can verify that."

"All right, Liza," Benjamin Fletcher said. "What time is good for you to go to the prosecutor's office?"

"I'll need to get my babysitter. About four o'clock would be all right." Or at least as "all right" as going into the Morris County courthouse will *ever* be for me, I thought.

"Four o'clock, it is," Fletcher said.

I hung up the phone, and from somewhere behind me, Jack asked, "Mommy, are you going to be arrested?"

72

M ost of the investigators in the prosecutor's office had been pulled off their own units to concentrate on the Mendham homicides. At three o'clock, the group analyzing the phone records of Charley Hatch, Ted Cartwright, Robin Carpenter, and Henry Paley were ready to report their findings to Jeff.

"In the last two months, Cartwright has been in touch with Zach Willet six times," Liz Reilly, a new investigator, announced. "The last time was yesterday afternoon at 3:06."

"Mrs. Nolan may have heard that call," Jeff commented. "That would be just about the time she'd have been finishing her ride with Zach."

"Cartwright and Henry Paley have been talking to each other a lot in the last few months," Nan Newman, one of the veteran investigators, reported, "but there was no contact on either of Henry's phones between him and Charley Hatch."

"We know Paley and Cartwright were working together to strong-arm Georgette Grove into selling that property on Route 24," Jeff said. "Paley's a low life, and he hasn't accounted for his whereabouts when Hatch was shot. I need to know where he was before I rule him out as a player in any of these crimes. I've asked him to come in with his lawyer. They'll be here at five o'clock, and Ted Cartwright is coming at six with his lawyer.

"We know Robin Carpenter is a liar," he continued. "She lied about the date in Patsy's with her brother. His E-ZPass shows that he drove into New York at six forty that night, which is exactly what his ex-wife told Angelo. In Patsy's Restaurant, Robin was seen giving Hatch what appeared to be two thousand dollars, which in my book is one generous birthday present, unless he was also going to do her a favor for it.

"There are no calls from Carpenter to Hatch since last Friday. I believe that she was using a prepaid phone with no subscriber name to contact him. She must have told him to get one, too, because the woman whose lawn he was cutting saw him holding two phones. My guess is that one was his usual cell phone and the other was unregistered. I also think that when he answered that call, he made an appointment to meet someone at the break in the hedge.

"Of course, we can't be sure that it was Robin who made that last call, but I'll bet the ranch that Charley Hatch was finished the minute whoever hired him learned that his jeans and sneakers and carvings had been confiscated. He wasn't the kind of guy who would have stood up to intense questioning."

The investigators were listening quietly, following Jeff's reasoning, hoping for an opportunity to make a significant contribution to his analysis of the series of events leading up to the homicides.

"Ted Cartwright hated Georgette Grove, and he wanted her property, which gives him at least a motive in killing her," Jeff continued. "We know he was working in some way with Robin Carpenter, and that they were dating, maybe still are. It's a possibility that Zach Willet has been bleeding Ted all these years since Will Barton died. We'll know more about that when we talk to Mrs. Nolan.

"I think that with any luck, we're going to crack these cases open in the next few days," he told the staff, then saw that Mort Shelley had opened the door to his office. They exchanged glances, and Shelley answered Jeff's unspoken question: "He's where he said he'd be. We've got a tag on him."

"Make sure you don't lose him," Jeff said quietly.

73

This was the courthouse in which the trial had taken place. As I walked through the corridors, I remembered those terrible days. I remembered the inscrutable gaze of the judge. I remembered being afraid of my lawyer, not trusting him, yet being forced to sit next to him. I remember listening to the witnesses who testified that I meant to kill my mother. I remember how I tried to sit up straight because my mother was always after me not to slouch. It was a problem for me, because I was tall for my age, even then.

Benjamin Fletcher was waiting for me inside the main door of the prosecutor's office. He was better dressed than he had been when we met in his office. His white shirt looked reasonably crisp; his dark blue suit was pressed; his tie was in place. He took my hand when I came in, and he held it for a moment. "It would seem I owe a little ten-year-old girl an apology," he said. "I got that child off, but I admit that I bought Cartwright's version of what happened."

"I know you did," I said, "but the important thing is that you did get me off."

"The verdict was not guilty," he continued, "but it was based on reasonable doubt. Most people, including the judge, including me, felt that you were probably guilty. When we get this latest episode behind us, I'm going to see that everyone understands what you have been through, so that everyone will know that you are and have been an innocent victim."

I could feel my eyes brighten, and I guess Fletcher noticed. "No charge," he added, "and it rattles my soul to utter those words."

I laughed, which was what he wanted. I suddenly felt comfortable, confident that this hulking septuagenarian would take care of me.

"I'm Anna Malloy, Mr. MacKingsley's secretary. Will you follow me, please?"

The sixtyish woman had a sweet face and a firm, quick step. As I followed her down the corridor, I had a hunch that she was one of those motherly type secretaries who think they know better than their boss.

Jeff MacKingsley's corner office was large and pleasant. I had always instinctively liked this man, even when I resented him showing up unannounced on my doorstep. Now he got up from his desk and came around it to greet us. I had done the best possible makeup job I could, trying to disguise my swollen eyes and eyelids, but I don't think I fooled him much, if at all.

With Benjamin Fletcher sitting beside me like an aging lion, ready to pounce at the scent of danger, I told Jeff everything I knew about Zach. I told him that as a ten-year-old in lockdown detention I would have spasms of grief at the sound of his name. I told him that it was only in these last two weeks that I had remembered clearly my mother's last words: "You told me when you were drunk. You killed my husband. You told me Zach saw you."

"That's why my mother threw him out," I told Jeff. Detective Ortiz and a stenographer were in the room, but I ignored them. I wanted this man who was sworn to protect the safety of the people of this county to understand that my mother was wise to be afraid of Ted Cartwright.

He let me talk almost without interruption. I guess in my own way, I was answering all the questions he had planned to ask me. When I described going to Zach's house, ringing the bell, and then seeing Zach in the car, he did prod me for additional details.

When I was finished, I looked at Benjamin Fletcher and, knowing he would be displeased, I said, "Mr. MacKingsley, I want you to ask me any questions you may have about Georgette Grove and Charley Hatch. I guess you know now why I made it home so fast from Holland Road. I knew that route from my childhood. My grandmother lived very near it."

"Wait a minute," Benjamin Fletcher interrupted. "We agreed we were not going to discuss those cases."

"We have to," I said. "It's going to get out that I'm Liza Barton." I looked at Jeff MacKingsley. "Does anyone in the media know yet?"

"In fact, it was a person in the media, Dru Perry, who first disclosed it to us," Jeff admitted. "At some point you may want to talk with her. I think she'd be very sympathetic." Then he added, "Is your husband aware that you are Liza Barton?"

"No he is not," I said. "It was a terrible mistake, but I promised Jack's father, my first husband, that I would not reveal my past to anyone. Of course, I will tell Alex now, and I can only hope that our relationship will survive."

For the next forty minutes I answered every question the prosecutor asked me about my brief acquaintance with Georgette Grove, and about my absolute lack of information on Charley Hatch. I even told him about the Little Lizzie phone calls and messages I had received.

At ten of five, I stood up, "If there's nothing more, I must get back," I said. "My little boy gets quite anxious if I'm away too long. If any other questions come up, just call. I'll be glad to answer them."

Jeff MacKingsley and Fletcher and Detective Ortiz got up, too. I don't know why, but I had the feeling that all three were hovering around me as though they thought I needed protection. Fletcher and I said goodbye and left the private office. There was a woman with wild gray hair at Jeff's secretary's desk. She was obviously very angry. I recognized her and remembered she had been at the house the day of the vandalism, a part of the media that surged onto the place.

Her back was to me, and I heard her say, "I told Jeff about Celia Nolan because I thought it was my duty to warn him about her. My thanks is that I lose my exclusive. The *New York Post* is giving all of page 3, and possibly its headline, to the 'Return of Little Lizzie' story, and they're practically going to accuse her of committing all three murders."

Somehow I made it to my car. Somehow I remained poised when I said goodbye to Benjamin Fletcher. Somehow I got home. I paid Sue and thanked her and turned down her offer to fix dinner for us, an offer she made because, as she said, I looked awfully pale to her. I'm sure she was right.

Jack was listless. I think he was starting to get a cold, or perhaps it was the heavy weight of my troubled aura that was making him ill. I sent out for a pizza, and before it came, I got him into pajamas and changed into my own pajamas and robe.

I decided I would go to bed after I tucked Jack in. All I wanted to do was to sleep and sleep and sleep. There were several phone calls. First from Mr. Fletcher, and then from Jeff MacKingsley. I did not answer either of them, and on the answering machine they both left messages expressing concern at how upset I must be.

Of course, I'm upset, I thought. Tomorrow I'll be starring in "The Return of Little Lizzie." From this day forward, I will never travel far enough or hide deep enough to escape being called Little Lizzie.

When the pizza came, Jack and I each had a couple of slices. Jack

definitely was catching some kind of bug. I took him upstairs at eight
o'clock. "Mom, I want to sleep with you," he said fretfully.

That was fine with me. I locked up and set the alarm; then I called
Alex's cell phone. He didn't answer, but I expected that. He had said
something about a dinner meeting. I left a message saying that I was
going to turn off the phone because I was going to bed early, and
to please call me at six o'clock A.M., Chicago time. I said there was
something important I had to tell him.

I took a sleeping pill, got into bed, and with Jack cuddled in my
arms, I fell fast asleep.

I don't know how long I slept, but it was pitch dark when I felt my
head being raised and heard a shadowy voice whispering, "Drink this,
Liza."

I tried to close my lips, but a strong hand was forcing them open,
and I was gulping a bitter liquid that I knew contained crushed sleeping pills.

From a distance, I heard Jack's wail as someone carried him away.

74

"Dru, that leak did not come from this office," Jeff snapped, finally out of patience with the reporter. "You seem to forget that Clyde Earley, among others, knows that Celia Nolan is Liza Barton. We don't know how many other people may have recognized her or been told who she is. Frankly, I think that whoever planned that vandalism at the Old Mill Lane house was well aware of Celia Nolan's identity. The *Post* is going to be rehashing an old story and trying to tie it to three recent homicides, but they're barking up the wrong tree. Hang around, and I may be able to give you the true story, and you'll have some real news for yourself."

"You're playing straight with me, Jeff?" Dru's anger began to subside, as her eyes relaxed and her lips became less compressed.

"I don't think I've ever been known not to play it straight with you," Jeff replied in a tone that reflected both annoyance and understanding.

"You're suggesting I wait around?"

"I'm suggesting that there's going to be a big story soon."

They were standing at the door of Jeff's office. Jeff had come out at the first sound of Dru's raised voice.

Anna came up to them. "You don't know what you did to that poor girl, Dru," she scolded. "You should have seen the look on her face when you were shouting about 'The Return of Little Lizzie.' She's stuck living in Little Lizzie's house, poor thing. She was devastated."

"Are you talking about Celia Nolan?" Dru asked.

"She walked right behind you on her way out," Anna snapped. "She was with her lawyer, Mr. Fletcher."

"Liza, I mean Celia, went back to *him? He's* representing her?" Too late Dru realized that Jeff had not told Anna who Celia was. "I'll hang around, Jeff," she added, an apologetic note in her voice.

"I'm expecting Henry Paley and his lawyer," Jeff told Anna. "It's five o'clock. You can go."

"Not a chance," Anna told him. "Jeff, is Celia Nolan really Liza Barton?"

Jeff's look made her next question die in her throat. "I'll send Mr. Paley in when he gets here," she said. "And whether you appreciate it or not, I *do* know when something is really confidential."

"I wasn't aware there was a difference between 'confidential' and '*really* confidential,' " Jeff said.

"Oh, there absolutely *is*," Anna assured him crisply. "Look, is that Mr. Paley heading this way?"

"Yes, it is," Jeff said. "And that's his lawyer behind him. Send them right in."

Henry Paley read a statement into the record that had obviously been prepared by his attorney.

He had been Georgette Grove's junior partner in the agency for more than twenty years. While he and Georgette had disagreed over the joint property they owned on Route 24, and about whether it was time for him to consider retirement, they had always been good friends. "It was personally very disappointing to me to realize that Georgette had gone through my desk and taken out the file of notes outlining my agreements with Ted Cartwright," he said, in a wooden voice.

Henry admitted that he had been at the Holland Road house several times more than he had indicated, but he insisted that it was only carelessness in keeping his daily reminder.

He went on to acknowledge that about a year ago he had been offered one hundred thousand dollars from Ted Cartwright if he was able to persuade Georgette to sell the land on Route 24 to make room for commercial development. He said she wasn't interested, so it never came to pass.

"There has been a question as to my whereabouts on or around the time of the demise of Charley Hatch, the landscaper," Henry read. "I left my office at one fifteen and went directly to the Mark Grannon Real Estate Agency. There I met Thomas Madison, who is Georgette Grove's cousin. Mr. Grannon had made an offer to buy our agency.

"As for the late Charley Hatch—I may have seen Mr. Hatch when I was showing properties where he was engaging in landscaping services. I do not remember ever exchanging a word with him.

"Referring to the most recent homicide that may have some connection to the Barton family, I never met the victim, Zach Willet, nor have I ever ridden a horse or taken riding lessons."

Looking pleased with himself, Henry folded his statement neatly and looked at Jeff. "I trust that covers the situation."

"Maybe," Jeff said pleasantly. "But I do have one question: Don't you think that Georgette Grove, knowing of your cozy relationship with Ted Cartwright, would have lived out her life holding onto the Route 24 property rather than go along with you and sell it commercially? From what I hear about her, that's exactly what she would do."

"I object to that question," Paley's lawyer said heatedly.

"You were in the vicinity of Holland Road when Georgette was shot, Mr. Paley, and her death made it possible for you to get a better deal than Cartwright was offering. That will be all for today. Thank you for coming in to make your statement, Mr. Paley."

75

The heavy frame that had once surrounded a mirror and then became the repository of Zach Willet's twenty-fifth anniversary memorabilia had been placed on top of a wide desk in a vacant office just down the hall from Jeff MacKingsley.

Investigator Liz Reilly had only been in the prosecutor's office a few months, and was champing at the bit to be involved in a murder case. She had been instructed to review every card and note pasted on the frame and to look carefully for any photograph that might show a bullet lodged in a tree, or in a structure such as a fence or shed. The photo, or photos, might have been enlarged, she was told. There also might be riding trails shown in them, and perhaps a sign indicating danger in front of one of the trails. Investigators were also going through everything found in Willet's apartment, hoping to find an actual spent bullet and casing.

Liz had a feeling that something important could emerge from this hopelessly cluttered object. She welcomed every chance she got to be at crime scenes because she loved the process of collecting evidence, and had arrived at the Zach Willet home shortly after the initial forensic team.

She was certain that the collage would be a perfect place to secrete a picture or any small object that might otherwise be easily discovered in a drawer or file.

The tape on the pictures and notes was cracked and dry, and easily separated from the corkboard that Zach had inserted for backing. Soon she had neat stacks of pictures around the frame. Liz got a kick out of reading the first several notes of congratulation: "Here's to another 25, Zach;" "Ride 'em cowboy;" "Happy trails to you."

She quickly got into a routine of glancing at them as she removed them, one by one.

It seemed to be turning into a useless exercise. Liz continued until only the caricature itself remained in the frame. It had been drawn in crayon on heavy cardboard, and was tacked rather than taped to the corkboard. Might as well take this one off, too, Liz thought. When she removed it, she turned the caricature over; taped to the back was a sealed 5-by-8 envelope. Liz decided to have a witness when she opened it.

She went down the hall to the prosecutor's office. The door was open and Jeff MacKingsley was standing at the window, stretching.

"Mr. MacKingsley, can I show you something?"

"Sure, Liz, what is it?"

"This envelope was taped behind that caricature of Zach Willet."

Jeff looked from the envelope to Liz and back to the envelope. "If this is what I hope it is . . ." he said. Without finishing the sentence, he went to his desk and got a letter opener from the drawer. He slit the tape, opened the envelope and shook it. Two metal objects clanked onto his desk.

Jeff reached into the envelope and pulled out a handwritten letter and a half dozen photographs. The first one was a close-up showing a bony hand pointing to a tree in which a bullet was clearly embedded. A newspaper was positioned below the hole to display the date—May 9th—and the year, which was the year Will Barton had died. A second picture, taken from the newspaper on that date, showed Ted Cartwright proudly displaying his pistol.

A two-page letter, neatly printed but filled with misspellings, and addressed to "Whoever it could concern," contained Zach's graphic yet oddly dignified description of how he had watched Will Barton die.

He described how Ted Cartwright, on his powerful horse, had charged the high-strung mare that the nervous and inexperienced Will Barton was riding. He related watching Ted's horse force the mare onto the dangerous trail. After she got close to the edge of the cliff, he saw Ted fire the shot that caused the panicking horse to bolt, sending both the horse and its doomed rider into the fatal plunge.

Jeff turned to Liz. "Good work. This is enormously important, and just might be the break we need."

Liz left Jeff's office, delighted with the prosecutor's reaction to the evidence she had found.

As Jeff stood alone, realizing that everything Celia had told him was true, he was interrupted again as Investigator Nan Newman rushed into his office. "Boss, you're not going to believe this. Rap Corrigan, the kid who found Zach Willet's body, came in to meet with me and give a statement. While he was there, Ted Cartwright came into the outer office with his attorney. Rap did a double-take when he saw Cartwright, and practically pulled me down the hall to talk to me.

"Jeff, Rap swears that Ted Cartwright, minus a dopey looking blond wig, is one of the two so-called moving men he let into Zach Willet's apartment yesterday."

76

Ted Cartwright was dressed in an impeccably tailored dark blue suit, a light blue shirt with French cuffs, and a red and blue tie. With his crown of white hair, piercing blue eyes, and imposing carriage, he was every inch the powerful executive as he strode ahead of his lawyer into Jeff's office.

Seated behind his desk, Jeff calmly observed the arrival and deliberately waited until Cartwright and his lawyer were standing in front of him before he got up. He did not offer to shake the hand of either man, but indicated the chairs that were pulled close to the desk.

As witnesses to this meeting, Jeff had invited Detectives Angelo Ortiz and Paul Walsh, who were already seated in chairs to the side of the prosecutor. The court reporter was in place, her face expressionless as always. It had been said of Louise Bentley that even if she had recorded the confession of Jack the Ripper, she would not have allowed a single muscle of her face to show reaction.

Cartwright's attorney introduced himself. "Prosecutor MacKingsley, I am Louis Buch, and I am counsel to Mr. Theodore Cartwright. I wish to state for the record that my client is extremely distressed by the death of Zach Willet, and has, in response to the request of your office, appeared here today voluntarily and with the strong desire to assist you in any way in your investigation of Mr. Willet's death."

His face impassive, Jeff MacKingsley looked at Ted. "How long have you known Zach Willet, Mr. Cartwright?"

"Oh, I think about twenty years," Ted answered.

"Think again, Mr. Cartwright. Isn't it well over thirty years?"

"Twenty, thirty." Cartwright shrugged. "A very long time, whichever it is, don't you agree?"

"Would you say you were friends?"

Ted hesitated. "It depends on how you define friendship. I knew Zach. I liked him. I love horses and he was a natural with them. I admired his skill at handling them. On the other hand, it wouldn't occur to me to invite him to my home for dinner, or really socialize with him in any way."

"Then you don't count having a drink with him at the bar at Sammy's as socializing with him?"

"Of course, if I bumped into him at a bar, I would have a drink with him, Mr. MacKingsley."

"I see. When was the last time you spoke with him?"

"Yesterday afternoon, around three o'clock."

"And what was the reason for the call?"

"We had a good laugh over the joke he pulled on me."

"What was that joke, Mr. Cartwright?"

"A few days ago Zach went over to my town house development in Madison and told my sales rep that I was giving him the model unit. We had a bet on the Yankee–Red Sox game, and he had kidded me that if the Red Sox won by more than ten runs, I would have to give him a unit."

"That's not what he told your sales rep," Jeff said. "He told her that he had saved your life."

"He was joking."

"When was the last time you saw Zach?"

"Yesterday, around noon."

"Where did you see him?"

"At the Washington Valley stables."

"Did you have a quarrel with him?"

"I blew off a little steam. Because of his joke, we almost lost a sale of that town house. My rep took him seriously and told a couple who were interested in it that it was no longer available. I simply wanted to tell Zach that his joke went too far. But later that couple *did* come back and made an offer on the unit, so I called Zach up at three o'clock and apologized."

"That's very odd, Mr. Cartwright," Jeff said, "because a witness heard Zach tell you that he didn't need the money the town house was worth because he had a better offer. Do you remember him saying that?"

"That wasn't the conversation we had," Ted said mildly. "You're mistaken, Mr. MacKingsley, as is your witness."

"I don't think so. Mr. Cartwright, did you ever promise Henry Paley one hundred thousand dollars if he could persuade Georgette Grove to sell the property Georgette and Henry jointly owned on Route 24?"

"I had a business arrangement with Henry Paley."

"Georgette was pretty much in your way, wasn't she, Mr. Cartwright?"

"Georgette had her way of doing things. I have mine."

"Where were you on the morning of Wednesday, September 4th at about ten A.M.?"

"I was out for an early morning ride on my horse."

"Weren't you on a trail that connects directly to the private trail in the woods behind the Holland Road house where Georgette died?"

"I do not ride on private trails."

"Mr. Cartwright, did you know Will Barton?"

"Yes, I did. He was the first husband of my late wife, Audrey."

"You were separated from your wife at the time of her death?"

"The evening of her death she had called me to discuss a reconciliation. We were very much in love. Her daughter, Liza, hated me
because she didn't want anyone to replace her father, and she hated
her mother for loving me."

"Why did you and your wife separate, Mr. Cartwright?"

"The strain of Liza's antagonism became too much for Audrey.
We only planned the separation to be temporary, until she could get
psychological help for her troubled daughter."

"You didn't separate because, when you were drunk one night,
you confessed to Audrey Barton that you had killed her first husband?"

"Don't answer that, Ted," Louis Buch ordered. He looked at Jeff
and angrily stated, "I thought we came here to talk about Zach Willet. I was never informed of other matters."

"It's all right, Lou. No problem. I'll answer their questions."

"Mr. Cartwright," Jeff said, "Audrey Barton was terrified of you.
Her mistake was that she didn't go to the police. She was horrified at
what it would do to her daughter to learn that you had killed her father so that Audrey could be free to marry you. But you were afraid,
weren't you? You were afraid that Audrey would have the courage to
go to the police one day. There was always some question about the
gunshot that was heard at the time Will Barton's horse went over the
cliff with him."

"This is ridiculous," Cartwright snapped.

"No, it's not. Zach Willet witnessed what you did to Will Barton.
We found some very interesting evidence in Zach's apartment—a
statement he had written about what he saw, plus he took a picture of
your bullet where it hit a tree near the trail. He described what you
did to Barton. He retrieved that bullet, and its casing, and kept them
all these years. Let me read his statement to you."

Jeff picked up Zach Willet's letter and read it with deliberate emphasis on the sentences describing Ted charging his horse into Will Barton's mare.

"That is a piece of fiction and inadmissible in court," Louis Buch snapped.

"Zach's murder isn't a piece of fiction," Jeff snapped. "He was bleeding you for twenty-seven years and finally got so cocksure of himself when he realized you killed Georgette Grove that he decided he ought to be taken care of on a higher scale."

"I did *not* kill Georgette Grove or Zach Willet," Cartwright said emphatically.

"Were you in Zach Willet's apartment yesterday?"

"No, I was not."

Jeff looked past him. "Angelo, will you ask Rap to come in?"

As they waited, Jeff said, "Mr. Cartwright, as you can see, I have here the evidence you were searching for in Zach's apartment—the bullet and casing from the gun that you fired to terrify Will Barton's horse, and the pictures that show where and when it happened. You'd just won a prize with that gun, hadn't you? Later you donated it to the permanent collection of firearms at a Washington museum, didn't you? You couldn't quite bear to throw it out, but you didn't want it in your home because you knew Zach had retrieved the bullet that sent Will Barton to his death. I am subpoenaing that gun from the museum so that we can compare the bullet and casing to it. We should be able to determine definitively if that bullet and casing were fired from that gun." Jeff looked up. "Oh, here's Zach's landlady's son."

At Angelo's prodding, Rap came forward to stand by the desk.

"Do you recognize anyone in this room, Rap?" Jeff asked.

The performer in Rap was clearly enjoying the spotlight. "I recognize you, Mr. MacKingsley," he said, "and I recognize Detective

Ortiz. You were both at my house yesterday after I found poor old Zach in his car."

"Do you recognize anyone else, Rap?"

"Yes, I do. This guy." He pointed at Ted. "Yesterday he came to our house dressed like a moving man. He had another guy with him. I gave him the key to Zach's apartment. Zach had told us he was moving over the weekend to some fancy town house in Madison."

"Are you positive this is the man who came to your home yesterday and went up to Zach Willet's apartment?"

"I'm positive. He had a dopey blond wig on. Made him look like a real jerk. But I'd know that face anywhere, and if you find the other guy, I'd know him, too. I remember more about him now. He has a little strawberry birthmark near his forehead, and he's missing half his right index finger."

"Thank you, Rap."

Jeff waited to speak until Rap reluctantly left the room and Angelo had closed the door behind him. "Robin Carpenter is your girlfriend," he told Cartwright. "You gave her the money to bribe her half brother Charley Hatch to vandalize the house known, thanks to you, as 'Little Lizzie's Place.' You shot Georgette Grove, and we will be able to prove it. Hatch became a threat and you, or Robin, took him out."

"That's not true," Cartwright shouted, jumping to his feet.

Louis Buch stood up, stunned and totally furious.

Jeff ignored the lawyer and glared at Cartwright. "We know that you went to Audrey Barton's home to kill her that night. We know that you caused Will Barton's death. We know that you killed Zach Willet. And we know that you're not in the moving business."

Jeff stood up. "Mr. Cartwright, you are under arrest for the burglary of Zach Willet's apartment. Mr. Buch, we are finishing our investigation, and we anticipate that Mr. Cartwright will be formally charged with these murders in the next several days. I am now instructing Detective Walsh to proceed to Mr. Cartwright's home and to secure that scene while we apply for a search warrant."

Jeff paused, then added sarcastically, "I anticipate that we will find a dopey blond wig and a moving man's outfit." He turned to Detective Ortiz and said, "Please read Mr. Cartwright his rights."

77

Twenty minutes after Ted Cartwright had been led out of Jeff MacKingsley's office, Jeff invited Dru Perry in to speak with him. "I promised you that you would have a story," he said, "and this is only the beginning of it. We have just arrested Ted Cartwright for the burglary of Zach Willet's apartment."

Experienced reporter though she was, Dru Perry felt her jaw drop.

"We anticipate filing far more serious charges against him in the next several days," Jeff continued. "These charges will relate to the deaths of Will Barton and Zach Willet. There may be other charges, depending upon the outcome of our investigation."

"Will Barton!" Dru exclaimed. "Ted Cartwright killed Liza Barton's father?"

"We have proof that he did, and the reason that he went to that house on Old Mill Lane that night was to kill his estranged wife Audrey Barton. Liza, that poor little ten-year-old, was only trying to protect her mother from Ted. For twenty-four years, Liza Barton, who is now known as Celia Nolan, has been tortured, not only by the loss of her mother, but by the nearly universal belief that she deliberately shot her mother and Ted because she resented their relationship."

Jeff wearily rubbed his eyes. "There will be a lot more details coming in the next couple of days, Dru, but you can rely on what I've just told you."

"I've been around for a long time, Jeff," Dru said, "but this is almost unimaginable. I'm so glad that that poor girl has a loving husband and a great kid. I guess that's what has helped her survive."

"Yes," Jeff replied carefully, "she has a really terrific kid, and he'll help her get through all this."

"You're telling me something," Dru said. "You didn't mention her devoted husband."

"No, I didn't," Jeff said quietly. "I can't comment further right now, but that might change very soon."

78

I am being carried downstairs. I can't open my eyes. "Jack." I try to call his name, but can only whisper it. My lips feel rubbery. I have to wake up. *Jack needs me.*

"It's all right, Liza. I'm taking you to Jack."

Alex is talking to me. Alex, my husband. He is home, not in Chicago. I have to tell him tomorrow that I'm really Liza Barton.

But he called me Liza.

There were sleeping pills in that glass.

Maybe I'm dreaming.

Jack. He's crying. He's calling me. "*Mommy. Mommy. Mommy.*"

"Jack. Jack." I try to scream, but can only mouth his name.

There is cold air on my face. Alex is carrying me. Where is he taking me? Where is Jack?

My eyes won't open. I hear a door opening—the garage door. Alex is laying me down. I know where I am. My car, the backseat of my car.

"Jack . . ."

"You want him? You can have him." It's a woman's voice, harsh and grating.

"Mommmmmmy!"

Jack's arms are around my neck. His head is buried against my heart. "Mommmmmmmmmy."

"Get outside, Robin, I'm starting the engine." Alex's voice.

I hear the garage door close. Jack and I are alone.

I'm so tired. I can't help it. I am falling asleep.

79

At 10:30 P.M., still in his office, Jeff waited for Detective Mort Shelley. He had already been notified that the search of Ted Cartwright's house had uncovered the blond wig, the movers' uniforms, and the boxes of papers that had been taken from Zach Willet's apartment. More important, a nine millimeter pistol had been found in the safe in his bedroom.

Jeff was virtually certain that the pistol would be matched to the nine millimeter bullet that had lodged in Zach Willet's brain.

We'll have Cartwright cold on this one, he thought, and with a plea agreement we may be able to get him to admit to Will Barton's murder. We may finally be able to also make him admit the truth of what he intended to do when he went to Audrey Barton's home the night she died.

The satisfaction Jeff would normally feel from the possibility of satisfactorily closing a case such as this one was outweighed by his concern for Celia Nolan. Or Liza Barton, he corrected himself. I'm going to have to be the one to tell her that her husband was setting her up to be accused of murdering Georgette Grove, he thought, and it's all about the money she inherited from his cousin, Laurence Foster.

There was a light tap at the door and Mort Shelley came in. "Jeff, how this guy Nolan has managed to stay out of prison beats me."

"What have you got, Mort?"

"Where do you want me to start?"

"You choose." Jeff had been leaning back in his chair. Now he straightened up.

"Alex Nolan is a phony," Mort said decisively. "He *is* a lawyer and he *is* affiliated with a law firm that used to be prestigious, but it's now just a two-man operation run by the grandson of the founder. He and Nolan basically go their own ways. Nolan claims to specialize in wills and trusts, but has only a handful of clients. He's had several ethics violations filed against him, and has been suspended twice. His defense has always been that he's a sloppy bookkeeper, not a thief, and he has managed to avoid prosecution."

The contempt in Shelley's voice deepened as he continued to read his notes and consult the thick file he was carrying. "He never made an honest dollar in his life. His money came from a bequest he received four years ago from a seventy-seven-year-old widow he was romancing. The family was outraged, but rather than allow a distinguished and cultured lady to become the butt of jokes, they didn't challenge the will in court. Nolan got three million dollars out of that scam."

"That's pretty good," Jeff said. "Most people would settle for it."

"Jeff, that kind of money is peanuts for someone like Alex Nolan. He wants real money, the kind that means private planes and yachts and mansions."

"Celia—I mean Liza—doesn't have that kind of money."

"*She* doesn't, but her *son* does. Don't misunderstand me. She does have plenty. Laurence Foster took good care of her, but the two-thirds of his estate that he left to Jack contain Foster's share of patents for research that he financed. There are three different companies that are about to go public, and that will mean tens of millions of dollars to Jack one day."

"And Nolan knew this?"

"It was public knowledge that Laurence Foster was an investor in start-up companies. Wills are on file in the county courthouse where they were probated. Nolan didn't need to be a genius."

Shelley picked another page out of the file. "As you suggested, we tracked down Foster's private nurses from the last time he was in the hospital. One of them admitted that she took big tips from Nolan to let him in to visit his cousin when Laurence Foster was dying and visitors were limited to the immediate family. Nolan was probably hoping to get himself written into the will, but Foster's mind was beginning to wander, so maybe it was he, himself, who told Nolan about Celia's past. Of course, we can't be sure, but it makes sense."

Jeff's mouth tightened as he listened.

"Nolan is all smoke and mirrors," Shelley continued. "He didn't own that apartment in SoHo. He sublet it on a month-to-month lease. The furniture wasn't his. None of it was. He was using the three million bucks his old—and I do mean old—girlfriend left him to convince Liza that he was a prominent and successful attorney.

"I spoke to Celia's investment advisor, Karl Winston. He told me that Celia's accident when she was hit by the limo last winter was Nolan's lucky break. She panicked at the thought that if she had died, Jack would have no close relative to care for him. Winston also told me that the way Laurence Foster set up his will, he left one-third of his estate to Celia and two thirds to Jack. If Jack dies before he reaches twenty-one, everything he has goes to Celia. After her marriage to Alex Nolan, except for a few charitable donations and a fund to care for her adoptive parents, Celia split her estate between Nolan and Jack. She also made Nolan Jack's guardian, as well as the trustee of his estate until the kid is twenty-one."

"I knew when Nolan sat in this office yesterday and referred to the picture Liza found taped in the barn as the one of the Barton family on the beach in Spring Lake, that he must be the one who put it there," Jeff said. "Last week I was in the kitchen when Liza gave it to me. Nolan came in as I was putting it in a plastic bag. He didn't ask to look at it then, so supposedly he had never seen it. But yesterday, despite all the Barton family pictures that have been in the newspapers, he knew exactly which picture it was."

"Robin has been his girlfriend for at least three years," Shelley said. "I took a picture of Nolan I got in the Bar Association Directory to Patsy's. One of the waiters started there three years ago and he remembers seeing them when he was new on the job. He said Nolan always paid cash, which figures."

"I guess Robin's been willing to stay under wraps because she wants him to hit the big bucks," Jeff said. "One thing that she may *not* have been lying about is that her dates with Ted Cartwright didn't amount to anything."

"I wonder if the plan to get Liza back into her old home was hatched after Robin went to work at the Grove Agency and the house came on the market," Jeff mused. "Buy the house as a gift. Move her into it. Vandalize it to rattle her. Expose her as Little Lizzie. Count on a psychological breakdown so he could get control of the estate. But then something went wrong. That last evening when Georgette stayed in the office, she must have found something that linked Robin to Alex. Henry told us that Georgette had gone through both their desks. Maybe Georgette found a picture of Alex and Robin together, or a note from him to her. Georgette made a call to Robin at ten o'clock Tuesday night. Unless Robin comes clean, we'll probably never know the reason for it."

"My guess is that Robin was the one waiting for Georgette in the house on Holland Road," Mort volunteered. "Between them, if she and Alex knew they had to get rid of Georgette, that may have been when they decided to try to point the finger at Celia by leaving her picture in Georgette's shoulder bag. And don't forget, if Robin put a picture in that bag, she then might have taken something out of the bag that Georgette had found in her desk. Then, when Charley Hatch's jeans and sneakers and carvings were confiscated by Sergeant Earley, he became too much of a danger to them. So their plot to get control of Liza and Jack's money caused them to commit two homicides. And if Celia ends up going to prison for these murders, that's a perfect ending."

"This may not be the first time Nolan has been involved in a homicide," Jeff told Shelley. "As you know, we had a number of our guys digging up information about his pre-law school days. He was a suspect in the death of a wealthy young woman he had dated in college. They never proved anything, but she had dropped him for someone else. He apparently went crazy and stalked her for over a year. She had to get a restraining order against him. I only learned that this afternoon."

Jeff's expression became grave. "First thing tomorrow morning, I'm going to drive to Mendham and tell Liza what we know. After that, I'll order around-the-clock protection for her and Jack. If Nolan weren't in Chicago, I'd have a 24/7 guard on them now. My guess is that Nolan and his girlfriend have to be getting very, very nervous at this point."

The phone rang. Anne, who was still at her desk with Dru Perry keeping her company, answered after the first ring, listened to the terse message, and turned on the intercom. "Jeff, there's a Detective Ryan on the phone from Chicago. He says that they've lost Alex Nolan. He slipped out of the dinner meeting he was attending more than three hours ago, and he hasn't showed up at the Ritz-Carlton."

Jeff and Mort jumped up. *"Three hours!"* Jeff exclaimed. "He could have flown back here by now!"

80

I had heard the garage door close. The car's engine was running. The fumes were making me drowsier, but I knew I had to fight it. Now that he was with me, Jack was falling asleep again. I tried to move him. I *had* to get into the front seat. I had to turn off the engine. If we stayed here, we were going to die. I had to move. But my limbs wouldn't function. What was it that Alex had forced me to drink?

I could not move. I was slumped against the cushion, half-lying, half-sitting. The sound of the car's engine was deafening. It was racing. Something must be wedged against the gas pedal. Soon we would be unconscious. Soon my little boy would die.

No. No. Please, no.

"Jack, Jack." My voice was a hushed, broken whisper, but it went directly into his ear, and he stirred. "Jack, Mommy is sick. Jack, help me."

He moved again, turning his head restlessly. Then he settled again under my neck.

"Jack, Jack, wake up, wake up."

I was starting to fall asleep again. I had to fight it. I bit my lip so hard that I could taste blood, but the pain helped keep me from losing consciousness. "Jack, help Mommy," I pleaded.

He lifted his head. I sensed that he was looking at me.

"Jack, climb . . . into front seat. Take . . . car key . . . out."

He was moving. He sat up and slid off my lap. "It's dark, Mommy," he said.

"Climb . . . in . . . front seat," I whispered. "Climb . . ." I could feel myself sinking slowly into unconsciousness. The words I was trying to say were disappearing from my mind. . . .

Jack's foot grazed my face. He was climbing over the seat.

"The key, Jack . . ."

From far off, I heard him say, "I can't get it out."

"Turn it, Jack. Turn it . . . then . . . pull . . . it . . . out."

Suddenly there was silence, total silence in the garage. Followed by Jack's sleepy but proud cry, "Mommy, I *did* it. I have the key."

I knew the fumes could still kill us. We had to get out. Jack would never be able to open the heavy garage door by himself.

He was leaning over the front seat, looking down at me. "Mommy, are you sick?"

The garage door opener, I thought—it's clipped onto the visor over the driver's seat. I often let Jack be the one to press it. "Jack, open . . . garage . . . door," I begged. "You know how."

I think I slipped away for a minute. The rumbling sound of the garage door slowly rising woke me up for a moment, and it was with a vast sense of deliverance and relief that I finally stopped fighting and lost consciousness.

I woke up in an ambulance. The first face I saw was Jeffrey MacKingsley's. The first words he said were the ones I wanted to hear: "Don't worry, Jack is fine." The second words seemed filled with promise. "Liza, I told you everything was going to be all right."

EPILOGUE

We have lived in the house for two years now. After much thought, I decided to stay there. For me it was no longer the house in which I had killed my mother, but the home in which I had tried to save her life. I have used my skills as an interior designer to complete my father's vision for it. It is truly beautiful, and each day we are building happy memories to add to the ones of my early childhood.

Ted Cartwright accepted a plea bargain. He got thirty years for murdering Zach Willet, fifteen years for killing my father, and twelve years for causing the death of my mother, the sentences to be served concurrently. Part of his agreement was that he would confess that he came to the house that night intending to kill my mother.

He had lived in the house while he was married to my mother, and he knew that there was one basement window that for some inexplicable reason had never been wired into the security system. That was the way he got in.

He admitted that he had planned to strangle my mother as she slept, and if I had awakened while he was there, he would have killed me, too.

Knowing that the impending divorce would make him a suspect in her death, he had placed a call from our basement phone to his home and waited an hour before starting upstairs on his murderous journey. He had planned to tell the police that my mother had asked him to come to our house the next day to discuss a reconciliation.

But that planned explanation for the phone call had to be changed when I awoke and the confrontation and shooting occurred. Instead, on the witness stand at my trial, he testified that my mother had called him late that evening and pleaded with him to come to the house while I was asleep.

Once he was in the house, Ted got the new code out of my mother's address book and disarmed the security system. He unlocked the kitchen door, again planning to make it seem that my mother's carelessness had allowed an intruder to sneak in. At my trial, his story was that my mother had disarmed it and unlocked the door because she was expecting him.

Ted also indicated that the other "moving man" was Sonny Ingers, a construction worker on his town-house project. His identification of Ingers was corroborated by Rap Corrigan's description of Ingers's strawberry birthmark and partially missing index finger. Since there was insufficient evidence linking Ingers to Zach's murder, he pled guilty to the burglary of Zach's apartment and got three years in prison.

When Ted's plea was entered in open court, and he related all of these details to the judge, I think that a lot of people in the community were ashamed that they had fallen for his story, and had condemned a little girl.

Henry Paley emerged from the investigation without any criminal charges. The prosecutor's office concluded that Henry's conspiracy with Ted Cartwright was limited to trying to convince Georgette Grove to sell the Route 24 property. None of the evidence indicated that he knew about or was involved in any plan to harm anyone.

It will be many, many years, if ever, before either Robin Carpenter or Alex Nolan will be released from prison. They are both serving life sentences for the murders of Georgette Grove and Charley Hatch, and for the attempted murders of Jack and me.

Robin admitted that she had been the one who shot both Georgette and her half brother Charley Hatch. She had taken from Georgette's shoulder bag the picture of Alex and Robin that Georgette had found in Robin's desk. She had placed my picture in Georgette's shoulder bag and my mother's picture in Charley Hatch's pocket.

So many people stopped by our house during those first weeks after Jack and I were nearly killed. They brought food and flowers and friendship. Some of them told me how their grandmothers and mine were schoolmates. I love it here. My roots are here. I've opened an interior design shop in Mendham, but I've had to limit my clients. Life is very busy. Jack is in the first grade and plays on every team he can find.

In the weeks and months following Alex's arrest, my relief over Ted's confession was overshadowed by my sadness at Alex's betrayal. It was Jeff who helped me to understand that the Alex I thought I knew had never existed.

I'm not exactly sure of the moment when I realized I was falling in love with Jeff. I think he knew before I did that we were meant to be together.

That's another reason why I am so busy. My husband, Jeffrey MacKingsley, is getting ready to run for governor.

POCKET
BOOKS

Also by
Mary Higgins Clark
NIGHT-TIME IS
MY TIME

The definition of an owl had always pleased him: *a night bird of prey . . . sharp talons and soft plumage which permits noiseless flight*. 'I am the owl,' he would whisper to himself after he had selected his prey, 'and night-time is my time.'

There is something uneasy about the twenty-year reunion of Stonecroft Academy, where Jean Sheridan is to be honored along with six other members of her class. A former classmate, now a high-powered Hollywood agent, has been found drowned in her pool. She is the fifth woman in Jean's year class whose life has come to a sudden, mysterious end.

Adding to Jean's apprehension is the anonymous fax she has just received, with its taunting reference to her daughter Lily, a child she had given up for adoption twenty years ago. No one had known – or so she thought.

The reunion assembles. Despite her fears, Jean does not suspect that the murderer is among the distinguished guests. Nor that she is her intended victim.

'Clark plays out her story like the pro that she is . . .
flawless' *DAILY MIRROR*

ISBN 0 7434 8959 4
PRICE £6.99

POCKET
BOOKS

Mary Higgins Clark
SECOND TIME AROUND

A gripping tale of deception and tantalizing suspense.

Nicholas Spencer, charismatic head of the medical research
company Gen-Stone, involved in the development of an
anticancer vaccine, suddenly disappears. His private plane
crashes en route to Puerto Rico, but his body is not found.

Rocking the financial and medical world even more,
comes the shocking revelation that Spencer had looted
Gen-Stone of huge sums of money – and that his wife,
Lynn, is accused of having participated in the scam.

Lynn Spencer, narrowly escaping death when her
mansion is set on fire, turns to her stepsister, Carley, a
columnist for the Wall Street Weekly, to help prove that
she was not her husband's accomplice.

As Carley proceeds with her investigation, she is confronted
by seemingly impenetrable questions: Is Nicholas Spencer
dead or in hiding? Was he guilty or set up? And as the facts
begin to unfold, she becomes the focus of a dangerous
group involved in a sinister and fraudulent scheme.

ISBN 0 7434 6773 6
PRICE £6.99

POCKET
BOOKS

Mary Higgins Clark
DADDY'S
LITTLE GIRL

Ellie Cavanaugh was only seven years old when her teenage sister, Andrea, was murdered. It was Ellie who led her parents to the secret hideout in which Andrea's body was found. And it was Ellie's testimony that led to the conviction of the man she firmly believed to be the killer.

Now, twenty-two years later, the convicted killer is set free from prison. He returns to Ellie's hometown intent on white-washing his reputation. Ellie, now an investigative reporter, also returns home determined to thwart his attempts and conclusively prove his guilt. As she delves deeper into her research, she uncovers horrifying facts that shed new light on her sister's murder. With each discovery, she comes closer to a confrontation with a desperate killer.

ISBN 0 7434 4937 1
PRICE £6.99

POCKET
BOOKS

Mary Higgins Clark
ON THE STREET WHERE YOU LIVE

In 1892, in the seaside resort town of Spring Lake, New Jersey, a young woman disappears and the house in which she grew up is immediately sold.

Now, more than a century later, Emily Graham buys back her ancestral home. Recovering from the bitter break up of her marriage, with a new position as criminal defence attorney in a major law firm, Emily begins renovating the Victorian house. In the backyard, the skeleton of a young woman is found, and identified as that of Martha Lawrence, the girl who disappeared from Spring Lake over four years ago. Within her skeletal hand is the finger bone of another woman, adorned with a ring – a family heirloom, Emily's family heirloom.

Seeking desperately to find the link between her forebear's past and this recent murder, Emily herself becomes a threat to the killer. Devious and seductive, he has chosen her as his next victim . . .

ISBN 0 7434 1499 3
PRICE £6.99

POCKET
BOOKS

This book and other **Mary Higgins Clark** titles are available from your
local bookshop or can be ordered direct from the publisher.

Please send cheque or postal order for the value of the book,
free postage and packing within the UK, to
SIMON & SCHUSTER CASH SALES
PO Box 29, Douglas Isle of Man, IM99 1BQ
Tel: 01624 677237, Fax: 01624 670923
Email: bookshop@enterprise.net
www.bookpost.co.uk

Please allow 14 days for delivery. Prices and availability
subject to change without notice